PENGUIN BOOKS

The Last Train Home

Elle Cook worked as a journalist and in PR before becoming a full-time novelist. She is the author of *The Man I Never Met* and *The Last Train Home*. She is also the author of five historical time-slip novels under her real name, Lorna Cook. *The Forgotten Village*, *The Forbidden Promise*, *The Girl from the Island*, *The Dressmaker's Secret* and *The Hidden Letters* have sold over 300,000 copies combined. She lives in coastal Essex with her husband and two daughters.

Praise for *The Last Train Home*:

'A heart-warming, heart-wrenching tale of two star-crossed
lovers that made me laugh, cry and sigh
in all the right places'
Virginia Heath

'Brimming with emotion and heart'
Fiona Gibson

'A heart-wrenching rollercoaster'
Caroline Khoury

'I absolutely devoured this funny, moving,
unputdownable novel'
Jenny Ashcroft

T0191257

Also by Elle Cook

The Man I Never Met

The Last Train Home

ELLE COOK

PENGUIN BOOKS

PENGUIN BOOKS

UK | USA | Canada | Ireland | Australia
India | New Zealand | South Africa

Penguin Books is part of the Penguin Random House group of companies
whose addresses can be found at global.penguinrandomhouse.com

Penguin
Random House
UK

First published in Penguin Books 2023

001

Typeset in 10.4/14 pt Palatino LT Pro
by Integra Software Services Pvt. Ltd, Pondicherry

Printed and bound in Great Britain by Clays Ltd, Elcograf S.p.A.

The authorised representative in the EEA is Penguin Random House Ireland,
Morrison Chambers, 32 Nassau Street, Dublin D02 YH68

A CIP catalogue record for this book is available from the British Library

ISBN: 978–1–529–15776–5

www.greenpenguin.co.uk

For the marvel that is Becky Ritchie, because of far too many reasons to list here, but mainly because you're a superstar agent and I'm so flipping lucky to have you.

Never go in search of love.
Go in search of life.
And life will find you the love you seek.

Atticus

Chapter 1

Abbie

October 2005

Why is it that so many of us can talk to the person opposite us on a train when it's midnight and everyone's been out having fun, but you would *never* in a hundred years do the same thing on the morning commute? And how is it that every train journey is the same as all the other journeys that have come before, until it's not? An ordinary day that becomes unlike any other. Because of a moment. Because of a person. Because of an event beyond anyone's control.

I dash down the Underground stairs at Tottenham Court Road and run onto the Central Line Tube just as the doors close. I lean back on the glass partition and breathe in with a sense of triumph. When I look back at this exact moment, I often wonder if it's fate that I made it in time. That I was supposed to be there, on the last eastbound train of the night. Supposed to meet Tom.

How different everything might have been if I hadn't run a bit faster, hadn't downed my drink and left the pub a little bit earlier. In the end, perhaps it was always meant to be like this.

'That was lucky. I didn't think you were going to make it in time.' I look up to see where the voice came from. There's a man about my age wearing a deep-grey suit, standing and looking up at me from his newspaper. He looks vaguely familiar, as if I might have passed him in the street. Maybe.

I give him a quick, polite smile, sharing in my silent joy that I didn't get stuck on the platform, missing the last train and having to get a taxi all the way home, or (and I think this might be worse) stuck between the doors as they closed, bouncing off me, prompting everyone to glance up and stare at the person causing the delay. That's happened to me before and it is humiliating.

There are no free seats, so I stay where I am as the train leaves the station.

'I didn't think I was going to make that, either,' I confess over the noise of other intoxicated and buoyant travellers making their way home on one of the last Tubes of the night. I'm breathless. I can hear it in my own voice. I open my nearly empty water bottle and drink the last of it.

'I've got one I've not opened yet,' he says in a slightly slurred voice. 'Do you want it?'

'Ah, that's really sweet, but it's OK. I'm sure I'll make it home without dehydrating.' No matter how parched and tipsy I am, I can't take someone's water bottle from them when I've only just met them. That's so weird.

He smiles, glances back down at his newspaper and I find myself watching him absent-mindedly as a bunch of blokes, dressed in matching football T-shirts with Hawaiian garlands draped round their necks, make their way towards us through the busy carriage, singing drunkenly. The man opposite me looks up. *Everyone* looks up with amused expressions. It's hard not to share in their joy, as they've brought the revelry in this carriage up about a hundred points.

They amble past, cheering and singing, and find a space further down the carriage. I'm still watching them and chuckling to myself when the man who offered me his water says, 'What do we think? Are they on a stag-do or on their way home from a match?'

Overcoming my reservations about conversing with strangers is easy when I'm half a bottle of wine and three cocktails into the night. 'Hmm, tough one,' I reply with an expression that pretends I'm really thinking about it. 'The Hawaiian garlands are throwing me.'

'Me too,' he says.

'Shall we ask them?' I offer.

'Go for it,' he replies with a smile that makes the sides of his blue eyes crinkle. 'Tenner says it's a stag-do.'

'But what if I also think it's a stag-do – then who wins the money?'

He narrows his eyes. 'I think I'm too drunk to understand what you've just asked me.'

'Excuse me!' I call down to the group of jubilant men. 'Have you had a really good night out or is one of you getting married?'

They cheer loudly and shove one of their number towards me. 'This is Jonno,' one cheers. 'He's just lost his virginity, so we're celebrating—'

'Sod off!' Jonno looks incensed and rolls his eyes. 'I'm getting married in a week. It's my stag-do.'

'Congratulations,' we say in unison.

Jonno leans forward and clinks his can of lager with us. 'Cheers,' he says loudly, and we cheers him in return.

'Where have you guys been?' the man opposite me asks Jonno, who is now swaying from side to side as the train carriage takes us through the network of tunnels carrying me towards Liverpool Street to catch my overground train home.

Jonno lists an American restaurant and a few bars near Oxford Street, then his mates start singing a song about him losing his virginity and Jonno turns back and gamely joins in.

'I remember those days,' the man opposite says to me. 'All those tourist traps luring me into London because we didn't know anywhere better to go.'

'Same,' I reply. 'I used to love getting dressed up and catching the train to go clubbing at Fabric.'

He makes a face. 'Fabric. I think I just travelled back in time.'

'Ha,' I laugh, noticing his playful smile. He's quite good-looking and fun, a combination I can really get behind. 'Where have you been tonight then?' I ask. The train doors open for the next station and someone does exactly what I did earlier and only just makes it into the carriage in time, slicing through the middle of our chat before we move off again.

He tells me the name of a private members' club. 'A friend goes there and I was thinking about joining, but I'm not sure I'd use it enough, so . . .'

'That sounds like a wild Thursday night out,' I deadpan.

'He thought I needed cheering up. I've recently called time on a relationship, and apparently extortionately priced drinks in graveyard-quiet surroundings are always the answer.'

'Sounds awful,' I say. 'I've never set foot in a private members' club, and this has probably confirmed that I'm not sure I'm supposed to.'

His eyes crinkle again as he smiles. 'It's not the most appropriate place to get wasted,' he agrees. 'Where've you been then?'

'A bar near my friend's work in Bond Street,' I say and then realise this also doesn't sound too wild.

'A few drinks after work in a bar turns into a few drinks in another bar, turns into going to a members' club,' he says knowingly.

'Oh,' I say teasingly, 'I see how easily it all gets out of hand.'

'Thursday's the new Friday – or so I keep hearing.' He chuckles and I lean back, relaxing against the glass partition. He watches me with that smile still on his face and I wonder if this silly chat is going to lead somewhere even flirtier. Probably not. I'm getting off in a few stops.

'Where are you headed then?' I ask over the increasing noise of the Tube as it speeds up over the tracks.

We have to lean in to hear each other, and there's a faint scent of pine or something similar on his skin as he dips his head and says, 'I'm off to meet someone at Bank.'

'Off to carry on the partying?'

'Something like that. You?'

'Home. Bed.'

'Home and bed sounds like a good idea,' he says wistfully.

Out of the corner of my eye I can see people giving each other looks. We're the drunk people on the train who can't stop talking, although Jonno and his crew are still going strong further down the carriage, still loudly trying to make something rhyme with the word 'virginity'.

'I really want to join in with the word "affinity",' I tell the guy. 'But I might not be drunk enough to take part in a stag-do singalong.'

'I am definitely drunk enough,' he says, as if trying to work himself up to chiming in, and then bottles it. 'No, I can't do it. What about the word "infinity"?' he suggests to me.

'"Infinity" works. I think.'

'Flexibility?' He's on a roll now.

'In the city?' I suggest, but fail to make it rhyme.

'Losing your virginity with flexibility to infinity in the city?' he says, and I laugh.

'We have a hit on our hands here,' I say. 'But I'm not sure it all rhymes.'

'Maybe it doesn't need to rhyme,' he says. 'Maybe it *shouldn't* rhyme. Also,' he says as if it's a huge secret, 'perhaps there are no words that truly rhyme with "virginity".'

'It's probably for the best or else there'd be more songs about it,' I say.

'Which would be weird,' he says.

'Which would be weird,' I echo.

I glance over at the guy who got on the train at the last stop. He is doing his best not to laugh at us, which in turn makes me smile. The train pulls into Chancery Lane station, he gets off, the doors close and we head off again.

'Are we the weirdos on the train?' my new friend says, echoing my thoughts.

'I think so, yes.'

'I can't believe I'm twenty-seven and I've never been the weirdo on the train before,' he says, opening his bottle and taking a sip. He sounds quite plummy, sort of posh, now that I'm paying attention. Although that might just be his slurring confusing me.

'Congratulations,' I say. 'I'm twenty-four and I think this is my first time too. Or maybe we *have* been the weirdos on the train, but we never realised it.'

'Profound,' he says with a mock-serious face.

'I know,' I return with a matching expression.

He drops his newspaper as he drinks and I bend to pick it up for him, passing it back. I look at the front page for a second as the train speeds up. The headline's talking about plans for the Olympics, now that London has won the bid to host them in 2012. That's for ever away.

Seven years.

A lot can happen in seven years.

A lot can happen in seven seconds.

At that moment there's an earth-shattering bang, followed by creaking and the noise of metal twisting. It's a sound unlike anything I've ever heard before. The man in front clutches the handrail and I do the same. There's confusion and crying and I reach up to touch my head and I'm sure there's blood, but the lights have gone out in the carriage and I can barely see anything. A few people issue a shocked kind of scream. And then there's crying. I think it's me. I think it's everyone.

And then there's nothing.

Chapter 2

Abbie

I'm half walking, half leaning against this man as he holds me, walks us over the tracks far away from our train, assuring me the live rail is switched off. How does he know that? Has someone told him? Have I blacked out? I must have, because I don't even know how I got out, how I'm on the tracks, walking. He must have pulled me from the carriage. I lift my head up and find I'm still looking down at the tracks as we walk. It's easier to look down. It hurts to lift my head. My legs are leaden, just about starting to work again, and for some reason I trust this man to take me out of here. I look up at him. He's staring intently straight ahead, while I concentrate on putting one foot in front of the other. I'm finally an active participant in my own rescue.

Someone in hi-viz runs towards us. Ahead of us the men from the stag-party lean against each other, walking in the same direction as us towards the next train platform. It's getting lighter as we walk through the tunnel because the station lights ahead glow like a guiding beacon. We don't have far to go. We stumble along, arm-in-arm, and he turns, pulls my hand to help me, and instinctively I walk with him as we climb up the little steps at the platform's edge. Station workers are there to check we're OK. The man next to me tells them that we are, even though I'm not sure I am. He's still having to hold me up and then he asks, 'What happened?'

'Train derailed,' someone answers.

The train derailed? How does that even happen?

'There are other people still in there,' the man holding me tells them, and I watch the station workers as they run towards the stricken train.

'Where are the paramedics?' I ask. Only a whisper comes out.

'What?' he asks, still holding me.

I can't remember what I've just tried to ask.

'Actually you're not OK, are you? We need to get you looked at,' he says.

Everything is fuggy and I'm only aware of the pain in my head, shooting into the back of my eyes.

'You were out for a while,' he says.

'Out?' I turn round and see a steady stream of passengers behind us making their way slowly along the tracks, climbing up onto the platform.

And then we're up the escalator at St Paul's station, at street level, into the open air, where lights from empty offices punctuate what passes for darkness in this city. Every street looks the same like this, littered with offices and coffee shops, pubs and bars. There's hardly anyone about at this time of night and something tells me we should probably go back and wait for the paramedics, although if people are still inside the derailed train, they presumably need help more than we do.

I look up and see the recognisable white Portland stone of St Paul's Cathedral up ahead. I'm back in the City again, vaguely near where I work, off Ludgate Hill. A late-night jogger pays little attention to us and I realise we're properly alone now, me and the guy from the train. We stop walking, unsure where we should go, what we should do. Paramedics rush past, blue lights swirling, sirens whirring. My clothes are dirty with train grime or something like it. His are the same.

'Come on,' he says. But I don't think he knows where we're going. Is he in shock? Am I in shock? What just happened? We pass the locked gates of St Paul's Churchyard and turn further down the road and soon we're on the patch of grass to the side of the cathedral, a quieter green space with the odd taxi driving past us. I've been across town tonight with a friend and have ended up back near where I work. I must have said it out loud because he replies, 'Me too.' He continues, 'I'm not even normally on the Tube.' His tone is quieter now, contemplative.

My head is thumping and I sit down on the patch of grass where I sometimes come in the summer and eat my lunch, and he crouches in front of me, sweeping hair back from my face.

He grimaces. 'That looks nasty.'

I touch my cut and blood comes away on my hand. It's sticky, the flow has eased off. 'Do you think we should go back?' I ask.

'And do what?' He runs his hand over his face. If anything, he's moved dirt around rather than removed it. I never realised how filthy the Tube tracks must be.

'We should go back to help others?' I suggest.

'No,' he replies gently, still crouched in front of me. 'I don't think you're in any condition to go back. I do think you need to be seen, though. We need to make that a priority. Let's rest for a minute until we work out which way's up.'

'The train derailed?' I say, baffled. 'Really? After everything that happened this summer, do we believe that?'

He knows what I'm talking about. I wasn't in London the day of the July bombings. I was at home, sick. I woke up to frenzied calls from my boss checking I was OK, as I was the only person from the office not accounted for that morning. Is it happening all over again?

'I saw it,' he says. 'I saw the other carriages behind ours. They must have . . . come off the tracks. I don't know. It *was* a mess, though. We were lucky.'

I wince as a searing pain shoots through my skull, and he looks at me with concern.

'I'll be fine,' I say. 'I want to go home. I need to ring my mum, let her know what's happened, so she knows I'll be home a bit later.' Mercifully I've still got my cross-shoulder bag. I'm missing my jacket, though. I think it was draped over my arm when the train derailed. I open my bag and pull out my phone. It's completely smashed, the screen unreadable, the buttons not lighting up under my fingers.

'Here,' he says, standing up and pulling his BlackBerry from his pocket. 'What's the number?'

I put the phone back in my bag and stare at the one he hands me. 'I don't know,' I confess. 'I can't remember.'

He crouches down, concerned.

'It's not because of the head injury,' I say. 'We moved house a few weeks ago and it's a new number.'

'Do you have a boyfriend or . . . someone else whose number you know?'

I shake my head, which sends the searing pain behind my eyes again. 'No boyfriend,' I say. There's never been anyone properly serious. Relationships have always fizzled out fairly rapidly, for various reasons.

'OK,' he replies distractedly, fiddling with his phone. 'I think I'm just going to search and see if there's any news about it.'

He's got one of those new phones with the internet on. 'Nothing yet,' he says.

'Don't *you* need to ring anyone?' I ask.

He shakes his head and sits down next to me. 'My parents don't live here. And they wouldn't worry about seeing news of a Tube derailment. Never in a million years would they think I might be on it.'

'Oh,' I say, because what else can I say? My parents are total worriers, expectantly awaiting a text from me that I'm on my way home and then listening out from their bed for the late-night click of the front door when I come home from a night out, before ever allowing themselves to fully embrace sleep.

I take a tissue from my bag to mop my head.

We sit in silence and I try to process what's happened – what's happening now, here. This man's presence makes me feel oddly safe. I turn to look at him but he's staring straight ahead, frown lines temporarily on his face. I wish I'd taken that bottle of water from him when he'd offered. I'm so thirsty. He's not holding it now. He must have dropped it in the confusion. My mouth is dusty and tastes tangy, like dirt and metal.

'Thank you,' I say eventually. 'For getting me off the train.'

'It's OK.'

12

'Were many people . . .'

He looks at me.

'Badly hurt?' I ask.

'Some.' He nods, looks at his hands, which only now do I notice are smothered in cuts.

'Was anyone—' I was going to say 'dead', but he doesn't give me the chance.

'Can you walk?' he cuts in.

'I think so.' My head still hurts, but I'm not shaking any more.

'We should go.'

'Where?'

'Hospital. Your head.'

'I'm OK,' I say. 'I don't want to go to hospital.'

It's only then that I notice more sirens. The street is alive with sirens and flashing lights everywhere, bouncing off the darkness of closed shop windows across the street. If I wanted to go to hospital, I could simply go and ask someone driving an emergency vehicle to take me.

I rise and walk past him, skirting the gates of the cathedral and into Paternoster Square. I look at my own hands, which are black with dirt. 'I need some water. And a shower. And then I need to go home.'

With my back towards the cathedral, I begin walking towards the City. Everything's gone a bit blurry and I stop.

'You're joking,' he says, catching up with me. 'You've just been involved in a train crash. You've banged your head. If you won't go to hospital, then come back to mine and I can clean you up and then see what's what. I'm not letting you go home on your own. What if you black out or . . . I don't know.'

'Where do you live?' I ask.

'Literally round the corner. About five roads in that direction.' He points somewhere vaguely towards Fleet Street. 'Do you think you can walk?'

'I can.'

We move off, neither of us speaking, but I wobble so obviously that he puts his arm around my shoulders and pulls me against him for support as we walk. I'm woozy and the closeness is comforting, necessary.

After a minute I ask in confusion, 'Do you live at work?'

'What do you mean?' he asks.

'You said you work near here and you live here too?' Funny how the mind picks up on the most random details.

'Oh, right, no. I live in a flat a few blocks from my office.'

We pass an all-night convenience store and I break away from him and head as purposefully as my legs will allow. 'I need water,' I say, entering the shop and walking straight towards the open fridge shelves.

He enters the shop behind me and pulls down a huge bottle of Evian. I grab one for myself and we turn to pay. He takes mine from me and puts it with his.

We both pause and look up at the TV screen positioned behind the counter. The man serving barely glances at us; instead he tots up how much we owe and mumbles the amount, while still staring at the twenty-four-hour news channel on the screen. Neither of us pays immediately. Instead we watch the presenter talk about the derailment. Eventually I pull out my purse and put a couple of pounds on the counter, and we turn and leave.

His flat is a tiny one-bed apartment on a lane running parallel to the river. It's modern and soulless and must have cost him a fortune. We stand in his open-plan kitchen/living room and he gives me painkillers, which I down with my water.

'What's your name?' I ask. It's strange not to know this most basic detail, given what we've just been through together.

He looks back at me. 'Tom. What's yours?'

'Abbie.'

He holds the phone to his ear, confirms he's reached Directory Enquiries and hands it to me, so I can see if my parents have already registered their new number. I write it down and then give Tom a look, silently asking if I can use the phone again.

'Of course.'

My dad answers our home phone groggily and I tell him what's happened. He listens in disbelief as to why I'm not home yet and springs into action.

'Are you hurt?' he asks.

'No, I'm fine. I was lucky.'

'Where are you?'

'I'm at someone's flat. But I'm OK, honestly. Don't worry. My phone's broken, so I'll ring you again soon, OK? I need to work out . . .' I don't know what I need to work out. How do I get home? Tom's given me some privacy and I assume he's gone to the bathroom, as he's not anywhere else in this tiny flat.

'If you tell me where you are, I'll come and get you,' Dad says.

'I'm not really sure. It's near St Paul's. I can ask Tom what street he lives on when he gets out of the bathroom.'

'Who's Tom?' my dad asks quickly, ever protective.

'Guy I work with,' I lie, because I don't want my dad to think I'm in a stranger's flat and I've no idea where it actually is. Which is what's happened.

I say goodbye to my dad and promise to ring him back shortly with more detail on where Tom lives. When he gets out the bathroom I'm going to ask if I can have a shower. I feel so grimy. Also, I really want to sit down, but I'm aware that I'm filthy and Tom's sofa is pristine white.

Chapter 3

Tom

I should ring my parents. I said I wouldn't, but I don't want the first thing they feel to be panic when they see messages on their phone from their friends checking if I'm OK, having seen news about the derailment. Their friends may worry, even if *they* probably won't. I pick up my landline and dial their number – working out the local time where they are. They're living the kind of life I can only dream of, as part of a British expat community in the Virgin Islands.

The shower's still running in my bathroom. The girl, Abbie, has been in there ages. I'll go and knock in a minute and check she's not slumped, passed out, drowning.

My parents don't pick up immediately, so I ring again. 'Hey,' I say when my mum eventually answers. 'I just want you to know I'm OK.'

'Why wouldn't you be?' she asks.

'When you switch on the news, you'll probably see. But I'm fine. I'm at home. I'm OK.'

'What's happened?' she asks.

'The train I was on got derailed.' Simple facts, no over-embellishment.

'But you're all right?' So cool, calm, unfazed by the daily goings-on in my world.

'Really. I'm good. I'll call you later, OK? I've got to go and check Abbie's all right.'

'Who's Abbie?'

'She's just a girl I helped get off the train.'

'You're a good boy,' my mum says.

I make a face that I'm glad she can't see. 'Yeah, I know.'

When I'm off the phone I go to knock on the bathroom door as Abbie switches the shower off. Then the door opens and she appears in the towel I've given her, which is unexpected. I thought she'd get dressed.

'Um,' she says, 'could I borrow some clothes? Mine are . . .'

'Sure. Of course.' I go to my bedroom and grab a T-shirt and some sports shorts that are far too small for me, but might be OK for Abbie, and hold them out to her. She takes them, mutters thanks and goes back into the bathroom to change. Her blonde hair is darker now it's wet. I put my hand through my own dark hair and although I washed my hands the moment I got home, they're grimy again.

I sit back in front of the TV and watch addictively. The news moves to and from the derailment, as other news from around the globe interrupts the cycle of doom on my doorstep that I can't stop watching. How weird to be wrapped up in something so serious and then to be home moments later, watching live coverage of it.

Abbie appears wearing my clothes. Why do men's clothes always look better on women?

'I need to call my dad back and tell him where you live, so he can come and get me.' But instead of doing that, she adopts the same look of pure bafflement as me as we watch a reporter on camera talk about how many derailments there have been on the Underground in the last few years. There are more than I'd imagined – three in 2003 alone. Three. And one last year. How did I not know this? Blue flashing lights are still showing on the TV. I'll never forget what I saw. So many injured people, but I'd only had one pair of hands and Abbie was slumped on the floor, blood all over her head. It seemed natural that I'd help her. I turn to Abbie. I don't think she saw all the injured.

'How do you feel?' I ask.

Her hand goes instinctively to her head. 'I think it looks worse than it is,' she replies.

It looks awful.

'Do you feel groggy or . . . anything?'

'No. I'm fine. It hurts. But I'm fine.'

I touch her face, tipping her head down so I can look at her wound. 'It actually looks a bit better, now you've cleaned the smeared blood off.'

Her hair's wet. She's used my eucalyptus and pine shampoo. It smells better on her than it does on me.

'I should shower,' I say as the news reporter repeats something they've said already.

Abbie sits on the edge of the sofa, looking uncomfortable in clothes that aren't hers.

When I emerge from the bathroom, feeling so much better than I did a few minutes ago, she's fast asleep. I watch her every now and again to check she's breathing and sit back down in fresh clothes, watching the endless reports running.

Chapter 4

Abbie

I'm woken up with the words 'Your parents are on the phone.'

I open my eyes to find a man's hand on my shoulder. He's smiling down at me and I look up at him, for a moment too confused to remember who he is, where I am. And then I realise and I run to the bathroom to be sick.

'She's just gone to the bathroom. I'll get her to call you back in a sec,' I hear him say calmly.

He runs in, pulls my hair back and holds it as I throw up into the toilet.

'This is definitely not good. We're going to hospital.'

'No,' I snap. 'I'm not throwing up because of—'

'Concussion?' he volunteers, still holding my hair.

'I just . . . I couldn't work out who you were or any of it, and then I remembered. I thought it was a dream. Or a nightmare. I don't need to be sick any more.'

'OK,' he says, letting go of my hair and standing. He opens his bathroom cabinet and reaches for mouthwash. 'Here,' he continues, handing it to me along with a clean tooth mug.

I wash my mouth out and then emerge from the bathroom, feeling ridiculous. I'm struggling to remember the finer details of what happened. I was sitting on the train. And now I'm here. Everything in between is in danger of vanishing. This man – I can't remember his name – pulled me out. I do my best to recall something, anything. And then his name comes to me. 'Tom,' I say to myself.

'Yeah?' he replies, lifting his head from his task in the kitchen. The kettle boils.

I shake my head. 'Nothing.'

'I've made tea,' he says, pouring hot water into two mugs.

'How long was I asleep?'

He hands me a steaming mug, and even though it's about a hundred degrees in here, I wrap my hands around it comfortingly.

'You're shivering,' he says, removing the cup from my hands and guiding me towards the sofa. He pulls a throw off the back and puts it over me. I look at the tea on the glass coffee table longingly and he hands it back to me, not quite letting go.

'I won't drop it,' I say. Though I'm not sure of that at all. I stare at the TV. He's muted it, but the breaking-news banner streaming along the bottom of the broadcast is giving an esti-mated number of severely injured. It's into the twenties now. I can barely speak. Emotionally I feel numb as I ask, 'Can you turn it up?'

'They've been saying the same thing for ages now.' He sits next to me and worries at his hand. He's got cuts, and I want to ask him what he had to do to get me out of the train, but he speaks first. 'Call your parents. Tell them where you are.'

Chapter 5

Tom

'Dad dialled 1471,' she tells me after she finishes the call with her parents. 'That's how he knew your number to ring me back . . .' She trails off, then starts up again. 'He's on his way to get me. It'll take him an hour or so to get in from Enfield, I think.'

'You're welcome to stay here as long as you need. You know that, right?' I say honestly.

'Thanks,' she says, hovering near the desk.

'Do you . . . want to sit down?'

She smiles, sighs exhaustedly. 'Yes, please.'

We sit and watch the news until we can't bear it any more. There's an injury toll and the numbers are rising. I think of what I saw on the train; what I wish I hadn't seen.

There's nothing new on the screen. It's just regurgitated pictures of a scene I'm now very familiar with. I can't watch this any more. And Abbie confesses that neither can she. We mute it and leave it running, in case of any new updates. Although what else they can have to say about this is beyond me. I wonder about people asleep, who have no idea what's happened. When they wake in a few hours' time will they be worried that friends, relatives, loved ones have been involved or will they simply get on with their day, wonder how their journey to work might be affected.

As if she can hear me thinking, Abbie says, 'We're so lucky to be alive.'

I pick at the cuts on my hand again. I'm sure there's bits of broken glass in there. 'Yeah.'

'Thank you,' she says, turning to me. She puts her hand on mine, stilling my action. It's nice, soft, comforting. It's something else as well – something I can't identify. And then it's gone, as she lifts her hand away.

I fumble for something to say. 'You'd have been fine without me,' I tell her. The emergency services and the train workers would have got her out. Or she'd have woken up and got herself out. She didn't need me.

'I'm not sure,' she says. And then she surprises me by saying, 'Do you work in the building opposite me?'

'I don't know. Do I?'

She smiles, ever so faintly. 'The big new financial one, with all the glass. I'm in the little courtyard office. I'm *sure* I recognise you. I'm sure you've been standing out the front, smoking, a few times when I've been on my way to get coffee.'

'I've been trying to quit,' I confess.

'How's that working for you?' She smiles.

'Not great.'

'You've not had one all evening, unless you had a secret smoke when I was passed out with concussion on your sofa?'

'I thought you didn't have a head injury?' I smile. 'And no, I didn't smoke at all today, but now you've mentioned it, it's all I can think about.'

'Sorry,' she says.

I'm picking at the glass in my hand again, making it bleed, and she puts her hand back on mine to still me. Oddly, it is actually very calming, as if she's cast a magic spell over me.

'Just have a bloody cigarette,' she says and follows me as I light up, hanging out of my window, looking into the lane below. It's dark; only the dim streetlights shine in this dark space, giving the alley full of Victorian buildings a Dickensian glow that I've always quite liked, in this city of steel and concrete. It's calm, quiet.

I hold the cigarette out of the window, which does no good at all because the smell is now filling my flat. I might as well be seated on the sofa with the windows closed. She gently takes it from me, holds it to her lips and inhales and I watch her, almost mesmerised.

'Nope,' she says, handing it back to me. 'These are still disgusting.'

I smile, inhale again. 'You're wrong. They're amazing. I've missed them this past week.'

'A week? Is that how long you'd quit for?'

'Sort of,' I say, out of the side of my mouth as I exhale. I flick ash, checking there's no one walking underneath the window as I do so. 'Bit hit-and-miss really. Job's been a bit stressful lately. And then . . . today.'

'What do you do?' she asks, taking the cigarette from me and trying again. She makes a face and I lift it out of her fingers when she offers.

'Analyst.'

'What's that?' I start to tell her and she interrupts me. 'Actually, I don't think my brain can take it. Tell me another time.'

I laugh. 'OK.'

We stand in companionable silence, passing my cigarette back and forth until it's finished and I stub it out on the windowsill, chucking it into the street. She gives me a look of horror. 'I'll pick it up later,' I lie. 'What do you do?'

'Retail journalist,' she says, returning to the sofa and sitting down slowly.

'What does that involve?'

She launches into a vague monologue and then I interrupt her. 'Actually, my brain can't take it. Tell me another time.'

A cushion flies through the air and hits me. 'Funny,' she says and then her face drops and she looks sad. 'It feels odd,' she says, 'making small talk after . . .'

I'm quiet and then, 'Yeah, I know.' At the bottom of the screen they're confirming a new death toll. The numbers are mounting. 'Fuck this. Are you hungry?'

'I guess.'

We stand in the kitchen – she's a bit steadier on her feet now – and make cheese on toast. It's the only food I have in. And Crunchy Nut cornflakes.

'Is all your food beige?' she queries as she looks in the fridge for me.

I ignore her. I don't really keep a rolling stock of supplies, because the corner shop and the canteen at work serve me well enough. And I'm out a lot.

She reaches for the cheese inside the fridge door, then spies two beers. 'Can I have one?' she asks.

'Sure.' I pop the lids on both and we drink while the toastie-maker sets to work. 'It's four a.m.,' I tell her. 'We should be closer to breakfast than to beer. Actually, do you think you should be drinking with your head inj—'

'Fuck off,' she teases, taking a deep swig.

'Fair enough.' I turn back to the toastie-maker and check it's not incinerating our food.

We eat standing up in the kitchen, and I watch her every now and again to check she's not about to fall over. Finally something clicks. 'You work on the same floor as me.'

She pauses and narrows her eyes.

'I mean . . . across the street, you're on the same floor as me. I think I've seen you from my office window.'

'Have you?' she says, her food halfway to her mouth.

'I recognise you, now I think about it. I recognise your profile. I see you laugh a lot on the phone. I didn't realise it was you until just now.'

She shifts on her feet, unsure if I'm taking the piss about her laughing.

I tell her I'm not and that I meant it kindly. 'Honestly,' I say. She plays with her hair a lot when she's on the phone, but I'm definitely not going to say that out loud. She's looking over my shoulder at the muted TV as the breaking-news banner keeps on rolling.

She stares at it as the casualty figure increases. 'Can we watch something else now?'

Chapter 6

Abbie

My dad arrives soon after. Tom and I have been cocooned in his flat and it's only as I leave, stepping into the street to greet my dad, that I realise I'd felt safe there. Dad holds me tightly in the street, his estate car practically wedged in the narrow lane outside Tom's. His tyres screeched against the edge of the kerb as he entered the road. Tom comes down, shakes hands with my dad, but my father swerves his handshake and embraces him as if he's a man who's saved his only daughter from a train crash. Which he has. I told my dad on the phone what Tom did because I had to, really. He deserves some recognition.

Tom and I had spent the last half-hour watching part of *The Matrix*. It was already in his DVD player and he just pushed play. It was easier to drift away watching Keanu Reeves save the world than think about the actual world outside.

At one point Tom drifted off to sleep and I watched his chest rise and fall, his head nodding to one side as he rested against the sofa. I thought back to the few times I'd seen him smoking outside his building before, laughing with his colleagues and intermittently checking his phone.

He has 'hero' written all over him. But that may be because of what he did for me today. He's tall, dark and I want to say handsome, but he's not traditionally handsome. He's good-looking, but I think it's because he looks a bit serious rather than Abercrombie-model handsome.

And now he's standing barefoot in the cold, dark street saying goodbye to me and fielding gushing remarks from my dad. Tom looks embarrassed, but has the good grace to say, 'You're welcome' in all the right places.

And then we're saying goodbye, and it feels rushed after everything we've been through tonight. Almost as if it shouldn't be like this. I have my clothes in a bundle under my arm and I'm still wearing Tom's things. 'I'll work out a way to give these back to you soon,' I say.

'Don't worry about it. Don't go to work today, will you?' he says softly and my dad agrees. 'Get your head looked at. Give yourself the weekend to recover. I'm sure your boss will understand.'

'Maybe.'

And then he pulls his phone from his pocket. 'What's your number? I assume you can remember your own, if not that of your immediate family,' he says with a knowing smile.

I tell him and he saves it into his phone. I don't take his because my phone is still in my bag in shattered pieces.

'Get some rest,' he says.

I look up at him and smile, despite the wave of all-out exhaustion that washes over me. 'Thank you,' I say, as my dad heads towards the driver's side of the car.

Tom opens the passenger door for me. 'It was nothing,' he replies. 'Anyone would have done it.'

And then I'm inside the car and Tom closes my door. I raise my hand to wave goodbye and he does the same, and then the car moves off. I turn round to glance at him through the rear window, but he's already looking away. Just before I face the front, I notice him stoop, pick up the cigarette end that he dropped from his window and then head back inside.

Chapter 7

Abbie

Safely at home, later that day, I wake from a nap, curled up in a little ball. My sheets and pyjamas are soaked with sweat and I shower immediately. I'd showered at Tom's, I showered when I got home. I can't stop showering – it's as if the grime and blood and dirt engulf me the moment I've finished washing them all off. I'm not sure what's wrong with me. My dad took me to A&E on the way home and we sat there for hours this morning until he adopted his best headmaster's voice, explained to the receptionist that I'd been on the derailed Tube and probably had concussion. I was triaged, examined and then sent home with a relatively clean bill of health, which is what I had assumed would happen – but it gave my mum and dad peace of mind. I'm sure it'll make Tom happy to know I went too.

I wonder how he is today. I don't have his number to call him – and I don't think I have the strength to yet, in any case. Yesterday was awful and I'm not ready to confront it all again by contacting Tom. I probably should try to track him down at his office after the weekend, to give him back his clothes and check he's OK. I wonder if he's a stronger person than I

30

am and has woken up, got dressed and gone to work without a second thought.

There's no way I could have done that today. When I told my boss what happened, there was no question of me returning to the office this afternoon. And she was surprised when I volunteered to work from home for the rest of today because I need something to keep me from thinking about it all. Although I'm fairly junior, I have an article to finish editing – I've been working on it for about a week and I am so close to filing it. I asked if she could log into my computer to email me my notes and what I've written so far, so that I could do something productive this afternoon. I've had enough of napping. At first she said no, but relented when it was clear I needed to be busy. But I'm jittery and I can't type anything coherent, so I give up, and Mum and I head into town, find a phone shop and sort out a replacement mobile.

And then we come home and I turn on the news. The focus has moved on to other matters now. I wonder what Tom saw last night that he didn't want me to see. I really wish I had his number.

I bin my clothes that had sat in the footwell of my dad's car on the journey home last night. They're black with dirt, and even if I could get them clean in the wash, I don't want them any more. I don't know why. I just don't.

I take the SIM card out of my old phone, lacerating my fingers in the process, and bin the remnants, before popping the SIM in the new one and charging it up. Then, when it's got enough juice in it, I call my best friend Natasha.

'Finally,' she says when I ring. I texted her from my mum's phone and gave her a debrief earlier today, and she's been patiently awaiting my call so that we can have a proper chat. She works in the head office of a major bank over in Canary Wharf, and I can hear the hustle and bustle of people shouting and swearing in the background. It's a stark contrast to my office, where we all type away quietly and where the silence is often broken only by a phone ringing or someone asking if anyone wants a coffee. Every time we skive off work for a few minutes to talk to each other in the working day, her office always sounds very . . . masculine.

'How are you?' she asks. 'Or are you already sick of people asking you that?'

'I'm fine,' I fib. Although I am, I guess. I tell her everything that happened, although I'd passed out for most of it. I mention Tom, because how could I not? His role in it, how we ended up at his flat for the rest of the night, how we work across the courtyard from each other. She's silent at that, obviously restraining herself from asking, 'Is he single', because I know how her mind works. She's forever trying to hook me up with people from her office. And because Natasha says nothing, I circle back, finish with, 'I'm not exactly laid up in hospital like so many others are. And I'm not dead, so I should count my lucky stars.'

'Sweetheart, it's not only about that, you know. It's big, what you went through. You and that guy, and everyone else on the train. Don't try to brush it off. Give it the time it deserves.'

'Yeah.'

'Is your mum pacing like she normally does when there's big stuff happening?' We've known each other since school, and my parents love Natasha, treating her like she's another daughter whenever they see her.

I glance over to my mum in the kitchen. She's waiting for the kettle to boil, pacing up and down the kitchen and issuing me worried glances.

'I think she believes I'm going to pass out again suddenly.'

'It's her job, as a mum, to worry.'

'She's taken the day off work to look after me, but I don't need it and I worry about the kids she's abandoned to the supply teacher.'

'Is your mum worried about the kids she's left with the supply teacher?' Natasha asks.

'I don't think so.'

'Then why are you?'

'Fair point,' I say, before signing off and agreeing that we'll catch up again properly later.

As I try to work, Mum takes Tom's clothes out of the tumble dryer for me, folds them neatly and puts them next to my temporary workspace on the dining table. I thank her and look at Tom's T-shirt and shorts, clean and ready to be returned, and wonder if he's had as rough a rest of his day as I have. In a way it's a blessing I don't really remember what happened, that I hit my head and blacked out the moment the train crashed. Whereas Tom, like countless others, was awake through the whole ordeal.

Chapter 8

Tom

I didn't realise at first that Abbie was the girl I'd stared at absent-mindedly from my office window every now and again since I moved to my new window desk a few weeks ago. Now it's Monday and she's back at her window desk. She's been on the phone off and on, but she's not laughing the way she normally does. She didn't go to work on Friday and every time I glanced up her desk was empty. I sort of missed the view and found my mind wandering towards her even more throughout the course of the evening. Easy to do when you're with colleagues, four pints down in The Dog & Sun at the corner and then moving on to Jägermeister. Disgusting, but that combination gets you hammered really fast, which is what I needed. Maybe not needed, but certainly wanted.

I didn't even make it home to my flat before I threw up in the entranceway. I tried to clean it up, but failed miserably. The weekly cleaning crew came on Saturday to clean the communal areas. I bunged the two of them £50 each. Again. I've done this too many times now. And then I slept, all of Saturday and most of Sunday, and opened the fridge to find those two beers I'd been saving had gone. And then I remembered who I'd drunk them with. And when. And why. And I forced my eyes closed for a few seconds to blacken out the memory of the train, Abbie smothered in blood and everything else I can't think about. Abbie passed out with her head covered in blood is not the worst memory of that day by a long shot.

And then I drowned my liver in a six-pack of Peroni from the corner shop. And then I threw up again, only this time in my own bathroom, so I don't have to bung anyone any cash.

But sitting here on Monday, nodding mutely in meetings, signing documents and generally being here but not here, I glance out of the window every now and again and see Abbie looking about as present as me. For a full six minutes she's been staring at her computer but I haven't seen her move a muscle; she hasn't once touched her keyboard or scrolled on the mouse. I think. She's quite far away. I might be wrong. I'm itching to message her. I don't want to look keen, needy, abnormal. But nothing about this is normal. I pick up my phone. Annoyed with myself, I put it down, glance at her again.

She also hasn't once looked across the courtyard at me. Not once. By mid-afternoon I can't take it any more and I grab my phone, ignoring the messages piling in from certain people, and open a new message window, texting her. It's a bland message asking how she is. I sign off with my name, because she's not got my number saved. I watch. She doesn't move. Maybe she's not yet managed to get hold of a new phone. And then she reaches forward, picks up what must be a replacement mobile and flips it open. I can't see what she's doing, but seconds later she replies with an equally bland message saying she's fine and then asking how I am.

This is bullshit.

I type, I'm going for a cigarette. Can you come outside?

She turns to me for the first time, looks right at me. How did she know I was watching? She nods, pushes her chair back and presumably heads for the stairwell.

Outside, she comes towards me holding a Sainsbury's carrier bag stuffed with something. I forgot how blonde her hair was. Now it's neat, styled in waves. She's wearing make-up. She doesn't need it. I've seen her bare-faced and she looks lovely like that. She's wearing nice jeans and a T-shirt, in stark contrast to my dark-blue suit. I loosen my collar.

We greet each other with a casual 'Hi' and strange smiles that look sympathetic rather than a genuine greeting.

'What's in the bag?' I ask as she holds it out to me.

'It's your clothes.'

I reach for them. 'Thanks.' I find myself actually caring about how this woman is – even though I hardly know her. 'How are you? And don't say "fine".'

She smiles, a bit less sympathetic, a bit more genuine this time. 'Oh, you know. You?'

I sigh, long and loud. 'Same. Your head looks better.'

She touches it self-consciously. 'I went to hospital after I left yours on Friday.'

'Did you?' I ask in surprise.

She nods proudly and then turns sheepish. 'My dad forced me.'

'Ah, that makes sense. There was no way you were going voluntarily.'

'Hey,' she says. 'I might have gone.'

'Hmm,' I respond.

'You're right. I wasn't going to go. Felt like a waste of the nurses' time when I knew I was OK, but it made Dad feel happy.'

'I'm pleased you went as well.'

She looks at me thoughtfully. 'Thanks. Are we having this cigarette or not?'

I laugh, pull out my pack and hand her one.

She shakes her head. 'No, thanks. I'm just going to stand here and smell yours.'

'*Smell* mine?'

'It smells better than it tastes.'

I light the cigarette, thinking about this. 'I suppose it does.'

But it doesn't stop her reaching for it, removing it from between my fingers and lifting it to her lips. I'm far too entranced by this move. Back in the flat, it felt so normal to share a cigarette with a girl I'd dragged off a mangled train. Here now, in front of my office, it feels oddly even more intimate than before.

She hands it back, gives me a look of concern. 'Have you talked to anyone about it?'

I shake my head. 'Have you?'

'Sort of . . . to my parents and my best friend. I'm not really sure what to say that doesn't make me sound mad. I think it's more the darkness of it all that's affecting me. The literal darkness. It's so strange – being unconscious throughout most of it. Everything's so . . . black. It's so uncontrollable, anyway. But everything is uncontrollable when you've blacked out. I could have been trampled on, I could have been . . . Oh, I don't know. And then there's the *what if*.'

'The "what if"?' I say, inhaling a long, deep drag on the cigarette. I watch her closely.

'What if I hadn't got on that particular train, what if I hadn't dashed through the doors in time, what if you hadn't been there to get me out, what if . . .'

'You're torturing yourself with that, are you? After everything you went through – don't do that to yourself as well.'

'I hate that I'd passed out, that I couldn't help someone else.'

'You were better off passed out, trust me,' I say quietly.

Silence. Then she prompts me. 'You were awake throughout the whole thing. You must have seen—'

I know what's coming next. She's going to ask me what I saw. I can't talk about it, so I cut her off quickly before she can ask me any more questions. 'I should go back in,' I say, offering her the rest of the cigarette.

She looks at it for a second, takes it. 'Thanks.'

Before I go I say, 'Do you want to meet for coffee or lunch or something one day?' I'm reluctant to finish things here.

She thinks about it. 'Yeah. That would be nice actually. Text me when you're free.'

When I get back to my desk she's not across the road at hers yet; instead she's finishing my cigarette and talking to some of her workmates. I turn back and stare at my screen, willing my presentation to finish itself.

Chapter 9

Abbie

Over the past few days since I met Tom outside our offices for a cigarette, it's taken every ounce of effort I have not to look out of the window at him across the courtyard all day. I never knew he was right there. I've never really had the urge to scan the windows to see other anonymous faces and wonder what they're doing. I'm usually so engrossed in my work, wading through retail data or deconstructing the non-news buried inside fluffy press releases. But now I know that he's there, my eyes are forever pulled in his direction and I have to fight so hard to stay focused on what I'm doing, which is sort of annoying me because I'm really busy today. I've let too much pile up, even though my boss is still being gentle, allowing me to go slowly, to extend my deadlines – which I don't want because I don't want to let the side down.

Tom and I are meeting for lunch today in a little Italian café round the corner. It was his suggestion and he offered to meet me outside our offices, so we can walk across together. I wonder now if this might be a little bit strange: Tom and I, hanging out. In ordinary circumstances I'd never be friends with someone like Tom, but I think that's because I immediately judged the kind of man he must be, from his suit and his job title. That's especially unfair of me because he's obviously so much more than that. And, more importantly, he rescued me.

We wave our greetings at each other from across the courtyard and meet in the middle. He looks good, a neat blue suit and dark-brown brogues. I've ditched my usual jeans and T-shirt ensemble and put a dress on today because the temperature's gone back to end-of-summer levels again.

I didn't think he'd notice my outfit really, but as we order paninis and coffees and sit on bar stools at the high tables in the back to await our food, he says, 'Nice dress.'

It's too short for these bar stools. I think he's spotted that too. He's making an effort only to look into my eyes while we talk. I try not to laugh. 'Thanks.'

Small talk is easier in here with him than it was in the courtyard because I knew some of my workmates had come outside and I felt watched, being, as I was, on the wrong side of the street. We often joked about Tom's building and the far more corporate people who work inside it, but I've heard they have an amazing subsidised canteen and their own coffee shop, so I think the joke is on us.

Tom takes his jacket off, rolls up his shirtsleeves and I look away from his forearms and into his blue eyes with the same level of concentration he's so far shown me. He tucks into his panini without a care that I'm watching him. I'm a bit more delicate, but melted cheese is still going everywhere.

'Your cut looks better,' he says, reaching up as if to touch it, then acknowledging that his fingers are a bit greasy from the food, he retreats. 'It looks orange, though,' he says.

'It's foundation,' I say. 'I'm covering it up. It's been a week and it's not healing as well as I'd like.'

'Don't cover it up,' he says and diffuses the command with a smile. 'It looks like you've taken that bit of you to a tanning salon and forgotten the rest.'

My mouth drops open. I've decided the man who heroically rescued me from the train is actually a bit forthright – or maybe he's just rude. I tell him this and Tom laughs loudly. 'You're not the first person to tell me that, and I'm sure you won't be the last.'

I look at his hands; the cuts have almost healed. 'Did you get all those from the train?' I ask.

'Yeah, the glass you were leaning against smashed. I crawled all over it when I pulled you up.'

'Thanks. I was leaning against glass? I don't remember that.'

He's finished his sandwich and I take his hand in mine to look at it, running my fingers gently over the marks on his palm where his cuts are healing. The air between us thickens. 'Did you have glass inside your hands?' I ask quietly.

'A bit,' he says after a beat, leaving his palm in mine. We're both looking down at our hands together. Is it my imagination or has the café become silent? I couldn't tell you how many people are in here, but I can't hear them, as if it's just Tom and me, and no one else.

I raise my eyes to look at his. 'How did you get it out?'

I think we're both feeling a bit awkward and so I let go of his hand and he lifts it out of my lap. And then the noise of the café seems to start up again, people ordering lattes and salads; and someone nudges me and apologises as they walk towards a spare bar stool near ours.

It takes him a moment to answer. 'Tweezers, pure deter-mination and a couple of beers.'

'A good combination,' I say because I can't think of any-thing else.

I look at my uneaten sandwich. I've ordered the wrong thing. It's too messy to eat like this. I wonder if I'll look like a moron if I ask for a knife and fork.

He's asked me something and I've obviously missed it and need him to repeat himself. 'I asked if you're seeing anyone?' he says. 'You said you didn't have a boyfriend before, but I wondered if you were . . .' He trails off.

'Dating?' I suggest. 'Playing the field?'

'That's such an old-fashioned way of putting it,' he laughs. 'But yeah, if you like, are you playing the field, Abbie? It's not *quite* what I meant, but let's run with it.'

It's such a sudden change in conversation. I wonder if my holding his hand prompted it, tilted us into a margin-ally different level of friendship. 'No,' I say truthfully. 'Are you?'

'No,' he says simply, and somewhere deep within me my stomach trips happily over itself, which is mental because I hardly know him. 'I'd just broken up with someone the night of the . . . whatever that was – derailment, crash.'

'I remember you saying that now,' I reply and try to resist the urge to prompt him into revealing more about this, despite the fact that I find I want to know every single detail.

But instead of opening up, he's staring at my sandwich. Is he dodging looking at me on purpose or does he actually want my panini?

'Samantha and I were friends and we fell into having sex, and then fell into dating and then, before I knew it, we were in a relationship, I guess. Which is what made it incredibly awkward when it dawned on me that we weren't right for each other.'

'Why awkward?' I ask.

'I had to make a decision: stay as I was and it would probably stay like that for ever.'

'Or . . . ?' I'm pushing now.

He inhales, exhales a sigh. 'Or lose a friend, because we could never really go back to what we were before. Even I'm not stupid enough to think you can be friends with someone, then have a relationship with them, and then you dump them and it's all fine.' He shrugs.

I think about this for a second or two and I wonder if he's right. I go to speak, but he slices in quickly, pointing at my panini. 'Are you going to eat that?'

I push the plate towards him. 'No, you can have it.'

'We should do this again,' he says with a grin.

'God help me.'

Chapter 10

Tom

A week later a fly's trying to get inside my office window, bashing into the thick pane of glass repeatedly. It must be doing itself an injury, the determined little fella. 'You don't want to come in here. And besides, it doesn't open, mate,' I say out loud and then catch myself.

Across the desk my colleague and friend Sean looks at me and then at the window and then back down again.

I stare at the fly as it gives one last attempt and then moves off to head-butt someone else's window. I'm quite jealous for a few seconds. That fly, out there, and me in this hermetically sealed environment. I push my chair back.

'I'm going for some fresh air,' I say.

'Fresh air or a cigarette?' Sean asks.

'Bit of both.'

The two of us were in early for a catch-up and we're now killing time before a big meeting. He's all right, Sean. We share the same sense of humour. In his interview he made me all sorts of promises about the kind of colleague he'd be. He's failed to deliver on quite a few of those and I'm working out how to broach that. I might do it in the pub one of these days.

Across the courtyard I see Abbie on her way into work. She's dismounting from a pushbike, removing her crash hat and clipping it onto her backpack. I instinctively cross the courtyard and say, 'Hi.'

She's got earphones in and they're blasting music from somewhere I can't fathom. She yanks them out.

'Do you usually cycle to work?' I gesture to the bike that she's chained up on the bike rack.

'I don't cycle all the way from home. I get the overground train. I just don't really want to get the Tube at the minute, so I'm cycling this little bit for now. It's not far. And besides, it's good for me.'

I put one hand in my pocket and give her a look. 'You won't want any of this then?' I say, holding my freshly lit cigarette.

She takes it from me and inhales, closes her eyes, which makes me smile, although she can't see me doing it. 'One or two drags on your cigarettes every few days won't undo the good work of my new cycling regime.' Her eyes open.

'It might. Cigarettes kill, remember.' I gently lift the cigarette out of her fingers. She's painted her nails some sort of pink. They look nice.

'Two weeks ago I was almost killed on a train,' she says. 'The cigarettes can get in the fucking queue.' And then she throws me a knowing smirk and strides off towards her office doors.

She's smart and funny, which I realise kind of turns me on. You never know what she's going to say next. Unpredictable. That's what she is. But in a good way. I message her later on, because a few of us are going to grab drinks and then head to a club after. We never admit that's what the plan is, but it goes in that order almost every time we head out. There are normally seven of us who go, and sometimes Sean pops his head in, if he thinks he can find someone to take home. It's brazen, I suppose, but he's got this confidence with women that I'm sort of envious of.

I have no idea if drinks and a club are Abbie's thing or not. I'm not really sure they're my thing, but what else am I going to do tonight?

Ugh, no thanks, she replies when I ask her, which surprises me. And then she follows it up with, I can't think of anything worse than a bunch of suits bumping and grinding in a club after work. So sad.

So sad? I suppose it is a bit, and I smile at her barbed response.

I can think of something worse, I reply. A bunch of suits who hardly know each other grinding at a conference after-party. I look across the courtyard and see her typing energetically on her phone.

I shift on my seat as I watch, entranced. Her shoulders are shaking and she's obviously making herself laugh, which makes me laugh. I'm still looking at her when my phone beeps in my hand. I look down expectantly.

Oh, I've seen that, she says. Totally awful. But in a way that makes you stare non-stop, and you can't wait to see who's going to snog who, and you put money on it—

She's obviously hit her 160-character limit per text message and I wait, because there has to be more. I'm still smiling when the next one arrives.

And then you see them the next morning, she continues. Full of regret, avoiding each other, knowing there's another day of the conference they've both got to suffer. And then a final message. Oooh, it's the best.

She looks across at me and we both laugh.

I'll buy all your drinks, I type. Just come.

All my drinks? she asks. And then: I can really drink, you know. I'm a journalist. They send us on courses to learn how to do features writing, news writing and serious hardcore drinking.

Really? Oh shit, I type. I look across the courtyard and she's not typing back, just looking at me, the humour evident in her face.

I'll buy some of your drinks then, I retort, and I watch her look down at her phone. Someone's standing next to Abbie, and she puts her phone down and starts pretending to be busy at her desk, knowing she's been rumbled, engrossed in her text messages. Then she gets up with a notebook and follows her colleague.

I'm left with disappointment that our conversation has come to a halt and I look back at my screen, still laughing to myself.

'What's so funny?' Sean asks, looking across the courtyard and then back at me, trying to work out what I'm chuckling about and where the hell I keep looking.

'Nothing,' I say, trying to look serious again.

It's a full three hours before I receive a reply. Fine, I'll come, she says and follows it with a colon, a dash and a bracket. I turn my phone to the side. Is that supposed to be a smiley face?

Chapter 11

Abbie

In the pub Tom and I spend all night talking. His colleagues come along and they're funny. He's telling me about how his work buddy Sean opted out, choosing instead to spend time with a few of his old workmates across town.

'He's all right. He sort of makes my days there slightly more bearable,' Tom says.

I wish I'd brought someone from work now, but my closest friend, Gary, had a date, and all the others in my office are quite a bit older than me. When I touted the idea of accompanying a bunch of bankers out to drinks and a City club, I'm not sure I sold it all too well. Natasha pencilled it into her diary and then pencilled right over the top of it with a client dinner. She still said I could stay at hers after, though, as it sounds like it'll be a late one, which meant I had to do an emergency run to Next earlier today for new knickers to wear tomorrow morning, as I couldn't remember if I'd left any clean ones at Natasha's or not. A shame she didn't come, because she was the only one up for the clubbing bit. She's up for almost any sort of night out. Her schedule is exhausting. I wonder if she and Tom might be quite a good fit? And then I remove that thought from my head immediately, as thinking of Natasha and Tom together makes me feel tense.

Tom looks at me as we talk, while I answer his question about my job.

'What kind of shops do you write about?' he asks, somewhat bemused.

'All sorts,' I say. 'It's a retail magazine, so if you're a retailer, in the magazine you go. This week I'm writing an article about Christmas windows.'

'It's October,' he says in a flat voice.

I laugh. 'I know. We start planning the main Christmas features in July. This is a pretty late one for us.'

'How did you get that gig?' he asks.

'I just applied,' I say. 'Went through a graduate trainee scheme.'

'It can't have been that easy,' he says. 'Isn't being a journalist one of those jobs that everyone wants to do, that hardly anyone gets a shot at and that everyone thinks is glamorous and fun?'

I nod along. I think he's right. It always raises a few add-on questions at parties, when people ask what I do for a living and I tell them. I usually leave out the bit about it paying peanuts. But I tell Tom and he delves deeper.

'Really? How many peanuts?' he asks. 'Actually, you don't have to answer that.'

I hesitate and then, 'Fifteen peanuts.'

'Thousand? Fifteen thousand peanuts?' he gasps. 'You're joking. I had no idea it paid so appallingly,' he states. 'How on earth does Boris Johnson swan about town living it large?' he questions.

'I think it might be something to do with inherited wealth, in addition to editing *The Spectator*. Plus, I don't think his basic salary is fifteen thousand,' I say as we're propping up the bar and I'm about to order. Buying a round for nine people is going to cripple my finances, and I see Tom wince on my behalf as I pay. I'm going to have to make my own lunches with scraps from home for the next few weeks, if I carry on like this.

'OK,' he says. 'The next twelve rounds are on me.'

I laugh.

'So what do you want to do – you know . . . long-term?' he asks.

'Is this a job interview?'

'Of course not.' He sips his pint. 'But you've been there a while, right?'

'Yeah,' I say. Doubt about where this conversation is heading enters my mind.

'And you like it?'

'I love it,' I enthuse. 'I'm having the best time. It doesn't really feel like work.'

'Lucky you. That's all right then,' he says.

'*Should* I want more?' I ask, although I don't know why I'm asking Tom.

'*Do* you want more?' he questions.

We're two drinks in and having a conversation about life goals. I wonder if I should want more or if that would be greedy. I'm not yet thirty. I'm not sure I should be stressing about career goals yet. Maybe if I don't see any progress over the next year or so, I'll engage panic stations.

'I think right now I'm just happy to be alive,' I tell him honestly.

'Amen to that,' he says and clinks his glass against mine.

*

A few hours later I'm glad I bought a round in the pub, because drinks in the club are treble the price. I'm so shocked when full bottles of Grey Goose vodka turn up in ice buckets at our table that I turn to Tom, seated next to me on the leather banquette. 'This cannot be a standard night out?'

He laughs. 'Sort of is, so far. Although normally the bar staff bring the bottles over with those attention-seeking indoor fireworks stuck in the top. I think they've run out tonight. Thank God.'

'Oh, that's so awful,' I cringe.

'I know,' he agrees. 'This is actually pretty low-key.'

I'm not sure how I feel about being here. This isn't very *me*. But then not long ago I almost died in a Tube crash. Perhaps I should live a bit more. I accept a shot of vodka from one of Tom's friends whose name I've already forgotten. My short-term memory is suffering since I bashed my head. I can't ask his name a second time and I just say, 'Thanks' while wondering how hungover I'm going to be tomorrow.

'Remind me where you live?' Tom asks after we've downed our drinks.

'Enfield,' I say.

'Have you always lived there?'

I nod. 'Where's home for you? Other than your swanky flat, I mean.'

'Nowhere else. Just my swanky flat,' he says teasingly.

'No, I mean where do you call home? Where do your parents live?'

'I don't really call anywhere home,' he says after a pause. 'Mum and Dad live in the British Virgin Islands. They own a small hotel out there. And before that Dad was a troubleshooter for a hotel chain and they moved around a lot, depending on which hotel he needed to go and spend time saving.'

'So where did you live?' I ask.

'School,' he says. 'Then university. Then I flat-shared for a bit.'

I look at him as another vodka is handed in my direction. I cannot do shots all night, and Tom sees this. 'You want a Coke or something to go with that?'

'Yes, please.'

He flags a passing waitress and orders me a mixer.

'So you never really lived with your parents?' I ask.

'Until I was about seven, I did. Then I was sent to school over here.'

I process this. Tom stopped living with his parents when he was seven years old. That must have had a massive impact on him.

My face obviously reflects this and he says, 'It's perfectly normal, you know, to go to boarding school.'

'At age seven?' I ask in horror.

'At age seven,' he says somewhat tersely.

'And you've not lived with your parents since?'

'Christ, now I can tell you're a journalist. Dig, dig, dig.'

I laugh and my drink arrives. I thank the waitress and decide to leave questioning Tom about his childhood. I feel a bit sorry for him, sent off to board at seven while his parents swanned around, doing God knows what. Poor Tom.

'So how often do you make it out to the Caribbean?' I ask.

'A couple of times a year: Christmas and sometimes in February, if I'm not skiing.'

'Oh, Tom,' I say and put my head in my hands, laughing to myself. He has no idea how posh he sounds.

'What?' he asks. 'What?' He gently lifts my head up to look into my eyes. 'Are you laughing at me?'

'No,' I say, straightening my face. 'I was. But I'm not now.'

His hand is still on my face and he's looking at me, his eyes full of amusement instead of annoyance. It feels nice, the warmth of his skin against mine.

'Sorry,' I say, collecting myself. 'It made me laugh. But I shouldn't posh-shame you.'

'Posh-shame?' he splutters and takes his hand away from my face, the physical connection between us lost. He tops up his vodka glass.

We sit companionably in the club, the thrum of the music making the banquette seating vibrate beneath us. The vodka is making me brave, and my journalism training is hard to shake. 'Can I ask you a personal question?'

'Uh-oh. Go on.'

'When we met . . .' I start.

'Yeah?' he says.

'You'd just finished a relationship.'

'Yeaaaah,' he draws out the word nervously, uncertainly.

'Did you finish it that day?'

He shakes his head. 'No, the night before.'

I draw in a breath. 'That's a dramatic twenty-four hours.'

He takes a sip of his drink. 'Agreed. As weeks go, that one was . . . fucking awful.'

He gives me a half-smile and attempts to laugh it off, but there's something in his eyes that tells me he's feeling the way I am, although I wish I knew what it actually *is* that I'm feeling.

And then he starts up. 'It wasn't right between us – Samantha and me. There was no *one thing*. It was a combination

53

of things, really. And you can either choose to ignore it all, hold on *really* tight, hope for the best, even though you *know* it's probably not going to work – not really. Or you can . . .'

He struggles for a word and, after a beat, I volunteer, 'Let go?'

Tom looks at me, thinking it over. 'Yeah,' he says slowly. 'Let go.' Another pause. 'It was the right thing to do, for both of us.'

I want so desperately to ask what she looked like, this woman, Samantha. Is she a lean, fit yoga bunny; a tall blonde from his office; a petite brunette he met at university? I think about how to position this question in the atmosphere, without sounding like I'm momentarily hung up on it, hung up on the type of woman Tom would date, the type of woman Tom would break up with – which obviously I *am* hung up on now – when a girl about my age walks past the table, her skirt short, her shirt open at the neck, and Tom looks at her for the briefest of seconds before returning his attention to me.

I look down at my work clothes – jeans, T-shirt – and am reminded that I don't fit in here. I pull my hair up in a high ponytail, fidgeting unnecessarily.

'You look great by the way,' he says softly. He leans in to tell me, so that I can hear him over the thumping noise the speakers are blasting. How could he tell I was stressing?

'You don't need to try like *that*.'

'I look like I don't try?' I ask over the thumping music.

'You look like you don't *need* to try,' he repeats, louder this time. 'Like that. You're effortless. There's a big difference. Trust me.'

He makes me smile and I don't know how he does it, but so far he's been an expert at making me feel relaxed. In the street, in his flat, here where I feel out of my depth, Tom is easy to be with. But despite his placatory words about my appearance, I still pull a lip gloss out of my bag. He looks at me while I apply it, but doesn't speak. He turns away while I finish, downs the rest of his shot and then turns back and grabs my hand.

'Come on,' he says as the DJ begins playing Rihanna's 'Pon de Replay'. I've been hearing this song everywhere for months, but I'm still not over it. Tom pulls me up from the seats, instructs his mates to watch my bag and drags me on to the dance floor, where I'm surprised to see so many people. I'm not drunk enough for this, but Tom has this good-humoured way of encouraging me to dance without forcing me. He's just going with the flow, and I'm going with him.

Under my shoes the dance floor is reassuringly sticky. While other couples seem to be grinding up against each other, Tom's still got hold of my hand, swirling and spinning me and then pulling me towards him. The music is fast and the beat's making my head spin. Tom being close is making my head spin too, but it feels natural, and he's making me laugh by singing all the words wrong. I think he's doing it on purpose.

'Are you going to grind on me, like we're at a conference?' I ask in my most teasingly seductive voice.

He laughs so hard and then says, 'Obviously.'

He gets closer and this has the potential to be something so very sexy, but I watch Tom as we dance together, putting his best super-serious backing-dancer face on as he moves and I think, *This is what I need. After the last few weeks, this is exactly what I need.* Dancing like this with Tom has made me forget. And then I realise I've remembered everything again, and it suddenly sobers me up.

'What's wrong?' he asks, his hands on my shoulders so he can look at me. He's noticed that I've stopped taking our dancing very seriously.

'I think I'm just hungry.' And then a bit more truthfully, 'I'm feeling a bit light-headed.'

'You want to get some food in here or are you done with this place?'

I look around at the girls in high heels and the men in suits. Rihanna's stopped singing and instead we're being treated to Kanye West's 'Gold Digger'. I do love this one, but the music, the darkness, the beat, the heat . . . 'I think I'm done. But you don't have to come with me.'

'Of course I do,' he says. 'Besides, I'm starving too. Let's find somewhere to grab some emergency dinner.'

I nod, smile gratefully. I didn't actually want to go on my own, but I would never have asked Tom to leave. He seemed so at ease. He appears to have slotted back into his normal life after everything. But maybe this isn't Tom's normal life. I don't actually know.

We say goodbye to everyone, and Tom drops some money onto the table to help pay for the oversized bottle of vodka that he barely touched. His friends give him a look that indicates he's scored with me. Tom misses it, but I don't. Has Tom scored with me? Do *I* want to score with *Tom*? I ponder this as I pull my backpack over one shoulder and find that Tom's hand has slotted into mine so naturally, leading me from the club. I hold his hand and wonder what it means. Holding hands is so innocent and yet . . . not.

Outside, the night is surprisingly warm for this time of year. It'll be winter soon, but autumn's mellow heat is still trying its best to cling to the season. Above us a few clouds scud slowly across the night sky.

'It's later than I thought it was,' Tom says, looking up. It's never quite dark enough in London to see stars. Far above us somewhere the stars are twinkling, unseen down here, but I know they're there, reminding me there are greater things in this universe; greater things than what's been happening to me, to Tom, to us.

Around us the buildings are lit up twenty-four hours a day, shining lights on empty desks; cranes assembling skyscrapers sputter red lights on and off, on and off, to tell helicopters to steer clear. Somewhere between the club and St Paul's Tom lets go of my hand and the welcoming lights of a McDonald's glow from across the road.

'Come on,' he says. 'I'll buy you some dinner. I think it's the only thing open.'

'You do know how to treat a girl,' I say as we enter the glaring brightness and step forward to place our order.

'I would take you to The Ivy, but you posh-shamed me, remember?' he teases, tilting his head up to look at the menu. 'So now we're in here, so I can prove to you I'm a man of the people. What do you normally have?'

'I have the same thing every time,' I confess. 'A Cheeseburger Happy Meal with a milkshake. The portion size just works for me.'

'What's a Happy Meal?' he asks, looking at the menu.

'Is this a trick question?'

He turns to me. 'No.'

'It's a kids' meal. It comes with a toy.'

'I've never had one,' he says.

I think of his confession that he never really lived with his parents as a child. When it's our turn, I step forward. 'Two Cheeseburger Happy Meals, please, with strawberry milkshakes.'

'Are you having two?' he asks with a look of mock-horror.

'They're not both for me,' I protest. 'You're about to have your first Happy Meal.' Then I remember they're for kids. 'And a portion of chicken nuggets and an extra pack of fries, please,' I tell the server. Then I turn to Tom. 'You're a big, strapping man and they are quite small portions actually, so we might need some top-up supplies.'

'Big, strapping man?' he repeats and his eyebrows lift. 'I can't work out if that's a compliment.'

'I think it is,' I say. 'I meant it as one. Although I've never quite understood what the word "strapping" means.'

He smiles. 'You're a journalist. Shouldn't you know?'

'Not really a word I use much when writing about shops.'

'I'm not sure either, actually,' he says as I find my gaze drawn towards his eyes. This is one of the least sexy conversations I've ever had, in one of the least sexy locations, and yet there is something strangely intoxicating about the whole thing. I wonder if Tom has recognised it too, because his look mirrors mine.

And then the server ruins it all by shouting out our order to alert us it's ready.

'I can't believe you've never had a Happy Meal,' I say as we collect our food.

'That's because I'm twenty-seven.'

'Ha-ha,' I reply. 'I meant when you were a kid.'

But Tom doesn't reply, just shrugs, clutching the paper bag full of food while I hold our milkshakes.

We walk back towards St Paul's to find somewhere to sit in the churchyard, choosing a patch of grass in the shadow of Wren's masterpiece. I glance at my watch, surprised to discover it's half eleven. I wonder if Natasha's home from her client dinner yet. Either way, I've got her spare key. I'm getting colder, now the heat of the club has shaken itself free of me. I shiver and Tom automatically takes off his suit jacket and puts it round my shoulders, leaving his hands on me for a fraction, before removing them from my arms.

'Thanks,' I say. 'You're quite the gentleman.'

'I try.'

I take the lid off my milkshake and dip one of my chips in and Tom stares at me.

'What on earth are you doing?' he baulks.

'It's really good – try it. There's something about the saltiness of the fries and the sweetness of the milkshake combined together.'

'Is this one of your quirks, like how cigarettes smell better than they taste?'

'I was wrong about that one,' I confess.

Tom dips a chip in his milkshake and then eats it. He frowns. I can't tell if he wants to admit I'm right or rejoice in telling me I'm wrong. He does neither.

I continue and he looks at me with increasing amusement while I watch the traffic on Cannon Street come and go. The traffic's light at this time of night, with only the occasional cyclist and a few black cabs passing by, mostly with their 'For hire' lights off, with inebriated passengers curled up inside being whisked to a mainline station or home.

Across the road, by the glass Tourist Information Centre, a man is drunkenly yelling into his phone that he's on his way home.

'That'll be us one day,' I say and Tom stares at me. 'Not us as in *us* . . . but us as in real grown-ups, adults – apologising for coming home late, missing dinner, hoping your other half will still love you and hold you at night.'

'Even if they're pissed off that we've let our dinner go cold and haven't rung until half eleven,' he plays along.

'Exactly. That would be nice,' I think out loud. 'To have someone to love, someone to . . . be with.' I'm aware of Tom's presence next to me, his shoulder near mine, our hands close together as we reach into the greasy paper bag for the food.

'Yeah,' he says when the taxi's pulled away. 'It would be.' He looks at me and I at him, and then he breaks eye contact as he tucks into his cheeseburger. Because Tom is a gentleman, we share the chicken nuggets and extra chips too. Alcohol makes me ravenous and I wish I'd got a bigger milkshake as well now.

'Kids' meals sounded quite funny, but the downside is all-out hunger if you're an adult,' Tom says with booze-laced wisdom.

'The upside is the toy, though,' I tell him and I dive into our Happy Meal boxes and pull out the same toy from each: a grey Beanie Babies bear.

I hand him one and position mine so it's sitting upright on the grass.

He looks at his thoughtfully. 'Kinda cute,' he says and then puts his next to mine while we finish our food.

I lie down on the grass and he lies next to me. I'm aware we look like drunkards sleeping in a churchyard with our fast-food packets piled up next to us, but even so it's nice, quiet, companionable.

'How are you getting home?' he asks me gently, but directs his voice towards the clouds.

'I'm not staying at home tonight,' I reply, turning on my side to face him. 'I've already organised to stay at my best friend Natasha's.'

'Where does she live?' he asks.

'Docklands.'

'Nice,' he replies, turning on his side to face me. The grass is cold even through Tom's suit jacket. Our Beanie Babies sit in the space between us, but I have this desire to move closer to Tom, close the gap. Just a little.

'I'll walk you to a station in a bit,' he says softly.

'It's fine. You don't need to do that. I'll grab a cab.'

He looks at me, seems to understand my reluctance to get on the Tube. 'OK. I'll pay, though. I did lure you out tonight.'

'I had a nice time,' I say.

'Really?' he asks.

'Yeah, it was nice to hang out, but you don't need to pay for my taxi.'

We stand up, dust grass off ourselves and scoop up our rubbish. I hand him back his jacket as I begin scanning the street for a cab. It's late. I need to get to Natasha's, but in a way I wish Tom and I could stay here all night.

'I'm paying,' he says and hands me £20. 'That'll cover Docklands, right?'

I don't reach for it.

'If you don't take it, I'll only hand it straight to the driver.'

'You really don't have to do this.'

'I can't *not*, now I know how much you earn. And also it's about staying safe, especially at this time of night.'

I reach reluctantly for the note. 'Thank you,' I say and walk towards a bin, piling our rubbish inside.

'Hey,' he says and points towards the grass. 'You forgot these little guys.' He bends down and picks up our bears, walking over and handing one to me. 'I might keep mine,' he says. 'I'll put it on my desk at work.'

'So that all your colleagues know Tom isn't just a numbers-and-statistics guy, that he actually has a hidden heart?'

He laughs and I put my bear in my rucksack. 'I think I'll keep mine on my desk too.'

'So it can join the hundred other soft toys sitting on it.'

'I don't have anything like that on my desk, thank you.' I give him a little shove and he fakes being mortally wounded.

A black cab drops someone off on the other side of the street and Tom whistles in his direction. We watch while the driver does a quick turn to pull up on our side of the road. I tell him Natasha's address.

'Thank you,' I say, turning back to Tom, 'for tonight, and for the taxi.'

'My pleasure,' he says and then follows it with, 'you're an unexpected friend, Abbie. I'm really glad I met you. Even though I wish we'd met under different circumstances.'

I climb inside the taxi.

'I'm really glad I met you too,' I say. He bends down, kisses me on the cheek. 'Especially now I know you own a hotel in the British Virgin Islands. *Hello*, free holidays.'

He chuckles, closes the cab door and the taxi pulls away. I turn back to wave at Tom, who raises his hand in return. And then I watch him put his Beanie Baby in his inside jacket pocket and begin walking the few streets home.

Chapter 12

Tom

I don't know what possessed me, but on the way back to my flat I responded to a text from Sean. He'd failed to get lucky and wanted to know which club we were in, then demanded to know where I was. Going back and joining them was inevitable, really. I don't know why I do this to myself, especially as I was practically at my front door when the message came through. I don't want to miss out, I guess. Although I never *quite* enjoy it as much as I think I'm going to. And then we ended up halfway across town at another club, and now it's eight a.m. and I'm bleary-headed and travelling back to mine, after crashing on our colleague Dave's sofa in the back end of Earls Court. Crashing. Crash. Poor choice of word, after what happened to me – what happened to us: me and Abbie, on the Tube. It's an especially poor choice of word given that I'm actually on the Tube for the first time since that day. I didn't think; too tired, I suppose. I just got on it.

The need hadn't arisen to get the Tube before this. And if it had and if I'd been thinking straighter, would I have done it so easily as I did just now? I simply walked towards the station on autopilot, tapped my Oyster card and took a seat, before it struck me what I was doing, where I was.

To say the Underground's not my favourite thing these days is a bit of an understatement. I wish I'd picked up a paper this morning to distract myself. There's no signal down here, either, so I can't even do anything useful on my phone. I crick my neck a few times, and the woman opposite me looks up to see where the sound of crunching bones is coming from. I give her a polite smile and will the journey to be over. I'm not prone to drama, I hope; and avoiding thinking back to that day has been relatively easy, what with work and going out drinking. But I'm actually in a carriage now, wondering if lightning *can* strike twice. What if *this* Tube derails? Or what if something else happens to it? Who would I save first, if it happened again – if I lived? There's a pregnant woman sitting further down the carriage. She's wearing one of those 'Baby on board' badges.

Her. I'd try to save her first. I might stand up actually. I might casually saunter over to her now, so I'm ready if it happens again.

I'm breathing so hard the woman opposite is still staring at me with a nervous expression on her face. Oh my God, what's wrong with me? I rub my forehead and sweat comes away in my hand. I must look deranged, unpredictable. The train pulls into Blackfriars station and I can't get out fast enough. My shirt is dripping by the time I make it back to my flat. I semi-needed a fresh change of clothes before, but now I definitely do.

It takes me ten minutes of letting cool water run over my body to finally calm down. And then I drink about a litre of water. I've run out of time to make coffee or grab breakfast from the Italian café, and I need to get to work.

As I exit my flat my phone beeps. I expect one of the lads from last night, but I get Abbie. Abbie – God, she feels like a lifeline today. Last night was fun. Do you fancy a quick drink in the pub after work? she asks.

I'm so hungover that the thought of a drink makes me heave, but the thought of seeing Abbie lifts me up so high. I don't want to reply; I want to phone her instead. I want to hear her voice. What's happening? But I don't call her, because that might be weird, so instead I adopt a tone that sounds like something Tom in normal times might say. Hey, I'll be in there with Sean and some others before we head off to Brick Lane for a curry. Come and find us? I reply.

I read what I've written three times. I'm sure I'm losing my mind. And then I hit send.

After a long day Sean and I arrive in the pub and find Abbie already at the bar with one of her workmates, Gary. Sean didn't meet Abbie last night, and I want him to now. She's cool and I'm sure he'll like her. I sort of want to show her off a bit, which sounds strange because we're just friends.

We shake hands all round and Sean, the absolute bastard, smarms all over Abbie, kissing her cheek when they're introduced. She kisses his cheek back and I feel a bit . . . odd. Why's he doing that? And then he offers to get everyone a round in. Abbie and her mate Gary look delighted and make self-deprecating jokes about being poverty-stricken journalists. She gives me a wink at this, and I remember I chatted shit about her living on such a low salary. Oh no. What else did I say last night?

I watch Sean and his easy confidence with Abbie. He's a good people person, which is why I hired him and why we became such easy friends, but I really wish I hadn't brought him now, especially because minutes later he's moved in for the kill, towering over Abbie like a silverback gorilla and topping up her glass from the bottle, ignoring me and her mate as we watch this with varying emotions. Gary looks amused. I'm fucking livid. I've barely had a chance to speak to Abbie, other than a quick hello. Why am I so pissed off? I reach for the bottle and fill up Gary's glass for him, swirl the dregs into mine and put the bottle on the bar. Gary is somewhere in the middle of being entertained at Sean's obviousness and recognising that our chat is in its dying throes. We've been comparing functions on our new phones for fifteen minutes. We're done with this conversation now.

I glance at the TV screen, which is always on the news channel in here, but it shows the time in the corner. I want to check how long before I can feasibly make a polite exit, under the guise of taking Sean for a curry, and vow never to let him anywhere near Abbie again. But I see what's on the TV and I stare.

Abbie's left Sean's side and has come to stand next to me. She sees it too. The news is reporting how the driver of the train we were on has died in hospital. I feel her hand slip into mine. I clutch it tightly while still watching the TV. I'm only vaguely aware that her face is upturned towards the screen as we stand in the pub, the only two people engrossed in this news story.

Chapter 13

Abbie

We walk towards St Paul's Cathedral. Somehow, automatically, wordlessly, Tom has steered me out of the pub, away from the TV and the busy noise of after-work drinkers. It was as if he knew I was going to break down and cry, which is what has just happened.

'I didn't even know him,' I say through my tears.

'I know,' Tom replies, handing me a tissue as we walk. 'But it's still . . . sad.'

'The front carriages were *fine*,' I say. 'We climbed out through them, didn't we?' Although I can't actually remember how we got out of the train. 'How can he have died?'

'The news said he suffered a heart attack in hospital,' Tom says mournfully. 'I don't know any more than that.'

'Oh,' I say pointlessly. I don't think this walk is helping at all, although it was kind of Tom to suggest it.

He extricates his hand from mine, which makes me notice that his hand must have been in mine to start with. When did that happen?

We go to the churchyard, back to where we'd sat before, on the grass by the cathedral railings. It's not dark yet and there are people in here who look so carefree: tourists taking pictures, a woman reading a book while nursing a take-away coffee. This news doesn't bother them. None of it affects them. But it does me. As we sit, Tom looks fine, his eyes closed, his head tipped back, raised to the skies.

The moment he entered my life was by far the worst experience I've ever lived through. But thank God he was there, although it was all over so soon and (as I keep reminding myself) I didn't really live through it. I'd passed out. Tom seems so fine, so strong. Whereas I can't even get on the Tube any more. I haven't got back on since that day. I'm petrified. I'd rather take my chances on my bike.

Tom's chin is still tipped up, but his jaw is clenched. *Is* he actually OK?

I start to ask him this, but instead different words exit my mouth. 'I don't want to go home tonight.'

'Stay at mine,' he volunteers immediately. 'Only if you want.'

That wasn't what I meant. I don't respond immediately. I think he's focused my mind a bit now. Is he being gentle-manly or does he want something else? He only has one bed. How would that work?

'Abbie?' He sounds kind of desperate. If I said no, he wouldn't make a big deal out of it, but he wants me to say yes or he wouldn't have asked. Tom's gaze connects with mine and I feel stilled, safe, calm.

I assume he'll take the sofa. It doesn't matter. I won't sleep anyway. It's been two weeks since the derailment and I've been restless every night since. I've almost forgotten what a proper night's sleep is.

'We'll get drunk and get takeaways and put on a few shit films.'

OK. He's won me over now, making me smile.

'Can we watch good films, though, not shit ones?'

He laughs, climbs to his feet, lowers his hand to pull me up. 'Let's do that,' he says, keeping his hand in mine as we walk. It feels so good, so natural. Somewhere an awkward boundary has been ushered away and now we're glued together. Perhaps it's the situation we've found ourselves in, but I could be glued to Tom quite readily, I think.

We pass a little Tesco and he says, 'Takeaway? Or shall we buy something prepared in a factory that we don't actually have to cook very much.'

'Cooking's not your thing?' I ask as we enter the shop.

'You've seen my empty fridge, right?' He lets go of my hand and takes a basket. 'The full works. Booze, ice cream, popcorn, pizza? Not in that order. Maybe in that order.'

He starts filling the basket up and sends me off to choose the ice cream. I text my parents en route to the freezer aisle, telling them where I'm staying tonight. My dad approves of Tom. It was definitely the heroics that clinched it.

I track Tom down to the snacks aisle, loading various packets of crisps and popcorn into the heaving basket. It's full of high-fat, high-sugar items. It's like two seven-year-olds have been let lose in a food shop for the very first time. Only with four bottles of wine on top.

'We're going to be comatose if we eat and drink all that,' I say appreciatively.

'Exactly,' Tom says.

'You'll have to hold my hair back again over the toilet, you know that, right?'

'I'd be disappointed if it was any other way.'

*

'Why do you always wear jeans to work?' he asks with his back to me as he's twiddling the nobs on the microwave. We are a bottle of wine in and have eaten all the crisps.

I walk over, take the pizza from his hand and put it on the work surface. We are not ruining this by microwaving it. I turn the oven on to preheat and he leaps to open the oven door, pulling out a cellophane-wrapped instruction manual.

'Have you never used the oven?' I ask.

He shakes his head. 'Everything I buy is microwavable.'

I ignore this sad state of affairs. 'I wear jeans because I can. I wore a dress the other day.'

'I remember,' he says with a sheepish grin. He opens the second bottle of wine and pours it liberally into our glasses. 'That dress was *very* short. Did you ride your bike with that short dress on?'

'I didn't realise until I'd left the house how short it was when I sat down.'

'*I* realised,' he says. 'It suited you.'

I look away, embarrassed. I should probably say something to set him straight at this point, but it's nice to be flirting with him.

'All this bike-riding – are you really on a health kick?' he asks. 'Because your drinking antics in the pub and nicking my cigarettes don't exactly go hand-in-hand with a health-and-fitness regime.'

I don't know how to answer this. I'm still thinking while I drink an unhealthy measure of wine. He's waiting for an actual answer. I'm about to make up a witty response, but he beats me to it.

'Have you still not got on the Tube since . . .' He doesn't need to finish the sentence.

If I'm going to talk about this to anyone, it's probably going to be Tom. I take a deep breath, let it out again. 'No.'

'Not once?' He looks concerned.

'No.'

He knows not to ask why. It's bloody obvious why. I'm scared.

'Oh,' he says.

'Have you?' I ask.

'Yeah. I wasn't keen, but . . .'

'Really?' My voice rises with shock. *How can he?*

He looks at me as if he's weighing up saying something else. And then he opts for, 'Life goes on. My life goes on. So does yours.'

'My life is still going on,' I say quietly.

'Is it? Have you been out much since that day?' he asks.

'A bit.' It's true. 'I've been out with friends from work and my best mate, Natasha, over in Docklands. It's only been two weeks and I'm on a journalist's salary, as you like pointing out to me. I can't go out every night. I can't afford it.'

He goes to cut in, but I stop him.

'Besides, it's not going out that frightens me; it's not drinks in pubs with friends that I can't get to grips with – it's getting around this bloody city that's giving me grief.'

'I get that. How did you get in from Docklands this morning then? You left your bike in the rack at work last night.'

'I took the DLR really early and then I walked the rest of the way.'

He tips his head to the side. 'You'll get on the Docklands Light Railway, but you won't get on the Tube?'

'The Tube's different,' I say.

71

'And you get on the mainline rail from your house into Liverpool Street,' he says.

'Again,' I say forcefully, 'The. Tube. Is. Different. And no, I can't make sense of it, either.'

I know why he's concerned. It's just how I feel, and I can't make it change.

'Give it time, I guess,' he suggests.

'Yeah, maybe.'

He folds his arms across his chest and looks at me as if there's more we both need to say. I wish he'd stop looking at me like that. I like it when he smiles, when he looks interested while I'm talking, not when he looks this concerned. But perhaps it's a good sign that Tom is concerned. He's such an unexpected friend, and I don't think any man (other than my dad) has ever cared about me like this before, even when I've been in relationships.

Tom drops the subject, rips the cellophane off the pizza and puts it into the oven.

'You need to take the cardboard disc out from underneath,' I tell him.

'Oh, for fuck's sake,' he says, opening the oven again.

I can't work out if this is the best thing for us – two tipsy people comforting each other while watching bad films from the nineties – or the worst thing ever. But I need this so much. This is the first proper night when I've let my hair down in . . . a long time. I couldn't do it before, in the club. But here, with Tom, I can.

We are dealing with our problems by not dealing with our problems. Instead he's teaching me how to do magic tricks with a pack of cards. We've resorted to this because when we tried to play an actual card game I lost every time and, far from Tom being pleased that he kept winning by default, he just lost interest. 'Where's the challenge?'

So now he's shuffling cards around and my eyes are swimming, trying to follow the ace of spades. 'Slower,' I say. 'I'm going to get it this time.'

'You're not,' he says.

'Where did you learn this?' I ask. 'It's really geeky.'

'It's not geeky. It's hot,' he says with confidence. 'I learned it at school.'

'Magic school?' I tease.

'No, actual school. Boarding school.'

'You really are a cliché,' I say, tapping one of the cards he lays down. He turns it over and it's the queen of diamonds.

'Ha,' he says and picks up the cards again. 'You lose. One more time.'

'Yes! We keep going until I get it.'

'We can't do that. I have to go to work in a few hours.'

'Ye of little faith,' I say, straightening up and topping up our glasses. 'Let's go.'

He shuffles the cards, maintaining eye contact, which is kind of eerie, but also kind of hot and kind of impressive. And then a thought enters my head and I say it out loud. 'The more I drink, the better looking you get,' I say.

'Thanks,' he says with genuine warmth. And then, 'Wait, what?'

I double over with laughter because that's not what I meant to say at all, but it's far funnier than what I was actually going to say.

'That sounded different in my head,' I say, trying not to snort.

He puts the cards down, our game abandoned. 'Why aren't you with someone?' he asks.

'Comments like the one I just made,' I say, taking a big drink from my glass. I pick up the discarded cards and start shuffling absent-mindedly. Even when drunk, I can't sit still these days – I need something to do or else I start thinking.

'You know you're really fun, right,' he says. 'And nice. And . . . gorgeous.' He takes a big swig from his glass. 'And those legs!' He whistles between his teeth.

'I haven't been single for long,' I say. 'About five months. I wasn't really into my last relationship and it sort of fizzled out. He was a bit of a workaholic.'

'I know the feeling,' Tom says.

'I've been speed-dating a couple of times since with Natasha,' I say in my own defence, although I'm not sure this is anything to be proud of.

'Christ, how desperate *were* you? Speed-dating is awful. I hated every second of it. Whoever invented it is a sadist.' Tom downs his drink and gets up to go to the kitchen.

I follow him. 'So you've been speed-dating.'

'Never again,' he vows. 'I went because Sean convinced me to join him. I'm better as a wingman.'

'Sean seems nice,' I say.

Tom's gone quiet now. All the fun of the fair is over and we've gone into serious territory again. This keeps happening.

'Yeah. He's all right.'

'You're a terrible wingman. Aren't you supposed to big up your friend?'

'To you?' he says. 'Why would I big him up to you?'

'He asked me for my number,' I confess.

'Did he?' Tom's voice just went really high. 'That's a bold move. Did you give it to him?'

'Yeah.'

He stops, stares at me. 'Why?'

'Why did I give him my number? Because he's friendly, we got on really well and, as I've discovered with you, it's nice to make new friends. And he got the first round in, even though he'd never met me before.'

'I knew that was going to come back to haunt me.'

'What do you mean?' I ask with a laugh.

'Never mind, go on.'

'There's not much more than that really. I met a nice guy in a bar, who comes . . . well, not highly recommended by his friend,' I shoot Tom a look, 'but with enough of a seal of approval to convince me he's not an axe murderer.'

'Sounds romantic,' he deadpans.

'It's not supposed to be romantic,' I say despairingly. 'It's to make a new friend. I've got Gary's number in my phone and I'm not dating *him*.'

Tom says nothing.

'This is where you tell me if Sean's an axe murderer or not, by the way,' I probe.

'Not as far as I'm aware,' Tom replies, but his voice is quiet, soft.

I have no intention of dating Sean, but now I'm worried I've upset Tom. I don't want to keep reiterating the point, but he's dwelling on it for some reason. I didn't say I'd given Sean my number to make him jealous or to stop our flirty chat, but I wonder, sadly, if I've just done both. I wish I'd said nothing now.

Tom opens the freezer and pulls out the tub of ice cream and places it on the side. He doesn't pull out any bowls; instead I join him and he hands me a spoon. We hover over his kitchen counter, lifting each spoon of ice cream directly out of the tub and into our mouths.

'I'm a bit worried about you,' he confides tenderly.

I turn to look at him and his face is so much closer than I expected it to be, even though our shoulders are touching while we stand and eat. Being close to Tom is nice and I can smell his shampoo, the same one I borrowed the last time I was here. I really like it. I might get some, even if it is for men.

'You're worried about me because I might go out for a drink with Sean?'

'Not because of Sean. I'm worried about you because of . . . you know. That day.' His expression is urgent.

'Don't be,' I tell him. 'I'll be OK. It'll just take time.'

Chapter 14

Tom

I look at her. She's so close I can see every single line and colour in her eyes. I've never noticed what an unusual tone they are: not blue and not green, something in between. 'Well, I'm here for you, whenever you need to talk to someone. You know that, don't you?' I say. Shit, this conversation's got serious again.

She nods.

'Do you think we should join a support group?' she asks.

I think about that for a while. 'I think we *are* a support group,' I say eventually. And although that doesn't really make sense, Abbie seems to know what I mean.

'We can go to one together if you want,' I offer, although I really don't want to.

'Maybe,' she replies.

I can see tears forming in her eyes and I reach up and brush them away as they fall.

'Sorry,' we both say together.

'Why are you apologising?' I ask.

'For being silly. We were having a nice time and I've ruined it.'

'You're not being silly,' I tell her, turning to face her properly now. 'And I always have a nice time with you. You're so easy to be with.'

She smiles at that. 'The same,' she says.

'I prefer being with you to being by myself,' I comment. But that's not what I mean. That didn't sound as nice out loud as it had in my head. I don't want to be by myself, I realise. I want to be near Abbie, with her. All the time. Oh, shit! Where did that thought come from? 'You know what I mean. I really like being with you,' I say. The cheap wine is making me incoherent.

I touch her face again, although there are no tears falling now. The room has gone quiet. We've gone quiet. And then, because Abbie is funny and pretty and sexy, and because we've somehow found ourselves inextricably intertwined in each other's lives since that awful day – because of that day – because I can't stop myself and because I don't want to stop myself, I do the most moronic thing I can think of.

I kiss her.

Chapter 15

Abbie

It feels so different from how I thought it would feel: Tom's lips on mine. So gentle at first, as if he's attempting to work out if I'm going to retreat quickly. But I don't. I close my eyes and let Tom kiss me so softly, so very gently that my body begs him to kiss me harder. And he does, but it's still wary, hesitant, until it's not. And we ease in so readily, so willingly. He touches my face, my neck and his hand edges into my hair, gently holding me.

I'm lost, but it's in such a good way. I never want this feeling to end – Tom wanting me. Me wanting Tom.

I hold onto his hips, hooking my fingers into his belt loops, pulling him towards me until our bodies are pressed against each other. We break for breath, for reassurance that this kiss is what we want, and then his mouth seeks mine again. I've never been kissed like this before.

He moves back ever so subtly and looks at me. I'm not sure if he's weighing up what we're doing, what we're about to do or if he's checking I'm OK.

I don't want him to check on me. I want him to have sex with me. But I can't say it out loud. I just want him to *know* that's what's happening.

His mouth is on mine again and I think he's finally got it, because our height difference gets the better of him and he finds a solution, lifting me onto the countertop, pushing the open tub of ice cream out of the way so that it flips over, the spoons clattering onto the floor.

I groan softly and, in doing so, I have made it abundantly clear where my head is at. But he's stalling, his hips in between my open legs, focused on kissing me. His hands rest on my waist and then they're around me, commanding me, pulling me into him.

I can't take this, I'm desperate now. I put my hands in his hair, pull him towards me and then I move, untucking his shirt from his trousers. His tie had come off the moment we entered his flat, and his top button's been undone all night. I don't think he gets how alluring it is, that little V of skin where his neck meets his collar. He's getting it now, though.

I lift my arms as he pulls my T-shirt up and over my head. He'd been a gentleman in the café that time, determinedly not looking at where my dress was so short, but he's far from that now. His eyes are on my chest and, because we both know where this is leading, he cuts to the chase, his hand unclipping my bra and pulling it away from me while I tackle his shirt buttons.

I mutter something provocative about how much I want him inside me and he pulls his belt off at such a speed it's dizzying. I slide off the work surface because I can't get my jeans off up here like this, and he holds me, kisses me. I pull back, fumble with the button, but my eyes are blurring and my hair falls in the way. He does it for me and I push my jeans down, almost falling over in the process as I stand there in my knickers. Tom pulls his socks off and his trousers hit the floor. Then he comes towards me again and scoops me into his arms, his metal watch cold against my back. I groan with desire as he kisses my neck, working his way seductively towards my mouth.

He pulls back, gently, slowly, reluctantly – leaving static charge in the space between us as he crouches on the floor, pulling his wallet out of his discarded trousers. In his haste his phone falls out of the upturned trouser pocket and crashes onto the floor. Tom pulls a condom out of his wallet, his phone screen lights up and he automatically glances at it. A perplexed expression descends on him and then he slowly stands up, clutching his phone.

'What?' I ask. 'What?'

He shakes his head.

'What?' I ask again. 'What's wrong?'

He skips a beat and then, 'Nothing.'

'That's not true. What's going on?'

But he pulls back and then draws out the words, 'Oh, fucking hell.'

'What?' I say. 'What?' *What's happening?*

'Oh, fuck, Abbie.' And then he issues a noise direct from the back of his throat. He moves backwards, away from me. 'Oh, fuck,' he repeats.

'What? What?' I'm not tipsy any more. I'm stone-cold sober.

He turns away from me and I know I've lost him at this point, as he exhales long and loud. 'I'm sorry,' he says and walks away, picking up our clothes one by one. 'Fuck. Fuck. Fuck.'

I'm so incredibly still, standing in his kitchen, half naked. I feel even more exposed now than I did when I was about to have sex with him. My breathing ramps up and I don't know what to say.

'We shouldn't do this,' he says. But what he means is: we're not doing this. There's no discussion. He's decided.

He's picked up his clothes, but he's not putting them on. He's standing in his tight boxer shorts, still hard. He's still hard, but he's not having sex with me. This makes no sense.

'Why not?' I ask. I am genuinely confused. Is it me? Is he not into me? His erection tells me otherwise. 'Talk to me. Tell me what's happening,' I beg.

He shakes his head. 'You should . . .' He gestures to the clothes scattered around us.

'Are you dismissing me?' I baulk. 'Are you kicking me out?'

'I just . . . you need to . . . Yeah. I'm sorry. Just – I'm sorry.'

I can't move. My mouth is open in horror, shock, humiliation, embarrassment. I'm naked. And I'm being kicked out because of something on his phone. 'Why?' I try again. 'Why are you doing this?'

'It's not my fault,' Tom says. And then his facial expression tells me he's reconsidering this.

'Is it *my* fault? Have I done something?' I plead, shamefully hearing the desperation in my own voice. I've hit a new low. He doesn't even answer. He's looking at the floor. What did I do wrong? 'I don't understand what I've done.'

'You haven't done anything wrong. We need to . . . God, I can't think. I need to deal with this when I'm sober.'

'You need to *deal with this* when you're *sober*?' I repeat disbelievingly. 'Are you joking? How can you talk to me like this. How can you do this to someone?'

He's looking at his phone now, his eyes purposefully avoiding mine.

My heart is racing. I want to shake him. I want Tom to admit he's an idiot, that he's sorry. I want him to tell me what's wrong. I want him to kiss me again. I want to punch his public-schoolboy middle-class face. I want him out of my sight for ever.

Through the red mist of anger I find my bra on the floor, turn my back to him and put it on, then my jeans and T-shirt go back on.

He turns away from me and puts his clothes back on with slow, laboured moves.

We neither of us say anything and then I'm gone, out of the door, my bag in one hand, my shoes in the other.

I'm not even crying. I'm too shocked. I'm angry and I stalk at speed round the corner out of sight of his window, leaning against the wall and pulling my shoes on. I flip open my phone and see it's almost 5.30 a.m. At some point a new day started and, inside Tom's flat, I didn't even notice. I don't know where to go. By the time I get home, I'll have to turn round and come back to work again. I could head to Natasha's, but she's probably already up and in the gym, and I can't sleep these days anyway.

Through the tears and anger and sadness I decide my only option is to go to work four hours early.

Chapter 16

Tom

I'm facing the wrong way when Abbie leaves. I only notice she's not here any more when my front door shuts. It's one of those fire doors that closes by itself painfully slowly, so by the time it clicks into place she's long gone. But it's this click that pulls me out of my thoughts. Why can't she see that I'm in turmoil? Why has she run? I race to the window to see which way she went, but she's fast when she wants to be and there's no sign of her.

I'm dressed, thank God, so I grab my keys, phone, trainers and I just run for it. I don't even close my front door. This isn't how tonight was supposed to go. It wasn't supposed to end like this. Where has she gone? Is she going home? I head towards the river, in the direction of Blackfriars Tube, and then I remember she won't get the Tube any more.

I stand by the Underground entrance, unsure of what to do. I dial her number and wait, holding my phone to my ear. It rings and rings. I dial again. The same thing happens. Where is she? What have I done?

I start walking back to my flat, ringing and ringing her. Every time the call ends, I redial. I need to speak to her. I need to tell her why I stopped. I need her to know why. 'Pick up,' I shout into the phone. A cabby with his window down at a set of red lights jumps in his seat and looks at me. He winds his window up. I'm the raving lunatic shouting in the street in the early hours of the morning.

I call again, but I get an annoying little triple beep. Abbie's switched her phone off. I turn to the nearest wall, which happens to be one of the walls to my office building. I make a fist and punch it so hard, while yelling the word 'Fuck!' at the top of my voice over and over. I hear the crunching sound before I acknowledge the pain.

Back in my flat, I lie down on my bed and stare up into the glare of the light bulb, wondering how that all went so horrifically wrong. I was about to have sex with Abbie. I wanted to. God, did I want to. And so did she. And now it's all gone wrong. And it's my fault. Everything about this is my fault.

I really like her. I'm not sure I understood how fast that feeling had crept up on me. We're friends, but not romantic friends. Flirty friends maybe? I'm so baffled about what's going on here.

Abbie and I, the way we met . . . People don't meet like this. People don't get together like this. I've either blown our friendship or I've saved it. I strongly suspect it's the former.

But I can't lose Abbie. I'm going to need her as a friend more than ever now. I look again at my phone and at the message that flashed up in the heat of the moment, drawing my eye when I was trying to find a condom. That fucking message. That fucking message changed everything.

I look at my right hand, crushed, covered in blood, the agony of it refusing to subside. I'm pretty damned sure I've broken every single bone in it.

Chapter 17

Abbie

November 2005

I watch the ice in my drink fracture and crack as the cold water hits the cubes. The noise of it is strangely satisfying and comforting. Funny how two things made of the same material can be so different, so at odds with each other, and then melt together as one anyway.

I'm at a bar near Canary Wharf waiting for Natasha. Despite the fact the buildings are so close to each other here, there's so much more space. Most of it is concrete or paving slabs, but the bars all have wide outdoor terraces, patio heaters and rugs in abundance so that it's quite nice to sit here, my coat wrapped around me, finishing my mulled wine as I watch the lapping of the river a few feet away.

I pull out my little foundation compact and look at my reflection to see what's going on with my head injury all these weeks later. The cut on my forehead has healed, but now there's a white line where I know it's forming a scar: a reminder of that day that I'll always have. I put a bit of foundation over it and it looks a bit better. Not much. But it's early days. It might go yet.

When Natasha eventually arrives, it's with her usual exuberance. Nothing ever fazes her. If it had been her and Tom on that train, Natasha would have been the one carrying Tom out, regardless of whether he'd wanted to be saved or not.

'Has Tom been messaging you?' she asks after she's ordered a bottle of champagne. She drinks it like it's water. Her job is entertaining bankers and their wives. I don't understand exactly what it entails, but she's used to a certain level of expense account and seems to apply that to her own free time as well. She forgets that our salaries are wildly different. She's also single and has barely any spare time. She's lovely and pretty, so it's only a matter of time before she finds someone, I'm sure. Then I'm stuffed, as she'll probably never have any time for me.

'Yeah, he's been messaging,' I admit. Although I don't know why he's bothering.

'Still?' she says, pulling a blanket around her and settling in. It's been a month since that night in his flat. 'He's clinging on, is he? Have you replied?'

I shake my head, sip my champagne. Champagne is expensive for a reason. It's delicious.

'I don't know what to say to him,' I tell her. We've spoken about this many times at length over the past month, but it's a subject that neither of us seems able to drop. 'We were standing there, I was practically naked.' I cringe at the memory and take another big glug of champagne. 'So was Tom, and we were on the verge of going to his bed, or back up on the counter.'

'Which would have been so, so hot,' Natasha unhelpfully points out.

'I'm not sure what we were going to do. But we categorically did not do it,' I say. 'And now he sends message after message saying how much he wants me as a friend – *needs* me as a friend. How he wants to explain in person.' Although the messages have drifted down to once every few days now, instead of every day.

'Urgh! A *friend*,' she interjects. 'That's the worst.'

'I know,' I say dejectedly. 'He wanted to have sex with me and then he backtracked, and now he thinks we're better off as friends.'

Natasha makes a face. This has never happened to her.

'I didn't even initiate it. He kissed me first. And then he changed his mind.' I'm whining now.

'It is his right as a human being to change his mind half-way through sex,' Natasha says as if she's doing the voice-over on a consent video.

I give her a look.

'If you'd changed your mind halfway through, do you think he'd be having this conversation with *his* mates?' she asks.

I think. 'Yes, actually. He would be bitching good and proper.'

'Yeah, he probably would,' Natasha says. 'Anyway. We're ignoring him for a bit longer, are we?'

'We are.'

'Cheers to that,' she says and we clink glasses. That feels a bit mean, so I clarify, 'Just until I can work out how I feel and if I want to see him again.'

But I'm not sure I do. I'm not sure I can look him in the eye ever again. How do I go from what happened in his kitchen to . . . 'Hey, how are you? Can I have another drag on your cigarette?' I simply can't. A few weeks ago I didn't even know Tom. How had he come to mean so much to me in such a short space of time? I think whatever our short-lived friendship was, that night ended it. And I hate that. I feel humiliated, embarrassed.

'Anyway, how are you?' I ask Natasha and listen like a good best friend while she tells me how she's just been promoted, how excited she is by her new job and how she's already got her eye on renting a bigger flat, 'with views of the river. It's incredible. It's got two bedrooms,' she says. 'Fancy the other one? You won't have to stay over on my sofa any more . . .' she continues in a sing-song voice. 'And instead of keeping spare knickers and a toothbrush stuffed in a zippy pouch in one of my drawers, you could have your *own* drawers in your *own* room.'

I doubt very much I could sleep on her sofa any more anyway. I can't even sleep well in my own bed very much. Sleep evades me these days.

'No, thanks. I doubt I could afford it.'

'I won't charge you too much. The second bedroom's tiny. And you spend so much time crashing at mine anyway, you might as well have a proper room for basic rent.'

I look at her. 'I don't need a pity-room,' I tell her.

'I get that. But you know what I'm like about sharing my personal space with people I don't know – if I have to advertise it and I end up accidentally inviting a murderer to live with me, then I won't be happy.'

'No,' I say with a smile. 'You'll probably be dead.'

'Exactly,' she says. 'Think about it. What if we come to some arrangement. I'm hardly ever there, but what if I put you in charge of food shopping to compensate for the reduced rent. I was going to rent the whole flat on my own anyway,' she reasons. 'This way, you can report into my mum that I'm eating vegetables, and we get to live together.'

I think about this. I don't mind living at home. I've lived there since I came home from university, whereas Natasha knew she was going to live under the City's bright lights the minute she got her first job. But I guess that now, as I head towards my twenty-fifth birthday, this arrangement might be wearing thin on my folks, although they'd never say. I could never afford to rent my own place, not on my salary. And flat-sharing with strangers . . .

Natasha reads my mind. 'It'll be fun, us living together. You know it will be.'

'I'll think about it,' I say with a smile. We both know that if I can make the financials work, she's almost got me.

'OK. Well, how about this much rent?'

She names a figure I'm sure I can stretch to, especially if I don't have to pay for an overground season ticket any more, which I won't have to, if I'm living so close to work.

'I'm meeting the estate agent in an hour, to sign for it,' she says. 'It's a brand-new development. It's only down there.' She points vaguely downriver. 'Come and see it? Then we can come back out and grab some dinner and you can decide how you feel.'

We're in the lift riding up to the fifteenth floor of a sleek, glass new-build complex. Natasha's on at me about how I don't want to live in Enfield with my parents for the rest of my life. If she takes this flat, she's about a ten-minute walk from her office block. She obviously has the same attitude to commuting as Tom.

The lift opens and we walk down a long, white marble corridor. At the end of it the estate agent is waiting in the open door to the flat, having buzzed us in. He greets us both warmly and opens the door fully, ushering us in to what turns out to be a high-ceilinged apartment with floor-to-ceiling windows with a view over the City. I stand at the window and look out in the general direction of where I work. I am speechless. You can see for miles.

'What do you think?' Natasha asks.

'I'll take it,' I tell her – sort of as a joke and sort of not. Behind me she whoops for joy.

'Really?' she questions.

'Maybe,' I say, laughing. 'If you're sure?'

I turn round to see her signing the rental paperwork and doing a little jig at the same time. I love Natasha so much.

And in only a couple of weeks I get to live with my best friend, in a deluxe pad in London. And even better than that, if I wake up early I can bike it to work from here, so I don't have to worry about getting on any form of public transport ever again.

Chapter 18

Tom

I see her every single day. She's at her desk, but she never looks at me, despite me boring my gaze into her, willing her to look. Abbie must know I'm looking. I don't bother messaging her any more. She doesn't reply, so there's no point.

I was right. I had broken my hand punching the wall when running after Abbie. I acted like a child doing that. Then I acted like an adult and took myself to A&E that morning. I looked more presentable than if I'd gone while still blind drunk. My hand was bound tightly for weeks, and so Sean's been opening all my packets of sandwiches and drinks bottles for me during the working day, literally turning into my right-hand man.

I reach for my water bottle and see it's open. 'Thanks, mate,' I tell him over our computer screens.

'No problem. I realise now I could have held you hostage for weeks over this: forced you to tell me how you did it or refuse to open your drinks and crisp packets.'

I smile. 'I'd have held out.'

'And be dead of starvation and dehydration within a week,' Sean deadpans.

'Maybe.'

'You still not going to tell me how you did it?' he probes, not for the first time and not for the last either, I reckon.

I shake my head. I'm not trying to be mysterious. I just don't want to lie. Neither do I want to tell the truth. It's private. It's between Abbie and me. Or rather, it would be, if she'd ever bloody speak to me again.

'Fair enough,' Sean says and resumes typing. He'll ask again in about an hour.

I consider going out for a cigarette, even though I've already been five times today. I go into the courtyard for cigarettes a bit more regularly than I should, in the hope I'll catch her, but Abbie never comes down. I never see her smoke any more, or beg cigarettes off anyone. She doesn't come down at all. Or if she does, she times it when I'm out for lunch or in a meeting, which means she must be looking, assessing the opportune time to leave. Maybe I'm overthinking it. Maybe she doesn't actually give a shit *where* I am. I look at the Beanie Baby that I put on my desk and adjust its legs, so it's sitting back up again. The little bugger keeps falling over.

I look back across the courtyard, but she's typing away. If I'd seen her once outside her building, I'd have been there like a shot. I meander down aimlessly now, stand outside my office on my own, with my hand in my pocket and a cigarette between my lips, and look up at her window every now and again, like some sort of Z-list Romeo, hoping I'll catch Abbie looking down at me. But she never does. Ever. She's got balls of steel.

In the pub, one lunchtime with Sean, we're standing at the bar on our second pint. We shouldn't have ordered a second one, for various reasons. We're putting together a presentation document in about twenty minutes, moaning relentlessly about it and, by the time we got served, we only have five minutes to neck it down. My senses are all off now. I'm not merry, though. The pint's having the opposite effect.

'Do you see that girl from the train much these days?' Sean asks conversationally. 'The one I met in here last month.'

I shake my head, sigh and put my pint on the bar. 'Not really. Not much.'

'Is she really just a friend?'

'Yep.' The answer is instinctive. I don't even need to think about it. 'But I think that friendship ran its course.'

'Let me guess: you tried to bang her and she turned you down?' That's not a bad guess. He's halfway there.

I force a laugh. 'Something like that.'

He nods, directs his attention to the dregs in his glass and I do the same, grateful I don't have to talk about this any more. I look at my watch. 'Come on, let's go.'

Chapter 19

Abbie

I'm at my desk when my phone beeps twice, letting me know I've got two messages back-to-back. I expect it to be my mum, because I've just messaged her to tell her I've been promoted. I'm now editing a geographical section of the magazine, covering features about retail in parts of Europe. It's on top of the UK features section I've already been editing, and it's for such a tiny bit more money that it's hardly worth discussing, but there's a bit of travel involved and it's all a leap and a bound to the next thing. Whatever the next thing is. But the message isn't from my mum. It's from a number I don't recognise. I click the messages and read the first one: Hi, it's Sean. I work with Tom. Don't know if you remember me? We met in the pub a while ago.

Well, this is curious, I think, as I read the second one, also from him: If you're up for a drink one day after work soon, let me know. It would be nice to get to know you. Sean x

I sit back and look at my phone. The message makes me smile. Is it because I'm flattered? Possibly. I do remember Sean. He was funny, nice and good-looking. But I wasn't interested in anything remotely romantic when I gave him my number. I simply thought it would be good to make a new friend. Perhaps this was somewhat naïve of me, but at the time Tom and I had been in the throes of . . . whatever was happening between us. And now we're firmly not doing that any more. I wonder if that's why Sean's messaging now, all this time later, because Tom's let on to him that whatever was happening between us has ended. So it *has* ended then.

I read Sean's messages again. They're written in a very low-pressure way and I quite like that. But Sean and Tom are friends. I put my phone down on my desk. I won't reply immediately. I need to think about this for a bit. I need to think about all of it.

Chapter 20

Tom

I've just walked into my annual review, and the bit where I start trying to negotiate higher pay is coming up, as is the bit where I get my Christmas bonus confirmed. I haven't exactly worked like a dog these past few months, but if I'd had this review prior to that day in October, I'd have knocked it right out of the park.

I worry if Sean's been carrying me recently. I worry if Sean's *told* them he's been carrying me. Prior to the Tube derailment, I was carrying Sean. But that's what friends do, right? Regardless, I look as if I mean business. I need the money or, rather, I want the money, so I'm giving this meeting my everything.

I sit down and start outlining everything we have achieved this year, and how much money my team and I have made the company and how much we've saved it, which adds up to a nice figure. 'And we've done this on reduced staff numbers, without hiring any extra personnel or having to let anyone go,' I say, which is my real ace card. They don't care about letting people go, but I do. People need to eat.

But because I have given my boss, Derek, zero time to lead his own meeting, he's giving me a look of impatience and I know it's time to shut up.

Throughout my speech he's written nothing down at all, despite the notepad and pen being the only things sitting prominently on the table that divides us. Nothing that's said in these annual reviews is ever a shocker. It would be a pretty sad state of affairs if we saved up all our news for a once-yearly meeting. The news would be bursting to get out of us, which is what I think has just happened actually.

'How are you doing in yourself, Tom?' Derek asks. His pudgy little eyes don't exactly look sympathetic, so I can't work out what's going on. When people ask this, I never quite know what it means. How does *How are you doing in yourself?* differ from a straight-up *How are you doing?*

'I'm great,' I lie. Let's get past this and crack on with the chat about my bonus.

'I've got to be honest,' Derek starts, and I know the conversation is about to go downhill. I feel my palms get sweaty and I rub them on my trousers. 'There have been some concerns raised lately.'

'What? About me?' I ask quickly.

'About the performance coming from your department.'

Oh, shit! It doesn't matter if it's not directly about me. My department is my responsibility. If we're underperforming, then it's on me. Although I didn't think we were underperforming. I've just spent the last twenty minutes outlining how we've excelled.

'Can I have some more details?' I ask with a calmness I don't feel, and Derek reels out a short list of minor offences that almost have me breathing an obvious sigh of relief. 'I will fix those,' I say. 'Not a problem.'

But he's giving me a look of sadness that makes me think he's about to start accusing us all of insider trading.

'There are other things we need to talk about,' he says, and I think, *This is it.* I start mentally spending my bonus. I've got my eye on a new watch and, man alive, I would love to fly over to my parents in the Caribbean in the first-class cabin this time. And then I realise my priorities are totally changing and I'm not buying any of this sort of stuff ever again probably. That's sobering.

But Derek stands up, wheels the TV over from the corner of the room, clicks a few buttons and faffs around for far too long with the VHS. Are we about to watch TV? What's on at this time of day? *Neighbours*? *Doctors*? Derek hovers next to the screen, clearly not at ease enough with all this fairly basic equipment to sit back down with any level of confidence.

A white-and-grey picture appears on the screen. CCTV images of our building appear. It takes me a few seconds to work out what I'm looking at, and then it all clicks into place as I see the date in October and the time marked at 5.32 a.m. I'd been running to catch up with Abbie, just after we'd been about to . . . I cringe, thinking about how badly I'd behaved. I'd been shocked and I'd reacted badly to a text message. It's good we didn't have sex. But no matter how many times I tell myself that, I'm not sure I believe it. That fucking message.

I stiffen in my seat as I watch a grainy image of me pulverising the wall of our office building as I admitted to myself that I'd lost Abbie – breaking my hand in the process. It's embarrassing to watch. I look like a twat, like I'm auditioning to be one of those sad men in *Fight Club*.

I don't speak. The image finishes, and the grainy me walks away cradling his hand. I don't remember cradling my hand. But it's all there. Exhibit A.

Derek sits back down and gives me the sympathetic look he's had on his face the entire meeting. I know how he's been positively itching to get to this point, and probably everything I've said prior to this has been irrelevant while he bided his time. This is the meaty bit, the juicy bit; the bit where Derek gets me to spill my guts. Well, not today.

The silence is uncomfortable and I'm worried I'm in danger of breaking.

'Do you want to tell me what's going on here?' he asks eventually.

'I was having a very bad day.'

'No kidding,' he says. 'The footage was time-stamped 5.32 a.m. How had your day gone so badly wrong, so early in the morning?'

I think he's attempting humour, and then it dawns on me that this is none of his business. He cannot possibly be disciplining me for this?

I attempt a tone that's not inflammatory. 'Am I in trouble?' I ask as if I'm twelve years old and petrified about getting suspended from school. 'It happened outside of work and outside of working hours,' I rush on. 'I know I punched the building, but I'll be honest, I didn't actually realise it was our building until it was over. I only live around the corner, and I was running past and . . . I'm assuming there was no damage.'

'Of course there was no damage, and of course you're not in trouble. But security picked up on this at the time and recognised you immediately. As your line manager, they told me, but I chose to sit on it. I thought I'd rather keep an eye on you from afar, see if you caused me any level of concern or if that was just a one-off. But it's been a little while since this night, and you don't seem yourself any more. I would be a fairly terrible line manager if I didn't check in on you about all of this, as I'm wondering if you're not actually OK. So that's what this is.'

'Good,' I joke. 'I was starting to worry I'd need a lawyer.'

Derek smiles, but it doesn't reach his eyes.

'That's nothing,' I say, gesturing to the TV. 'Don't worry about it. I'm fine. More than fine. If I've been a bit off, then I apologise. I'll fix it. And I'll fix the issues with my team.'

Derek nods, unconvinced, but at least he's willing to change the subject. 'Perhaps you could all go on a team-building day, white-water rafting or something.'

'Sounds fantastic,' I say. *Shoot me now.*

Chapter 21

Abbie

December 2005

I didn't mean to play hard to get with Sean. That wasn't my intention at all. But in between him texting me a few weeks ago and today I've been far busier than I expected.

I moved in with Natasha at the start of this month and we've enjoyed endless drinks after work whenever we're both in, on our new balcony – despite the fact it's bitterly cold now – in our new flat, with views of the river. I cannot stop saying that to anyone who listens: 'my new flat, with views of the river'.

And work has been a bit frantic. My promotion means I get to travel, for work, on company expenses. Travel that someone else pays for . . . I can't get my head around that. I can eat and drink whatever I want (within reason; it turns out that caviar and champagne are on the 'no' list). All I have to do is submit receipts and someone puts money in my bank account. I've only been away twice, and just for two days here, two days there, but it's addictive and I can't wait to go again.

Sean and I have texted back and forth a bit and it's getting flirtier. I quite like it. We're going to meet tonight for a drink. He suggested our work local, but I don't really go in there any more. I don't want to risk running into Tom. Every time I think about that night in his flat – me standing in my knickers while he rejected me – I close my eyes to shut out the humiliation. And then the usual cascade of sadness falls onto me, which is the order of it all when I think about losing Tom: humiliation, followed by sadness at missing him, every single time. Because I have lost him. I have. We've lost each other. He must feel it too, if his frequent I'm sorry text messaging was anything to go by. But that's all stopped now.

No, I can't run into Tom ever again, which might be a bit impossible if I start dating his friend. But we'll cross that bridge if, and when, we come to it.

We meet in a cellar bar, where upturned whisky barrels form tables and red candles are held in old wine bottles. There's sawdust on the floor. I can't tell if this is an ironic-themed bar. It's dim, dark, muted, a bit sexy and we're on our second bottle of wine. We've not eaten, but the girl behind the bar keeps bringing out those little dishes of wasabi nuts, which I assume are free. They're making my eyes water, but I need to keep eating them because I'm so hungry.

We've accidentally ended up playing a game where we position beer mats on the edge of the table, flick them up into the air and catch them with the same hand. It's tougher than it looks. Sean's a pro, which is why I suspect he started showing me how to do it.

'So where are they sending you next then?' he asks.

'Andorra,' I say, focusing on flicking my mat. I knock it with my fingertips and it flies towards his face, hitting him on the nose. 'Sorry,' I giggle.

'Wow! To do what?' he says, handing the mat back for me to try again.

'Interview the tourism minister and talk about ski resorts for an online feature about Christmas sales predictions.' I neglect to tell him that I had to look up on a map where Andorra was.

He nods, expecting more. There is no more. That's about the whole of it.

'Great,' he says, catching my mat for me again. 'When are you going?'

'Next week.'

He makes a huge jokey show of looking put out. 'It takes weeks for me to get you on a date and I can't even arrange a second one in a week's time because you're away.'

He's cute. He's making me feel important, which is very sweet of him. But it's just drinks. For now. We'll see how we go. The reality of sitting here, leaning awkwardly across this whisky barrel with Sean, makes me feel a bit like I probably shouldn't be on a date with one of Tom's friends. Although I don't know why I feel that. I'm certainly not worried about hurting Tom, because he wouldn't care at all, I think. He rejected me. Not the other way round. But it still feels a bit odd. So I reason this is probably a two-date thing and then we'll call it a day. But it's fun to go out. Now I think about it, we've not mentioned Tom once. He's like the elephant in the room. Maybe not to Sean. Maybe it's only me.

'OK, so how about this?' he asks when we've settled up the bar bill. He's helping me on with my coat and, in doing so, gets closer to me than he's been all evening. He smells nice, of a musky, wintery aftershave. 'I've been invited to the opening night of a new bar soon,' he tells me. 'There'll be free drinks and canapés. You up for it? A few friends are going, so there'll be a little gang of us.'

'Yeah, all right.' Oh, this is good. This next meet-up isn't a date, by the sounds of it. Free booze and canapés sounds great, and Sean is actually quite good company. He's fun, easy to talk to, asks questions instead of solely talking about himself. We haven't stopped talking all evening, and being with him isn't stilted at all. I hope the friends he's going with to this bar opening don't include Tom. I'm assuming Sean doesn't know what happened between us. Is it wrong of me to assume that? I can't ask that. I can't ask anything really. Perhaps going on a couple of dates with Sean is a really bad idea, now I think about it.

'Do you fancy some dinner?' he says, halting my inner angst.

'Now? Or after the bar opening?'

'Now. *And* after the bar opening,' he says, with the kind of smile that makes his eyes crinkle, the kind of smile that weakens my resolve a tad. We leave the bar, climbing the stairs and entering the streets of the City once again. The sun was still out this time last month, although not as fierce as it had been the month before. But we're tantalisingly close to Christmas now, and I'm permanently cold. They never turn the heating on in my building. But they do make up for it with an enormous expenses budget, so I'm feeling forgiving.

Sean pulls up the collar of his coat to shield him against the biting winter wind. I love a man in a peacoat, collar up or down. *Oh dear, what's happening?*

'OK, dinner sounds nice.'

'There's a great little Vietnamese place I know,' he says, taking charge. 'We might have to wait for a table, but they have a bar. So we can brush up on your beer-mat catching skills while we wait,' he teases. 'Although I'm not sure they have mats, now I think about it.'

'Not to worry,' I say, opening my bag to show him the contents within. 'I've stolen two from in there, so I could practise at home. They only throw them away when they get wet anyway.'

He laughs, puts his arm around my shoulders and we huddle together against the chill as he takes me out for dinner.

Andorra is cold but fun, cosmopolitan and full of snow-capped mountains. Everywhere I turn I feel I'm looking at a postcard. It's making me feel incredibly Christmassy and I've only been here twenty-four hours. It's also full of very rich people who like to ski. I haven't had time to get out on the slopes, but I do get to go Christmas shopping – it's tax-free – and eat very well indeed, on company money. This is the dream job, surely. I just wish I got paid a bit more, so I could actually afford to start saving. I have nothing saved, which financially-minded Natasha tells me is a crime. I'm not sure it's that bad, but she has encouraged me to start thinking about a pension. When I get home I find pension leaflets artfully fanned out next to the kettle, which makes me laugh. But I vow to take it seriously. I'm living like a grown-up, so I should start taking some grown-up financial decisions.

I'm telling Sean about Andorra while we're sipping free cocktails at the bar launch. We're waiting for his friends to arrive.

Obviously we are both ridiculously keen, because we're among the first there. He's never been to Andorra, either, and he tells me he's off on holiday for two weeks to the Maldives in the New Year.

'Two weeks?' I ask, as a waitress comes past carrying mini-hamburger canapés. We take one each. 'Wow!'

'Promise not to laugh if I tell you I'm going with my parents?'

'Why would I laugh?' I ask.

'It's a bit sad, isn't it? A bit lame?' He looks at me through his eyelashes, thick and dark, shadowing captivating eyes. I didn't notice that on our first date.

I swallow. 'No. If my parents stumped up for me to go to the Maldives, I'd be packing my bags to go quite happily.' I adjust my bag on my arm.

'Yeah, I really like going away with my parents,' he says, 'which is definitely sad. But it's all right. We go and see stuff, I spend time with them because I hardly see them the rest of the year, we sit around on sun loungers a lot and prop the bar up each night. It's actually pretty decent.'

'It sounds it,' I respond.

'It's also a good way to kill off some time.'

'What do you mean?' I ask.

'I'm leaving my job – I'm handing in my notice tomorrow. And because I'm going to a rival, the moment I tell Tom, he'll put me on gardening leave, so I've booked this holiday during my eight weeks off.'

My stomach clenches at hearing Tom's name and I try to ignore that Sean's even said it. 'What's gardening leave?'

'It's when your boss assumes you're leaving to hand over all the company secrets to your next employer, so they march you out the door there and then, so you can't start nicking all the files.'

I blink. 'Mercenary!' And then, 'Tom wouldn't think you'd do that, surely.'

'No, he wouldn't, but it doesn't matter what Tom thinks. It's company policy. It'll have to happen. So I've got eight weeks off. Paid.'

I raise my glass and we clink to 'Cheers'. 'Congratulations on your new job,' I say.

'Thanks,' he replies with a warm smile. 'Tom's been a bit weird of late, so I'm not sure how he's going to take it. You two don't talk much any more?' he probes.

'No, not really,' I say casually, praying Tom never told Sean what happened in his flat.

I change the subject and ask Sean what his new job is. But when people in finance start talking to me about what they do, I can't seem to differentiate between one job and another. Tom, Sean and Natasha may have wildly different jobs, they may also have *exactly* the same job, and no matter how many times I'm told, I'll never grasp it. It's like someone's trying to explain the offside rule to me while using terminology from the *Financial Times*.

'How does this work then?' Sean asks me when he's finished his dizzying explanation about mergers and acquisitions.

'How does what work?' I say, scooping up two mini fish-and-chip canapés presented in tiny sheets of newspaper. I hand him one.

'Thanks,' he says and starts on one of the two chips inside. 'So you and Tom meet on the Tube, you hang out a bit, you

manage to throw each other firmly into the friend zone and
then what . . . ?'

I want to tell him we're not even friends any more. In
a matter of weeks I met a man, became his friend, I nearly
became something else entirely too, although I'm not sure
what. What would have happened if we'd kept going? Would
we be together now? Would I be out on a date with Tom *right
now* instead of with Sean? I'll never know.

'What has he said?' I ask tentatively.

'That you don't really hang out any more.'

OK, good. Tom's been vague with Sean and I can work
with this. I like Sean. I'm not sure I want to tell him *exactly*
what happened between us, especially as it's so humiliating.
But I might open up a little bit to him. 'I don't really think
we're friends any more,' I say. 'Actually, I think it's the fastest
I've made and lost a friend.' And then . . . Hang on. 'He said
we met on the Tube?' I ask slowly.

Sean nods, puts the world's smallest fish goujon into his
mouth.

'On the Tube?' I ask again and then look at Sean for more
information. 'Nothing else? No sort of . . . other information?'

'No,' he looks puzzled.

I start on my own mini fish-and-chips, chewing slowly.
Tom hasn't told him. Tom hasn't told his workmate that he
was on the Tube derailment. He hasn't told Sean he pulled
me from the wreckage. He hasn't told him any of it. I don't
know what to make of this. *Why* hasn't he told him? Does
anyone else at his work know about that day?

Sean's looking for more information, so I nod. 'That's
about it, yeah. Shame, really,' I say far too casually.

'He's been a bit odd for a while,' Sean reiterates. 'Especially more recently. There's something going on with him and he won't say what. I thought you might know.'

I'm not going to put Sean straight about how we met. If Tom hasn't done it, then there's a reason. What else could be going on with him?

I don't want to talk about him any more, it's only going to ruin the night, and up until now I was having a really nice time with Sean. I don't need to tell him what happened. But I do want to know why Tom's keeping it all secret.

Chapter 22

Abbie

1 January 2006

Goodbye, 2005. That was one of the worst and best years of my life. I don't want to reflect too long on last autumn, but I think it's fair to say that day in October almost overshadowed everything else.

But what came after it . . . a promotion, a new flat, a new man. The last few weeks of December had been dizzying.

Sean pops the cork on a bottle of pink champagne and we stand on the balcony of our hotel suite near Trafalgar Square, which he's hired so we can watch the fireworks explode across the London skyline. The colours dot the sky in effervescent shards of neon and gold and I pull my coat around me a bit more, even though my bloodstream is warmed from all the delicious champagne Sean's been plying me with. We've only been dating for about four weeks, but he's sweet, kind, easy to be with. I really like him.

'Anyone would think you're trying to get me drunk?' I tease as he kisses my neck. I'm not sure he's watching the fireworks with the same level of enthusiasm as me.

'Me? No. No way. Perfect gentleman,' he says, which he is.

'They only last a short while,' I say, enjoying the feeling of him nestling into me. 'Didn't you spend a fortune on this suite so we could watch the fireworks?' I don't wait for an answer. 'So watch them,' I giggle as he carries on nuzzling me. I point to the sky, as if he can't see where the fireworks are.

'I spent a fortune on the suite,' he clarifies, lifting his head to watch the sky. 'So we could have a night away together, in style, alone for once, without your flatmate sleeping in the next room at yours, or my flatmate in the next room at mine.'

There's a tiny gap between us and I lean back against him, closing the distance. 'Sean,' I sigh happily.

'Mmm,' he says as we watch blue-and-pink sparkles dot the sky. He's not really expecting me to speak. I'm content, safe, happy. I'm actually happy. Sean is perfect – my safe harbour.

He makes so much time for me and makes plans to do 'stuff': a concert booking here, a restaurant booking there. We went ice-skating at Somerset House a few days ago, in that down-period between Christmas and New Year when nothing interesting ever happens. But this year it did. He told me he wanted me to be his girlfriend while he was trying to hold me up, and I felt my breath catch in my throat.

'None of this *just-seeing-each-other* bollocks,' he'd said. I wondered if it might be a bit too soon, but we've seen so much of each other over recent weeks that I've lost count of how many proper dates we've been on.

We were both laughing so hard because I was skidding around on the blades that I didn't hear him at first and asked him to repeat himself. At first it stunned me so much I didn't know what to say. I let down my guard with Tom. I put it back up with Sean and, despite wanting to say yes, I just . . . couldn't. Tom's made me fear rejection; it was almost as if I didn't trust Sean's declaration of commitment.

Without explaining my reasons, I asked if I could think about it. Sean took it so gracefully it endeared him to me even more. And then we bought hot, steaming cups of mulled wine and went for a walk along the Embankment, holding hands and making plans to see each other tonight before he goes away to the Maldives. And I felt so safe, so happy, so content that I knew that yes, I did want to be Sean's girlfriend. I want everything that entails, but the moment had passed to say it back.

And now I'm in a hotel suite with Sean, and it's midnight as one year finishes and a new one starts. He wraps his arms around me and I turn away from the sparks shooting through the sky and look at him – right at him. I trace the curve of his mouth with my finger and he closes his dark eyes. Then I pull back, and his eyes open and he looks at me with a hint of amusement. 'What?' he asks, softly.

'Yes, please,' I say shyly, days after he asked me. 'I would like to be your girlfriend.'

His smile widens and his eyes crease at the edges in happiness. 'What took you so long?' he asks.

I lean in to kiss him. 'I have no idea.'

Chapter 23

Tom

February 2006

I wake to find my hands shaking and my heart racing. Am I having some kind of panic attack *while I'm asleep*? Is that even possible? I sit up, pull on my running gear and decide I'm going to have to run this all out of my head. Running always stops me thinking.

I head down towards the river and join the few others who are also out bright and early, stopping by the coffee shop at Embankment Tube to get an early-morning coffee and croissant fix. I think I'm their first customer of the day; they look a bit startled, but it might have been the way I entered the shop, suddenly and with no care as to whether the door hit the wall, swung back and then hit me in the face.

I've got plenty of time before I need to be at work, so I can afford to linger, walking through Embankment Gardens where in the summer they put deckchairs out. I must come here one day in summer and just sit. I won't do that, though. As I walk back towards the river there's a homeless guy and I open my wallet to hand him a fiver, although I remember all my notes have gone. I had to use them to bung the cleaning team some cash again. I give him a couple of quid, because it's all I've got, and then I turn back and hand him the still-wrapped croissant in its paper bag. He thanks me and tucks in eagerly.

I enter the network of little lanes near my office. I reckon half the people who wander near Fleet Street and St Paul's never even know this lot's here, which is why I like living where I do. It's right in the centre of the City, close to my office, and it's so quiet at weekends that it doesn't feel much like London at all.

As I take in the scene around me, I suddenly notice Abbie riding past on her bike. I don't immediately realise it's her. But it is.

'Abbie!' I yell her name and she skids to a startled stop, puts both her feet on the ground and turns in her seat to look at me.

Her face falls immediately, which cuts me so hard. I'd never have expected her to look so devastated at seeing me. The few times I imagined this happening I thought she'd be shy, and so would I, that we'd hug awkwardly and possibly even joke about what a dick I'd been that night. But four months on, I didn't expect her to look at me the way you look at the underside of your shoe when you step in dog shit.

'Yeah?' she says without any hint of emotion whatsoever.

I walk towards her to close the gap between us. I'm going to have to ignore her ambivalence and make small talk, regardless. It looks as if me walking towards her is the very last thing she wants.

'Hi,' I say.

With some effort she says 'Hi' back and waits for me to continue. She really has nothing to say to me, after all this time?

'How are you?' I ask.

'I'm OK.' She sounds stilted. 'How are you?'

God, this is awkward. 'Yeah, good.' I have nothing else in the reserve tank. I don't know what else to say now.

I miss you. That's what I want to say. It's the truth. So I'm going in for it. 'I mi—'

But she opens a verbal assault on me. 'Why didn't you tell Sean how we met?'

'Sorry?' I ask.

'You told Sean we met on the Tube.'

'Yeah?'

She looks at me. 'Why didn't you tell him what actually happened?'

'Oh, I don't know. He asked me how we met and I think I did just utter the words "on the Tube", and I wasn't really able to think or do anything useful, much, immediately after that day. He assumed I'd been out and was on the Tube, drunk, and that we'd started talking. And because that *is* how we met, I didn't bother filling in the rest of it. I didn't tell him what happened immediately afterwards.'

She's staring at me uncomprehendingly. 'Why not? Why didn't you correct him?'

'Because I . . . didn't want to.' I sound like a child. I know this. I might as well have stamped a foot on the ground to illustrate my point. 'It seemed best all round to leave it there.'

'I see,' she says quietly. But I can see that she doesn't see. Abbie doesn't see at all. She goes to get back on her bike, but she's here and I'm here, after all this time, so I can't let her go. Not yet.

I walk in front of the bike. 'Abbie,' I start. 'I really miss you.'

She ignores this. 'Have you told *anyone* at work what happened that night? Not mentioned it in passing to anyone: "Oh, by the way, last night I was on a train that derailed quite badly – you know, the one that was all over the news – and I helped a girl off the train . . ."'?'

'No.'

'Have you told anyone other than your parents?'

'No.'

'Why not?' she asks. 'Sean said you were acting really odd before he left, and I thought to myself, *Of course Tom's acting really odd, Tom almost died on a train*. But it turns out Sean didn't know.'

'Did you tell him?' I ask in a far-too-snappy voice if I want her to hang around here a bit longer.

Her voice is soft. I think I might be getting somewhere. 'No, I didn't tell him.'

'Do you speak to Sean?' I ask, suddenly working out the finer intricacies of this chat.

'Yes,' she says.

'Regularly?' I ask.

'Yes,' she says again.

'Why?' I'm incredulous. Why are the two of them talking to each other and yet neither of them is talking to me? It was as if the very moment Sean went on gardening leave, I didn't exist to him any more. I've texted a few times and received short replies, but they've dwindled to nothing.

Somewhere in the depths of her backpack her phone rings. 'Hang on,' she says and pulls her bag round to get to it. She answers it, tells someone she's round the corner. 'I have to go,' she continues to me when she hangs up. 'It's press day and we're supposed to be in early, to proof pages and—'

I have to get in before she goes. 'Can we go for a drink or a coffee or something? I could really do with a friend right now.' That last sentence was a manipulative low blow, and I feel a bit ashamed about it, but it achieves the desired effect because she looks at me sympathetically.

'OK,' she says after a while. She's putting her phone in her bag. She's going to leave.

'Tonight?' I ask.

'I can't,' she says. 'It's Valentine's Day.'

Is it? Bloody hell. I need to book a dinner reservation somewhere. And flowers. I need to arm myself with flowers if I'm going to make it through tonight alive.

'I'm seeing Sean. But I'm free tomorrow,' she suggests.

'Yes,' I say far too keenly. 'Tomorrow. Six-ish? In the pub?'

She nods and then she's gone.

'Bye,' I call to her retreating figure and she turns the corner in the direction of her office without even raising a hand to say goodbye.

It's only as I'm unlocking my front door to shower and change for work that I start to wonder seriously why it is that she's seeing Sean on Valentine's Day. And then it hits me, and everything hurts. And it's not because I didn't warm up before my run.

Chapter 24

Abbie

We're in the cinema watching *Brokeback Mountain*. Sean looks quite puzzled for the first portion of the film and I suspect he had zero idea what this film was about. I've seen the trailer, he clearly hasn't. But he did insist on planning the perfect Valentine's Day, or so he told me, and that involved choosing a romantic film to watch. I keep glancing at him to see his reaction, but he's expressionless, just watching it.

He perks up whenever Michelle Williams appears on the screen in the same way I perk up whenever Heath Ledger does. Afterwards he confesses he saw an advert for the film on the side of a bus, spotted Michelle Williams and made a point of booking it, the minute he was sitting back in front of a computer.

'Well . . .' he starts slowly. 'That was . . . romantic. Not in the way I thought it was going to be.' He laughs at himself and I can't help but chuckle in return. 'I'll admit gay cowboys was not where I saw that film going.'

'You had no idea what it was about before you booked it, did you?'

'Not a clue. I enjoyed it, though.'

'Good. I loved it,' I tell him, planting a quick kiss on his mouth as we enter the ever-manic throng of Leicester Square. 'As our options were basically *Brokeback Mountain* or *Chicken Little*, I'm pleased you chose the first one.'

He nods. 'Good,' he says. 'Although I've seen the trailer for *Chicken Little* twice and I laughed both times, so if you want to go see that too, just say the word.

'Now?' I tease.

'No, not now,' he says pulling me towards him and draping his arm around my shoulder, warming me on this cold February night. 'We've got somewhere to be in about half an hour.'

'Where?' I ask excitedly. I am having the best time.

'I've booked The Ivy.'

'The Ivy?' I squeak with even more excitement. 'I've never been there.'

'I know. You mentioned it about a thousand times when I told you I'd had a client dinner there. That's why I booked it.'

'Sean . . .' I sigh happily. I'm smiling to myself as we walk hand-in-hand through Covent Garden, killing time and feeling like tourists. It's still buzzing with crowds, entertainers, revellers, lovers. A flower seller is offering single-stem roses and Sean pulls out his wallet, pays for one and hands it to me.

'You really are too cute,' I say. 'Thank you.'

He smiles and we move away from the flower seller, stand in the cobbled Piazza as the lights shine down on us and, despite the cold, I feel warm, cared for, appreciated, happy. I turn to Sean to tell him all of this, to tell him how happy he makes me and how I hope I do the same for him. He's smiling the whole way through, and when I finish my jubilant monologue he brushes his hand against my cold cheek, looks into my eyes and tells me he loves me.

Chapter 25

Tom

'OK,' I say, cradling my phone to my ear as I'm running. I'm on the phone to The Ivy. 'If you get any cancellations, will you let me know? Even if it's twenty minutes before, ten minutes before, call me and we'll be there.'

Samantha and I are back together. I cannot believe the way my life has panned out over the last few months. Was it fate it all happened like this? I often think back to that night in my flat, Abbie and I . . . I shake the thought away because that's not helpful now. Samantha and me: that's what I need to think about. That's what I need to focus on. Not Abbie and me. That's gone. I ruined it. If only we hadn't nearly . . . If I'd just not bloody kissed her, we might have managed to still be in each other's lives. Because of that kiss and where it almost led. But it was the right thing we stopped – the right thing. Only now I don't have her in my life.

Another thing I don't have is a dinner reservation. I can't believe I forgot it was Valentine's Day. I've made a total hash of this. Samantha is not going to forgive me, and I need to rush to the florist and see what they've got left. I meant to go at lunch, but I got called into a meeting, ate a quick sandwich at my desk and all thoughts of Valentine's Day went out the window.

The florist's prices have gone up, I swear, but at least they're still open. I buy twenty-four red roses and hand over the GDP of a small country in exchange for flowers and a lot of foliage. Even if the rest of the evening is me apologising for messing up tonight, these flowers are actually quite impressive and should go some way towards making her feel special.

I shouldn't have held out for The Ivy to pick up their phone. I should have rung around a bit more. *Of course* they were going to be fully booked. Maybe I could try the Oxo instead.

I see Samantha in front of St Paul's, her curly brown hair streaked with red. I raise my hand to wave, and the first thing she does is smile at me across the lanes of traffic. The next thing she does is tap her watch to indicate I'm late. I glance at my watch, before weaving through the slow-moving congestion on Cannon Street. I'm three minutes late. *Three*.

When I reach her I pull her into an embrace and give her a kiss. She sees the huge bunch of flowers and her face moves into a big smile.

'Tom, these are massive,' she says. 'How many are there?'

'Twenty-four,' I say.

Her gaze darts across the roses, appreciating them, and then she says nothing.

'What?' I query.

'There's twenty-three, but it doesn't matter.'

'No, there's not. I watched him count them out.' I do a quick tally. 'Shit, where's the other one?'

She inhales, squeezes my arm. 'Ah, shame they don't smell, but they are still so, so gorgeous.'

I don't reply. Just smile. I've presented her with twenty-three red roses that don't have any scent. The wind is out of my sails now. She doesn't seem annoyed, but I am. I was hoping the flowers would be advance recompense for what I'm about to say, but I don't think it's going to work now.

'I've messed up on the dinner booking,' I tell her. Let's get this out of the way early. 'I'm so sorry. I thought I'd booked The Ivy, but it turns out I booked it on the wrong day.' This is a lie that I hadn't planned. I'm not sure why I'm saying it now. Perhaps because the truth – that I hadn't booked anything – is awful, and this lie is still awful, but not as bad as the truth.

'The wrong day?' she says, lowering the flowers.

'I thought Valentine's Day was tomorrow. The restaurant called to check my reservation and . . . I'm sorry.'

'That's OK,' she says with a genuine smile. 'I'm a bit tired today anyway. Let's just go tomorrow. We'll have our Valentine's Day tomorrow.'

I freeze. I don't have a booking at all, let alone for tomorrow. 'I let the booking go.' The lies keep coming. 'I didn't want it for tomorrow. I wanted it for tonight.'

'Oh,' she says and then hands the flowers back to me. 'Can you carry these, they're really awkward.'

I take them from her, but don't speak. I'm not sure what to do now.

'What shall we do instead then?' she asks.

'Something low-key?' I offer. 'If you're tired?'

She shrugs. 'Yeah. OK. It's been a long day.'

I rack my brains and then work out what to do. I feel like a genius. I take her hand. 'I've got an idea. Come on.'

*

'You're joking?' Samantha says, pulling her hair back off her shoulders and foraging distractedly for a hairband on her wrist that isn't there. She's looking around as if she doesn't want to touch anything in here, let alone eat the food. 'You've brought me *here*, on Valentine's Day?'

'Yeah,' I say. 'It'll be fun. Trust me.'

'It's McDonald's,' she says dubiously. 'Why is this fun?'

'It just is.'

'I don't remember the last time I was in one of these places.'

One of these places? 'When was the last time you had a Happy Meal?' I ask, changing tack.

'A what?'

'You know, the kids' meals. You've never had a Happy Meal?'

'I don't remember.'

'They come with a nice little toy,' I say. I'm going to claw this situation back. I am. But Samantha's looking at me as if I've lost my mind. I think I probably have.

'Come on,' I say as we move forward in the queue. I'm committed. I'm forcing this to happen. And we don't have a dinner reservation. We need to eat and neither of us can cook. I hold her hand, smile at her. But she's not smiling back. I had her onside earlier with the flowers, and I've lost her now that I've brought her here. And who can blame her.

'I really shouldn't eat this kind of food. You know that.'

'You always eat healthily,' I reply. 'Have a night off. If we'd been in The Ivy, you'd have been eating something covered in cream and butter and . . . whatever. So let loose a little. Which flavour milkshake do you want?'

'I'll just have a Diet Coke or maybe a bottle of water? I assume they sell bottled water?' She glances up at the menu, the confused expression refusing to depart.

'You can't dip your chips in either of those,' I say knowingly.

She turns to me. 'What?'

'Never mind. Water and a Happy Meal. Nuggets or something else? Burger? I can vouch for the cheeseburger.'

'You choose.' She's lost interest.

I order the same thing I had with Abbie all those months ago, including the nuggets and extra fries.

'That sounds like a lot of food,' she says. 'Do we need all that?'

'The Happy Meals are kind of small, if you're an adult,' I reason.

'So why are you buying them then?'

'Er . . .' I mumble something about the toy and then I stop. I can't be bothered any more. I feel worn down. I've tried. Actually I haven't tried, and that's why we're in here, having this passive-aggressive exchange at the counter in McDonald's.

When the server lays it all out in bags and a cup holder, I pay and grab as much as I can. Samantha looks at the cup holder the same way she's looked at me, as if she can't fathom what's going on, how we ended up in here on Valentine's Day, which is fair enough, I guess.

'Could you grab the drinks?' I ask. I'm holding twenty-three red roses and all the food. I've got nothing left, both physically and mentally.

She sighs, her shoulders rising and falling visibly. She reaches forward and takes them.

'Are we going back to yours to eat?'

I look down the road at St Paul's Cathedral, where I'd sat with Abbie last autumn. It's a Tuesday night in February and it's bloody cold now, so much so that I think it's going to snow. Perhaps this idea has no legs whatsoever. Besides, I don't want to take Samantha there. It's kind of sacred to me. I'm already trying to replicate something fun that I did spontaneously with Abbie, but to replicate the location too feels wrong.

'Yeah, let's go to mine. I've got a bottle of champagne in the fridge that I bought when I got my bonus. Let's have McDonald's and champagne. Might taste odd when we dip our chips in, but—'

'I'm not drinking, remember?'

'Yes, yes, I do now. Sorry.' *How could I forget?*

Back at my flat, the first thing I do is open the little toy that comes with my meal. They've obviously moved on from Beanie Babies, because it's a plastic *Chicken Little* toy this time. I wonder how often they change the free toys. Weekly? Monthly? I've not seen the film yet, so I've no idea who this little fella is.

Samantha's automatically switched on the TV and is picking through her chips. She's taken one bite from her burger and decided it's not for her. I offer her the nuggets, but she shakes her head, opens her bottle of water and drinks as if she's cleansing herself. When she gathers up all her rubbish, I notice she's included the toy as part of it. She didn't even break it free from its plastic wrapper.

Chapter 26

Tom

15 February 2006

I've already got Abbie a drink when she arrives. And I've snagged a good table in the corner where the old Victorian windows swoop round to the side. I'm amazed she came, actually. It's clear from yesterday that she's angry with me. I give her a smile and she gives me one back as she walks towards me, but it doesn't look real.

Abbie's here, but I don't think she wants to be. At least when she says 'Hi' to me it's not snappy and angry, like her greeting yesterday morning.

'How are you?' I ask.

'Good. You?' she sips her wine. 'Thanks for this.'

'No problem.'

We both shift in our chairs. Why is this so awkward?

'So why do you need a friend?' she asks, getting straight to the point. She doesn't let me answer. 'I thought about that a lot yesterday.'

'Did you?'

She nods, sips again. 'It worried me.'

I don't know how to answer that, so I don't.

'Why did you react the way you did in your flat? I have to know. What's going on with you, Tom?'

I see the pain in her eyes as she reminds me how I treated her in my flat, how we almost . . .

'Oh God, I don't know,' I say. I push my hand through my hair and I think it's now a bit of a mess. She's waiting for something more concrete. 'Actually I do know. I've fucked everything up,' I confess.

'Everything?' she asks.

'Yeah, pretty much,' I tell her.

'Go on,' she says. 'Tell me.'

I look into the depths of my pint. I could tell her how much I miss her, how I should never have pulled any moves on her in my flat, because I ruined everything. I could tell her how being with her felt like the most wonderful thing I'd ever done, how it made perfect sense – the feel of her skin on mine – but that I panicked and said all the wrong things because I didn't know the right thing to say; because I'd glimpsed a text message that I wish I'd never seen, and it threw chaos at me, and chaos keeps coming. It just keeps coming. I could tell her how I am an expert at believing I'm doing the right thing and it always, *always*, turns out to be the wrong thing, with the exception of carrying her off that train. I could tell her that the day I met her was both the worst and the best day of my life. I could tell her how I have fears that she's dating Sean, and how I'm scared that after today I'll never see her again.

But I don't. Instead I tell her the thing that's eating me up the most, the thing that's going to impact on my life more than any of this.

'I'm going to be a father.'

Chapter 27

Abbie

I stare at him, open-mouthed. He's just said words that make no sense. Is it the order of the words that make no sense or the sentence itself?

'Say that again,' I say slowly.

Tom repeats himself. I'm waiting for the punchline. But if there is one, it's well hidden.

'You're going to be a dad?'

He nods.

I sit back, lean forward again. I need to do something with my hands, so I lift my wine glass and drink. I really need a water and so I rifle in my backpack for my bottle. This is a lot to take in.

Tom's squirming in his seat. I think he expected me to take charge of this conversation, but I'm too stunned to think or speak.

'It's Samantha,' he says in answer to a question I haven't asked.

'The girl you broke up with the week we met?' I ask, dumbfounded.

He nods, reaches for his pint. 'We're back together. We're having the baby together.'

I look down at the table, trying to process this. My stomach hurts.

'How?' I ask and then realise that's not what I mean at all. I don't know what I mean.

'The usual way,' he says and smiles, but it's a sad smile.

'I don't know what to say. Are you happy?'

He blinks as if he's never asked himself this.

'I don't have much choice,' is the surprising answer he settles on, but he hasn't answered my question. That's a no. 'I'm doing the right thing,' he continues. 'It's important I do the right thing.'

I nod. 'I suppose it is, yes,'

'I'm going to marry her.'

'Wow,' I say. 'Marry her?'

'It's the right thing to do,' he says simply.

I'm incredibly still, working out how to phrase this next bit. I think it is the right thing to do if you're in the 1940s. But he's not. He's Tom in 2006, and people don't simply get married these days if they knock someone up. 'Both parties have to be in love, to be married,' I say. I wait for him to confirm or deny if he's in love with Samantha. I'm not sure I'm going to like the answer, either way.

He doesn't move. Just looks at me, waiting.

'And if you're not, then a little baby will grow up with two parents who start despising each other, having trapped one another into a loveless marriage. This is your life, Tom. And Samantha's. And a baby's. Don't rush in. Why don't you think about it?'

'I've been thinking about it for months,' he says.

My eyes open so wide. 'Months?'

It happened before you and I met. Just. Only I didn't

know. Samantha didn't either, until . . . I found out she was pregnant that night in my flat.'

I narrow my eyes. 'What? When? Before we started . . .' I trail off, trying to work this out. 'Your phone?'

He nods, slowly. 'She – Samantha,' he makes a pointed effort to use her name, 'messaged me earlier in the day telling me she was late and I didn't understand what she was on about. I was too busy to comprehend. Late for what? And besides, we'd broken up. And then I was with you. And finally she messaged me when you and I – you know – saying, *I'm pregnant*.'

I don't know what to say, so I don't say anything. Tom's wittering on about baby scans and the health of his unborn child, and I'm replaying that night in my head, every hot and heavy minute of it, from magic tricks to wine, ice cream to kissing, our clothes coming off, him reaching for a condom.

Did he forget with Samantha – is that why they're in this situation? Was she on the pill? I want to know. Or maybe I don't. I pick up my wine and drink, grateful this isn't happening to me. I don't want to be a parent at my age. I look at Tom as he talks about his baby, with a perpetual look of confusion on his face. I empty my wine glass into my mouth. When I next see Sean, we're going to discuss this at length and we are never, *ever* having unprotected sex. I am never, *ever* skipping taking my pill. Ever.

'She's due in July,' he says. I've missed everything he's said before that. 'Time's running out,' he finishes.

I don't think I can argue with that. Tom is going to be a dad. 'My God,' I say and reach for my empty glass. These 175-millilitre glasses are too small.

'Do you want another?' he asks. He's barely touched his pint.

'Yes, I do.' I think I need it. He gets up to buy another round, even though it's my turn. I feel a bit numb and I can't work out why. Maybe if he was happier about all this, I'd be happier. I watch Tom at the bar, waiting his turn, fiddling with the contents of his wallet. In five months he's going to be a dad. This. Is. Unbelievable.

He hasn't told me he's happy, but he hasn't told me he's unhappy, either, and I watch his face when he returns and sits opposite me. 'Thanks,' I mumble when he places my drink down.

'There's a part of me,' he starts up again, 'that thinks, *This is it – this is the family life*. I've never really had that.'

'I know,' I say.

'Do you?' He looks surprised.

'You got shipped off to boarding school at age seven, Tom. I get it.'

He bristles, clearly hates me referencing it again. 'I understand, in part, that you feel you need to create a family environment, when one presents itself to you. But . . .'

'But what?'

It's not my place to say, *But it's all wrong. This is all wrong*. Is it wrong because somewhere deep inside me thoughts of Tom and this Samantha girl, and their unborn baby, creating a Happy Ever After isn't the way I thought this would all end between us. Looking back, I thought Tom and I would be together, but the upshot of it all ending so sourly is that it ended for a reason. A big reason, it now transpires. And more importantly, *it has ended*. Now that I know why, it's like some sort of closure that I wasn't sure I needed has arisen from the ashes of that night. We've both gone in different directions. He's having a baby and getting married, and I'm with Sean and I'm *happy* with Sean, I'm genuinely happy. So it's not fair of me to stop Tom looking for happiness too, even if I don't think he's necessarily looking in the right direction.

'But what?' he asks again. He's waiting for an answer. I don't have one. Not one I can say out loud. Not one he'd like.

'I hope . . .' Tom fills the silence, 'that it's going to be so cool, such an adventure. And there's this other part that thinks, *I'm twenty-seven. I'm too young to be a dad*.'

'You're going to have to grow up then,' I say and it sounds mean, the way I've shot that out of my mouth. 'Or you'll be forced to grow up.'

'I know,' he says.

'I suppose I should say congratulations.' I force a bright smile onto my face, because this is happening. Tom's on board with having a baby, so I suppose I should be, too. 'To family life and getting married.'

I raise my glass and he raises his. He is making the biggest mistake of his life, but he seems set on this path of self-destruction – and what is Tom to me any more, anyway? What was he to me before that night at his? I didn't even know him this time last year. Our friendship was fast, intense and then I thought it was over.

'I hope you're happy, or that you will be happy,' I say, because I can't resist getting a little nudge of doubt into his mind. Just in case he's not too far gone. But he doesn't take the bait, merely smiles genuinely at me.

'Thanks,' he replies. 'Thanks for being a friend. Thanks for talking to me. Thanks for not riding off on your bike the moment you saw me yesterday.'

I laugh. 'I considered it.'

'I know. I could see you working out whether you could push your feet off the ground before I caught up with you,' he says.

I laugh loudly now. 'Would you have broken into a run? Tackled me to the ground?'

'No,' he says softly. 'But I'd have been devastated. That really would have been it for us.'

Us. A strange thing to say. We're not an us. We're just two people who met under awful circumstances and couldn't make it work as friends, or as anything else. Although I did meet Sean through him, so I suppose Tom entering my life brought me that.

'Tom,' I start.

He downs the dregs of his first pint and moves the glass to the side, pulling his second towards him.

'Why don't you talk to Sean?' I ask.

He shrugs. 'He left, and I had a lot going on in my life. I messaged him a bit, but maybe he's been too busy to reply. I assume you're in contact with him, given what you said yesterday.'

I know he knows. Or rather, I know he's worked it out, but he still wants me to say it.

So I tell him how it was only supposed to be a two-date thing, but the dates kept coming and we started to like each other. 'We really get on,' I tell him. I find myself justifying my decision to be with Sean. 'He's really nice.'

Tom smiles. 'I'm pleased it's working out for you both.'

'We have fun together, and he loves me,' I say. Tom's head jerks a bit and I wonder if this is an oddly boastful thing to say, given I'm not sure where Tom and Samantha are at in the love department.

'I wasn't expecting . . .' he says and then stops. 'Do *you* love *him*?' he asks.

I pause. Why am I worried I'm going to hurt Tom? We were never a couple. We never got that far. I need to remind myself of that. 'Yes,' I say. 'I do love him.'

He doesn't speak. Just sort of stares at me. 'How long have you been together?' he asks eventually.

'Since early December.'

He lifts his pint glass to his lips, drinks, puts it back down again.

'December,' he mutters, as if trying to place what he was doing then or working out how it happened without him noticing. 'Why didn't you reply to any of my texts?' he asks.

I should go. This was only meant to be a quick drink.

'Oh, Tom. What do you want me to say?'

'The truth,' he says. 'I was so sorry, and you didn't want to hear it.'

'No, I didn't. I felt angry and humiliated. And you didn't give me a reason why you did what you did. You left me standing there. Naked.'

'I know,' he says quietly. 'And I'm so, so sorry. But it wasn't meant to be like that, honestly. It's pretty hard to keep going with it all, when I'm staring at a message telling me my life's about to change. I couldn't work out what to think, let alone what to say to you. I just had to stop. I had to . . . stop, Abbie. Do you think I wanted to get so close to doing – you know – what we were about to do and then simply walk away halfway through? Do you think I got off on that?'

'I don't know what you get off on, Tom. I really don't. You baffle me.'

'I baffle myself,' he says into his raised glass. He drinks, puts it down. 'I wanted you,' he says, and I think an electrical current must be passing through my chair because every nerve in my body flickers to life. 'You know that, right? And *you* wanted *me*,' he says, when I don't speak. He needs to stop now. This isn't helpful. 'And I fucked it up,' he finishes.

'Yes, you did,' I respond and I feel a bit smug at that, and also a bit destroyed at the memory, despite the fact that I can't even look at Tom while he's talking about us having got so close to sleeping together.

'It was for the best,' he explains. 'You and I *not* sleeping together. It was the right thing to do.'

'In hindsight . . . it was,' I concur.

'Also, I was a bit off my game after that message.' He's shooting for humour. I'm not sure he hit the target.

'I'm not surprised.' I'm aiming for humour too, because what else is there?

'I'm sorry,' he says again. 'Please forgive me for making you feel so shit – for all of it. Can we go back to what we were before?'

'We weren't anything before,' I say and, as cruel as it sounds, it's the truth. 'Not really.'

Tom looks a bit taken aback. 'Can we start again then?' he asks. 'Please?'

'What's the point?' I ask him. 'Why are we forcing this friendship?'

'Because . . .' He grapples for something. 'We're good as friends, and I would rather have you in my life than not in it. We had fun together, until I ruined things.'

'True,' I confirm.

'Please,' he says. 'You've moved on with Sean. I've got Samantha, and a baby on the way. We met each other in the most awful of circumstances, but that's got to mean something, hasn't it? That connection, we must have been thrown together like that for a reason. I don't know if you feel that, but I do. We haven't got to see each other loads, unless you want to. But when someone comes into your life who you really get on with, why wouldn't you want to keep them as a friend?'

He puts forward a good argument. I'm not committing to anything, but the concept of being able to even think about Tom without wanting to stick pins in his eyes might be good for my mental health. And actually I sort of feel a bit sorry for him, now I know what's been going on this whole time. And, annoyingly, he is right. When you meet someone like that and you connect, throwing them to the wolves in their hour of darkness is not the right reaction.

'Start again?' he suggests.

I nod, ever so gently, so that I'm not sure whether I've actually done it or not. He's obviously been waiting for any kind of sign, and his shoulders relax for the first time since we met up tonight.

'Great,' he says with obvious relief. And then he leans over the table, extends his hand. 'Hi,' he says. A small smile edges its way onto his lips. 'I'm Tom.'

I inhale and can't stop a smile working its way onto my face. I extend my hand. 'You're such a dick,' I mutter, and he tells me he knows this, but his hand is still out. And then I play along, reach out and take his hand. 'Hi, Tom,' I say with a reluctant sigh. 'I'm Abbie.'

*

Sean stands at his kitchen island in his flat in Highgate, chopping vegetables, when I tell him later that week how Tom and I really met. The awful thing is that because Tom never told Sean how he and I met, and because I wanted to find out why Tom never told people (although I've still not got to the bottom of that), *I'd* also never told Sean that I was on the derailed train.

It's all coming out of my mouth in a garbled mess, concluding with the words, 'And I didn't tell you when we started dating because I thought you *knew*.'

He puts the knife down and rubs his forehead. 'I didn't,' he says. 'I had no idea.'

'I'm sorry,' I say. I feel I've duped him in some way.

'Don't be sorry,' he says. He's stunned, I can see that. 'I had no idea,' he repeats again. We stand in silence, Sean giving me such a sympathetic expression.

'But nothing happened to me,' I say. 'Not really. I got hurt. I passed out. Tom carried me off the train. It's Tom who saw everything. Tom who lived through the horror of it all. I know he saw some horrible things, only he won't say what. He walked me away from all of that and then managed to take care of me. All night long.'

Sean speaks. 'Tom carried you off the train,' he repeats.

'Yes.'

He's looking at me differently. 'That's huge,' he says. 'He saved your life.'

'Tom assures me, in no uncertain terms, that he didn't save my life, that I'd have been fine sitting in a pile of glass, waiting for the emergency services.'

'And now he's a modest kind of hero,' Sean jokes. 'My absolute favourite.'

'Are you upset?' I ask.

'Of course I'm not upset,' he says soothingly. 'He saved your life. And now you're with me, I should thank him, really.'

I'm not too sure Tom would actually like that, although I'm going to work that one out later.

I can see Sean thinking. He picks up the knife and starts cutting a cucumber for the salad we're making. I move round the island, stand next to him, take another knife from the holder and a pile of tomatoes and start chopping them. This silence is odd.

He puts the knife down and turns to me. 'Were you two really just friends?'

I should have seen this coming. Only I didn't. I didn't see it coming at all and I'm paralysed suddenly. I love Sean. Sean loves me. I'm not sure I really subscribe to the theory of *what he doesn't know can't hurt him*. What happened – or didn't happen – between Tom and me has no bearing on what's going on between Sean and me.

'It's complicated,' I say.

Sean closes his eyes as a level of obvious exasperation moves through him. 'Why is it complicated?' he asks.

'We *were* just friends, and then one night—'

'Oh, I knew it,' he says. 'I bloody knew it. People don't stop being friends for no reason. I knew Tom was lying when I asked him. And I still went ahead and asked you out.'

'Nothing happened,' I interject. 'Nothing at all.' I realise that's a lie. 'I mean, something happened, but not what you think. We didn't . . .'

He waits. I think he's stopped breathing.

'We didn't have sex. And even if we had . . .' I realise this train of thought is unhelpful, 'I wasn't seeing you, remember?

It was before you and I even went on our first date. By that point Tom and I – we were done. It was over. Whatever *it* was.'

Sean picks up the knife and starts chopping again, his brow furrowed. I think he's completely forgotten about the fact that I've just told him I'd been in a train crash. I know it was last year, but a little sympathy would have been nice. Instead he's fixated on . . .

'Tell me *exactly* what happened between you,' he says, pointing the knife at me. He lowers it and mumbles, 'Sorry. But I need to know. What did you . . . *do*?'

'You want graphic details?' I'm being crass now, and I shouldn't be. He's perfectly within his rights to know if the woman he's in love with once hooked up with one of his mates. He's shocked, needs talking down from the edge. 'You can't possibly want to hear that,' I try. 'And it's not even that graphic. And if it makes you feel any better, Tom didn't want to have sex with me.' This is sort of true. 'Tom and I were in our underwear, and that's when he decided he did not want to have sex with me. Does that make you feel a little bit better?' (I'm skipping over the bit about Tom finding out Samantha was pregnant and that's why we stopped. That might only muddy the waters.)

'Of course I don't feel any better,' Sean says. 'You wanted to have sex with Tom. Why would anything else you say after that make me feel better?'

I open my mouth and then close it again. This conversation hasn't gone the way I'd hoped at all.

'You wanted to have sex with Tom,' he says, to himself. 'Abbie,' he exhales loudly.

'What?' I say soothingly.

'Do you still see him?' He looks pained. 'Because I don't really want you to meet up with him again,' he says quietly. 'It scares me. What if the two of you—'

'That's not going to happen,' I interject quickly.

'I don't want him anywhere *near* you.'

'He's with someone. And I'm with you. And Tom and I . . . we're friends,' I say helplessly.

'No, you aren't. You haven't spoken to him in months.' He looks at me. 'Have you?'

I don't know what to do now. I don't want to lie. I don't want to tell the truth, either, and risk upsetting him further. I don't want to hurt Sean. Sean is in my future, and Tom is firmly in my past. I feel I've got no choice but to shake my head and utter the smallest of white lies. 'No, I've not spoken to him in months.'

'Good,' he says, visibly relieved. 'I wish I'd known all of this before. I'd never have asked you out, if I'd thought you and he . . .' He turns his head away. 'Is it because he saved you? Is that why you did it? Did you feel you *owed* him something?'

'No,' I say. 'It was just two drunk people in a kitchen. And *nothing happened*.'

'And nothing's going to happen,' he says, mostly to himself, as he dices the cucumber with more gusto than he did a few minutes ago.

'Understood,' I concede. I need to move this on. 'Why don't you speak to Tom any more? You were friends.'

'I'd started a new job. I wanted a fresh start.'

'And cut your old friends out of your life?'

'Tom went a bit strange,' Sean says.

'Because of the train, probably,' I suggest.

'Yeah, I guess so now. But . . . as well as being my friend, he was my boss,' Sean continues. 'And then he got promoted again and I thought I'd end up in his old job, but that didn't happen. No one got his old job. He could have promoted me, but it was some sort of cost-saving bullshit. I wasn't buying it. I think I held it against Tom a bit and then realised it was time to move on.'

'I didn't know he'd got a promotion,' I mention. Tom tells people nothing about himself. 'You went speed-dating once together, so I heard.' I'm aiming for a light-hearted tone and I think Sean's coming round now.

'That was before,' he says. 'I felt my wings were a bit clipped and, in part, that's because of Tom. I couldn't wait to get out of there, after all that. I didn't feel very valued. Anyway it all worked out in the end. I'm at a better company, better pension, better bonus scheme. Better all round. And I'm in a more senior role.'

I cosy up to him. 'Because you're brilliant,' I say, turning his body so that he's forced to stop chopping up salad items and moves into my embrace. I'm holding him tightly, this man I love, and he holds me back in return.

And then I think of the lengths I'd have to go to, to calm Sean down, if I *had* actually slept with Tom. I can't imagine.

Chapter 28

Tom

May 2006

Samantha's started sending out 'Save the Date' cards. She's determined she's not going to be pregnant when we get married, nor is she going to be 'the size of a house', so we've scheduled the wedding for September 2007, instead of having what she called 'a shotgun wedding' *before* the baby is due, which is in two months' time. I'm not sure what fills me with fear more: a wedding or a baby. I need to wrap my head around both, because they are happening. But I want this baby and so does Samantha; I want this baby to *feel* that love, and I want to share that love with Samantha.

What Abbie said to me in the pub rang true. She wasn't telling me anything I didn't already know. But how on earth is she ever going to understand why I'm doing what I'm doing? She comes from a lovely family. I've met her dad. He's decent. Really cares about his daughter, and I'm sure her mum's the same. A stable family background – that's what she has, that's what Samantha has. I had two parents, but the way they show love is . . . different.

I don't want that for this little baby. And I'm sure as hell not going to be responsible for bringing a baby into the world to find that his or her parents couldn't even be arsed to make a go of it. My baby *will* come from a stable family background. It won't be packed off to boarding school, like I was. We are going to be a family. A good one, a proper one. I'm going to be part of a family. But it doesn't mean I'm not freaking out.

The wedding is more than a year away. I had no idea weddings take this long to plan, but Samantha assures me they do. This is all so huge. And expensive.

I lift my shoulders higher, give myself a good talking-to. Abbie was right. I do need to grow up, be responsible, because I'm going to be a father. I'm going to be a husband. I'm finally going to be part of a proper family.

Chapter 29

Abbie

July 2006

I've made good on my promise to Sean not to see Tom. I felt awful telling him I wouldn't when I really wanted to, especially now that Tom and I have reconnected again, and now that I understand why things ended between us the way they did. But I understand Sean's concerns. I see his point of view. How would I feel if it had been the other way round; if Sean had wanted to sleep with someone, had got so incredibly close to it happening and the other person had backed out – and then had kept meeting up with that person? I doubt very much I'd be happy about it. Actually I'd be nervous, on tenterhooks, checking that Sean actually came home to me. So I see what he means.

It's been a few months since that day in the pub with Tom when I said we could be friends again. I've glimpsed him across the courtyard from my office window and we've waved. But while I'm avoiding seeing him in person, so as not to upset Sean, we've messaged a few times, exchanged views on England's performance during the World Cup: that getting knocked out of a tournament on penalties is cruel and how, in his next life, Tom says he's coming back as Frank Lampard.

He makes me smile. When I eventually thought I'd mention to Sean that I'd like to meet up with Tom, just for a drink or a coffee or something innocent, I chose the wrong time and decided against it. With England getting knocked out of the World Cup, Sean's been in a sore mood for weeks, like most of the nation.

On the two occasions Tom's suggested we meet up, I've fobbed him off. Actually I've typed out messages agreeing to it, but my stomach twisted so much, as a result of the deceit, that I couldn't go through with it. He's stopped asking now.

And then one day in July I look across the courtyard, which I try not to do too often, and see Tom's not at his desk. Nor is he in later that day. He never takes a day off. Perhaps he's on holiday.

I send him a message. 'How are you? The England team's getting a new manager,' I type inanely. I wonder if his interest in football has waned. I look across at Tom's empty desk, my mind whirring as to where he is.

Chapter 30

Tom

I am a father. I have a son. I have a *son*.

Samantha was about to be induced, after the baby was determined it was staying put, sailing past his due date by miles. But after her waters finally broke and our baby worked his way into the world, it was as if a miracle had happened right in front of me. I've never known anything like it. Childbirth is kind of cool. And also pretty grim. But mostly cool.

No one tells you how long it's going to take. He was an outrageous little fighter, though, really fought to stay in there. When he did emerge, screaming his lungs out in annoyance at Samantha having evicted him from his little home, I fell in love.

I wasn't prepared for the sudden rush that hit me, as if my heart had never truly known love before, which actually I don't think it ever had, now that I think about it. After they cleaned him up and handed him to me for a quick hold, I vowed there and then that I would never let any harm come to him. I actually cried.

And then he went off to Samantha, who was a trooper the whole way through. She's so elegant and collected in her everyday life, but she swore like a scaffolder every time the midwife told her to push. He lay on her chest and then fed for what felt like hours. He's marvellous. Just the best little man. I'm so lucky. I can't believe I thought this was going to ruin my life. This has *made* my life. I'm still shit-scared, though. I have to keep him alive. I can't even keep plants alive. Thank God Samantha and I are in this together. I'm so glad I made that decision. I glance over at her as she's looking at our son and I think, *I have a family. I've done it, I've made a family. My God, I'm so lucky.*

'What shall we call him?' she asks.

We've been debating this for months and we still can't find an answer. We were both hoping something would come to us the moment we saw him. But he's here and it hasn't.

'It'll come to us eventually,' I say. 'He's perfect. You were perfect.'

She looks up at me. 'I love you.'

'I love you too,' I say. And I mean it. The endorphins rushing through me are off the chart. I am the happiest man alive.

I get a taxi back to Samantha's house and leave her and our beautiful baby to sleep in the hospital. I'll be back to pick them up tomorrow. I live at Samantha's house now, although she insists I call it 'our house', which I don't seem to be able to remember to do. I could hardly carry on living in my flat, by myself, while my girlfriend has my baby. When I closed the door for the last time and handed my keys to the rental agent, it felt so strange. I'd lived there for five years. But that chapter of my life has ended – single Tom who can't get his shit together has gone. He's been replaced by this guy who lives in a three-bed town house in Islington with his girlfriend and his new baby. I like this version of Tom. This version of Tom has got his life together. Finally.

Chapter 31

Abbie

The words I'm a father! I'm so happy and in love with him! The baby is amazing! appear on my phone the next morning. It's Saturday and I'm waking up with an enormous hangover. Natasha should also be in bed nursing a headache, given the amount we both drank, but I heard the front door bang as she went downstairs to use the gym in our building, so it can't be too bad. I don't use the gym. I cycle a billion miles a week instead.

I read the message again and smile. Tom's happy. And I'm happy for him. I sit up in bed and reply: Congratulations! How are you all doing? How's Samantha? How's the baby? Have you picked a name?

We don't have a name yet! I laugh because he's using exclamation marks on every sentence. I can feel his excitement.

You'll find a name soon. I'm so happy for you.

Thanks! I've even given up smoking!

Good move. You're going to be a great dad, I tell him.

Let's hope so! No going back now!

I put the phone down as I curl back up, to sleep away the rest of my hangover.

No, Tom. There's no going back now.

Chapter 32

Abbie

September 2006

'Singapore?' I stop what I'm doing and stare at Sean. It's a Saturday afternoon and we're curled up on his sofa together, both of us with our laptops, me with a Word document open and him with Excel. The TV's showing some sort of travel programme on low in the background, which is probably why he's started talking about Asia. 'Singapore?' I ask again.

He laughs. 'Yeah, what do you think?'

I blink. 'What do I think about Singapore?'

'About moving there,' he says. 'Just for a while.'

I sit back against the sofa. I'd been writing up an article and he caught me mid-flow. I should really have finished this at work yesterday, but I've got so much on and it's filtered into my weekend, and now Sean's talking to me about moving. To Singapore.

'I've been looking at jobs,' he continues.

'In Singapore?' I repeat. If there was a game where you had to say the word 'Singapore' over and over again, I'd be winning.

'Yeah. It's either there or Dubai, I've decided.'

'You've decided?'

'If we want this tax-free lifestyle where we can bank a load of cash and live like kings . . . yeah, pretty much Dubai or Singapore. There's a few other places, but I think they're the best for my job prospects.'

'Right,' I say. We'd talked about this in passing a few weeks ago – our hopes and dreams, and our travel bucket lists – and I'll admit it did get me thinking, and possibly looking up foreign climes on the internet, but Sean's obviously being a bit more urgent about it than I imagined.

And when I don't say anything else, because I feel a bit blindsided, Sean continues, 'So what do you think? Do you hate the idea?'

'Are you being serious?' I ask uncertainly.

'Of course,' he laughs.

'Do you want me to come with you?' I ask.

He looks at me like I'm mad. 'Of course,' he repeats.

I need to think. 'What would you do if I said no?'

'I hadn't envisaged you saying no.'

'So what if I *do* say no?' I push.

'Then I won't go,' he says.

'Really? You won't go?'

'I haven't even applied yet. I wanted to talk to you about it before I did.'

I smile at that. He's not making big, life-altering decisions without me. He's factoring me in. And we've not been together a year yet.

'You've not been at your new job all that long,' I say.

'Yeah,' he says with a shrug. 'But I can put in for a transfer.'

'What's brought this on?'

'I want to earn more.'

I laugh. 'We all want that.'

'I reckon you could earn more too, out there.'

'I reckon I could earn more literally anywhere else than where I currently am,' I confess.

Sean laughs. 'That's true.'

But now I'm thinking. Over the last few months I've been away for work quite a bit and I've a few more trips planned, but I only go away in Europe. 'I've never been to Asia before,' I say.

'Do you fancy it?' he asks. 'Or not really?'

'That's a leading question,' I reply, abandoning my laptop on the coffee table. 'I don't *not* fancy it.'

'So why don't we think about it? Why don't you do a bit of research and see how you feel. The expat life over there sounds great. Weather's always good too.' He brushes my fringe out of my eyes. I had it cut in a few weeks ago, when I realised the scar I gained on my forehead from the glass on the train wasn't ever going to go away and foundation wasn't quite fixing it.

'I love you, you know,' he says.

'I know,' I reply. 'You honestly wouldn't go without me?'

'I don't think so, no. No, I wouldn't. I want to be with you, Abbie. I think you and I are meant to be. I think we're supposed to do all that crazy shit, like get married and have kids. But I think we're also supposed to live a bit first. Why not, let's move country, do something wild. Although I'll be moving country to take up another job in banking, so it's not that wild really.'

I laugh again. His enthusiasm is infectious.

'We can save some really decent money, come home and buy a great big house somewhere to raise a little brood of kids.'

'Whoa, Cowboy!' I say. And then, 'Are we going to be together for ever?' I ask.

'Sure,' he says, as if it's so simple, as if it doesn't need thinking about. 'What are we doing this for, if we're not in it for good?'

I swallow. He has a point. I guess I was going with the flow. I was just living . . . not thinking about living. Just getting on with it.

'Wow,' I say.

But he reins himself back in. 'Look, I've not even applied yet. I've been thinking about it since we spoke about it the other week, but I didn't want to pursue it until I thought it might actually work for us. I've had a brief look, and there's a few jobs that look good. Why don't you see what's out there and we'll talk about it another day? If you think you could move countries with me, for a while – not for ever, obviously – I'll start applying for some jobs.'

I breathe in hard, exhale. 'OK,' I agree. 'I'll have a good look online and . . . wow, we might be moving to another country.'

Sean moves in to kiss me, and I kiss him back. I'm still too stunned to do anything else.

'Singapore?' Natasha says one evening while we're enjoying drinks on our balcony. I've not been at the flat in about a week, so I thought I needed to put in an appearance. Our deal, that I'd be on reduced rent in exchange for making sure Natasha eats all her vegetables, has backfired on both of us.

I'm relaxed, sitting here with my best friend, and that's when it often happens: flashbacks of that night, as a whoosh of bright light enters my mind. And then it's replaced by darkness. I flinch at the sudden memory of the train derailment that I've allowed to enter my brain, then close my eyes and count to five. I thought these flashbacks would have eased off a bit more, given that it's been almost a year since that night on the train.

Natasha sees my reaction. 'You OK?' she asks.

I swallow, my mouth dry. 'Yep,' I say.

The sun is retreating behind the horizon and we're sticking it out until the bitter end. I pull my cardigan closer around me. Summer's coming to a close. But things always end.

And new things begin.

'Singapore,' I repeat. 'I think Sean's really keen. And I think I am too.'

'It's nice there,' Natasha says, still watching me warily to check I'm OK. 'I was there for a fortnight for work a couple of years back and decided I could very easily live there.'

'Really?' I ask. And Natasha tells me more. Although I think, at this point, I need very little encouragement. I have spent hours on expat forums looking at advice, and on tourism websites staring at the white colonial buildings, the beautiful hotels and bars, the rooftop nightclubs, the museums, the restaurants. It looks like Singapore knows how to eat well. And then, when I'd satisfied my idle curiosity, I realised it was no longer idle curiosity. And I went on jobs forums and looked into how much I could earn, and explored editorial jobs in magazines and supplements. I got carried away, set up an account with a recruitment website and started adding jobs to my favourites list. I think even Sean hasn't made this step yet.

'I haven't told Sean I'm on board with this idea yet, though,' I tell Natasha. 'He's been patient and hasn't even mentioned it once, although I can tell he's itching to talk to me about it. It's been a fortnight since we spoke about moving there together and he's been out at work functions, and so have I.'

'You've been thinking about moving to Singapore for a fortnight?' she asks. 'And you've not told me?'

'I just wanted to be sure before I said anything.'

'But you're sure now?' she asks. And then, 'Oh, crap, I haven't thought this through. My best friend is moving away.'

'Possibly moving away,' I clarify.

'No, it's awful in Singapore,' she says. 'You don't want to go, actually. Nasty place. Horrific. Big mistake. Stay here with me in our flat for ever.'

'I'm hardly ever here anyway,' I reason.

She nods. 'Neither am I much, really.'

'I'll miss you,' I say.

'I'll miss you too.'

I've decided I am going to say yes to Sean's idea. And then he's going to start applying for jobs or putting in for a transfer and, once that wheel is in motion, he'll be unstoppable. Perhaps I'll tell him tomorrow, so I can enjoy one last day of calm before the storm begins.

Chapter 33

Tom

November 2006

'It's your turn,' Samantha says as I hear Teddy crank up on the baby monitor. He's upstairs in a crib in our room and we're downstairs trying to watch a rerun of *GoldenEye*. I don't think either of us is really into it. We know we get a good ten-minute run in and then Teddy will cry again. It puts us both on edge, never quite able to settle in, relax.

'I don't know why we don't leave him down here with us in the evenings. I could hold him on my chest, if you don't want to,' I say as I stand to go and fetch our son. 'Or we could pop him in a Moses basket.'

'Because he needs stability and routine,' Samantha says.

'He needs to feed off your boobs,' I retort. 'And they're down here and he's up there.'

I go upstairs, pick him up and he stops crying immediately. Samantha hates that I can always calm him down. She says Teddy just cries when she holds him, which I didn't think was true, but now she's said it, I notice that unless he's on her boobs he really does kick off when she holds him.

I change him before his feed. I've learned about the order of things the hard way. If he gets all sleepy after his milk and I rustle him around changing his nappy, he's a total sod to get off to sleep after that. Now I've mastered the art of winding him and then laying him down and backing away gently.

'He's four months old. How can he still be this hungry? I think we might need to start him on solids a bit early,' Samantha says as Teddy settles in for a feed.

I nod along, watching his little fingers grab at Samantha's boobs as if his life depends on it, which it does, I suppose. His little mouth is sucking away. 'You're a hungry little fella, aren't you, Tedster?'

'Don't call him that,' Samantha says. 'It's awful.'

'It's nice to have a nickname,' I protest. 'My parents never gave me one.'

'Me neither,' Samantha says.

This I can believe. The one time I called her Sam I thought she was going to claw my eyes out. I've never made that mistake again.

'It's just Teddy, OK?' she says. 'Not Tedster. Not Ted. Just Teddy. I wish we hadn't given our child a name that can be shortened. We didn't think that through.'

It takes him ages to feed and, when he's done with one of Samantha's breasts, she moves him to the next.

'Do you want me to try him on a bottle next time? Might be easier.'

She sighs. 'Maybe.'

'It might be nice to try a bottle before we whip him straight onto solids. Four months seems a bit early for actual food.'

'Fine,' she says.

Teddy resurfaces for air, looks at me triumphantly and makes a loud burp, which I know has halved the amount of time it'll take to put him down in his crib and get him to sleep. I thank him silently.

'Right, shall I?' I offer to take him and Samantha gives him up easily.

'Why did no one tell me this was going to be so hard?' she asks. 'And boring. It's really boring, don't you think?'

I hold Teddy upright and rub his back in case there's more secret wind that he's holding on to. I bob from side to side automatically. I often catch myself doing this while standing in the queue at the coffee shop, and in the lift at work. I must look like a total weirdo, swaying to my own beat.

'It's not boring. It's amazing,' I say.

'Speak for yourself,' she says. 'I can't wait to get back to work.'

'Really?'

She nods. 'I need to use my brain. I need to stop feeling so tired. I'm *so* tired.'

'I know. Me too. But we're over the worst of it. We're pros now.'

I glance at the TV. Pierce Brosnan's been on pause, while jumping off the cliff, for about thirty minutes. I love this scene, but the screen's going to burn out at this rate.

'Go to bed,' I tell her. 'I'll clear up down here and lock up.'

'Really?' Samantha says gratefully. 'Thanks.' I expect her to scoop Teddy up from me as she goes upstairs, but she walks past us both and continues on. I follow behind her, with Teddy looking at me with his big blue eyes, his hand grabbing at my shirt collar.

'OK, little man. It's sleepy time. Don't let me down now,' I say, popping a kiss on his gorgeous downy head.

I can't help noticing that he looks suspiciously wide awake for a baby who's supposed to be heading back to bed.

Chapter 34

Abbie

December 2006

'Happy Christmas,' I say as my mum opens the front door.

'Happy Christmas, darling,' she trills. I suspect she's already had a few Buck's Fizzes and it's only 11.30 a.m.

'Sorry we're late,' Sean calls over my shoulder.

'You two are always late, I'm used to it,' my mum says cheerily. 'Anyone for a Buck's Fizz? I'm on my third!'

I knew it.

Sean gives me a knowing look that asks, 'Is your mum drunk?' as we dive in from the cold. I ignore the look. We'd tossed a coin to decide whose parents we'd spend Christmas Day with, and I won. We're with his family tomorrow for Boxing Day. I haven't seen my parents in ages and I feel so bad for having left it this long. I live in London and so do they – well, technically on the out-skirts – but I've hardly seen them since I moved out. Week-ends are so precious. I read somewhere that you only get 4,000 Saturdays in your lifetime. If it's true, then that is a sobering thought. I should spend more of them with my mum and dad.

I've already broken to my parents the concept of moving to Singapore. My mum cried. My dad put on a brave face and, sitting around the dinner table, popping champagne corks, pulling crackers and wearing silly wafer-thin party hats, we talk about the kind of jobs that Sean's applied for, and my parents, being discreet, don't ask about the salary. Sean tells them anyway, because he's proud (and so he should be), and I watch their varying reactions. My dad looks aghast and my mum smiles wildly and gives me a satisfied look. She's always jokingly wanted me to end up with someone who'd keep me 'in the lifestyle to which you wish to become accustomed', which she laughs at every time she mentions it.

I give her a silent 'Don't say it' look.

There are many things I should probably have given my parents a briefing on not mentioning in front of Sean. One of them is Tom. It did not even *occur* to me that my dad would talk about Tom. Why would he? They only met once, but because of Tom's brief but important stint as my rescuer and the fact that he and I became friends, my dad asks after him every now and again, despite the fact that I hardly ever mention him. Perhaps it's because I make a point of hardly ever mentioning Tom that their curiosity is piqued.

They ask after all my friends that they know and eventually land on Tom, and I glance immediately at Sean. But he's three glasses of champagne in and, if he's noticed, he doesn't even blink.

'I think he's fine, Dad,' I say. 'He's got a baby now.'

'Has he?' my mum chimes in. 'Boy or girl?'

'Boy. I think he'll be . . .' I calculate, 'five months old by now.'

'What's he like? What's his name? Do you have a picture?'

'I do. He emailed me a picture. He's called Teddy.'

Sean looks at me across the table. I know what he's thinking. I said I wouldn't see Tom, and I haven't. But the messaging clearly upsets him too. I continue, far too casually, 'He did this group email thing and bundled me in. Let me find it.'

I go off to find my new phone. I've succumbed to one that's got email and internet on it. I've finally given up my beloved Nokia. I really miss playing Snake. While I'm rifling in my bag in the hall, I hear my dad tell Sean how lovely Tom is. I wonder what Sean's thinking about that.

'He's getting married next year,' I tell my parents as I re-enter the room, but I direct the comment at Sean.

'How do you know?' Sean asks. 'Group email?' he enquires in a tone that I'm not sure I'm reading correctly.

'He messaged me. We're invited,' I say.

'Are we? When is it?' he asks.

'September.'

'We'll be in Singapore then,' he says.

'But we'll come home for a wedding, won't we?'

He pauses. 'Maybe. Flights are thousands.'

'No they're not,' I say.

'It's still really expensive.'

My parents' heads are going back and forth watching us descend into this exchange. 'Let's discuss it later,' I suggest.

'OK,' Sean says. And then carries on regardless. 'You can fly home if you want to. I don't mind. But I'm not flying home for Tom's wedding. I doubt I'll get the time off so soon, either. We're not really friends any more.'

'Aren't you?' my mum asks, sniffing gossip. 'Why not?'

Oh God, what's happening?

'We're just not,' Sean says, lifting his champagne glass and looking at the crystal glint in the light. He's examining the glass too closely for it to be natural. I wonder if he's regretting having said that now and if this is a cover.

Oh no, I'm wrong. Sean's off . . .

'I know he's a bit of a hero and everything, but since he tried it on with Abbie and then treated her like shit, I sort of can't bring myself to like him much any more.'

My parents both look at me. I wish the dining chair was an ejector seat.

I smile, shrug. 'These roast potatoes are yum.'

My parents look from me to each other. They don't know what to make of that revelation. Unexpectedly it's Sean who saves the situation. 'Any more Yorkshires?' he asks and my mum leaps up to fetch them, clearly relieved to be leaving the table.

'What time's the Queen's speech on?' I ask. I have never once sat and watched the Queen's speech, but I can't think of anything else to say to break this awkward silence.

'I don't know, love,' my dad says. 'Let's look in the *Radio Times*.'

The table goes silent again and I drain my champagne glass, watching Sean drain his too.

'Are you still worried about me and Tom?' I hiss as quietly as I can when we're in my old room later that night. I've been hanging on to this comment all day, waiting for the Christmas pudding to be munched, the presents to be opened, the Queen's speech to be shown (because my dad put it on, thinking I actually wanted to watch it). I've been waiting for the end of the most awkward Christmas I've ever had.

'I don't like the fact he's been emailing you,' he says.

I want to soothe Sean, agree with him, but I've been such a pathetic person avoiding this subject for all this time that I tell him the truth. 'I want to see Tom. I want to meet Samantha. I want to meet Teddy.'

'Who's Teddy?'

'The baby. You could come too?'

'No, thanks.'

'But then how are you going to keep an eye on me, if you don't come along?' That was probably unnecessary.

'Is that what you think I want to do: keep an eye on you?'

'Don't you?' I ask.

He sits on the edge of my bed. He's actually thinking about this.

'Tom's too good to be true, isn't he?' Sean says eventually in a deflated sort of voice. 'Heroic. Saves you from a train. And then there's what you told me about nearly sleeping with him. And I don't like it. I don't like that he's there in the background, just being . . . Tom.'

'Exactly,' I say. 'He's in the background. I've not seen him in for ever. And you're here with me. And you're amazing. I love you and I'm moving to Singapore with you.'

'Yeah, I know.'

'Isn't that enough?' I ask.

He shrugs. 'I suppose.'

But it's not. I can tell it's not. 'I won't see him if you still don't want me to.'

'Can I think about it?' he asks.

I nod, although my stomach hurts. I've eaten too much. Or not enough. Or I'm feeling something resembling disappointment. But I don't want to hurt Sean. I don't want to ruin this. 'OK,' I say. Because we are good together. We are.

As long as we're not talking about Tom.

Chapter 35

Tom

February 2007

'You've got to be joking, Samantha,' I say down the phone as I'm heading away from work to Gianni's to grab a panini for lunch. 'You can't go on a work trip the weekend we move house. It's just not on. Tell them. Tell them you'll have to reschedule. I can't move house on my own.'

'You won't be on your own – you'll have the removal company.'

'You've got to be joking,' I say again. 'What will I do with Teddy while I'm moving house?'

'He'll be at nursery that Friday,' she replies.

'But the nursery's closed at the weekend, so I'll have to look after him and try and sort out boxes?'

'Tom, don't give me this. Do you think I want to go away for a weekend for work?'

Yes, I think. *Yes, you bloody do.*

'There's nothing I can do,' she says. 'I'm sorry.'

'Fine. OK. We'll talk about this later,' I respond as I enter the shop. I'm raging. How can she think this is remotely acceptable? We're supposed to be a team. I didn't even want to move house, but Samantha wanted somewhere bigger. It's 2.30 p.m. The day has run away with me. I think this is the latest I've ever eaten lunch at work, but I'm up against it and only remembered that I needed to eat when my new assistant, Debbie, offered to go and buy me something to eat. I said I'd go, because I needed to get away from the stress for a few minutes. And then Samantha piled a whole lot more on me.

I've got a face like thunder when Gianni serves me. He raises an eyebrow.

'Woman trouble,' I volunteer, for no reason at all other than not speaking felt odd. Then I remember why I'm there. 'Double-meatball melt, please, and you choose all the salad bits,' I say, swishing my hand around in front of the salad bar and hoping Gianni can work out what goes best in the sandwich.

'Women are always trouble,' he says sagely. 'Even when they're not trouble, they're trouble.'

I look to the side, trying to work that one out. I'm not sure it's true, but I'm annoyed and not inclined to contradict him.

'Always trouble,' he says, nodding emphatically again. Discussion closed, I guess. 'Or . . .' he starts back up again. I brace myself. 'If we don't wish to tar all women with the same brush, maybe it is that you and I do not choose the right women.'

I look at the salad bar as he loads up the sandwich. I'm thinking about what he said. I don't think that's true, either. I don't choose the wrong women. Samantha's not wrong for me. We just bicker a lot. We've got a baby. It's hard going. And she keeps dicking off on work weekend trips. This isn't the first, but she's going for a partner's position at her law firm. I didn't ask her where the trip was or what it's even for.

Gianni says something else that I miss and I look up, wondering what else he's going to say that might add fuel to the fire already raging in my head. 'Sorry?'

'I said, four pounds and fifty pence, please.'

That's gone up since yesterday.

'Right. Yeah.' I hand over the cash and walk out with the sandwich. I don't think I'm going to go back there again.

It's when I turn the corner that I finally see her. Abbie – after all this time. She stops in front of me and I struggle to catch my breath.

'Hello, stranger,' she says, and I'm too stunned to speak. Not that I can, because I've got a meatball and a giant lump of bread still in my mouth.

I swallow and the bread scratches my throat all the way down. 'Hi,' I say in a croaky voice and then recover. 'You're a fine one to talk. Where the hell have you been all this time?'

'I get sent all over the world now,' she says. 'Far too busy for the likes of you.'

I'm glad it's as easy as this, because we've been chatting a bit on text, but we've never managed to pin down a date to meet up. 'I wasn't sure you even worked there any more. I never see you.'

'I got moved,' she says with a sigh. 'Office refurb. Partitions flippin' everywhere now. I'm over on the other side. Miss my window view.'

'How have you been?' I ask.

'I'm good. How are you?'

'Same. I'm moving house.' I feel I need to wow her with some actual news. 'Putney.'

'F-a-n-c-y.' She draws the word out.

'It's going to take sodding ages to get to work, though.'
She laughs.

'Are you still in Docklands?' I ask.

'Technically. Although I pass back and forth to Sean's in
Highgate quite a lot.'

'Highgate. Nice.'

'Yeah, it's pretty.'

The conversation has stalled. 'Were you going somewhere? Can I walk with you?' Now that I've finally seen
her, I know the timer will reset and it'll be months before it
happens again.

'Gianni's for lunch.'

'OK.' I turn and walk back towards the café with her.
She looks a bit startled at my abrupt about-turn in the
street.

'Do you normally grab lunch here?' I ask, because something has dawned on me.

'Yeah, when I'm feeling flush. I think their prices are
creeping up.'

'They are. Do you normally eat at this time?'

'I guess,' she says, looking at her watch. 'I don't really take
a lunch hour any more, so I cram it in when I can.'

'Hmm,' I say out loud.

'Hmm, what?'

'I just wondered if you emerge from your office so late
because you're avoiding me.'

She stops outside Gianni's. 'Why would I do that?'

'I don't know.'

She looks at me. 'It's not all about you, Tom.'

Ouch! 'I know.'

She enters the café and I follow, despite the put-down. She orders a salad and Gianni whizzes round assembling it with tongs. I continue munching my panini.

'I need your address,' I say between mouthfuls.

'Why?'

'So I can send you a wedding invite. You got the "Save the Date" email thing I sent you?'

'Yeah. I hope I can come. I'll text you my address when I know it.'

'When you know it?'

'I'm moving,' she says.

'You've been in Highgate for all of five minutes and decided it's not for you?' I quip.

'Something like that,' she says, handing over her money for the salad. 'Actually,' she continues, clearly steeling herself for something as we leave the shop and enter the cobbled lanes, 'Sean and I are moving to Singapore.'

I can feel my mouth try to say something, but nothing comes out.

'Singapore?' I say eventually. And then I mutter something between 'wow' and 'why' and it comes out as 'wah?'

'Wah?' she laughs. 'Because Sean and I are getting jobs out there, and we really fancy a change. That's wah.' She laughs, but I'm not sure if it's at me or at her own play on my garbled words. 'So I guess I'll be needing *your* address, so I can send you a leaving-party invite, or maybe I should email them out. I'm not sure.'

I give her the address of the house I'm moving to in Putney and she types it into her phone. 'When are you leaving?' I ask.

'Sometime in May, we think.'

I can't speak. Abbie is moving to the other side of the world. I breathe in and out, then I speak. 'How long for?'

'I'm not sure. It might be the start of some serious country-hopping or it might not be. Maybe until we have kids and need to settle them somewhere permanent.'

My voice goes up an octave. 'Kids?' I'm blindsided. She's talking about having kids with Sean.

'Yeah, children. You know those little things that walk and talk and, by all accounts, drain your finances. You've got one, remember? How is Teddy? Do you have a recent picture?'

We stop in the street and I pull out my wallet, opening it to show Abbie a picture taken at my parents' hotel at Christmas. I'm in swim shorts and Samantha's in a tiny little white bikini on the beach, and held between us is Teddy, done up head to toe in a sunsuit and matching hat. I'm so proud of my family.

'Oh, he's gorgeous. He's grown so much.'

I look at her, waiting for her to acknowledge that she's never once met him, having turned down all my invitations to the point where I gave up issuing any more.

'You've done really well, Tom,' she says and puts her hand on my arm.

I look at it. 'Thanks. So have you.'

'Thanks.'

We resume walking and I decide I'm not going to tell her I miss her any more. I tell her this far too often by email, and the last time I saw her in the pub around Valentine's Day I told her. I thought it would reignite our friendship. It did, in a way, but Abbie is definitely keeping me at arm's length. I can see that now. I need to let her go.

'It's good to see you, Abbie,' I say as we enter the court-yard. She'll turn right towards her office, I'll go left to mine. And that will be that.

'You will come, won't you?' she says suddenly, almost desperately.

'Come where?'

'To our leaving drinks. It'll only be somewhere nearby on a Friday. I'll give you plenty of notice. Please come.'

I'm not sure I want to. I'm not sure I want to see Abbie in the arms of Sean as they chat happily about how they're leaving London, moving far away to be together.

I shouldn't feel like this. I shouldn't feel annoyed that she's happy. I don't have the right to feel anything. I'm with someone. She's with someone. I have a baby. I should be happy that Abbie's happy, but somehow I can't summon that emotion.

'I do want you there,' she says. 'I've really missed you.'

'You wait until you leave to invite me to something. And you've only done it because I bumped into you in the street.'

She recoils in shock that I've spoken to her like that. 'No,' she says. 'I was going to invite you anyway. It's just . . .'

'You *have* been avoiding me, haven't you?' I ask. I'm going for this. I'm going in hard because I have to know.

She sighs. 'A bit.'

'Why?'

'I don't know. It's still a bit raw.'

'What is?'

'What happened between us. Or didn't happen. And then it all sort of went weird.'

'It went weird because you let it go weird. We met in the pub. We said we'd be friends. We had a lot of good banter afterwards – admittedly only by text. Then I had a baby and you went . . . cold. You didn't want to come and see Teddy. You didn't even want to come and see me after work one night for a quick drink. You never had time to meet for lunch or a quick coffee or a cigarette.'

'I don't smoke any more,' she says.

'Neither do I,' I reply.

'It's one of those things,' she says, moving the conversation on. 'Friendships fall away sometimes.'

Neither of us speaks for a few seconds. She looks at me and then at the ground.

And then I say. 'I didn't think that would happen to us.'

'We didn't know each other very long,' she fires back.

'I didn't think that mattered. It just felt different.'

'Different?' she asks.

'Special, in some way.'

'Because of the train?' She frowns. But it's not mocking. She's being serious.

'Yeah,' I say. 'Because of the train.'

'I don't think you can hold on to that,' she says. 'People come and people go. You and I would never have been friends, or even met, in ordinary life. I'd have been a few people behind you in the queue in Gianni's one day, or maybe even every single day of every single working week for years, and you'd never have looked at me or known who I was. If the train hadn't derailed the night you and I both happened to be on it together, we'd have exited at our stops, merged into the crowd of people on their way home and that would have been that. We'd never have become friends.'

'That's not true,' I say. 'We started talking before the accident. It was . . . good – fun.'

'For five minutes, and only because we were drunk!' she hurls back at me. 'None of it was real.'

'This friendship *is* real,' I say, moving towards her. Then I doubt myself. Am I deluded?

She doesn't speak. She looks sad. There are tears in Abbie's eyes.

'I'm sorry,' I say. 'You're right.' She's not. She's massively wrong. 'We can leave it there, if you want. We don't have to keep doing this.' Although, really, what *are* we doing? We've not seen each other once in a whole year, but even so, all we seem to do is hurt each other.

'You don't understand,' she says. 'I do want to be your friend, Tom. I do. And I miss you. And I'm sorry I haven't seen Teddy yet. I feel awful. And I want you to come to our leaving party. I don't know when I'll be back in London again, once I'm gone, and—'

'OK,' I cut in, because I can see she's trying not to cry again. 'I'll come.'

She lifts her eyes to mine and her smile returns slowly. 'Will you?'

I nod. 'Yeah, I'll come. If you do actually want me to. I don't want to turn up and you just blank me.'

'I wouldn't do that, and I do actually want you there,' she says, moving closer towards me. I can smell her perfume. I need to back away, but I can't. 'Promise me,' she says. 'I know I sound like a five-year-old, but promise me you'll come, because yours is one of the last faces I want to see before I get on that plane.'

I inhale, exhale, look her in the eyes. 'I promise I'll come.'

Chapter 36

Abbie

I have to stand in the toilet cubicle at work for a few minutes, my back against the door. Why is seeing Tom always so painful? He's right. We did let it go weird, or rather I did. I shouldn't have given in so easily to Sean's request for me not to meet up with Tom. I should have negotiated harder, so I could just have gone to see him. I'd be a part of his life now. I'd have held his son. I'd have known that he'd gone away at Christmas to his parents'. He was in the Caribbean, sunning himself with Samantha. My God, she's stunning in that picture. I had no idea. But then Tom's attractive, so of course he was going to end up with someone like her.

He's lucky to have her. I'm lucky to have Sean. But I really wish he hadn't been so jealous of Tom. I wish he'd let me see him, because it wouldn't be so painful every time I do. It would have been normal – we'd have got used to seeing each other. Now, Tom's coming to the leaving party. That'll please Sean no end, but I meant what I said to Tom: I really want him there. I've missed out on so much of his life by keeping him at arm's length. I regret every second of it.

Chapter 37

Tom

April 2007

I lift Teddy's little hand up into the air and place my palm against his. 'High five,' I say as he splashes in his baby bath. I'm seated on the floor next to him. 'We did it. We can tell Mummy that Teddy and Daddy moved house and sorted boxes into all the right places, found all your little onesies and nappies, and everyone's clean and bathed and it's all under control.'

Teddy smiles up at me and makes a noise that I take as total agreement. I pick him up when he's done, wrap him in his hooded towel and carry him to his new bedroom, which is twice the size of the little boxroom he used to be in.

'I know,' I say to him. 'This place is a palace compared to our last home, and our last place was awesome. Daddy has to work like a dog to pay the mortgage, but it's all good. Mummy too,' I say, remembering that Samantha's not here today for a perfectly good reason, which I've almost come to terms with. 'Mummy also works like a dog.'

I make a barking noise like a dog and Teddy laughs. 'You're a good audience, Ted. Never change.'

I give him his night-time bottle once he's in his onesie for bed and we settle in downstairs. Teddy's sitting up against the back of the sofa. 'Boys' night,' I say, clinking my bottle of Peroni against his Tommy Tippee bottle. 'Cheers.'

He holds his bottle out to me to do it again. And then again. He loves this. I love this.

'Ted, you're awesome,' I say, taking a sip of my beer. He sucks his milk down greedily while I fiddle with the TV remote. 'We can watch children's TV or . . .' I flick through the channels, '*Star Wars*.'

He looks at me, his mouth never leaving his bottle.

'*Star Wars* it is,' I say and settle back in, cosying up to my son. 'I won't tell Mummy you went to bed late, if you don't. We can have a lie-in tomorrow to make up for it.'

Teddy pulls his bottle away from his mouth and holds it out to me. We clink bottles.

'Cheers,' I say, putting my feet up on the coffee table. 'This is the life.'

My phone beeps. It's an invite from Abbie. Even though I gave her my address, she's emailing them out. It looks like a generic copy-and-paste job that's gone out to everyone in her phonebook: Leaving Party! Sean and Abbie are leaving for Singapore! Celebrate with us at Coq d'Argent, Friday 11 May. We'll be there straight after work at 6 p.m. and have an area reserved on the roof terrace.

So she's going then. It's actually happening. It had been a few weeks and I hadn't heard anything, so I assumed either she'd had the party and gone without saying, which I wouldn't have put past Abbie, or she wasn't going at all. I was hoping for the latter.

I was wrong.

Chapter 38

Abbie

May 2007

It has taken ages to sort moving overseas. Sean's new job provides him with a relocation specialist and so we've done our flat-hunting practically blind, with someone called Amanda being our eyes and ears on the ground. She's been sending us specs of flats, sorting out visas for us. It's like having a PA we've never met. Thankfully, Sean, who is very used to having a PA, took charge of Amanda's demands – paperwork being his forte. We are finally going at the end of the month.

I'm in the flat with Natasha and we're on our balcony, for what is going to be one of our final nights in together. I'm packed. I've sent a lot of things back to my mum and dad's, including my winter wardrobe. The average temperature in Singapore is twenty-seven degrees and it changes only one degree up or down mostly throughout the entire year.

I have two suitcases of summer clothes, and all the items I couldn't bear to part with, ready to go. My suitcases are in my room and it's odd, walking past them every day and knowing my life is packed up in them.

'I won't replace you,' Natasha says.

'That sounds businesslike,' I tease.

'I don't want another flatmate. If I can't have you, I don't want anyone else.'

'Now you've gone from businesslike to child.'

She laughs. 'I still dread a murderer moving in, and I don't need the money, so I'm leaving your room empty.'

'A tenner says you've got someone else living here within the month.'

'You're on.'

I've bought us a bottle of Moët & Chandon from the supermarket, because who knows when we'll get to do this again. We're sitting on chairs on the balcony and our bare feet are up against the glass balustrade. I look out at the view of London. The red light of Canary Wharf blinks out at me. In the distance, further into the City, skyscrapers are being built. A bird flies past us, and all feels right with the world. I top up our glasses of fizz.

'I'll miss you,' Natasha says.

'Me too. I'm supposed to be back for Tom's wedding in September, so let's make sure we fix a date to meet. I could even come back here and sleep in my old room, so it'll be like old times.'

'Oh, I'll have replaced you by then,' she teases.

'Charming!'

She laughs and so do I.

'Might have replaced you with a man.'

'A man?' I ask. 'A real one?'

'Piss off,' she says. 'Yes, a real one.'

'But you don't want to settle down,' I point out. 'You like the easy, flirty nights out that don't go anywhere.'

'I did,' she says. 'But I've met someone.'

'Tell me.'

'Remember the hot estate agent, Will, who rented us this place?'

No. 'Sure.'

'It's him. I had to re-sign the tenancy and we got chatting. We've been out a few times over the past couple of months.'

'You never told me.'

'You've not been here much to tell.'

'Sorry.'

'Plus, anyway, I thought it would go the way of the others: a couple of dates, a couple of drunken fumbles and then done. But actually it's past that now. It's moved towards something else – something good.'

'That's wonderful.'

'I really like him. You know that feeling you get when you want to be with someone the whole time. When you want to wake up next to them, go to bed with them, hold their hand. I can't stop touching him when we're out. It's automatic. I just reach out for him and Will reaches out for me when we're walking, or he puts his hand across the table in restaurants to hold my hand. I also find myself touching him inappropriately when we're alone in lifts. I can't stop myself.'

I laugh and spit out my champagne. 'Natasha!'

'It's fine. He wants to be touched inappropriately in lifts, believe me.'

'Oh my God,' I say, trying not to laugh again.

'But there's something else. It's not only lust. It's something . . . bigger.'

'Is it love?' I dare.

'I'm not sure!' she says. And then, 'Maybe . . . No. It's too soon. But there's something there. Is that what it's like for you and Sean?' she asks. 'Is that what love is like? Do you want him, not just sexually, but do you want to be with him all the time? Do you want to reach out and touch him, tell him everything, be one hundred per cent completely his, and have him be yours?'

I've never heard Natasha speak like this about anyone in all the years I've known her. She's got it bad for this guy. He is a lucky man.

I nod. 'Yes,' I say, because what else can I say? Of course it was like that at the start, with Sean and me. But that's the honeymoon period. It doesn't last for ever, as Natasha is going to find out. But if I say that out loud, it's going to come out wrong. It's going to sound bad. So I don't say it. Sean and I aren't like that any more, but we're planning our life, making decisions together. I am jealous of the honeymoon stage that Natasha's got going on. I don't think I'd realised it was over for me.

Chapter 39

Tom

I'm out of work on time, for once. I'm dreading going to Abbie's party. I don't want to say goodbye. I don't want to see her go. I'm worried I'll say all the wrong things. I also won't know anyone else there, other than her dad – who I've only met once, very fleetingly – and Sean, but I don't fancy getting embroiled in any kind of chat with him.

My phone rings and I reach into my inside jacket pocket. The number for Teddy's nursery flashes up on the screen.

'Hello?' I ask, warily. The nursery staff never call.

'Mr Archer, it's Lizzie from Little Faces nursery. You didn't request a late pick-up and tea for Teddy tonight and I'm afraid we don't have the staffing numbers planned to accommodate him.'

I'm not quite sure what they're asking me. 'Has Samantha not arrived yet to collect him?'

'I'm afraid not. We've tried calling Teddy's mother and have had no reply.'

What's happened to Samantha? 'OK. OK, leave it with me. I'll try her and I'll call you back.' I put my bag down on the courtyard pavement and ring Samantha.

No answer.

I try again. And then again.

She picks up finally. 'Yes?'

'Where are you? Nursery's been on the phone. You didn't sign Teddy up for a late pick-up and you've not arrived.'

'I'm not there.'

'Where are you?'

'I told you I was going away again. It's our team-building weekend,' she says.

'What? When did you tell me this?'

'It's been on the calendar on the wall for ages. If you bothered to look at it, you'd know.'

'So you didn't tell me.'

'I did tell you. Weeks ago.'

'But you didn't remind me this morning before you went to work. You got up and left before I was even awake.'

'But I told you weeks ago, and it's on the calendar. I can't bloody do it for you, Tom. You have to think for yourself every now and again.'

I can't believe what I'm hearing. 'I *do* think for myself! I just need you to tell me this kind of stuff. I need a reminder.'

'You had a reminder. I told you, and it's on the calendar. How many more reminders do you need?'

I run my hand through my hair. 'Samantha, I'm at a leaving party.'

'Then you need to leave it and go and pick up Teddy, or else we'll get some kind of super-bill as punishment for an evening and dinner session we didn't request.'

That nursery already robs me blind. I'm going to have to sell a kidney soon to fund Teddy's place. 'They can't keep him there anyway. They don't have the staffing ratio or some bullshit.'

'Problem solved, then. Leave the party and go and get him.'

'I haven't even made it to the party!'

'Even better,' she says. 'Get on the train and collect our son.'

'When are you back?' I ask. I can't fight any more.

'Monday.'

'Monday? You're away for three nights?'

'Yes, it's a work event.'

'On a weekend? Why does this stuff keep falling on a weekend? Don't they know you've got a family?'

'Tom, I'm in the running for partner and I need to be present. I keep reminding you of *this* too. I'm back in the office on Monday morning, and I'm home Monday evening. If we want this nice life and this nice new house, you need to suck it up. We need all the money we can get.'

Teddy's at nursery and he's being kicked out because we didn't fill in a form. His parents are rowing about collecting him. I'm mortgaged up to my eyeballs, and my fiancée is nowhere to be seen at weekends these days. Even when she's at home, she's always working in her office. This isn't how it's supposed to be.

'Fine,' I say and because I'm so bloody angry, I hang up without saying goodbye.

I call the nursery back. 'Hi. I'm leaving right now. I'm on my way.'

Chapter 40

Abbie

Sean and his mates are in the middle of a drinking game. I'm not sure if he's aware that he's managed to successfully exclude half the party by doing this. There are about thirty people here on the roof of Coq d'Argent. It's one of my favourite bars in the City because it sits on top of Poultry, in a building that houses a few of my go-to high-street fashion shops. It has a lovely beach-club vibe in summer, with white umbrellas, good cocktails and rooftop views down towards the Bank of England. Right now, Sean has organised bottles of Prosecco to be dotted around our area, and people are chuffed to bits there's free booze available.

The sun is beating down. We've managed to successfully choose a day without rain. I really didn't want to go inside to have the party or to have to huddle under umbrellas. Everything is perfect.

This feels like a final fling, a last hurrah. I don't know when I'll be back here again, with any of these people. Natasha and Will are cosied up in the corner, chatting to my parents.

Gary's pretending he won't miss me but he's sidled over to me a few times this evening and enveloped me in a bear hug, telling me how the person replacing me isn't as much fun as me, or checking if my drink needs topping up, or generally finding a reason to keep me talking to him, much to the amusement of his new girlfriend. And all my workmates have shuffled down here to bid me farewell, even if it's just for a quick one before they head home for the weekend.

I've dressed up for the occasion, wearing a leather mini-skirt and a white peasant blouse. Sean looks up and gives me appreciative glances, but he's doing something that involves repeating a sequence of numbers back and if he gets it wrong, he has to down a shot. For a guy who works with numbers all day long, he's getting quite a lot of these wrong. I wave at him from time to time as he looks up and around, checking if anyone he knows has entered our area.

I choose a quiet moment to readjust my sunglasses, take a long drink of cold water and pull out my phone to check if people are running late or can't find it and need directing towards the lifts, which are well hidden.

On my phone is a message. I click it open: Abbie, I'm so sorry. I can't come. Samantha's away and I'm stuck at home with Teddy. I hope you have a lovely party. Tom x

I stare at his message for what feels like ages. Samantha's away? He must have known that before now. Why has he left it until the middle of our party to message me this? He clearly doesn't want to come. He's bottled it and has made up the most transparent excuse I've ever heard.

I take a sip of my cocktail and slam it down so hard that most of the pink liquid inside slops over the top and onto my hand. I wipe my sticky hand on a napkin. What is wrong with him? He makes all this effort to try to be in my life and then decides it's not worth it, after all. Who plays a game like that? It's just cruel. I want to tell him this and I'm halfway through typing back an angry rant about how he promised he'd come, when a friend of mine I used to work with enters and I'm forced to put my phone away and say hi, make polite conversation and answer questions about my new life in Singapore.

All the answers I give are speculative – I have no idea really what's in store. I haven't found a job yet and have agreed to take on some freelance work. Most of the jobs I looked at wanted someone to start within four weeks, and Sean and I didn't know when his start date was going to be. It looks like I'll be at a loose end for the first few weeks. I suppose that time will be good to settle into our new apartment, but I've never been unemployed. It frightens me, even though Sean's new salary is more than enough for both of us. I'm just not used to the uncertainty.

By 11 p.m. our friends and family are filtering out. I've hugged my parents goodbye and I'm going to spend my last night with them tomorrow. They're taking us to the airport on Sunday, so I wave them off as they head towards the lifts. I won't see Sean's parents again before we fly, so we hug for ages and then I watch his mum hold him, brushing his hair back from his forehead and then give me a talking-to about looking after him. Sean and I share an amused look throughout.

Natasha gives me a quick wave and heads off with Will, saying she'll see me at home when I'm finished here. I'm staying in our flat tonight for the last time. And then it won't be *our* flat any more, because I won't live there. This is starting to feel very real now. Before, I was swept along in the planning stage, but now the party's over there's no planning to do, just tickets to print and flights to board. It's happening. I'm really leaving.

Sean wanders over, pulls me towards him. 'That's that, then,' he says. 'Nothing left to do now except board that plane.'

'I'm sure we can manage that,' I say. 'This is really, really happening.'

'It really, really is. You OK?'

'Yes. Are you?'

'Of course. I'm excited,' he says.

'Me too.' I'm something like excited. I think I'm actually quite scared. This is huge.

'Some of us are going on to a club. You coming?'

'No thanks. I think I'm going to wander down to the river for a bit, take in the view one last time. Do you want to come with me?'

He makes a stricken sort of face. 'I sort of promised the guys I'd go with them.'

'Only for a few minutes?' I say. 'We can hold hands and say goodbye to London together.'

He looks at his watch. His mates are putting on their jackets, their ties tucked into their pockets and their top buttons undone. Sean's done the same at some point.

'You go,' he says. 'Have a moment by yourself. We'll be stuck together like glue over the next few weeks, so enjoy the peace and quiet.'

'OK,' I say. He's only got this night with his friends, because he too is back to his parents' for one final night tomorrow. I don't want to steal this last moment with his mates from him. 'Have fun.'

'I will,' he says as his friends head past, gesturing for Sean to go with them. They say goodbye to me and things like 'Look after our boy', 'Don't let him get up to his usual tricks' and 'Keep him in check, won't you?'

Sean rolls his eyes. 'Ignore them.' He leans in to kiss me and then says, 'Catch up with you later. Text me to let me know you've got back home all right?'

'OK. Bye.' I wave him off and gather my things, standing on the rooftop terrace, looking out one last time at the view, before making my way down in the lift. I laugh as I watch Sean and his mates rounding the corner ahead of me. They're giving each other piggybacks and trying to push one another over. I turn in the opposite direction, down towards the river, passing my office, closed up for the night. The night security guard is reading a paper and I give him a wave, although he doesn't see me. I walk past Tom's old flat and see the lights on inside. Someone else is living there now. I detour past Gianni's, and the curved Victorian windows show that a light has accidentally been left on in the kitchen at the back.

And then I stand down by the river at Embankment. The London Eye is stationary, lit up, and the Oxo Tower's red lights shine down. The South Bank is a sea of light. I'll miss this view. I'll miss London. I'll miss everyone here. I'll miss all of it.

I should think about getting myself over to Natasha's. But somehow I don't want to go. I don't want to draw a line under my last night in London. I don't want to wake up and go out for my last breakfast with Natasha; I don't want to take my suitcases to my parents' in Enfield tomorrow afternoon and sleep there one last time. I don't want to wake up on Sunday morning, pick up Sean and be driven to the airport, kiss my parents goodbye and walk through the barrier towards our flight. But I know I have to do it. I'm committed. It's too late to do anything else. I'll be fine when I arrive in Singapore.

But before all of that, there's one last thing I have to do.

Chapter 41

Tom

Who the hell is ringing our doorbell at this time of night? Actually it's more like the early hours of the morning. I'm holding Teddy in my arms because he's been up for hours, and so have I. Why he's awake now is beyond me – no amount of nappy changes, nursery rhymes or cuddling with me in bed is making him sleepy. So we're in front of the TV and I'm hoping this selection of children's shows on DVD are going to send him off to sleep. The volume's down low, but I suspect all those bright colours on the screen are not going to do the trick. If it's some little punk outside playing Knock Down Ginger at 1 a.m., then I'm going to lose it.

I pull open the door. Teddy's in my arms and I'm braced to shout, but my mouth just falls open. I can't say hi. I can't even say her name. How does she manage to do this to me every single time?

She's obviously steeled herself for this. Her stance is aggressive. So is her voice. 'Hi,' she says. 'You gave me your new address when we were outside Gianni's that time.'

I'd forgotten that and am still feeling the shock of her presence.

'So I decided to call your bluff. Are you really alone? A simple Yes or No will do it.'

I find my voice. 'No.'

'I knew it.' She turns.

'I'm with Teddy.' I have to talk quickly to stop her reaching the end of the path. 'I wasn't lying. Samantha's away.'

Teddy looks from me to Abbie, and her expression softens as she turns back. 'He's cute,' she comments. And then she smiles at him and says, 'Hello.' He makes a happy noise and buries his head into my neck. But Abbie's expression has changed to one of sadness and she can't meet my gaze.

'Abbie, it's nearly one a.m. What are you doing here?'

She walks towards me, takes a deep breath. 'I don't know.'

'Look, just come in.' I step back and she walks in slowly, looking around the hallway, which is dimly lit by only a table lamp.

We walk past the large mirror above the radiator and I catch sight of myself holding Teddy. I forgot I'm only wearing boxer shorts.

'Go through,' I say. 'I'm going to put some clothes on.'

I carry Teddy upstairs, place him on the bed and pull on a pair of shorts and a T-shirt. When we go back downstairs, I find Abbie standing in the kitchen. She looks lost and awkward in such a huge space, even with all the baby crap and bottles and takeaway boxes littering the counter.

'You still don't cook then,' she says.

I smile. 'What are you doing here?' I ask again. Teddy grumbles in my arms, swivelling his head to try to see the TV. I put him on his play mat and he crawls into a slumped sort of sitting position in order to watch *Teletubbies*.

All this has spared Abbie from answering and so I offer her a cup of tea, which she accepts. As the kettle boils, I put my back against the counter and watch her while she looks around the room, taking in the family photos, the books on the shelves, my collection of films, Teddy's toys and nappies stashed under his changing unit. She looks back at me, surprised to see me with my arms folded, watching her.

'You didn't come,' she says.

I shake my head. 'I couldn't.'

'You promised,' she goes on, but not in anger, or petulantly. It's just a statement.

'I know. I'm sorry. I had no choice. I didn't know Samantha was going away until the nursery called me. I had to rush and pick him up.'

'I wanted to say goodbye to you,' she says.

'I know,' I reply, although I didn't really know that, but what else can I say? I've apologised once. I can't keep doing it. I want to tell her I've missed her. Instead we stand in relative silence, with the sound of the kettle mixing with the TV.

'Where's Samantha?' she asks.

I look past her to check Teddy's all right. He's lying down on his mat, his thumb in his mouth. If I'm not mistaken, I think his eyes might be closing. I'll leave him a bit longer.

'Some kind of work event. Team-building weekend, I think.'

'And you didn't know she was going?' Abbie asks. She thinks I set out to hurt her on purpose. I would never do that to her.

'I really didn't. We had an almighty row, if that makes you feel any better.'

'Why would that make me feel better?' she asks.

I don't know. I don't know why I said that now. I don't answer. I also don't think either of us really knows what to say. Abbie looks embarrassed that she's here, in the middle of the night.

'How did you get here?' I ask. I assume she still doesn't get the Tube.

'Taxi.'

'Is he waiting outside?' I ask.

'Who, Sean?'

Fuck Sean. 'No, the driver.'

'Oh . . . no. I let him go.'

'What if I hadn't been in?'

'Then I'd have known you were lying about being left home alone with Teddy and that would have been the end of us.'

The end of us. 'Fair point. What if Samantha had answered the door?'

'See above comment,' she says.

I can't help but laugh, and the kettle clicks off. I pour us both a mug of tea. Teddy's asleep on the mat. 'Finally.' I go towards the remote, turn the volume down so gently that Teddy won't wake up, startled. There are no other lights on in here, so in order not to plunge us into darkness I leave the TV on, and the swirling images blur the room.

I regret turning the volume down now. The silence is all-encompassing.

'When do you leave?' I ask.

Abbie moves over to collect her tea and stands against the sleek silver American double fridge that Samantha insisted we buy, and which I could only afford on interest-free credit.

'We fly on Sunday.'

'*This* Sunday – as in the day after tomorrow?'

She nods, looks at her watch. 'Technically it's tomorrow, I suppose.'

'That's . . . soon.'

'It is.'

'When will you be back?' This sounds desperate. I'm not sure why I asked in that tone.

She shrugs. Sips her tea, winces at the heat and puts it on the side. 'I don't know.'

'Will you be back for our wedding at the end of summer?'

'I'd like to come, but Sean's not sure he'll be able to take time off so soon into his new job.'

'I don't care if Sean comes or not – the invite was for you. Can *you* come?'

'I don't know, Tom. Can I let you know?'

'I guess.' Samantha will go nuts if she thinks someone's going to renege after having already agreed to *save the date*. I won't tell her. Not yet. I can't have another row. I'm exhausted by all the rowing.

But the thought of Abbie not wanting to come to my wedding, having already not wanted to come and actually meet my baby in all this time, is . . . disappointing, upsetting. And yet she's got the gall to come to my house at 1 a.m. and call me out on not coming to her leaving party. Anger builds and I turn away from her for a moment, so that she can't see how pissed off I've suddenly become.

'I really messed things up, didn't I?' she says suddenly.

I spin round. 'What?'

'I messed everything up.'

'*You* messed everything up? Are you joking?'

She shakes her head and looks at the marble floor that cost me ten grand, and which I regret bitterly every time I look at it. 'No, I'm not joking. I could have been a better friend to you. A few emails and texts here and there weren't enough to keep our friendship alive. And I didn't come and see Teddy. I'm so sorry.'

'It's OK,' I say.

'It's not. I'm a bad person.'

I issue a dry kind of laugh. 'You're really not, Abbie.'

'How old is he now?' she asks.

'Ten months.'

'Oh my God.' She puts her head in her hands.

Is she crying? She says something into her hands that sounds a lot like, 'How is he nearly a year old and I've not even held him? This is you . . . This is your son and I didn't come and see him.'

'Why didn't you?' I ask. Because I have to know, now that she's raised the subject. She shrugs, but that's not enough for me. 'Tell me,' I say. 'Did you hate me that much you couldn't even come near me? Couldn't even come near my son?'

Oh, shit. Abbie's really crying now. I move towards her because she's speaking into her hands and I can't understand a word of what's she's on about. I pull her towards me, but her hands don't leave her face. My arms are around her hunched figure. It feels good holding her again, after all this time. 'Come here . . . It's OK. Don't cry. Don't wake Teddy up, for God's sake.'

She laughs. 'Sorry.'

'It's OK.' I lean us towards the counter and hand her a piece of kitchen roll. She wipes her eyes. She's managed to smudge her eye make-up everywhere, so I grab another piece. 'Let me.'

She stands obediently while I wipe softly under her eyes. I'd forgotten how much of a mix of green and blue her eyes are. Like the ocean. Being this close to her is dangerous. It always has been.

I move back a bit. 'I didn't hear what you said,' I confess. 'But you don't have to repeat it.'

'Sean didn't want me to,' she blurts out.

My eyebrows shoot up. 'Sean didn't want you to come and meet my son?'

She shakes her head.

'Why not?'

'He didn't want me seeing you.'

I pull back from her, lean against the counter. 'Why not?' I ask again.

'He was jealous – worried.'

'About what?'

'You and me.'

'You and me?' I repeat.

'I told him about what almost happened between us.'

'It was so long ago,' I say.

'I know. But he wouldn't listen. He hated the idea. And I loved him – love him – and we're making a life together, and I had to choose between hurting him or hurting you.'

'No-brainer,' I say sarcastically and it's a bit of a low blow.

'For you, maybe. But it was tough. I was emailing you and he didn't know, and it just made me feel . . . deceitful.'

'I take it he doesn't know you're here.'

She smiles wryly. 'Of course not.'

I pick up my tea, drink it, put it back down again. 'In which case, I think you should go,' I say, and her face visibly falls. 'You're putting your relationship on the line to stand in my kitchen at one a.m. Why did you think this was a good idea?'

'Because I had to say goodbye.'

'Why? What are we to each other, that you want to put your relationship in jeopardy forty-eight hours before we probably never see each other again?'

'Don't say that,' she says. 'Of course we'll see each other again.'

'No, we won't,' I reply, and I genuinely believe this.

She's crying again now and I know I'm being a total shit, but I'm too locked in the punch to pull back now.

'You won't come back for my wedding. You know you won't. You worked in the building opposite me and we never saw each other there. Sean says he doesn't want you seeing me, and so we don't meet up. And all the while I want to see you, want to know how you are, want to know if you're OK. We went through something awful together – what's wrong with checking in on each other every now and again?' Abbie's tears are really falling now, but I can't stop. 'You just want to airbrush me out of your life? And then, what? You decide tonight that actually you do want to see me. So it all happens on your terms, despite the fact that I wanted to see you for so long. Did it never occur to you that *I* might not be OK?'

Her head lifts. Her make-up is everywhere again, smudged. I hand her more kitchen roll. She can deal with it herself now.

'Aren't you OK?' she asks.

'Of course I'm not,' I raise my voice.

Teddy stirs on the mat.

I lower my voice. 'I'm a mess. I've got myself knee-deep in debt for a house I can't afford, I hate my job, I'm pretty sure my girlfriend hates me, and every time I close my eyes to fall asleep, I see—' I stop. I'm going too far. My chest is rising and falling in anger, but it's not anger at her. Not now. It's everything. I can't face her. I turn away, run my hand over my mouth.

She's not speaking. It must be the three Peronis I've had tonight, the lack of sleep, the despair that hits me every time I think about that day or the fact that she's standing in front of me, for what will possibly be the last time ever, that makes me decide, foolishly, that I'm going all the way with this. 'And then there's you,' I say.

'Me?' she questions.

I turn round. Her voice is soft and she's backed away from my onslaught and is now completely still, standing against the fridge, not moving.

'You,' I repeat.

'What about me?' Her voice is shaking. She thinks she's about to get another verbal hammering.

'Everything about you, Abbie. I have a lot of regrets, believe me. A lot. And one of the biggest ones is letting you go, the way you did, that night. Not explaining myself better. I couldn't comprehend what was happening. Samantha had just told me she was pregnant. And I turned round and you were gone. I think about that a lot. I keep telling myself: us not being together was the right thing – for you, for me, for Samantha. But what if it *wasn't* the right thing?'

'What do you mean?' she breathes.

'Because after that everything went sideways.'

She's staring at me. 'No, it didn't,' she says. 'Even if the rest of your life has gone a bit shit, you have Teddy and he's beautiful.'

'Teddy's the best thing that has ever happened to me,' I say. 'And I wouldn't undo it for the world.'

I'm so tired I don't know what I mean, so I don't say any more. I'm being a bastard. Poor little rich boy, good job, nice house, hot fiancée, perfect son: this is everything I ever wanted. I'm lucky. I know I'm lucky. Maybe one day soon I'll start feeling it.

'I wish it had been different.' She says it so quickly I don't quite catch it.

'What?'

'I wish you hadn't seen that message,' she clarifies. 'If I could go back to that night, knowing what I know now. I would have moved your phone away – far out of reach.'

'But then—' I start.

'Yes,' she cuts in. 'We'd have slept together . . .'

She's clearly nervous. And all I can do is watch, because I can't go to her. I can't stop her. I need to hear this. I'm desperate to hear this.

'And I think,' she says, 'I think it would have been the start of something and not the end, even with Samantha being pregnant. It would have been a messy situation, but if you'd have wanted to – we could have made it work. And I think it would have just . . . I think it would have helped make me realise what I already knew.'

'Which is what?' I ask. I think I've stopped breathing.

'That I loved you.'

I've definitely stopped breathing. I had no idea how much I needed to hear that.

Chapter 42

Abbie

'Say something, for God's sake.'

He's not speaking, why isn't he speaking? I'm an idiot. I've put my heart on the line. I've confessed too much.

'And now?' he says slowly.

'And now what?' I ask. I don't understand the question.

'You don't love me now?' he says carefully. His eyes are scanning mine.

I don't want to say it. I don't want to say what I'm feeling, because I love Sean. I do. I love him. But I love Tom too. I thought I didn't. I thought the feelings that had grown between us would diminish. But they haven't.

I could lie. Or I could tell the truth.

'Yes,' I whisper.

'Yes?' he asks quickly. 'Yes, you do love me?'

He's stepped forward. If he comes any closer I think I'm going to collapse. I don't know how my legs are holding me up. 'Yes, yes, I do love you.' *Oh God, make it stop. Why am I doing this?*

Tom breathes in sharply, rubs his hand over the stubble on his face. I'm pressed against the fridge. I've got nowhere to go, to get away from this awful situation I've just created. Why did I have to do this?

'Say something,' I beg. 'Even if you're only telling me to get out.'

'I'm not going to tell you that,' he says after a painfully long silence in which he's been analysing the floor.

I'm not sure what I expect him to do. What can he do? We can't do anything. Even though we can't do anything, I simply want to hear him say—

'I love you.' He's running his teeth over his lower lip and he's lifted his gaze, staring straight at me.

Tom loves me. Everything feels brighter. And now I know it's about to get darker.

'I'm in love with you,' he says, his gaze holds mine, and I know tears are about to come again and I can't let them. I do my absolute best to stop the lump in my throat from getting the better of me. He's looking at me, his expression pained. He looks like he's got tears in his eyes. And mine arrive again, because my eyes blur and I can't see him any more, only a faint outline. I blink the tears away.

He steps forward and gently touches my cheek, silently wiping my tears away with his fingertips.

'Abbie,' he says and his voice catches.

'I know,' I soothe.

He doesn't speak, just watches me. I want him to kiss me. I don't want him to kiss me. I wish I'd never come here.

'We can't . . .' His gaze drifts towards my mouth.

'I know,' I repeat. But I don't know. I don't know anything any more.

On the mat Teddy wakes, cries out for Tom, and I watch this man I love back away from me slowly, reluctantly, before his gaze disconnects from mine and he turns towards his son.

'It's OK, Teddy,' he says, 'Daddy's here.' He moves around the kitchen island towards his baby.

I'm a mixture of emotions. Bereft, devastated, relieved we didn't go further. I think of Sean. 'Oh God,' I say.

Tom picks Teddy up, soothing him gently.

What happens now? Nothing. Tom and I were almost friends again. Now we can't be anything to each other. We can't risk it.

'I have to go,' I say.

'Not like this. Wait. Just give me five minutes to sort Teddy and we can talk.'

'No,' I reply, walking towards the door. 'What is there to say? We can't be together. This is your life,' I say to him, gesturing to his house. 'You're getting married, you have a child. I'm going to leave,' I say and I'm in the hallway, heading towards the front door.

'Don't,' he pleads. He's at a disadvantage, holding a squirming ten-month-old, but he's still faster than I am. His hand grabs hold of mine as I reach out to open the front door. 'Abbie,' he says. 'Wait. Please. We can sort this.'

I pause. He so very nearly has me. But I don't know what we can do to sort this.

'I can't,' I whisper. My throat is tight as I try not to burst into tears.

'I'm so sorry,' he says after a second or two. 'I'm so sorry. I'm fucking everything up again.'

'Don't, Tom. This is my fault. I'm sorry I came tonight. I'm sorry I told you.'

I open the door and leave, walk down the path, towards the gate. Behind me he calls out, 'Abbie, don't get on that plane. Please! Let's talk about this.'

But I'm already running down the road, away from Tom, as I allow myself to cry.

Chapter 43

Tom

September 2007

'Tom, will you take Samantha to be your wife? Will you love her, comfort her, honour and protect her and, forsaking all others, be faithful to her as long as you both shall live?'

'I will.' I mean it. Samantha and I love each other. We've committed to having a child together, a life together, a marriage together. I'm going to be thirty soon, as if this makes a difference. We've pulled out all the stops. She wants to be married. She wants Teddy to have parents who are married. This matters to Samantha. It's important to her. And if it's important to her, then it's important to me too. That's how this works, isn't it? That's how a relationship works. I'm a parent, a father, a family man, a husband. I need to give Teddy the kind of stability I never had; the kind of loving family environment my parents didn't go in for. What happened with Abbie was a fuck-up.

I glance around the church while the vicar is busy doing his thing. Samantha replies, 'I will' in the right place and looks up at me from beneath her veil. She smiles, I smile back. This is happening. This train has well and truly left the station.

My side of the church looks pretty slim. A few work friends, my family. Mum and Dad flew over. There's no Abbie, though. As I predicted. I'll never see her again, although whether that's because of what we said to each other or simply because it was the inevitable conclusion for us, I'll never know.

She wouldn't answer my messages or my calls. And when I phoned the last time, the number no longer worked. She must have a Singaporean number now. But she's not told me what it is.

And so we're back where we started, sort of: friends who don't talk to each other, friends who hurt each other, friends who admitted they're in love with each other, friends who have made the adult decision to do nothing about it, because it's wrong and it will hurt people. So why did being with her feel so right?

I've mulled over that for a long time. I could have left Samantha. Abbie could have left Sean. We could have been together. But then I'd have seen Teddy only at weekends, because Samantha's a lawyer and she would have taken me to the cleaner's.

She'd probably have filed for sole custody and would have cited the occasion when I didn't get Teddy from nursery when she went away. And then I might not even get to see Teddy at weekends. I look at Teddy in the front row, being held by Samantha's mum.

I can't lose him.

Chapter 44

Abbie

January 2008

I've been in Singapore for just over seven months. A lot can happen in seven months. A lot can happen in seven seconds. My mind jogs back to a different year, a different moment. It's been over two years since the crash and it still happens when I least expect it: that flash of light. And then the darkness. I close my eyes and count to five. It helps shift the sudden unwanted memory of the train derailment. A bit. And I go out onto our balcony and let the heat and the humidity of the Singaporean night engulf me.

It never fails to surprise me, even after all this time, that outside means heat and inside means life-threatening pneumonia, thanks to the intense air-conditioning. I've had to rebuy a lot of winter clothes, after I foolishly stored all mine at my parents'. Everywhere is air-conditioned and Marks & Spencer has served me well out here, with its range of oddly out-of-place seasonal apparel. Sean and I laughed when we first saw Marks & Spencer in the malls. A little slice of Britain. And we laughed even louder at their range of coats and jumpers, laid out on a twenty-eight-degree day. And then a week later I returned and handed over a lot of cash for a lot of jumpers, so that I wouldn't risk hypothermia every time we went out to eat.

Our first apartment turned out to be a dud. But once we'd settled, after a few months we managed to move into a fantastic new, high-rise block. I've never seen so many shiny surfaces in one space. It's all so white.

The rent is eye-wateringly expensive. But Sean's new salary more than covers it, and our low living expenses and excess of money enable us to do anything we want, which is kind of amazing. I'm not used to living like this. My mum's thrilled.

I stand here, on the balcony, watching another day roll into another night, nursing a faint hangover from a champagne-fuelled party that Sean and I had with some of the friends we've met through the expat network. How Sean went to work this morning is beyond me.

I stare up into the night sky and stars flicker and glare, brighten and diminish. All around me it's an intense display. As if bright-white dimmer switches are being turned on and off by an invisible hand, adjusted up and down all over the wide expanse of sky.

Sometimes I stand here and see the flicker of Venus in the clear night sky and I'm reminded I'm in the eastern hemisphere, seeing a different constellation of stars and planets from everyone I love. Everyone except Sean, of course.

I hear the front door bang shut and Sean goes to the store cupboard, which is actually a bomb shelter. He dumps his bag, then cranks the air-con up. I've never quite understood why these apartments all have bomb shelters. We're on the nineteenth floor. If a nuclear bomb goes off, we're screwed, surely.

'I'm so late. I'm sorry,' he says, moving forward to kiss me. He looks tired, his jaw etched in stubble. His tie's askew and he yanks at it, curls it into a ball and throws it in the direction of our bedroom, where it hits the floor, awaiting collection later.

'You're always late home,' I say, but it's meant consolingly, sympathetically.

'It's not my fault,' he says. 'It's gone haywire.'

'I'm not accusing,' I say softly.

He slumps on the sofa, kicks off his shoes, sighs and closes his eyes.

'Do you want a drink?'

'Mmm,' he says.

This is our nightly routine. So much so that I feel like one of the wives in *Mad Men*, that I should be in a pinafore and have a shiny Martini ready to hand over to my hard-working man. Only I don't know how to make cocktails that fast, so I pull a beer from the fridge and open it. Sean's eyes open at the sound of the bottle top clattering onto the granite work surface.

I grab one for myself. It's my reward for doing fifty laps of the pool this morning.

'How was your day?' he asks. The air-con blows remnants of his aftershave and sweat towards me. I find it strangely intoxicating. He goes out to work intensely clean, but by the end of the day the ride on the MRT underground, rammed with other people, tips him towards needing another shower. I still don't take the underground. Instead I've mastered the bus situation.

'My day was good,' I reply.

'What did you get up to?'

'Fifty laps of the pool, a bit of reading and then, after lunch, I finished that feature I was working on and sent it to my editor, before Gary and I Skyped each other for a catch-up. He was in his office with his headset on, pretending it was a work-related call. I'm not sure he got away with it.'

'How is he?' Sean asks.

'Good. Got a new girlfriend.'

'A new one? Newer than the one who came to our leaving do?'

'Newer than that,' I say, chuckling at Sean's surprise.

'I'm glad you had a good day,' he says. He's been really sound about the fact that he works unbelievably hard and, in comparison, I've got it so easy. I couldn't find a job, despite my best efforts, so in the end we agreed I'd freelance for my old magazine along with a handful of others, as and when I found the opportunities. Gary let slip in an email that my old magazine needed an Asia correspondent and I leapt on it, contacting my former editor to throw my hat into the ring. I played it cool but, in truth, I was desperate.

I had a month with their outgoing correspondent while he finished up, and now I'm a few months into doing the job solo and have easily found my feet. Most days I interview people on the phone, dig around for news stories and come up with features ideas. Today was, admittedly, a bit of a lazy day, work-wise, but the hangover didn't help. The work isn't very challenging, but it keeps me busy and, importantly, means I'm earning something. It in no way compares to what Sean earns, but he's adamant it doesn't matter. He made no secret that this relocation was all about him earning as much money as possible, and not really about me having to do the same. It makes sense. As a journalist, I'm never going to be able to buy the kind of house Sean wants us to own when we eventually move back home. If only I worked in banking. But that kind of job isn't a reality for someone who uses her fingers to count.

'I could really use a holiday,' he says. Now is not the time for me to point out that every day here feels like a holiday to me.

'Where do you want to go?' I ask. I start to sit down next to him, but he pulls me onto his lap. There's that musky scent of aftershave again. I inhale greedily.

'Where do *you* want to go?' he asks and then continues, 'we can travel literally anywhere. The USA. Dubai. Australia. Ten days? A fortnight? What do you fancy? First-class flights. Spa treatments every day. Champagne on ice. God, I can almost taste it,' he says. 'Where does Ritz-Carlton have properties? Let's five-star the shit out of this.'

I laugh at his enthusiasm and can't help dipping my head to kiss him. I'm rewarded with a beer-laced kiss that does certain things to me. I was worried, after my chat with Natasha – it feels so long ago now – that Sean and I might have lost that spark. I know now that we haven't. I've made sure of it. I've never invested so much of my earnings in so much lacy underwear. Another thing I'm grateful to Marks & Spencer for. I miss home so much that sometimes I just wander into good old M&S and pretend I'm in the one in Enfield, reminded of home. Which is odd because I never even used to shop in M&S when I lived in England.

We pull apart, both of us looking flushed. There's nothing stopping us from ravishing each other, right here, right now, other than the fact that I'll have to close the blinds. We're quite close to other modern high-rises. Yet Sean has only one thing on his mind and it isn't sex. He sips his beer again and says, 'Vietnam?'

'Can we go home?' I ask.

'Home?' He looks utterly confused by this.

I nod. 'Have you forgotten where home is?'

'It's here,' he says. 'With you. Home's wherever you are.'

'Sean,' I draw out his name happily, 'that's so sweet.'

He smiles, like a child rewarded.

'Don't you want to go back to London at all?'

He shakes his head. 'We've only just left.'

'Seven months ago. Nearly eight.'

'That's not that long, Abbie.'

'I know. But it feels like it is.'

He sits up a bit straighter and I shuffle off his lap, taking a seat next to him on the sofa, my legs draped over his thighs at a bit of an odd angle.

'We'll go home. Of course we will,' he placates.

I brighten. 'Now? Soon?'

Sean makes a face. 'I really need a holiday,' he repeats.

'So not back to London?'

'Sorry, Abbie. I need somewhere sunny, with a beach and champagne on ice. I need to relax. I can't relax back at home. I'll have to see my folks, you'll have to see your folks, we'll end up out with my mates, and then we'll have to factor in Natasha and Gary and all your other lot and, before you know it, we've been in England for a week or two, sat down for twenty minutes total and I'll be back at work, wondering why the hell I'm still drained of all energy.'

'When you put it like that, it's hard not to agree,' I say.

He continues, 'And where would we stay?'

'A hotel?' I say sensibly. 'There are plenty of them in London.' I don't know why I'm trying, I've already lost this one, but I admire him for humouring me. 'We could go back to that one in Trafalgar Square where we watched the fireworks?'

Sean makes a noise from the back of his throat, which goes some way towards saying no without actually having to. But I get the hint.

'It's fine,' I say, touching his leg. 'We'll go another time.'

'You could always go without me,' he offers quietly. 'If you want to?'

It's my turn to make a face. 'I don't want to go home without you. It would be weird.' I pull my cardigan tighter around me. It's freezing in here.

'No, it wouldn't,' he says, lifting his beer and drinking. I watch his jaw move as he drinks, his Adam's apple bob in his throat. I want to kiss him. He looks knackered. He works so hard for us.

We didn't go home at Christmas. I didn't quite promise my parents that we would, but I think it was expected. I was a bit shocked Sean didn't want to. That was only a few weeks ago, so I don't know why I'm surprised that he hasn't changed his tune. I was just hoping really.

Before that, there was September, and Tom and Samantha's wedding. I'd told my parents I'd be back for that. Then I'd swiftly had to tell them I wasn't coming home after all. I couldn't. How could I sit in a church and watch him marry her, after what we'd said to each other?

I think constantly about that night I went to his house. I *hate* that I relive it in my head as often as I do. We told each other we loved each other and it was . . . wonderful, incredible and dreadful.

I hate myself for all of it: for going there, for telling him how I felt, for trying to play make-believe. I hate that we did that while his sleeping baby was in the room, in the house that Tom shares with the mother of his child. I hate that I did that a day before I got on a flight with Sean and started the rest of our life together.

I have a long list of regrets. They're stacked like building blocks, one upon the other. I know now that it's possible to love two people at the same time. I love Tom in a way that's different from how I love Sean. I can't explain it. I love them both, in such different ways.

That day on the train bound us together. But now we're nearly 7,000 miles apart.

Sean's waiting for my reaction; he's said something and is looking at me expectantly. 'So . . . you OK with it?'

I don't know what he's just suggested. I nod all the same.

'Good,' he says, sitting back and closing his eyes. 'Dubai it is, then. I'll book it tomorrow.'

And then I climb onto his lap again and kiss him seductively. Closing the blinds, be damned.

Chapter 45

Tom

March 2008

I didn't realise how much I'd needed a fresh start. I just had to leave.

Now is a bit of a strange time to change jobs, given that we're probably about to enter a recession. But the pay's more and I desperately need the money. Our living expenses are out of control and the mortgage on our house is a killer. I was offered the job eight weeks ago, after I received my bonus – I timed that right. And now I'm on gardening leave. A shame the weather's been so bad that I've not been able to actually sit in the garden. I've played a lot of *Call of Duty*, though. And I've been able to take Teddy to and from nursery every day, allowing Samantha to put in the hours at work. I've snuck him off for the odd day here and there but, as Samantha points out, if we withdraw him for the eight weeks to save some money, they'll fill his space up with another kid on the waiting list almost immediately.

We go to the park most afternoons when the weather's not totally dire and I've met a few of the nursery mums and their children.

I cannot stress how relieved I am that Teddy is a happy little kid, that he's not going to be shipped off to boarding school, as I was; that he's going to make local friends at the local school – which has an excellent Ofsted track record, so Samantha tells me. Apparently this is why we moved to this neck of the woods. I did not know that until a few weeks ago.

Teddy toddles up to me and hands me another stone he wants to take home. This is his new thing – stones. Samantha thinks he's going to be a geologist. Last week he collected leaves. I think Samantha's getting ahead of herself in predicting job prospects for a child who's nearly two.

My pockets are full of stones and I feel my new iPhone screen paying the price of Teddy's environmental interest. I wonder if I can sift out a few and drop them when he's not looking. I move my phone to my back pocket.

I'm trying to have a conversation with the only other dad, Andy, who picks up from nursery. We spotted each other and bonded in that forced way that only two men in a sea of women at the nursery gate can. Andy's all right. He's a children's book illustrator, but harbours dreams of creating a cartoon to rival Peppa Pig, 'Although a bit less annoying, you know?' He's a single dad and said my arrival took the pressure off him. He's been struggling to fight off 'the hot European nannies'.

'Really?'

'Nah, not really,' he says, pulling his hoody over his head like some thirty-year-old middle-class gangster. 'I wouldn't date one of the women at the gate. Too risky. What if it doesn't work out? Then I've got to see them every day, at the kids' birthday parties and that sort of thing. Not worth it. I've got to stay strong, though. Some of them are really hot.'

'Some of them *are* really hot,' I concur.

'So how long have you got until you callously abandon me at pick-up time and start your swanky new job?' he asks.

'One week to go,' I say. 'I'll miss this. I love picking up Teddy. We have so much fun together. I'll miss pushing him on the swings and standing in the park and chatting shit with you.'

'Yeah,' Andy says. 'It's all right. Bloody cold. But all right.'

'We'll get the kids together for some weekend playdates perhaps?' I offer.

Andy nods. 'Or we could sack that idea off and go to the pub instead.'

'That'll work.'

I watch our sons toddling around together, exchanging stones. I really am incredibly lucky. I think I'm starting to feel it now. I'm settling into the hand that I got dealt. It's a good hand, I think. I got dealt a bloody good hand.

Our sons run towards us, their coats flapping as they gather pace, each carrying an armload of rocks, ready to be shoved into our jeans.

'No!' Andy and I holler and we back away at the same time.

Chapter 46

Abbie

May 2008

It is so hot I think I am actually melting. My sunscreen is running sweat lines down my face. This hotel in Dubai is meant to be glamorous and I am not fitting in very well. Why are other women walking around the edge of the pool in heels and wedges? And what's with all the jewellery?

I've been swimming almost every day for the past year since we moved to Singapore, so I'm fairly comfortable in my varying selection of bikinis, but the jewellery-and-heels thing is ridiculous. Also, no one seems to be reading a book. They're all just drinking cocktails. It's 11 a.m. This I might be able to get on board with.

'Do you want a drink?' I ask Sean. He's asleep on the sun lounger next to me. Although how he can sleep when the poolside speakers are blasting out Ibiza beach-club tunes is beyond me.

'Mmm? Yeah.' He falls asleep again. He's been working so hard, and by day three of our holiday he's slept pretty much every day, which means that every night he's raring to go. It's like we're in completely different time zones. The heat and the daytime drinking are zonking me out by 10 p.m., but Sean wants to hit the bars and stay out as late as possible.

Today I'm going to get with it. I grab myself a juice at the bar and some waters for both of us, along with Sean's beer. I won't have anything alcoholic today and I will be able to stay out all night and enjoy being with my boyfriend. At the moment I feel I'm almost on holiday by myself. Just me and a few books.

Sean rolls over and looks at me as I return, shuffles himself into an upright position. My sunglasses slide down my nose with the heat. I think my hair's gone a bit frizzy, so I pull it back into a tighter ponytail and hope for the best.

'I've booked us somewhere amazing for dinner,' he says.

'Have you?' So far we've been heading to various hotel bars and restaurants that I've found us on Tripadvisor.

'Mmm,' he says and gives me a knowing look. 'Wear something *very* nice.'

'I always wear something *very* nice,' I say in mock-defence. 'I've only bought nice things with me.' And then I think. 'Do I own clothes that you don't think are nice, then?'

He laughs. 'Some.'

Sean's actually booked a restaurant. He used to do this all the time in England when we were dating. The old Sean has been resuscitated, and I like it.

'What are you reading?' he asks me.

'*Harry Potter and the Deathly Hallows*. It's the final one.' It came out last year and I've been saving it for a holiday read.

'What's it about?'

I stare at him. 'You are joking, right?'

He smiles. 'Maybe. Do you think he dies in the end?'

'Voldemort? Flipping hope so.'

'No – Harry.'

'Harry?' I splutter. 'No way. I look at the sheer size of the book I'm reading. 'He'd better not die. Jesus! I don't think I could cope with that. Imagine reading these books to your kids over the last few years and you get to the final chapter and Harry dies. You'd have to make something up, wouldn't you?'

'You'd lie? To your kids about the ending of a book?'

I nod. 'I would about this one.' I deliberate flicking to the end of the book. Harry had better not die.

'Interesting,' he says.

'Why is that interesting?'

'You'd lie to protect someone.'

'Depends on the lie.'

He thinks about that for a while.

'What else have you lied about to protect someone?' Sean says eventually.

'I don't think I've lied about anything,' I say honestly. And then the memory of Tom and me in his kitchen, telling each other how we feel, hits me hard and fast. I realise the sentence I've just uttered is itself a lie. I went to see Tom, after Sean asked me not to.

He puts his empty beer bottle down on the table that divides us. 'Will you read our kids Harry Potter?'

'Yeah.' I'm distracted, trying to push Tom out of my head.

'How many?'

'How many books?' I ask.

'How many kids . . . I mean, how many kids do you want?'

'Um . . . I'm not sure. Two?' I've thought about this over the years. They say you can't miss what you never had, but

I know that growing up a single child, I missed not having a sibling.

'Two sounds nice. A boy and a girl?' he questions.

'I don't think you get to pick like that,' I laugh.

'Little versions of us, scampering around. Rugby at weekends for little man. And a bit of ballet for her – or whatever girls get up to.'

'Maybe if we have a son, *he* might like to do ballet?' I suggest.

Sean rolls his eyes at me. 'Maybe.'

I sit back, put Harry Potter down, indulge Sean in this fantasy life.

'It's good to be on the same page,' he says. 'About life. We are, aren't we?'

'I think so.'

'We want the same things,' he says. It's a statement, not a question.

'I guess so.' What do we want? What do I want? What does Sean want? I ask him this.

'Nice life. Nice house. Nice car. Nice kids. Excellent job. What about you, what do you want?' he asks.

'I suppose what you've said sounds good – it's hard to argue against having a nice life.' To want the opposite of that seems counterproductive.

'That's what I thought,' he says. 'Good. Just checking.'

I smile, look out at the sun shimmering on the pool water. No one's swimming; everyone's posing. 'I might do some laps,' I say.

'Don't wear yourself out again,' Sean warns. 'We're going out tonight, remember.'

*

I'd only seen the sail-shaped Burj Al Arab building on TV and once in real life before, when we drove past on our way to a champagne brunch. But now we're in a taxi pulling up to it.

'Sean, is this where we're having dinner?'

He grins. 'Yup.'

'Wow,' I say, because I can't think of anything else. It's one of the most magnificent buildings I've ever seen. Inside, a floor-to-ceiling fish tank lines either side of the reception walls and spans up to about the size of a house, or so it looks. We head to the escalators, agreeing that we need to go up and then down, then up again, so we can really take in the immense display. We ride up and down, giggling like children, a few times before agreeing that people are starting to look at us.

Then we're in the lift to the twenty-seventh floor and Sean looks at me in the mirror. He pulls me towards him, spins me round so that I can see myself – us. 'We look good,' he says. 'Don't we?'

I'm wearing a red dress, tight but not too tight, above the knee but not too high. Sean's in his dark-grey suit, his shirt open at the neck. We're groomed, tanned, smiling.

I lean towards him, rest my head on his chest. 'We do.'

'We're a good couple,' he says.

I smile. I want to touch him. I laugh, thinking of Natasha telling me how she can't help touching Will inappropriately in lifts. It turns out I want to touch Sean inappropriately in lifts too. That's a good sign.

'I'm really happy,' I tell him instead. Because if there's a security camera in here and I touch Sean somewhere inappropriate, we are both probably getting arrested.

'Me too,' he says.

The lift doors open and we walk towards the restaurant, where we're greeted and shown to our table next to the floor-to-ceiling windows. Everything in Dubai appears to be floor-to-ceiling. We look out over Jumeirah Beach and the view of the city beyond. Our white-tableclothed table is small, just for two, and we both sit on little chairs with a cushion propped behind us. It's formal, but relaxed. Sean looks relaxed. I'm relaxed. It's perfect.

He takes my hand as he orders us a bottle of champagne, and we talk all the way through dinner about life and where we want to be, the kinds of people we want to grow into. The restaurant is full, there are so many other people eating and drinking, but it's almost as if there's no one else here. We agree to be together through everything life can throw at us, and that nothing will ever rip us apart.

This dinner has refocused me. I'm falling in love with Sean all over again, and because we've entered a conversational world where I feel I can say this to him, I do.

He looks a bit taken aback and then says he thinks he knows what I mean. 'I've been so busy at work. I'm sorry,' he says. 'I've ignored you a bit.'

'You haven't. You come home to me every night,' I say.

'Where else am I going to go?' he says and takes my hand in his as the waiter clears our dinner plates, rakes the crumbs from the table into a little dish and the sommelier returns to top up our champagne.

'Good point,' I say.

'I'll always come home to you,' he says.

We order pudding, even though I am stuffed. But I don't want to go yet, don't want to get the bill and leave the heavenly confines of this dinner, where Sean and I have refocused our energies on each other. Tonight is perfect. Tonight could not be more perfect.

And then my pudding arrives, presented without show or fanfare, just placed delicately in front of me with a small display of edible flowers and some swirly chocolate garnish etched onto the plate.

I read the swirly chocolate words and then, because I think I'm hallucinating, I read them again. Sean's smiling, looking a mix of nervous and proud of himself for having pulled this off without a hitch. I look back at the chocolate writing on the plate one more time, to be completely sure I'm not going mad.

Marry me.

Sean moves slowly from his chair, opens a small black box and drops to one knee.

Chapter 47

Tom

July 2008

Today is Teddy's second birthday. He wakes up late and Samantha and I have to go and nudge him out of his little bed, because she needs to leave for work. He's spending the day with me. I've pulled a sicky, as I'm not permitted holiday leave yet. It's a bit underhand and Samantha doesn't approve, but I reason that when Teddy eventually starts school it'll be illegal – or some such shit – to pull him out for his birthday, so it's only this once. And maybe next year too. We'll see.

But today I've suggested the park, with Andy and his son, Oliver. Andy needed no encouragement to skive off work, and so the four of us are meeting in an hour, after we've done presents and cards. Teddy's not interested in his birthday cards – only the ones with badges appear to cut the mustard. And he rips the paper off his presents and delights in the Peppa Pig toys and Fireman Sam paraphernalia. My star present is a goal for the garden, and he goes outside to find it with bows and ribbons that I left Samantha to tie on. He wears his '2' badges on his T-shirt and we wave Samantha off for work, after she's winced her way through half a grapefruit and a coffee.

Then it's just me and Teddy, and we play football in the garden for a bit, taking turns to be in goal, before it's time to meet Andy.

Andy brings a beer each and we stand in the sunshine, kicking a football between us and the little ones, feeling very smug with ourselves for being out in the middle of a working Monday with our children.

'How's the job going?' he asks.

'Better than the last one.' I kick the ball to Oliver and watch as he and Teddy kick it back and forth between themselves, missing and having to chase it around the park. Andy and I have just been benched from the team by a couple of two-year-olds.

'What is it you do again?' Andy asks me for the third time since I've known him.

'Analyst,' I tell him. I should have said, 'Astronaut', to see if he was paying attention any of the previous two times.

'And what have you analysed recently?' he asks, sipping his beer. 'Do you think we're going to feel the fallout of all that financial stuff going down in America?'

'Yes,' I say. 'Yes, I do.'

'Really?' he asks. 'How bad? And what the hell even is a subprime mortgage anyway?'

I shrug, sip my beer. I've clocked a sign saying the park is a no-alcohol zone. Whoops. 'Mate, I don't know what's going on over there. It's trickling through here, and it could be a gentle current or it could be a storm.'

'I think you've mixed your weather metaphors,' he says. 'So a little old illustrator like me had best stop spending money on new phones and start hunkering down, do you reckon – just in case? It's always the little guy who suffers, isn't it?'

'Usually,' I say. 'But don't panic too soon, you know? I'm not sure it's going to be quite like the last recession. I knew someone whose parents walked into their building society and simply handed their house keys over. They couldn't pay their mortgage.'

'I remember seeing it all on the news,' he says. 'I was only a kid, though. My parents worked so hard to come out of that on the other side with a roof over our heads. Shielded me from all the panic, I reckon.'

I look at Teddy and Oliver – so small.

Andy says, 'It's our job, though, isn't it, as parents, to shield our kids from all the panic?'

We watch them kicking a ball back and forth, missing each other by miles, as usual. 'Yeah,' I reply. 'It is.'

'Right.' Andy pulls me out of the very unbirthday-like funk we've pushed ourselves into. 'Where did you say we're feeding the kids? McDonald's is easy. Oliver likes the nuggets.'

I give Andy a look. 'Samantha won't like that,' I reply. 'Teddy's never been to McDonald's. He's only on organic food.'

'I don't miss being married.' Andy shudders suddenly. 'Imagine being told by your missus you can't go and eat where you want. It's barbaric.'

He has a point. Teddy catches on. 'Nuggets,' he shouts, despite not actually knowing what they are. Oliver and Teddy shout together, both of them laughing because they know I'm about to cave in. I didn't need much of a push.

'Come on then,' I say, picking up the football and shoving it into my rucksack. I clutch Teddy's hand and we make our way to McDonald's with our friends.

Of all the presents totalling about £200 that Samantha and I bought Teddy, his prize possession of the whole day is the Kung Fu Panda toy that he got with his Happy Meal.

He's chuffed to pieces with it, and clutches it the whole way through our dinner in a local pizza restaurant that I've chosen for tonight. Samantha eyes it curiously. We're sharing a bottle of red wine and she's granted Teddy the rare privilege of an apple juice, rather than his usual rations of water with his children's pasta. I don't tell her about the chocolate milkshake he's also downed today. I tried to bow to her ideas about salt by licking some of it off Teddy's chips, but after the fifth one I gave up. It was arduous. A little bit of salt once in a while won't kill him. And sugar, there's been a lot of that too, but he's still going to get an ice cream in a few minutes, and birthday cake when we get home.

'I can't believe we have a two-year-old,' Samantha says. 'Makes me feel old.'

'Me too, but in a good way. Like an adult.' I sit with my wife and my child and I do feel a sense of achievement and pride. 'Do you think Teddy might like a little playmate?' I've had a good amount of Chianti, so I wonder if tonight's the night we might actually have this discussion.

She doesn't understand what I'm driving at. 'He's got friends at nursery,' she says. 'Wait, what do you mean?'

'I mean, do you think we should . . . have another?'

She sort of recoils her head back into her neck, which was not quite the reaction I expected. 'No,' she says, glancing at

Teddy, who's going great guns with his felt tips in his new Peppa Pig colouring book. 'I don't want any more. I've just made partner, which took me years, and I've got my life back. Why would I want to undo all that with another one?'

I don't reply, toying with the stem of my wine glass.

'You can't seriously want to do it all again?' she asks.

'Why not? It wasn't that bad. It was good, in fact.'

'It wasn't,' she says. 'You took two weeks' paternity leave and then left me to deal with it on my own.'

That's not quite how it went. Samantha's mum came to look after Teddy two days a week, so she could go to the gym, have lunch with her friends and check in on her work emails. And then she signed him up for nursery and went back to work. She went to mother-and-baby groups. I dropped him to nursery and picked him up most nights. I think we had it easier than most people. Night-times were hard for a while in the early days, but they're hard in the early days for everyone, surely.

'What if we hired a nanny?' I offer, despite knowing that would be the world's largest financial stretch for us.

'A nanny?'

'To take the pressure off, right from the start. Five days a week, if you like. Until we're comfortable with sending the baby to nursery.'

She sits back, mulling this over. I think I've got her now. 'I'll still need to take maternity leave,' she says.

'You don't *have* to take maternity leave, do you? If you don't want to – which I'm guessing you don't. If you feel you can't, you could work from home unofficially or . . . do what you like, if we've got a nanny.'

She sips a bit more wine. 'Can I think about it?'

'Well, I want to put a baby inside you in about two hours' time, so you've got until then to think about it,' I say.

She stares at me.

'I'm joking!' Samantha never gets my sense of humour.

Teddy says, 'Baby?' and I wonder if he and I can work on her together over the next few weeks. I want her to want this too. And it might help mend us, Samantha and me. Teddy brought us back together, and another baby soon might be the perfect timing. I smile, remembering those scans, seeing Teddy for the first time, the way Samantha and I held hands waiting to hear if Teddy was healthy, if his measurements were what they were supposed to be. It was perfect. We were so *together* then.

We go home, sing 'Happy Birthday' to Teddy and he blows out his candles. He's having a proper party at the weekend but today has been nice. It's been more than nice – it's been perfect.

And it's made even more perfect when, after Teddy goes to sleep in his little car-shaped bed, Samantha and I creep into our room and have sex for the first time in . . . I've lost count how many months it's been since we last had sex.

She still popped her contraceptive pill into her mouth as standard the next morning before breakfast, though.

I've got tickets to the Wimbledon men's singles final. This was very much luck of the draw through work, and I never thought I'd get one. Nor could I ever have afforded it, and anyway I never do anything at the weekends any more. I don't think I realise that until I'm sitting here, wearing a crisp white shirt that Teddy isn't here to spill stuff on, surrounded by hundreds of people.

I've never seen anything as nail-biting in my life. Federer and Nadal play for almost five hours. If only the sodding rain hadn't delayed the start. They need some sort of retractable roof in here.

It's only as I'm leaving, buoyant on corporate hospitality and full of Pimm's, champagne, strawberries and cream, that I bump headlong into a man using his hat to fan himself as we queue to exit. The chatter is so loud and excited and I apologise for nudging him.

He brushes it off as no bother, and then says, 'Good match.'

'The best,' I say. 'Incredible.'

And then he looks up at me and does a double-take. I smile politely and he says, 'It's Tom, isn't it?'

'Yes,' I say and I realise I'm doing that recoil-of-the-neck thing that I hate so much when Samantha does it.

'It's Ken – Abbie's dad.'

This is crazy. 'Oh my God! How are you?' I ask. 'I'm so sorry I didn't recognise you.'

'I never forget a face,' he tells me. 'Especially the face of the man who rescued my daughter from death.'

'Ah, it wasn't, you know, quite like that.'

'Don't be modest,' he says as we filter out into the street. 'If it wasn't for you, I might not have had a daughter to come home to. You took very good care of her that night, and for that we are eternally grateful.'

'Thanks,' I say and look down at the pavement, embarrassed and avoiding his gaze. 'Are you headed this way?' I ask.

'I've got the day to myself,' he says. 'Thought I might try to find a pub and waste a bit of time.'

'Sounds like a *great* plan.'

'Could I buy you a drink?' he asks.

I'm ready to instinctively politely decline, but something stops me. I've also got the day to myself. If I go home now I'll have to change the beds, put away Teddy's laundry and get the towels in the tumble dryer. But if I don't go home yet, maybe Samantha might step up and do at least one of those jobs, in addition to keeping Teddy occupied all day. 'Yeah,' I say, still thinking about it. 'Yeah, that would be great.'

The pub is packed, but we squeeze in and Abbie's dad is eagle-eyed, spotting two bar stools becoming vacant at the end of the bar. He moves fast and secures them and I carry our two pints over to him, where we sit and drink companionably.

'How's Abbie getting on?' I ask when we're settled and have finished analysing the match, like two BBC pundits. I assume she's not told her dad *any* of what happened between us, so I hope this comes across as an innocent question.

'She's very well, thank you.'

'Is she enjoying Singapore?'

'Yes, she complains about the heat and says she misses the seasons, but she and Sean seem to have found their feet, made some nice friends, settled in well. Did you know they're engaged?' he asks me.

I cough on my pint, but I don't know why I'm surprised. It was bound to happen. In fact it was inevitable really, wasn't it?

'No,' I say. 'I didn't know that.'

'I'm surprised she didn't tell you,' he says. 'I thought you and she were . . .' He doesn't finish his sentence.

'You thought Abbie and I were what?' I ask carefully.

'Good friends,' he says, equally cautiously.

'Yeah, I thought we were too, but . . .' Now it's my turn to leave my words in the air.

'That's a shame,' he says.

'Mmm, yeah, it is.' I'm not going to say anything else. I think it's best we leave it there.

'Was it because you didn't attend their leaving party?' He's choosing to keep going with this. 'Abbie told me you were coming, but I noticed at the time you didn't pop in.'

I make a noise in my throat and I'm not quite sure what I'm supposed to say to this.

'Or . . .' he's offering me a lifeline, 'did something happen before the party that stopped you going?' Nope, there's no lifeline there.

'It's complicated,' I say.

'I thought as much.'

'I don't . . .' I start and then, sod it, I'm going to say it, 'I don't have her number and so . . . if you could say hi to her for me, I'd really appreciate it.'

'I will,' he says. 'Any other message?' I notice he's not offering to give me her number. I respect this. Abbie wouldn't reply to me anyway.

'No,' I say after a few seconds. 'Just hi. And maybe . . . that I'm glad she's doing well. I'm really happy for her.'

'I'll tell her.' Before the jubilant mood descends too deeply into morose territory, he follows it up conversationally with, 'And how is that son of yours getting on? Abbie told me you'd had a little boy. Freddie?'

'Teddy,' I say and he nods. 'He's two now. He's such a little character. Has a thing about stones, has nice little buddies in nursery. Loves cars – mainly red ones. We're toying with the idea of having another baby, actually.' I'm not quite sure why I've said this.

'That would be a nice age gap,' Ken says thoughtfully.

'I think so. Not sure Samantha's so up for it, though. We'll see what happens.'

Ken nods and then mercifully changes the subject. 'If your little boy loves cars, there's a classic-car rally on at Audley End next weekend. You should take him.'

'I don't think we've got anything in the diary for next weekend,' I say, thinking about it.

'Trish and I are going. She hates cars, but we do keep each other company at weekends every now and again.'

'Sounds fair.'

'Why don't you buy a couple of tickets and come with us? Or we could meet you there for a quick drink, if you didn't fancy hanging around with us all day. Trish would love the chance to meet you, after all these years.'

I think about it. I'm not sure it's Samantha's cup of tea, hanging out with Abbie's parents at a classic-car rally, but Teddy would love it. I nod.

'Yeah, that would be great. I'll buy us some tickets.'

Chapter 48

Abbie

August 2008

'Let me get this straight,' I say to my mum after my dad has picked up and we've had a very brief 'hello', before my mum leaps onto the call. I'm not sure if I'm annoyed yet. For now, I'm just thoroughly confused. 'Dad and Tom went to Wimbledon together?'

My mum cuts in. 'No, love, they bumped into each other afterwards and then went for a drink.'

I haven't managed to speak to my parents in weeks, which is a huge oversight, but work has been non-stop and the time-zone clash has been an issue. Normally my parents have nothing to report, other than work woes and Ofsted inspections. But now . . . now I discover that a whole bunch of stuff has happened.

'But they *did* plan to go to a classic-car rally together?' I ask.

'Yes.' There's a hint of exasperation in my mum's voice, as if I'm grilling her. I *am* grilling her. I need to work out the finer details of what has gone on here, and then I'll be fine.

'And so you went – you and Dad, him and Teddy – and hung out together at a country-house car-show thing?'

'Ye-es,' my mum draws out the word.

I transfer my phone to the other ear. This Skype connection is a bit hazy.

'OK,' I say. But I'm not OK. Why am I not OK? Why are my parents hanging out with Tom?

My mum's quiet. She's expecting me to say something mature at this point.

I sigh. 'How is he?'

'He seems very well, but you are, of course, free to ask him this yourself.'

I'm not going to do that. 'We don't really talk any more,' I say.

'You could do the mature thing and send him a little message,' my mum offers.

'Yes, I know,' I say. 'Did he mention me?'

'Not that I'm aware of,' Mum says. 'But your dad had a good chat with him in the pub, so maybe—'

'Can you put Dad back on, please,' I say, far too quickly. I turn round to check where Sean is in the flat. He's on the balcony with a beer and his phone. I turn the air-con down a bit while he's not in the apartment.

My mum breathes deeply. 'Ken!' she calls and then my dad's voice sounds.

'Hello again,' he says.

'So you and Tom are now a thing?' I tease, trying to make light of the conversation I'm about to embark on. 'Why didn't you tell me you were seeing him?'

'We're telling you now,' Dad says.

'But you didn't tell me you'd bumped into him, and you didn't tell me you'd made *plans* with him.'

'They weren't really *plans* – more that I mentioned the rally and we swapped numbers, in case he wanted to meet while we were there.'

'And he messaged you when he arrived and you spent the whole day with him?' I prompt. I have no idea why I need to know every single detail of what happened and what they talked about.

'Ye-es,' Dad says in exactly the same tone my mum used on that word a few minutes ago.

I force a light and breezy tone into my voice. 'What did you talk about?'

'Cars,' my dad replies.

'Ha-ha.'

'It's the truth,' he says. 'Abbie, what's going on? I know you two don't talk any more, so is this conversation upsetting you?'

'No, this conversation isn't upsetting me,' I say through gritted teeth. 'I just want to know how Tom is.'

'All right,' my dad says. 'He's fine. He seems happy; his son is delightful, a real credit to him, very well behaved. Not like you were at that age.'

'Thanks,' I say.

My dad's getting into the swing of this now. 'They're thinking about having another baby—'

'They're *what*?' I ask and hate that I've said it aloud.

'He said it's something they're considering – having another child.'

I don't know what to do with this information. My body has tensed without me realising. I remember Tom's face when he told me Samantha was pregnant the first time. It was panic, fear, and maybe I'm remembering this wrong, maybe

I'm remembering that conversation from years ago how I want to remember it, but I swear to God he was devastated. And now they're actively planning to grow their family.

'Oh,' I say. 'Right.'

'I told him you were engaged. I hope that was all right?'

Yes, I think savagely. I'm glad Tom knows I'm engaged. I want him to know I'm happy, doing well. And then I hate myself all over again and I can feel tears welling up. I have no right to feel like this. I walked away from Tom. I don't want him to be unhappy. But I don't want him to be ecstatically happy, either.

'He wanted me to pass on a message to you. He said *hi* and that he was happy for you.'

'He was happy for me? When did he say that?'

'In the pub after Wimbledon,' my dad replies.

'But that was weeks ago,' I say.

'I didn't think it was a *vital* message,' he replies. 'I was going to tell you as and when I next spoke to you, which is today.'

'Are you going to see him again?' I ask.

My dad breathes in. 'I won a golf day at the school raffle and invited Tom along. He plays, apparently. I'm thinking about getting into it for when I retire.'

It's my turn to make an exasperated noise.

'But I will retract the invitation, if you don't want me to see him again. Just say the word.'

Sean re-enters, sliding the balcony door closed. He walks towards the air-con and cranks it back up again.

'Dad, I've got to go. Sean and I are going out for dinner.' My dad starts to ask me something quickly and I cut him off. 'Love you, Dad, bye!'

I hang up. Sean looks at me. 'That sounded a bit . . . abrupt.'

'Not really.' I put my phone down.

'*Are* we going out for dinner?' he asks. 'I didn't know that.'

'Yes,' I say, sidling towards him. I need to get out of the flat right now. I need to process that conversation with my parents, but I'm not going to do it here, now. Instead, I file it away for analysis later. My head's a mess. I'm not sure how to process this, but I need to focus on something else – anything else. I run my hands over the thin cotton fabric of Sean's shirt. 'Or we could just stay in,' I say seductively.

'And eat what?' he says provocatively, looking down at my crotch.

'Are you being gross?' I ask.

'Yeah,' he chuckles. 'A bit.'

The moment's lost and I'm not in the mood to play this game. 'Fine, let's go out,' I say.

'Oh no, come on, you were being seductive. Any second now you were going to bust one of those lacy pink numbers out of the naughty drawer and we were about to go at it, like only unmarried people do.'

'Don't say that,' I reply desperately, tuning back into the here and now. 'Sex will still be fantastic when we're married.'

'Pfft! You say that now.'

'Then let's not get married,' I say urgently. 'Let's just be like this, for ever.'

Sean seems to be weighing this up. 'No,' he says. 'I want to be married to you.'

'Even if the sex is bad?'

'Even if the sex is *non-existent*,' he enthuses.

I force a laugh. I do hope the sex isn't non-existent.

'So are we eating out or *eating in*?' he asks, his eyebrows going up and down for sordid effect.

'We're going out, Sean.'

He grabs his keys. 'Fair enough.'

Chapter 49

Tom

September 2008

I'm frozen to the spot in my office. Normally by now I'd be on my second coffee, with both my oversized computer screens loading graphs and data, and I'd be typing, dialling, writing. I'd be in a frenzy of non-stop work. But today's not like that.

It's been going steadily wrong for the best part of a year, ever since a Spanish bank discovered how tied up they were in subprime mortgages and began withdrawing credit. And one by one the dominoes have fallen down, as other banks finally worked out where the hell all their money had been going and, more importantly, that they were never going to get it back.

My job focuses mainly on analysing specific mergers and acquisitions. But even I can see what's been going on, down on the investment coal face – the day-to-day trades and the freefall of money to who-knows-where that came to a grinding halt earlier in the year. And our company has been all over the news for months. Our share price has tanked to the point of no return; we can't find a buyer, we've been shedding divisions, hoping for a bail-out. Other banks have been squeezed down to their bare bones and have gone, cap in hand, for financial help from the government – from anyone.

Shortly after I joined, the company went on a hiring freeze. No one new joined and, if you left, you weren't replaced. The last few months have been like circling around the fire pits of hell, all of us working flat out to avoid falling into the flames. But today we've been kicked into the fire head-first, and none of us is coming out of this intact.

My team and I stand in front of the news that's on rotation on the TV. We're watching the end of the financial world as we know it. There's swearing, crying, phones are ringing off the hook as investors panic about the location of their money. It's too late. Across the floor we can see the money guys flat out, trying to get the bank – and themselves – out of this. But it's no good. We're a bank without money. It's laughable. It's tragic.

'My parents had money with Northern Rock bank last year,' one of our graduate trainees, Samuel, tells me. He's twenty-one and has just left university. He thought this would be the start of his career in banking. Only now I have a feeling he'll be one of the first to go. I'll be operating on a skeleton team, going forward. 'My parents stood outside their local branch, queuing for hours on day two of the bank run, but by that point it was too late. There was no cash left. They were offered a cheque for all their funds. They thought it was going to bounce. They were going to lose everything,' he says. 'Everything they'd ever saved was in that account.'

I can't take my eyes off the TV, but I'm listening to Samuel. 'What happened?' I ask.

'They went home in fear, clutching this cheque, with no idea what to do with it. Where could they put it? What if the bank had gone bust and then there'd be no way to cash it – no Northern Rock to honour it. When the government announced it was nationalising the bank and honouring all account holders' money, my dad cried with relief. My dad. Not even my mum. I don't think my mum knew what to do. It was awful. Just awful.'

A bank running out of money *is* awful. It's a one-off – a one-in-a-100-year event. Something I didn't think I'd see in my lifetime, considering that we had a huge recession when I was a child. But Northern Rock was the precursor to this total downfall. 'And now this,' I say, our eyes are still on the TV.

'It's going to get worse, isn't it?'

I look back at Samuel, his face stricken in panic. This isn't how his first job after university was supposed to end. Around our wide open-plan office, hundreds of people are standing at their desks, yelling into phones, gesturing loudly to other team members, with people running frantically, clutching files. 'Yes, I think it is going to get a whole lot worse.'

My boss has been in since the early hours of the morning. In fact I don't think he went home last night. I'm not sure how many people actually went home last night.

'Tom,' he says. 'Can you come in here?'

I nod, go towards his office. I brace myself, because this isn't going to be good.

'I'm sorry it's taken me so long to get to you,' he says. 'As head of your team, I need to give you the news. Today the bank's head office in New York is filing for Chapter Eleven bankruptcy protection. I'm telling you before the news breaks and you have to watch it play out on TV. As such, we've been working all weekend to present a restructure plan. I'm sorry,

Tom, but in front of me is a list of names of people who are leaving, with immediate effect. I know you'll want to ask questions and I know you'll want to speak to HR, both of which you are within your rights to do.' He stops speaking, pushes the sheet of paper towards me.

My eyes are a blur. 'This is my entire team,' I say, scanning the list.

'Yes, I'm sorry, Tom. We aren't the only bank this is happening to. We've been holding on for a bail-out, but over the weekend it became apparent that isn't going to happen.' He's got tears in his eyes. 'I need you to gather your team together and tell them in the best possible way, before they see it on the news. We owe them that much. You haven't got long.'

I nod. 'Right.'

'I'm sorry, Tom, but I have to go and bring the next person in now.'

I raise my eyes to him. 'Is everyone losing their job?'

'Most people,' he says, straight to the point.

'Am I losing mine?' I look down the list again. Is my name there? Oh my God, it is. How did I miss it?

'You're a good analyst, Tom. You'll find another job soon enough, I'm sure.'

'Are we staying until the end of the week, or the month, or—'

'No,' he says. 'It's today. Everyone's leaving today.'

This can't be happening. I think my windpipe is closing up. I'd only just got this job.

He stands, extends his hand. 'Thank you for taking it so well.' He looks haggard, unshaven, with sweat patches under his armpits. That will be me soon.

I extend my hand, shake his, because what else am I going to do? This isn't his fault, and the cut and thrust of his role today is distributing execution orders in order to try to help save a bank that can't be saved.

I leave the room, the piece of paper shaking in my hand, but I don't need to look at it. The fifteen faces of my team slowly turn to look at me. I can't work out what to think, what to feel. This is a dream, a nightmare. I'm losing my job. But so are they.

They know what's coming. Around the floor it's the same story: people being brought into the meeting room, individuals, whole teams. There are no meeting rooms left. A few of the marketing guys are already sitting in the room where I was, fixed expressions of horror evident through the glass. My ashen-faced boss is delivering the same speech to them that he just delivered to me.

My team is waiting for me and so I steel myself. I have nowhere to do this, other than out here by our desks in the middle of the room. I'm holding the execution order. Now I need to carry it out.

The queue outside the post room says it all, as people queue to grab packaging boxes to put their stuff in. Samuel's emptied out a box of printer paper, its pristine white pages scattered all over the floor, trodden on. No one cares. No one's using that paper now. There's still a frenzy of people, but most of them on my side of the office are subdued, shocked, echoing each other's words of 'I can't believe this is really happening.'

We can hear the TV, now that the noise has quietened down on our side of the office. Across the City, the financial industry is in turmoil. The news gathers pace; the presenters look far too excited for their own good, reporting on job losses, bank closures. News about our Chapter 11 bankruptcy file has hit, as New York wakes up for business and the documents are submitted.

My lot took their job losses as well as could be expected, helped by the fact that I, too, was walking out the door for the last time with them.

My desk is packed up: pictures of Teddy and Samantha, books and notepads, a few bottles of whisky that we cracked open to celebrate a merger going well as a result of our diligent reporting. I hand one to Samuel, who looks forlorn.

'You're twenty-one,' I remind him. 'You'll be fine.'

He nods.

'Start applying for other jobs immediately. Start today. Ring around everyone you know, see what openings they've got. Do it before everyone else gets in there. Do it before the dust settles. Be proactive, OK?'

He's too stunned to reply. I put my hand on his shoulder.

'Yep,' he replies. It's all he can say.

'Good' is all I can say in return. I'm only just thirty and I'm offering forward operating advice like a wizened troop commander who's seen it all. I've seen nothing. I know nothing about job-hunting in a recession. I'm fucked. We're all fucked.

Like the captain going down with his ship, I wait for everyone to leave the vessel first. They go at varying paces, some stopping to look around their desk, their office, to say goodbye to others who are busy packing, to wave sadly to friends on the other side of the office. There are two paces of speed to this floor: frenzied phone calls or silent packing, depending on whether you've kept your job or not.

When the last of my team goes, I don't glance back forlornly at where I worked, one last time. I turn my back on it, bitterness and confusion unravelling in equal measure. I put my rucksack on over my suit jacket, take the escalator down the sleek marble interior, hand my pass over to the security guy, who utters a sympathetic phrase I barely acknowledge, haul my box further up my arms and then walk out into the bright sunshine.

Out in the square in front of me, a few colleagues are walking away, hunched over their boxes as they head towards the Tube station or the bus stop. A BBC News van's over in the corner; Channel 4, ITV, Sky News and Channel 5 News are setting up cameras. I stare at them all for a while. This is unreal. Reporters are gesturing towards the building and directing their talk to the cameras. It's as frenzied out here as it was in there. I don't know where to go. I watched *Alice in Wonderland* with Teddy last week, and I think of that scene where the broom wipes out the path in front of Alice, moves around her and wipes out the path behind her too. She's rooted to the spot then, with nowhere to go, exactly as I am now.

My phone rings in my pocket. I put the box down and lift my phone out. It's Andy.

'Mate, keep walking,' he instructs.

'What?'

'You're on TV.'

'I've just been fired,' I say. The words sound alien to me. *I've just been fired.* 'We all have.'

'I know. I'm watching it. Your company's all over the news. You look really lost, mate. BBC News has zoomed in on your face. Pick up that box and get the hell out of there. Chin up. Head high. Go.'

'OK,' I say quickly, doing as I'm instructed. I hang up on Andy without saying goodbye, pick up the box and walk with a purpose that I no longer feel towards the Underground.

Chapter 50

Abbie

Sean bursts into the bedroom, where I've got my notes spread out on the bed and I'm propped up against the pillows, working with my laptop on my thighs. He's working from home today too and he needs the desk space for all his paperwork, so I've relocated to the bedroom.

'Guess who I've just seen on TV, getting the sack?' he says, so quickly it takes me a second to de-jumble his sentence. His eyes are wide with excitement and he's holding on to the doorframe with one hand, as if to steady himself. As if the electrical current of excitement threatens to unbalance him.

I look up at his sudden entrance. The news has been running all day as Sean's industry grinds to a crashing halt. As a retail journalist, I'll be writing about the downfall of various companies as they begin throwing in the towel. We're heading into a serious recession. Sean's been warning me about this for months. He's relatively calm about the whole thing, considering his bank wouldn't touch subprime and they've been invited by numerous banks across the world to dig deep and form a merger. They're still considering their options, Sean says, based on a number of factors that I don't even pretend to understand.

'Someone we know is on TV?' I ask, rising from the bed. 'Who?'

'Come and see.' He leaps back out the room like Tigger on steroids, crosses his arms over his chest. He's got a financial news channel on, and an American reporter is analysing facts that have led to a major New York-based bank's collapse.

'I don't think I know anyone in New York,' I tell Sean.

'It's London,' he says. 'Just wait.'

'And someone we know has been fired? That's awful, Sean.' *Oh God, is it Natasha? Please let it not be Natasha.*

'It's life. Wait, they'll show it again in a minute. I've seen it twice. I didn't think it was him at first. It's on some kind of rotation where they keep showing the same footage over and over, people walking out the office, looking all sad and holding— There he is!'

I look at the TV as a man in a suit exits a bank building in London, nearly 7,000 miles away. I don't have a clue who it is, and I tell Sean as much.

'Wait for it,' he says.

And then the camera zooms in on Tom's face and I breathe in so sharply, my hand flying to my mouth.

'Tom,' he announces. 'Tom's bank has just gone bust.'

My hand is still over my mouth. I watch a close-up of Tom putting a box down, taking his phone out of his pocket. He looks stricken, says a few words, puts his phone away, picks up his box and quickly walks on. It's about ten or fifteen seconds of footage, max.

Tom.

'I've been watching this play out since the markets opened,' Sean says knowledgeably. 'And do you know the most bizarre thing: our bank was approached to merge with them, to help bail them out. We said no, obviously. No one's touching that bank with a bargepole.'

I turn to stare at him. I can't work out what he's saying. 'You're not actually *happy* about this, are you?'

'No! I'm not happy but, you know, caught up in the excitement.'

'The excitement of an entire industry collapsing? One of our friends has lost his job.' I point to the TV, which is now showing the presenter again. 'Publicly. He's lost his job so publicly.'

Sean adopts a soothing tone, but says, 'He's not really my friend any more. Just someone I used to work with. And Tom's not exactly the Second Coming. The world doesn't know who he is, so . . . it's not *that* public.' He has the good grace to look a bit ashamed now, but only because I'm so utterly disapproving. Until then he was only too happy to crow over this fifteen seconds of awful TV. I sit down on the sofa and watch the news.

Sean walks off. 'Want a coffee?' I shake my head and mumble, 'No', but he can't have heard me, so he shouts back, 'What?'

'No, no, thank you.'

'OK,' he says and heads to the kitchen.

I stand up again. I don't quite know what to do. I have to file an article and I'm nearly finished, so I retrieve my laptop from the bedroom and the last remaining notes I need and position myself on the sofa for the rest of the afternoon, watching, waiting.

Every now and again they show the same piece of footage. Each time they do, I turn to see where Sean is. The fifth time they show it, about two hours later, Sean is in the bathroom. Without him here to see me, I dare to move over to the TV.

Tom.

He looks good, physically. Despite the fact that he's lost his job and everything has collapsed on top of him. I kneel down. I have only a few seconds left before they cut away from him again. I reach out and touch the moving image of a stricken Tom. I want to comfort him and tell him everything will be OK, the way he did to me years ago.

As he picks up his box onscreen, my eyes are drawn to its contents. My gaze locks onto something I recognise sitting on top. It's the grey Beanie Baby. My heart somersaults, my stomach too. He'd taken it with him from his last job to his new one. And it's with him now. What does that mean?

And then he's gone and they cut live to the roving reporter, outside the very same building, although there's no one coming or going now. It's all so still. It feels strange to think of Tom being anywhere other than across the courtyard from my old building, in the office window.

He got a new job. Although that's ended today, clearly. What else have I missed? Has he moved house again? How has he spent his birthdays? His Christmases? Are he and Samantha *actually* trying for a baby, after all? I didn't want to know any of this, and now I need to know everything.

'I didn't know he worked there. I didn't know he'd got a new job,' I say out loud as Sean re-enters the room and I move back towards the sofa. But it's too late. Sean's already seen me kneeling in front of the TV. He must know it was in order to get a better look at Tom. I wish I'd stood up quicker and not let him catch me.

'How *would* you know he'd moved job? You don't talk to him, do you?'

'No,' I say, purposefully staring at the TV, although I've no idea what's being said. More of the same, probably.

'I thought – you know – you might be chatting to him, in the background,' Sean says.

I turn to look at him. 'In the background?'

He nods. 'You two . . . did for a while. Emails or whatever.' He sounds lost.

'I wouldn't do that,' I say. 'I wouldn't do that to you.' I think back to that night in Tom's kitchen after the leaving party, when I did far, far worse than simply chat in the background. His words – 'I'm in love with you' – echo over and over.

It shouldn't have happened. We shouldn't have said these things to each other, not when I'm with Sean and Tom's with Samantha. It was wrong. I turn away.

'It doesn't happen any more: no emails, no texts, nothing. Not since before we came here,' I say.

Sean seems content with this and then rounds off with, 'I feel sorry for him. Losing his job like that.'

'I think I'm going to message him,' I say. It's not a question, it's not a request for permission. It's a statement. And I'm telling Sean because it's the truth – I want to talk to Tom – and because I don't want to hide this from him.

Sean seems immediately stressed. 'Why?'

'To commiserate,' I say.

'That's all the poor sod needs,' he replies. 'Imagine losing your job, and someone on the other side of the world lets slip they've seen you crash and burn on TV. I'd be mortified.'

He has a point. I think for a while. Maybe I won't message Tom. Not yet anyway. He'll be going through hell. The last thing he wants is to hear from me.

Chapter 51

Tom

March 2009

I don't know how I ever made Christmas work. By mid-November our finances were dwindling, but I dug deep because I couldn't let Teddy know, in a roundabout way via Father Christmas, that things were tight here. I never expected money to be this stretched, what with Samantha having been made partner. But it turns out our outgoings very much rely on a two-person-salary kind of set-up.

No longer doing the weekly food shop in Waitrose was about the only concession I was able to make – that and negotiating a better package with Sky, so I could keep the sports channels. But I'm going to have to get rid of them altogether. The film channels went months ago. I am remarkably low-maintenance. I rarely go out drinking, don't remember the last time I bought clothes and I don't have a gym membership. Running is free.

Samantha needs to be out a lot for work, which I get, and not all of it can be claimed back on expenses. I've started ignoring the credit-card bill, which makes for painful reading. It's money spent in bars and restaurants, the odd hotel for conferences.

I think of Abbie joking with me about how we should grind on each other, like we were at a conference gala night, and I laugh out loud. And then I'm sober. I hope Samantha's not grinding on anyone at a conference gala night.

I'm so grateful she's keeping us afloat, just. But this mortgage. I don't know how long we can keep it up. I can't seem to get a job at the minute. I'm unemployable. And as an ex-member of the banking industry, I'm the Devil. According to one of the nursery mums whose husband's building company has just gone under, thanks to his bank calling in his loan early, I am the root cause of everything wrong with the world. The fallout is astronomical.

I need to find something else to do. It might be for the best if I don't go back into finance. But I don't know how to do anything else.

Samantha's home from work early and she's in her office, which used to be our office, but I've got no use for it any more and notice all my stuff's been pushed to the far end of the long workbench we had installed. I wander in and hand her a glass of wine.

'Thanks,' she says. I watch her fingers fly over the keyboard, bashing out an angry email. She stops, turns. 'Yes?'

I baulk at her tone. I'm not one of her little apprentices, or whatever you call them. I decide I'm not going to comment. 'The weather's looking good for the weekend. I thought we could take Teddy to the seaside.'

'Yes, lovely.' She turns back to her screen. I look around at all her legal textbooks and journals. She moves back from her screen, takes a sip of wine and I think she realises I'm not leaving quite yet.

'So you're coming?' I say.

'I have a lot on, Tom. I'm earning for two now.'

I try my best not to rise to that. But then I cave and say, 'You know I've been looking, applying.'

'Yes, I know. But nothing's arisen, and consequently I need to keep going over the weekend.'

'It's only a day. I thought Brighton.'

'I'll have to let you know in the morning,' she snaps and turns back to her screen. There's no point me pushing the fact that we hardly ever do anything as a family these days.

'The nursery fees need paying,' she reminds me.

'Oh God, really? I feel like we only just paid them. We could probably send Teddy to Eton, for what we pay that place. Why don't we pull him out of nursery a couple of days a week? That would take the pressure off a bit.' I've suggested this before and Samantha always says no.

'He needs the stability,' she says. 'And what if you come down with some sort of bug on one of the days he's not in nursery . . . and what if my mum's not free to help? I'll have to stay at home with Teddy.'

'That combination of events is quite unlikely,' I say. 'The bills are mounting. We can't afford to keep living like this.'

'Tom, you'll have a job soon. Don't tell me you're planning to sit around here like this for much longer?'

'I wasn't planning on it. I didn't plan any of this.'

She ignores me. Her voice is shrill. 'Let's review things in September, when we renew the nursery place. If you don't have a job by September, that will be a whole year. You'll have been unemployed for a *whole year*, which *cannot* be possible.'

Fuck me. All I did was bring her a glass of wine and ask if she wanted to go to the beach.

'It's not my fault,' I say.

'Of course it's your fault. Whose fault is it then?' she shouts back.

I blink. Samantha can't be serious. But my anger has seen hers and it's ready for the fight.

'I didn't cause the credit crunch,' I shout back at her. 'I didn't cause the global economy to tank.'

She stands up. 'But you switched jobs. You should have stayed where you were. What kind of idiot moves jobs in the middle of a fucking credit crunch?'

There it is. That's what I've known myself, but I've been waiting for her to throw it at me. I moved because she can't stop spending money. I moved jobs because the new one paid loads more than I previously earned, and the bonus scheme was better. I moved to do the right thing for my family.

I can't win. Whatever I do, it's wrong. And then it's as if the universe has decided to stop firing warning shots at me. This time it's the real deal, and I feel pain galloping up my arm as if the Four Horsemen of the Apocalypse are riding up it, bringing death and destruction. Something's happening inside my chest. I feel the shock and agony gather all the way up towards my throat, towards my eyes, sending a blackout instruction to my retinas.

It's so sudden – the darkened collapse – that I don't even know it's coming. It's forcing the breath from my body. I clutch at my chest, but something's going on inside and I can't stop it. I can't stop it.

Chapter 52

Abbie

I've just gone cold. I don't know why, but I've gone cold. Something's happened. But I don't know what. I glance around the beach. It's boiling, only I'm not. What's happening? And then the cold, awful feeling ebbs away slowly, to be replaced by the heat again. Goodness knows what that was about.

I fan myself as a waiter brings me a fresh bottle of water; condensation runs down the side of it, pooling onto the table next to me. I gulp the water down and collect myself. I've been presented with a menu for lunch, and I'm watching a bride and groom walk past, barefoot on the sand. She's got a crown of flowers on her head and her light white dress is floating out behind her.

'The Seychelles are incredible,' Sean says, staring out to sea as I watch the couple have their picture taken. It's only them. There appears to be no family with them. I ponder this for a moment.

We've already been for a swim to cool off. I'm sure we're due another soon. Maybe after lunch.

'Can't think why I've never thought to come here before,' he continues.

We fell for an advert in *Condé Nast Traveller*, hook, line and sinker, and Sean splashed out on the nicest hotel I've ever been to. Although to Sean it's not splashing out; it's par for the course for him these days. How we live our lives now is so at odds with how I was brought up, and how I'd been living until very recently. It feels ridiculous to have this much money floating around, especially given what's been going on in the world.

The hotel is in a horseshoe-shaped bay with tranquil turquoise waters, lush jungle behind us, all colonial-style low-level wooden buildings – the lot. I thought they must Photoshop a few of these images, but it turns out this is real. Our room is actually a cottage, high up the hillside with pano-ramic views of the ocean, kitted out in muted soft greys and beiges, white cushions, its own veranda with a daybed. And the main bed is a four-poster. I've never slept in a four-poster. Not that much sleeping is getting done. There's something about hotel rooms, isn't there? Some underlying connotation, some sort of sexual expectation.

We're on day three of a ten-day breather from the stresses of Sean's work. He's been working so hard, he puts me to shame. Although I have got another magazine gig lined up when I return, so I'll be sacrificing my morning swims, by the look of things. No time for fifty lengths a day any more. I eye up the ocean. Maybe I should be doing some strokes now.

I pull Sean up. 'Come on,' I say. 'We're going back in.'
'Already?'
'Yes, before lunch, let's just have a quick dip.'

He groans, hauls himself up. 'OK, OK.'

In the water he pulls me towards him as I'm about to start swimming. 'Oh no you don't,' he says, kissing me.

'Sean, this is a family beach.'

'Yeah, yeah – no one's watching. Tell me how much you love me,' he says.

'A lot,' I reply, squirming in his wet arms.

'Do you see that couple?' he asks.

'The newly-weds?'

'Yeah, what do you think?'

'I'm not sure I think anything,' I say as he brushes my wet hair back off my shoulders.

'I do,' he says. He moves in to kiss my neck. It's too gentle, too seductive for an open space such as this. 'I'll tell you what I think. I think we should get married.'

'We *are* getting married,' I say, flashing him the huge diamond ring that never leaves my finger. 'That's what engaged means.'

'Now. Here,' he says.

'Now hear what?' I ask in confusion.

He laughs. 'Not hear as in listen. Here as in here. We should get married now. We should get married here.'

'Now?' I squeak.

'This week. Here. Just us.'

I pull back and look at him seriously. 'For real?'

He looks at the bride and groom kissing in wedded bliss on the beach, the photographer snapping away. 'Yeah,' he says slowly. 'For real.'

'By ourselves? Our parents will kill us.'

'Mine won't,' he says.

'Mine will.'

'It's only an idea. We don't have to. I thought it would be romantic, suggesting that I whisk you down the aisle – down the beach, I mean – and make you my wife. Because we want to. Because we're here. Because it's never going to get more perfect than this.' He gestures around the bay: the gentle breeze, the lapping waters.

'I suppose it would be romantic,' I agree.

'It saves a lot of fuss,' he continues. 'This way, you don't have to keep worrying about venues in England that you can't view because you're stuck in Singapore. And we don't have to worry about guests not being able to afford a trip to Singapore, if we do it there. We can do it here,' he ploughs on. 'Now. And then . . . what if next time we go home to London, we have a huge party to celebrate getting married? All the pressure's off then, isn't it, and we still get to see all our friends and family.'

'But what about our parents?' I ask. 'My mum will miss the chance to wear a hat, and have people congratulating her about her being mother of the bride. I'm her only child. She won't get the chance to do it again.'

Sean has no answer to that. 'It's up to you,' he says. 'We don't have to. No pressure.'

He spins me round so that my back is against him, and kisses the top of my sea-salty hair. We look at the view of the beach, the hotel laid out in varying wooden lodges up and down the verdant hillside. If I don't marry him now, then he's right. I will struggle to plan a wedding taking place in England, from the depths of Singapore; and asking people to travel to Asia to watch us wed is a huge, expensive demand. Ideally, I'd like to have flown home to see venues, but it's costly and time consuming going home to do that. And what if Sean didn't like the one I picked? It's his wedding too.

This way it's low pressure – just Sean and me.

He hears my thoughts. 'It's special here, like this,' he says. 'It's just us. Romantic. Picture-perfect. Impromptu.'

I turn back to Sean and scan his eyes. 'You really want to do this here?'

'Yeah,' he says. 'I really do. With you. Because of you. I love you.'

'I love you too,' I say. And I think, hard, one last time before I kiss him on the lips and then, when we're finished being slightly inappropriate in open water, I whisper, 'Let's get married.'

We're on the plane home, in business class as usual. I never normally understand why Sean forks out so much to go in the business-class cabin when he sleeps the entire flight away, rather than making good use of the never-ending free champagne and nibbles that come past, and the delicious aeroplane meals that are *not* like any aeroplane food I'd ever tasted until I met him. But this time he's not asleep. He's gazing into my eyes, stroking my face, resisting the urge to kiss me over and over again.

I hold up my hand and gaze again at my wedding ring, chosen from a little jeweller on Mahé. I'd picked a sleek little platinum band and he'd chosen his to match, but slightly thicker. He holds his tanned hand up to me, and I run my fingers over it. 'I can't believe I'm Mrs O'Hara. I'm your *wife*.'

He looks around to check we're not being watched and kisses me so deeply that if I wasn't already sitting down, I'd have had to seek out a chair.

'Mr O'Hara, please – my dignity,' I say.

'Damn your dignity, Mrs O'Hara,' he teases and then laughs with embarrassment as the cabin crew hand us two fresh glasses of champagne, pretending not to notice our behaviour.

I look through pictures of our special day on my phone, while Sean puts his headset on and scans the films. I never envisaged choosing my wedding dress from a bridal outfitter on an island off the coast of Africa. I also thought when I did choose my dress it wouldn't be with the help of a friendly sales assistant, but with my mum and Natasha.

I've got some explaining to do when I speak to them. I didn't want a row with my mum or my best friend; although I know they'd have been happy for me, there would have been some 'What the hell?' conversations. So I thought I'd put those phone calls off until we're back home in Singapore.

Sean takes his headset off. 'Nothing on that we haven't already seen,' he says.

'I was thinking,' I say, toying with the sleeve of his T-shirt.

'You want to go in the toilets with me?' he asks.

'No, that's not what I was thinking.' I bat his arm. 'I was wondering if . . . now we're married, if you want to think about – I'm not saying we have to do it immediately – but maybe think about . . . talk about . . .'

'Spit it out, Abbie.'

'A baby,' I say. 'If you wanted to think about trying; not seriously, just see what happens and maybe . . . have a baby.'

He looks at me and a huge smile spreads across his face. We've talked about this many times before, but we've always agreed *when we're married*. 'What does try, but not seriously, mean?' he asks.

'It means I don't want to get stuck in that zone where we're having sex due to ovulation schedules and it sucks all the fun out of it. Low-pressure sex. I'll come off the pill and we'll see what happens. It'll take my body months to resettle itself anyway, so nothing will happen for ages yet. We'll have plenty of "honeymoon period" to enjoy.'

He takes my hand and I can see Sean thinking, giving it the serious thought a question like this deserves. 'Wow, yeah, OK. Let's make a baby.' And then he says, 'But when you say not try seriously, we're still going to be having sex frequently, right?'

'Obviously,' I say.

'Get in!' he says with a mini cheer.

Chapter 53

Tom

September 2009

As I sit here in the kitchen, pushing a chicken kebab around my plate that I've got no intention of eating, now I've collected it from the takeaway, I think again of that night in Samantha's office when I collapsed. It's been playing over and over in my head for months now.

I'd woken in hospital, rigged to tubes and wires, to discover that I'd had a panic attack. A really fucking big one. If that's what a panic attack does to me – sending me clutching my chest and dropping to the floor, passing out through the pain – then I dread to think what an actual cardiac arrest would be like.

I'd thought that was the end. I thought the universe couldn't hit me with any more warning shots. But that was the warning shot I couldn't fail to ignore. I can't do this any more. I can't live like this. Something has to change.

I'm going to do something I should have done a while back. I'm going to end things with Samantha.

I've spent years trying to do the right thing. And it always, always turns out to be the wrong thing. So today I'm going to do the hard thing, and I just have to hope for the best, especially where Teddy is concerned. I've sought advice and I'm not rushing into this, by anyone's standards. Andy's divorce lawyer is a devil in a sharp suit and he says I've got a strong case for sole custody, given that Samantha works away a lot and shows zero interest in Teddy. I'm ready for the outcome of joint custody, though. I think I could be happy with that. I'm not prepared to see Teddy only during weekend visits, though. I want joint custody as a bare minimum, and I will fight hard.

I wait for Samantha to get home from work on Monday evening. Teddy's gone for a sleepover at Andy's house. When I had the anxiety attack, Teddy was in bed when I collapsed and had to endure being woken up, going to the hospital with Samantha, because she didn't have the foresight to ask anyone to look after him, tell him it would all be OK. He's not been the same since. He watched oxygen masks being strapped around my unconscious face, saw me lifted onto a trolley bed and hauled into an ambulance, blue lights flashing. He thought his dad was dying.

So I need him gone tonight. I don't want him subjected to any drama. I'm calm, collected, I've not had a beer. I need a clear head.

Samantha walks through the door, roller suitcase behind her. She sees me at the table and disappointment floods her face.

'You're here,' she starts.

Where did she expect me to be? I live here.

'We need to talk,' she says, as she lets go of her suitcase and pulls the cork from the open bottle of red wine on the side. She pours herself a healthy measure and doesn't offer me one. She drinks, heavily.

'Yes, we do,' I say tentatively.

'This isn't working,' she says, and I'm stunned. Not because her words aren't true, but because she's the one saying it. Samantha has come through the door, guns blazing. 'It's not been working for a long time,' she reiterates. 'And we can't go on like this.'

I nod in agreement. 'No, we can't.'

'This is going to hurt, Tom, so I'm going to say it quickly. I don't think it will come as any surprise to you to find out I don't respect you any more.'

Ouch. That is actually a surprise.

'You've not had a job in a year. I know you've tried,' she puts her hands up, heading me off at the pass, 'and I know you've had interviews. And I know that getting a financial job in the middle of a financial crisis was always going to be tough. But a year, Tom. I've been carrying you for a year.'

If the shoe was on the other foot, I'd have done it for her, no question. That's what love is. But this isn't love. It hasn't been for a long time. I wonder if it ever was. I don't say any of this. I don't want to fight. I want this over.

I sit up in my chair, look alert. 'I'll move into the spare room,' I say. 'And then I'll pack and . . .' Shit, I haven't thought this through at all. Where am I going to go?

'There's no need,' she says. 'I'm leaving you.'

My head snaps up. 'Leaving me?'

'Yes. I've been seeing someone else.'

The air in the room has just turned cold; all my failures have risen, taken seats around the dining table and are staring me in the face.

'You've . . . been cheating on me?'

'Yes,' she admits.

That's brave – a lawyer admitting she's been having an affair.

'Who?'

'Someone from work. I've . . . we've fallen in love. I couldn't help it, I couldn't stop it.'

I know how hard it can be to control feelings for someone you can't have. I've been doing it for years. I'll bet Samantha never even tried to stop.

'How long?' I ask.

'A year.'

'A *year*?' I try to think back to last year. I was losing my job, my career, my self-respect, my whole self. And she just started shagging someone else. This is a joke, surely.

'I thought you and I . . . I thought we would get better,' she continues, 'but this last year things have been the worst they've ever been between us. A job isn't going to fix this. And, Tom, I'm sorry but I don't want to fix this. I want to move on.'

I need to refocus. 'What about Teddy?' I ask.

'You've been his primary caregiver' – *primary caregiver?* – 'and he needs to be here, in his home, in order to get him into the school we want.'

'He needs to be here for stability,' I counter, more calmly than I feel, 'not for a school place.' And then I realise she's walking out on Teddy too. This is unreal.

I don't know what to say.

'We don't have to talk about things like school now,' she says. 'You've taken this so much better than I thought you were going to. So for now, let's say Teddy and you live here for the foreseeable future. You and I will maintain a dialogue' – *a dialogue?* – 'about Teddy's care, and I'll continue to pay the household bills. But, Tom, this isn't a permanent solution. This is temporary; the fiscal side is temporary, while you sort yourself out. And then we'll sit down in the next couple of weeks and let the dust settle, talk about legal separation and then . . .'

'And then?'

'All the things that will naturally follow after that.'

'I want Teddy,' I say, getting my point in now. 'That's all I want. I want Teddy, here with me, or wherever we end up living eventually. I won't fight you for anything else, but I *will* fight you for custody over Teddy. I want joint custody, minimum. None of this weekends-only shit. You can see him whenever you want, but Teddy lives with me.'

Samantha blinks rapidly at my torrent of demands and then gives me a small smile. 'I didn't think it was possible for you to earn back my respect,' she says. 'That might just have done it. I'm too busy to be Teddy's primary caregiver, Tom. It might have escaped your notice, but I work very hard, and looking after a small child doesn't fit too well with that. Even I can see that. I don't want to commit to anything now, but I don't think it's in Teddy's best interests to be dragged from his home, and his father, to move in with me and Ronald in central London, and then be dumped on a nanny every day after school.'

Ronald? Is that the name of the bastard she's been seeing? How old is this guy, if he's called Ronald? But I can't voice any of this, so instead I mumble, 'Central London?'

'Ronald has a penthouse on the South Bank.'

Of course he does. I don't reply. As long as I've got Teddy, I don't care what happens next.

She finishes her wine. Puts the glass on the table. 'I'm going to go and pack a few things now, and I'll come back tomorrow to talk to Teddy after school, explain that nothing's changing for him, but that Mummy is going to be around a little less than usual. If anything, if I take him out some weekends he might actually see *more* of me.'

This is actually true.

'OK,' I agree.

She goes upstairs and I hear drawers opening and closing, cupboard doors banging shut, and when she finishes taking things from the bathroom she comes downstairs.

'Bye, Tom,' she says meaningfully.

I look up at this woman I know, but hardly know. 'Bye, Samantha.'

She shuts the front door behind her and I hear a car door close. Has *Ronald* been out there the entire time, waiting for her? Or was it a taxi? I realise I don't actually care. *I don't actually care.* I stand up, put Samantha's glass in the sink, head towards the fridge and pull out a beer.

I pop it open and let the cap tumble like a spinning top until it eventually settles itself on the granite counter. Samantha's left me. I was trying to leave Samantha, putting it off ever since I'd had that panic attack – petrified that she was going to punish me by taking my son from me – but she's not taking Teddy and *she's left me*. I lift the beer to my lips, but I can't even get the first mouthful in because I'm laughing so bloody hard.

Chapter 54

Abbie

November 2009

'You're pregnant?' Sean asks. 'Really?'

'Yes,' I squeal, waving the little stick with its two red lines. 'Yes! Only a few weeks, at a guess.'

'Oh my God', Sean says. 'Oh my God. I'm going to be a father. I'm going to be a father!' He looks a bit confounded. 'That was fast,' he says after a moment, pulling me towards him. He's still not smiled yet. I think he's in shock.

'Not really. We started trying in March, when we got married.'

'That went quickly.'

Actually I thought it had dragged and, in the end, I did succumb to ovulation kits, peeing on sticks in secret, waiting for smiley faces to tell me I was ovulating. If Sean found himself getting sexually jumped at the most random times of the day, he chose not to comment on it. Low-pressure sex became high-pressure sex, for me at any rate. But we've done it. We're having a baby.

'I thought it would take years,' he says. 'Years and years. I'm shocked. I genuinely thought we'd have more time.'

'More time?' I ask.

'Yeah, more time.'

'What did you want to do with more time?'

'I dunno,' he says. 'More of the same, I guess.'

I'm voicing a question I never thought I'd have to ask. 'Are you happy about this?'

He looks at me, blinks. 'Yes,' he says, alert now, paying attention. 'Yes, I'm very happy.' He sounds wooden, stunned.

'We wanted this,' I say.

'We did.'

'You don't, now? Because, Sean . . . it's too fucking late.'

'I want a baby,' he continues. 'With you. I just . . . I'm . . . I thought we'd have longer. You never mentioned it really, after we spoke about it on the way back from the Seychelles.'

'I didn't want to go on about it the entire time, Sean. And you knew I was coming off the pill. We agreed.'

'We did,' he consents. 'We did.' He exhales loudly. 'I'm happy, Abbie. I think I'm happy. I just need a minute to process this.' He moves towards me. 'OK, that was a shit reaction. I realise that now. I'm stunned. Good stunned. Oh, Christ, I'm so sorry. I've sorted it in my head, almost.' He puts his hand on my stomach. 'Wow,' he says again. 'Wow.'

'OK,' I say warily. 'Are you sure? You're happy about this?'

'I'm happy about this. We're having a baby.'

'We're having a baby,' I repeat.

He exhales loudly again, kisses me. His hand is still on my stomach. He rubs it up and down and looks down at the place where his hand rests. 'There's a baby in there.'

'There is,' I say, trying not to laugh.

'You know I'm going to keep saying "Wow" all afternoon, don't you?'

'Yes.' I smile.

'And most of tomorrow,' he says. 'And possibly for a while after.'

'And then, when my stomach really starts to show . . .'

'That's going to be really weird,' he says. He's looking at my stomach still. 'I'm going to be touching your stomach all the time now. I hope you're ready for that.'

Oh, thank God, it's not as I feared. He's coming round now. 'I am more than ready for that.'

'And I'm going to protect you, and this little . . . thing.'

'Thing?'

'Baby,' he clarifies. 'I'm going to do everything in my power to protect you and this baby. My baby. Our baby.' And then he says, 'Wow' again and I laugh.

I put the pregnancy test on the dining table and allow him to envelop me in his arms as he mutters, 'Wow' a few more times into my hair.

And then he looks at the pregnancy test, resting on the dining table, and frowns. 'Didn't you pee on that?' he asks.

I pick it up again, fetch a disinfectant wipe and clean the table, just in case. I'm not ready to put the stick in the bin, though. I want to keep looking at it. Inside me there's a little life growing.

Chapter 55

Abbie

December 2009

I stroke my stomach as we exit Heathrow Airport, out into the cold. Sean's lugging our suitcases, his flight pillow draped around his neck. Holy hell, it's cold. We were last here, waving goodbye to our London lives, more than two and a half years ago and I'd forgotten how cold it gets in England in the depths of midwinter. I love it. I feel all snug in one of my latest M&S coat purchases.

It's dark and it's only 4 p.m. I'd forgotten how dark it gets here, too, this time of year. I can't wait to have my first mulled wine in for ever. My mum's bought some non-alcoholic stuff from the food section in IKEA. It's the best. I'm going to eat and drink all those stodgy things I can't possibly face in the humidity of Asia. And if I don't get one of those so-bad-they're-good steak-and-kidney pies from the chippy at least once, I'm going to return to Singapore very unhappy.

I can't believe it's taken so long to get Sean to come home. But finally we're returning to see my parents and spend Christmas with our loved ones. I am so excited. I've told my mum and dad we're pregnant, even though it's only the early stages, but I've not told Natasha yet. We've spoken quite a lot recently and I can't wait to hug her and tell her our good news.

I've contacted all my friends who I really want to see and my diary has a smattering of breakfast, lunch and dinner dates. It's funny how so few friends are actually still in London these days, some scattered to the Home Counties, married, getting ready to have babies. But there are plans to commute in and meet up in all our favourite old haunts. A shame I can't drink now.

Sean and I talked about throwing a wedding party, but it never got any further than just talking about it. And now we're actually here, and it's a bit late to organise anything. Plus it's Christmas and everyone's diaries are full enough already.

I think of my old office Christmas parties and how I miss out on all of that, now I'm a freelancer. But life changes. People change. I stroke my stomach again as we wait for my dad to pull up and collect us – yes, I've become one of those women who strokes their baby bump, although mine is barely showing at only a few weeks.

When I'd scrolled through my phonebook to organise meet-ups with friends, my finger had paused on Tom's name. I'd stared at it for ages, deciding what to do. What good would have come from tapping on his name, firing a message, organising to meet? We're completely different people now; we have different lives, in different continents. Would seeing him merely slice open a wound that had nearly healed? I don't even know if we'd still get on. I'd have to tell Sean I was seeing Tom. And he'd want to come too, to keep an eye on things. No. Seeing Tom is a bad idea. It ended so badly last time. Again.

So I'm home for Christmas and I'm not seeing him. My dad told me he'd made an excuse not to meet Tom for golf in the end, because it had clearly upset me. I feel awful about that. What if Tom had needed a friend in my dad? What if I had taken that away from him? I'm overthinking it, I'm sure. I'm sure Tom's been fine.

But I do wonder if we'll ever speak again. That thought shocks me as we stand in the cold, dark airport pick-up point and I see my dad's car turn the corner towards us. I wish I could stop this feeling every time I think of Tom – the strange knot that presents itself in my stomach. He's still there deep down, in my heart, in my head, and being back home reminds me of that. That night, in his kitchen. My words to him; his words to me. *I love you. I love you.*

Natasha and I have been chatting for an hour. We've covered life, love, everything in between. All the good TV that I've missed because I can't get certain channels in Singapore. We've covered Christmas, the baby and *her engagement*. She was waiting to see me, so I could be one of the first to know. I spotted the ring before she'd even said hello, and I wouldn't let her talk about anything else until she'd dished all the details.

'I didn't even put it on Facebook,' she says. 'I was waiting to tell you. I've written the post on a note in my phone and am ready to hook it up to a picture of Will and me, smiling, on the London Eye.'

'The London Eye?' I ask enthusiastically.

'Will's an estate agent – he loves a view.'

I laugh.

'He hired a pod, just for us, with champagne and strawberries and chocolates. It was so romantic. Although I'd rumbled what was going on, because no one else got in with us and there was all this romantic paraphernalia. But he didn't want to propose until we'd got right to the top, so I was sort of waiting expectantly for what felt like *ages* for the wheel to reach the top, and *he* was waiting ages and he looked all nervous, and I knew, I just knew . . .'

She goes on, telling me about how Will fumbled for the ring, dropped it and how he proposed, the words he used, the love they share. I'm so happy for her. Also this means I get to come home again for the wedding next summer.

'Tell me your due date again. I'm going to write it into my diary, so I can begin texting you every hour, on the hour, to see if there's any progress,' she says.

'The twentieth of July.'

'Twentieth of July,' she writes down. 'Four weeks before our wedding. We've booked the venue for the fourteenth of August. That's bad timing, isn't it? You won't want to fly over here with a four-week-old.'

'I suppose not, no. Depends if Sean comes over or not. I could probably do it with a bit of help – one of us carries baby, one of us carries cases . . .'

Natasha looks dubious. Then she says, 'Sean will come, won't he? You don't want to be at a wedding on your own with a baby.'

'I don't know if he'll come home. He doesn't really like it here any more. He doesn't seem to have the same pull towards London as I do.'

'Can't think why,' she says sarcastically, pointing out the window of the bar we're in, to where a thick blanket of cloud has smothered the low winter sun. I think it's going to rain.

'*I* want to come,' I say to Natasha. 'I'm coming. It's happening. I'm not sure how but, Natasha, I'm not missing your wedding. Babies are really transportable at that age, aren't they?' I ask desperately. 'They feed and poop and sleep. I'm sure I can handle that' – *on a thirteen-hour fight, on my own*, I think even more desperately.

'Do you know what you're having?' she interrupts my doom-laden thoughts.

'No. I don't want to find out,' I say.

'I couldn't do that,' Natasha replies. 'It's all enough of a shock and a surprise that adding another surprise into the mix seems bonkers. But if that's your strategy, you ride it out.'

'I intend to.'

'Does Sean want to know?'

'He's desperate for a boy,' I say. 'Desperate. It's killing him, the not-knowing.'

'How's he been?' she asks.

I tell Natasha how hard he's been working, how he was a bit worried at first about having a baby, but how he's on board with the idea now. 'He's been promoted. He's a regional director now. It's huge. A big deal.'

'And have you made any nice new friends?'

She always asks me this, whenever we talk, expecting my answer to change from my usual, 'A few – you know. It's quite transient, Singapore. People come, people go. People don't seem to stick around for a great deal of time.' I'm sure she expects me to say, 'Yes, I have a new best friend and so I can kiss *you* goodbye, Natasha Young.'

She looks relieved at my answer. Natasha was first on my list of friends to see, and I have two more this afternoon – one of whom is Gary, who has thoughtfully already ordered me a wine when I arrive in the pub, although I'll have to break it to him in a minute that I can't drink it. It's already so festive in here, but Gary's wearing a Christmas jumper with lights rigged up inside it that flash on and off. He's putting the pub to shame with its comparatively low effort.

He stands up to greet me, and I can't help but laugh at his jumper as the lights flash blindingly. He points at his jumper as if I can't see it. 'How've you *been*?' he says in an excited voice.

'Pardon?' I joke, 'I can't hear you over your jumper.'

'It is a bit loud, isn't it?' he laughs, fumbling inside to switch the lights off.' 'We're having our work Christmas party tonight,' he says, by way of explanation.

'And that's the dress code, is it?'

We hug each other tightly. It's been so long.

He smiles, drinks his pint and I watch him jealously. 'Thanks for the wine,' I say, 'although . . . I can't drink it because . . .'

'You're up the duff.'

'How the hell did you know that?' I ask, my mouth dropping open.

'It was inevitable, wasn't it?' he states simply, standing up.

'Was it? Where are you going?'

'To the bar to get you something non-boozy and . . .' he says, lifting the wine glass and parking it next to his pint, 'I will take one for the team and drink this too.'

'Gary. You're such a champion,' I say fondly. I've really missed him – I've missed this.

'I know. Wine and a pint here, and then a Christmas party. I'll be calling in sick tomorrow, unsurprisingly,' he says as he moves towards the bar.

'Congratulations, by the way,' he continues when he sits down, after ordering me a mineral water. And then, after we've discussed when the baby's due and how we've both been, he says, 'Two and a half years, Abbie. That's a long time to have been away.'

'I know. It's ridiculous. It wasn't supposed to have been that long.'

'I've missed you,' he says. 'All my co-workers are boring.'

'Well, I don't have *any* co-workers,' I tell him soberly.

'I think that might be better actually,' he jokes.

'I've missed you too, by the way. I kind of miss all of it, you know . . . the way it used to be.'

'Yeah, I know. Fun times. You know the company had an office move?'

'I did *not* know that. Where are they now?'

'Closer to Oxford Street.'

'Oooh, that could have been handy for shopping. Not so handy for my bank balance.' And then I think about the kind of trek that would have been from Natasha's flat in Docklands. I couldn't have done that on a pushbike.

'I've got a new girlfriend,' Gary interrupts my thoughts, announcing it proudly. 'I'm taking her skating at Somerset House tomorrow evening, if I can stand up straight and get rid of the impending hangover.'

'I did that with Sean when we first got together,' I tell him.

'And look at you now,' Gary says. 'From meeting him in the pub that time with me, to getting married and becoming pregnant.'

'Nothing stays the same,' I say.

'Thank God for that,' Gary replies wisely.

Chapter 56

Abbie

January 2010

Sean straps himself into his airline seat as we prepare to leave our friends and family far behind, once again. It's been a wonderful Christmas. And such a chilled New Year's Eve, which we spent with Natasha and Will at their flat – our old flat – watching the fireworks go off all across the City, lighting up the London skyline. I'm sure more skyscrapers have gone up while I've been away. Sean looks relaxed for the first time since we left Singapore, back in his spiritual home – business class.

'Let's never do that again,' he says, pulling his belt tighter and casting his eyes around for the cabin crew and the tray of champagne.

My eyes shoot wide open. 'What? Come home? Didn't you enjoy seeing your parents over Christmas?'

'Yeah, that was nice. But other than that, the trip was . . . awful.'

My mouth drops open to link the rest of my face in a totally startled look of shock. 'No, it wasn't.'

'Was for me.'

'Oh, Sean, I had no idea. Why didn't you say?'

'You were having a nice time. I hardly saw you the whole trip.'

'I was catching up with friends I hadn't seen in so long. Why weren't you doing the same?'

'I did. I don't have as many friends as you,' he says bitterly.

I think of how he willingly let Tom go, and wonder who else he's done that to. The steward arrives with a tray and I take an orange juice, eyeing Sean's champagne greedily. It's torture, watching other people drink. Nine months of not-drinking, and then the breastfeeding period. I do a mental calculation of when I can start drinking again and it's probably another year away yet.

'Can I have a sip of your champagne,' I say. 'Only a really, really tiny sip.' I feel I'm going to need something to get me through the rest of the conversation. 'Actually no, don't worry.' I change my mind guiltily and then sigh longingly as he glugs most of his drink in one go. 'Was it that bad?' I ask.

He signals for the steward to come back with another drink.

'Yes,' Sean harrumphs. 'And I said we should have stayed at a hotel in central London. When you were out busy with your mates, I had to spend so much time with your parents at theirs.'

'*Had* to? I asked if you wanted to come and meet people. You didn't want to.'

'I thought I'd have the house to myself – that your folks would be out at work and I could relax, watch films or whatever. But your parents are always around.'

'It's the school Christmas holidays. They're off work.'

'Yes, I realised that quite early on in proceedings, actually.'

The steward arrives with more drinks for both of us on a tray. Sean forgets to say thank you, so I make mine extra clear and polite as I take a second orange juice. I haven't touched my first one yet, and I am left with one in each hand. I hate putting them on the little tables in case they jerk and fall off as the plane begins moving away from the gate.

'I guess now isn't a good time to tell you I'm thinking of coming back home to have the baby, then.'

He turns to look at me so quickly I hear a bone click.

'Ow!' he says, rubbing his neck. 'You're not serious?'

'I can't think how else to do it,' I tell him. 'Natasha's booked her wedding date for four weeks after the baby's born. I don't think I can get on a thirteen-hour flight a month after I've given birth. If I did, would you come with me?'

He necks the second glass of champagne. 'I don't know,' he says. 'I can't keep taking time off for trips back to the UK.'

'It's Natasha's wedding. She's my best friend.'

'She wasn't at *our* wedding.'

'No one was at our wedding.' This is a pointless argument. I should never have said anything.

But he continues, 'Healthcare in Singapore is amongst the best in the world. Why would you want to fly back here to have the baby?'

'I wouldn't normally, but it just works, with Natasha getting married. And my mum and dad would love to see the baby hours after it's born, and all the days after, instead of having to book a last-minute flight and only spend a little bit of time with us. Your parents too. Everyone we know and love is here. It makes perfect sense.'

'To you,' he says.

Sean's jaw is clenched. But I'm persevering with this, regardless. 'It's my body,' I plead. 'Where I give birth and how – it should be up to me. This is what I want.'

He's quiet.

I've switched from pleading to accusing in my tone when I ask, 'You will come, won't you?'

'For the birth of my child. Of course,' he snaps. 'But I'd really rather not have to travel. I can't afford to take this level of time off again.'

'You get paid paternity leave.'

'Only one week.'

'But your company *gives* you another week as well.'

'It's not good form to take it, though.'

My mouth drops again. 'But you'd take it if we were in Singapore.'

He frowns. 'I'm not sure I would.'

'So you weren't going to spend the first fortnight of being a new parent actually being a parent?'

'Don't put it like that,' he snaps.

I drink one of my orange juices, thinking. *What's happening here? If we're like this now, how will it be after the baby is born?*

We haven't reached a conclusion to this. I have no idea if Sean's going to fly over; he doesn't seem to respect my decision about giving birth, and he gets two weeks' paternity leave, so what's the big problem? I don't want to give birth in Singapore at all now, if he's not even going to take his paternity leave. This changes everything. Even if Natasha wasn't getting married, I don't want to do this alone. My mum and dad are in the UK, my best friend is in the UK. I'll be alone in Singapore. For the first two weeks of being a mum, when I'm finding my feet, no idea what I'm doing, Sean's not even going to be with me. Is that what he's saying?

I don't know what to do with this information. I can't leave it there. We have to talk about this again another day. There's plenty of time to discuss it before July, plenty of time.

But I hate that we've argued about this. I hate that we've argued at all.

Chapter 57

Tom

February 2010

I've started investing in the stock market from home. I started with my own money, what little of it I had left out of my savings, and then Andy wanted a piece of the action when I confessed I was finally starting to make quite a profit. Not millionaire-worthy, but quite a tidy sum, given how poor I've been this past year, running my meagre savings down and living off Samantha's benevolence so that Teddy could have basics like food and new shoes.

I said no to investing Andy's money, at first, not wanting to put his finances at risk as well as mine, but he's a persuasive sod.

I don't touch Samantha's money. That's for Teddy and the house, to keep a roof over his head. I was beholden to my wife for well over a year and we're not even together any more. It's far too embarrassing. Andy thinks it's great. He wishes he'd managed to get his ex, Annabel, to fund him and Oliver living what he calls *the high life* while the divorce went through. Maybe Samantha's not as bad as all that after all, because I never asked her for it. She just offered.

I've had to make that money go a long way, though. But now, with the investments in stocks and shares I've been making, it's actually paying off quite well, so I don't have to make what I call 'Samantha's handouts' go quite so far. I hope I can ditch them entirely soon, regain a bit of self-respect. I don't know why I didn't think of this before. I'm only re-investing half of what I make each time and then banking the rest, for both Andy and me, so we're never down on our original investment. It's bloody nail-biting stuff. I work most of the day on my investment portfolio, and prep something on the hob or slow cooker for Teddy and me to eat when he finishes pre-school.

I'd had no idea about slow cookers. You basically just shove all the ingredients in and turn it on. That's it. Why did no one tell me about this years ago?

Andy knocks at the door with Oliver for a playdate. The boys disappear upstairs and start playing with all Teddy's plastic tat immediately, and Andy and I pop open a few beers and chew the cud. He's impressed that I'm cooking.

'Still don't know how to use the oven, then?' he asks, clocking the slow cooker.

I look at the oven and all its sleek dials. 'No idea,' I say. 'Way too complicated. It came with the house when we bought it. If I'd had my way, the instruction manual would still be inside it. Samantha cooked most nights, moaned incessantly about it, but she knew I was a lost cause. Cooking was the one job in this house I didn't do, so it was fair she stepped up and did something.'

'I think that's probably the worst thing you've ever said about her.'

'Really? I shouldn't be too nasty about the mother of my child.'

I look around at how we live now, Teddy and me. Samantha's dusty collection of Jamie Oliver cookbooks is long gone. She took everything, and it's nice, actually, her not being here any more. She was never very present anyway, but I've got more room for my computer games, now her books aren't on the shelves. Teddy's toys have filtered down here as well, and we bundle them into the space where Samantha's collection of legal journals used to live. It means he plays downstairs a lot more with me, instead of being banished upstairs. We live differently now, Teddy and I. It's kind of great.

'You never say anything bad about her actually,' Andy points out. 'And seeing how she cheated on you, you're well within your rights to.'

I shrug, take the lid off the slow cooker and peer inside. 'We have to talk all the time about Teddy, so there's no point every conversation being some shitty accusation about neglect, on both our sides.'

'You're being more mature than I was,' he admits.

I look from the slow cooker to Andy, echoing the sentiment that someone I still care about said to me years ago. 'It was probably about time I grew up.'

'It's *Peppa Pig* meets *South Park*, but not as gross.' Andy's leaning across the table, sketching something out in one of Teddy's drawing books. 'The kind of cartoon kids will love; funny, though, and true to life. Parents will snigger at it. It's the kind of cartoon they'll leave running in the background after the kids have gone to bed, rather than switch channels.' I'm listening as Andy outlines his grand plans to scupper

Peppa Pig's impending world domination. 'It's about two single dads and their sons.'

'Where'd you get that idea from?' I deadpan.

'Ah, you know. Genius just arrives, doesn't it?' he sniggers.

'Maybe one should be a daughter,' I suggest. 'Might alienate a few girls if the show's too boy-centric.'

He nods, 'Yeah. Yeah, true. Then it can be about how dads navigate raising girls alone, as well. But funny,' he's quick to say.

I watch Teddy and Oliver as they both bundle downstairs, raid Teddy's crate of toys for something specific each and then hurl themselves back up the stairs again.

'Maybe make it a little bit close to the bone,' I suggest. 'But not close enough that five-year-olds start asking awkward questions.'

'Two single dads trying not to fuck up their kids,' Andy says. 'Obviously that's not going to be the pitch I'll go in with.'

'Go in with?'

'To investors or production companies, or whoever. I'm not really sure how it works. I'm serious about this, though,' he enthuses. 'I've been thinking about it for a long time, but it's only since getting to know you that it's really come to me how this could work. I've tweaked the original concept a bit, you know. Because we actually live this life,' he says. 'It's painful, it's funny, it's energy-zapping, it's brilliant.'

It *is* all of those things, and so much more. 'Will it be humans or animals?' I ask.

He turns the drawing round to show me a tired-looking dog, upright – not quite a Labrador, but not quite identifiable as any breed I know, either. Beside it is a bright-eyed puppy with a football shirt on.

'Dogs? That could work. Who'd write it?'

'I'm a book illustrator, but I know loads of funny children's authors. We can rope a couple of them in.'

'We?'

'You're coming in on this, aren't you?' he says as if it was never in question. 'You know finance people, and you've got a brain. Two things I don't really have going for me.'

I raise an eyebrow. 'You've got a brain – you've created a children's cartoon.' I sip my beer thoughtfully. 'I do know people,' I say. 'Quite a few actually.' I've kept up with people in the City, even if I haven't managed to *really* keep up with them. My old graduate trainee, Samuel, works at an investment bank now and has his own graduate trainee to look after. And Debbie, who I worked with years ago and always got on with, is now PA for the director of a hedge fund. And there's loads of others I know in good positions around the City. Not sure how I never managed to slot back in. Perhaps I never really wanted it. 'I suppose I could ask around, see what investors we could be introduced to. Our investments are doing pretty well. We could cash out a bit more and put in a healthy chunk, to show serious willing.'

'Tell me again what you used to do in the banking world?' he asks.

This must be the hundredth time I'll have told him. 'Analyst.'

'That's right.' He sits up straight, clicks his fingers for emphasis. 'You can analyse the children's cartoon market – make our pitch strong.'

'That's not quite what—' I start, but Andy's in full flow now.

'Find out where we'd sit in the market, which production companies have room for another cartoon, which don't have any at all, and who might be interested. What are our strengths? What are our weaknesses, opportunities, threats?' he says as if reading from a business-studies textbook. 'Who's our competition?'

'*Peppa Pig*,' I say without hesitation.

He tuts. 'Other than the sodding pig.'

We sit quietly, each drifting off into another world, five years from now when we've done really well out of a children's cartoon.

'Just think,' he says. 'This year, it's a pilot episode—'

'This year?' I cut in. 'Running before we can walk a bit, aren't we? Let me guess: next year it's a range of backpacks, lunchboxes and pyjamas?'

'Nah, mate,' Andy says, raising his beer to cheers me. 'Next year it's a BAFTA.'

Chapter 58

Abbie

March 2010

I'm researching the maternity unit at the hospital nearest my parents in Enfield. It's only four months until the baby arrives. I'm over the halfway mark now and am settling into being pregnant. I *feel* pregnant – not just bloated and a bit sick if I even so much as smell coffee. I wasn't expecting to pour a cup of decaf one day around six weeks in and retch uncontrollably. Now I can't sit in coffee shops any more, even if I'm ordering a juice.

I've got used to sharing my body with this little person who's now the size of a salad item. 'Hi, little avocado,' I say as I feel a small flutter inside me. I look pregnant too. A bump has well and truly formed. I've been reading all the baby books, and have been updating Sean regularly as he or she grows. Creating new life is a miracle and it's also fascinating. Sean can't deal with the pictures showing the womb and what's going to happen. It's one of the reasons he won't let us join a group birthing class.

'I can't even think about it or talk about it on my own terms, Abbie. How am I going to be able to sit and listen to a lecture, week in, week out, on someone else's terms? I can't force the class leader to stop talking if I don't like what she's saying, can I?'

Maybe I should join a group on my own, but I'd probably have to dip out early if I'm going to fly home to have the baby. I've looked into flying when heavily pregnant and I have until thirty-six weeks, latest, to get a flight back to London. That means I have to be gone from Singapore by the end of June or the airline won't let me fly. The last thing the cabin crew needs is me giving birth in the aisle of a 747.

And then I'll have a month to myself, cocooned in my family home and waiting for the little avocado to grow into a melon that'll emerge into the world. I'm having a baby. This is still so . . . foreign, but so utterly, unbelievably wonderful.

I feel secure knowing that Mum, Dad and Natasha are on standby. And Sean will fly over a few days before my due date, I guess, so he can make it on time. Hopefully I won't go into labour early. Although we've not really discussed any of this in great depth. There's plenty of time to work out the finer details, though.

And then, when the baby is established in the world and after I've been to Natasha and Will's wedding, we will fly back to Singapore to be with Sean. Maybe I'll be able to join a mother-and-baby group, so I can make some more friends and not feel so lonely. I think that's what's crept up on me recently as some of our European friends have relocated to pastures new. Perhaps it's been the high level of work I've had that's staved off the loneliness, keeping me busy. But it's been there, slowly bubbling under the surface, rising effervescently to the top. I'm sure I'll be fine when I'm back, with a baby, being busy.

I look around our sleek apartment, where I spend most of my days working. This is where my life is, sort of, although I feel pulled towards the life I left behind in London. Sean is here. His job is here. He'll never leave, not now he's been made regional director. Our plan to make this the starting point as we moved around the world has ended. His ambition is admirable. But I think it might be costing us . . . something. I'm just not sure what, yet.

Chapter 59

Abbie

April 2010

It's Natasha and Will's engagement party today. Obviously I'm not there – stuck as I am on the other side of the world. And even if I was going, flights over Europe have been disrupted, thanks to an Icelandic volcano going off and there being ash clouds everywhere. Natasha's been sending me pictures of the dresses she's chosen and we're having a Skype video call, so we can talk through all the options.

'The black one,' I say. It's night-time for me and morning for her so, Natasha's got plenty of time to decide after we've spoken. While I'm asleep tonight she'll be partying with lots of her nearest and dearest. I hate missing out, but at least I get to celebrate the wedding when I'm over in a few months.

'I'm not sure about the black one,' Natasha ponders. 'It doesn't do much for my boobs. Whereas the yellow one,' she holds it up, 'makes them look enormous. But,' she reasons, 'the yellow one isn't the *best* for my waist.'

'It's a conundrum, isn't it?' I laugh.

The data connection is a bit hazy, so I can't make out the detail on the yellow dress. 'I wish I was there in person,' I say.

'So do I. But soon you will be.'

'I know.' And then, because I'm pregnant, hormonal, lonely and because Sean and I have just had another huge row about London versus Singapore, which I always lose, I burst into tears.

'Oh, Abbie, no,' Natasha soothes from so far away. 'No, don't cry. What's wrong?'

'Nothing, I'm sorry. I'm being really silly.'

She's quiet, waiting for me to finish sniffling and wiping my nose with a tissue. My nose always runs when I cry. I'm a really ugly crier.

'What's happened?' she asks. 'I know the waistline on the yellow dress isn't ideal, but you don't need to *cry*.' She succeeds in doing what she intended to and raises a smile from me.

I take a deep breath. If I tell her how horrid it's been here recently, will that be disloyal to Sean? Natasha's my best friend. I really don't want to withhold things from her, and if I can't talk to anyone, where will that land me?

So I tell her. I tell her how miserable I've been and how I'd put it down to hormones, but how I'm worried Sean's not in the same headspace as me. 'And I don't know how to win him back round,' I say at the end. Even I can hear how pathetic I sound. But I can't give up. 'We love each other and we're having a baby together. We're just having a blip.'

'Is this about living in Asia or is this about having a baby?' she asks.

'I'm not sure. Both, maybe? I think the two go hand-in-hand. Sean won't move home. He won't even entertain the idea of moving home. And he won't take his full paternity leave. He says he'll be too busy.'

'So how long is he going to spend in London, when you actually have the baby?'

'I don't know,' I say. 'I'm sort of too scared to ask, because I'm not sure I'm going to like the answer.'

'Oh, Abbie, this isn't good.'

'I know.'

'This isn't even remotely normal,' she says and that strikes an icicle into me.

'Don't most men get spooked when a baby's on the way?' I plead.

She thinks hard about this. 'I *think* they worry about losing their freedom, sure. But not taking his paternity—'

'He's taking some of it.' I've done Sean a disservice – I've made him sound really bad and he's not.

'But not all of it?' Natasha asks. 'Even though it's only two measly weeks?'

I don't reply. I'm too ashamed.

'Could he work from home during that time?' Natasha offers Sean a way out.

'I've tried that argument,' I say. It's true. I have. So many times. 'He says he needs to be in the office.'

'How's he going to do that from London? Is he going to go and work from the London office? He won't have any of his files, though, so . . . as long as he's got access to the system on his laptop, he *should* just be able to work from home, in theory.'

I shrug, but the picture is hazy and I'm not sure she can see me. I don't think Natasha's expecting an answer, which is good, because I don't have one.

It feels like Sean and I are fading and I don't have the answer.

'I suppose you could *not* come home and have the baby there. And miss the wedding. I won't mind,' she says in a voice that indicates she really does mind. 'If it makes all the difference between saving your marriage and . . .' She doesn't even say the words.

'It shouldn't have to be like this,' I go on, crying. 'I give in on everything. I want to come home and have the baby. I want my mum.' I sound like a child, I'm aware of that. 'I want my mum and I want my dad, and I want you. I miss my friends. I don't want to be here, alone, any more.'

'Just for a while, though, right?' she encourages. 'You don't want to leave Singapore for ever, leave Sean for ever?'

'No,' I say, 'I don't want to leave Sean. I don't want that at all. But we're not getting on, when it comes to anything to do with the baby, and we've not even *had* the baby yet. He's making it really hard for me to go, and I'm finding it too hard to stay.'

'You need to talk to him,' Natasha says, as if I've not tried this.

I nod, because there's nothing else to do.

There's nothing else to say.

Chapter 60

Abbie

May 2010

'I'm going next month,' I tell Sean. We've been avoiding this subject, but it's the elephant in the room. It's the thing he skirts around on his way out of the door for work. It's the barrier I have to edge my way around when we sit down to eat dinner. 'It's time to strategise,' I say in a businesslike language I think he'll understand. 'I'm due on the twentieth of July. But that date's not set in stone as the day the baby will actually arrive. So . . .' I must remain factual, not emotional, if I'm going to win him round. 'We need to set a date when you will arrive.'

He starts to speak, but I cut him off, because I know that once he's launched into me with his defence, I won't get a word in edgeways. And then the silent treatment will begin. So I keep going, quickly. *Keep to the facts, Abbie. Keep to the facts.*

'Here's what I suggest. You fly out two days before, if you really can't take much time off work. Then it gives us a tiny bit of leeway. And we hope the baby arrives within the week.'

He nods, but he's looking at his dinner plate. He's nearly finished his food and I've only picked at mine. I'm too nervous to eat. I'll be fine in a minute, once I've dealt with this situation, because we need to draw a line under it once and for all.

'What if . . .' he says and I sit up, excited that we're going to get somewhere. 'What if the baby doesn't come that week. I can hardly go home when my pregnant wife hasn't had the baby yet.'

Damn. This is what I was hoping I could avoid, because this *had* occurred to me. I'd thought, somewhat sneakily, that if this did end up happening, Sean would automatically stay. He would, wouldn't he? He'd just stay and wait for his first child to be born. First child. A shudder runs through me. I can't have these discussions again for our second. I'm stilled. Our second child. Will we have a second child? I can't see it happening, if this is what we're going through for the first. But surely it'll be better once the baby is born.

In a way I'm grateful my mind has gone to this worrying topic because it means I don't answer his question. I need him to answer his own question. I need Sean to decide what he wants to do.

'I have a better plan,' he says enthusiastically.

The sigh of relief reverberates through my entire body, from my hair to my toes. I even feel myself smile. I reach for his hand, encouraging him out from the mist and into the light, where he finally becomes part of all this.

He speaks slowly, thinking while he's talking. 'Why don't you go home, if that's where you want to be.'

'It is where I want to be, Sean, it really is.'

He nods, squeezes my hand in return. 'OK. So you go home and then, to make it work with paternity leave and all that, why don't you message me to say you're going into labour? I'll get on the first available flight. I won't spend any days of my paternity hanging around London, waiting for the baby to appear. This way, it's much more time-efficient.'

He's joking, surely. Only he looks serious.

I loosen my grip on his hand. 'But you'll miss the birth.'

'I've been thinking about this,' he says and I wait, expectantly, because I cannot fathom what words are possibly going to come out of his mouth next. 'I don't think you're going to need me at the birth. It's not the best use of what limited time I have.'

My head jolts so quickly that a sudden pain forms behind my eyes.

'Sean . . .' But I can't speak for a moment. I try to collect myself and then a whisper is all that emerges. 'You're not going to be at the birth?'

'I don't see how I can be, what with you being on the other side of the world. And I'll be honest, Abbie. I don't think I can stomach seeing a baby come out of your vagina.'

The pain deepens, sears itself into me.

'I read in a magazine that it's a bit like watching your favourite pub being blown up,' he says.

'What?'

'Watching a baby rip your wife's vagina to shreds – it's like watching your favourite pub exploding.' He laughs.

I'm not laughing.

But he's on this trajectory and he continues, despite seeing my horror and all-out confusion. 'And then you have to look at this baby and know that he or she is the very thing that caused your sex life to turn to rubble, probably for ever.'

I can't quite catch my breath. I let go of Sean's hand entirely.

'You wouldn't be there for the birth . . . even if I was having the baby in Singapore?'

He makes a face. 'I'd really rather not,' he replies, as if I was asking him if he wanted sugar in his tea, instead of asking if he's going to be present to usher our newborn into the world.

'I'll be there in spirit,' he offers as the worst kind of consolation prize.

I count to ten, because if I say what I really want to, I can't see a way back. And then I reach ten and I say it anyway. 'Fuck off, Sean.'

'What?' he splutters.

'How can you say that to me?' I explode. 'How can you sit there and tell me you don't want to be there when I have your baby – that you don't even want to be in the same country, let alone the same room. I can understand that your job is busy and important. I can, just about, understand why you're not taking your entire paternity entitlement. Just about. But I can't understand your attitude. You wanted a baby. You wanted *this* baby. But now you don't. You're going to let me go to London alone, have this baby alone, you're not coming to Natasha's wedding and, even if I was staying right here, you still wouldn't be there to hold my hand and tell me everything was going to be OK while I squeeze your baby out of me.'

I don't know why I expect Sean to placate me and tell me everything's going to be OK right now, because he's just told me he's not going to be there to do any of that, at the exact moment I'll need it most. But I'm still surprised when he snaps, 'This is my solution to the problem. It's the best I've got. I'm willing to hear a better one.'

'Problem?' I say. 'Problem? Am I the problem, Sean? Or is it the baby? Is the baby a *problem*?'

'That's not what I mean,' he says. 'Although the baby isn't a problem per se, it's not even here yet and it's already messing with our lives. What's it going to be like when it's born?'

'*Messing* with our lives?' I can't stop repeating everything he says. He's setting off fires everywhere and I can't put them out quickly enough. I stand up. 'You're right,' I say. 'You're right. What is it going to be like when it's actually here?'

He nods, but he's misunderstood my meaning.

'I don't think I can do this any more,' I say. I'm exhausted.

'What do you mean?' he asks, a hint of nervousness in his voice.

'I think . . .' I start and I count to ten again, because if I suggest this, I don't think I could take it back. 'I think I need some space.'

'What kind of space?' he asks.

'Seven thousand miles.'

'You're going back to London? Now?'

'Tomorrow,' I say because I need to give him a chance to sleep on it, to wake up in the morning, retract what he's said, apologise and stop me from leaving. And then we can try to move forward, take it from there.

'Are you leaving me?' he asks.

'No,' I say. 'I'm leaving. But I'm not leaving you. We just need some serious space. We can talk about it in the morning and maybe . . . you won't feel this way, once you've slept on it.' I stop talking. I can't put words in his mouth. Sean needs to reach a conclusion himself. When I think about this later I'm sure he'll be able to reassure me, but at the moment he's floored me.

The sun streams down as I stand by the taxi's door. Sean stands with his hands in his pockets, watching me as I put my cardigan for the flight and my carry-on luggage into the car. He's booked the taxi to take me to the airport. He doesn't know what to say or do. So far he's said and done all the wrong things. Only I don't think he's realised that yet. I don't know if he'll ever realise that.

'You know where I am, Sean. If you decide you want us in your life . . . you know where I am.'

'I didn't think you were leaving me?' he pleads. 'I thought you were only leaving for a bit.'

'I don't know what's happening,' I cry.

'I didn't want it to be like this,' he says. 'We were so good.'

'We were.'

He's said all this before. I feel numb. I can't hear it again. It's doing neither of us any good.

'How will we make this work, with you there and me here?' he asks again.

'We won't,' I say. 'We can't. You can't be a father from the other side of the world. You can't be a husband from that distance, either.'

We'd talked late into the night. We'd talked through the early hours of this morning and at no point did Sean volunteer to be part of the family he'd helped create. At no point did he volunteer to apply for a transfer to the London office. At no point did he beg me to stay, which was the thing that hurt the most. I can't be here with him any more. I just can't. It's scaring me that I might descend into full loneliness when my husband doesn't really want the family he's created. We're getting in his way.

'Hasn't it occurred to you that I might be a bit scared?' I asked him when we woke, bleary-eyed and both of us crying when the argument started again. 'That I need you?'

Now we're here, by the taxi, it seems as if both of us are resigning ourselves to the facts. Our marriage is ending. Neither of us wants to make it work with the parameters each has set the other. We hold each other, because there's still love there, but it's clear that this is the end.

'We don't fit your ambition. We don't fit the life you're trying to create for yourself. I'm not enough. Collectively, the baby and I . . . we're not enough.'

'Don't say it like that,' he protests, but deep down I'm sure he knows I'm right. His ambition didn't encompass living well with a family, although at one point I think he thought it did. There's no room for us in the picture of his day-to-day life that Sean's painted.

I'm leaving and he's not even trying to stop me. Instead he booked the car.

'Will you . . .' he asks as I start to climb into the taxi. 'Will you message me, when you've had it, please.'

It.

'For what purpose?' I say, rather horridly.

'So I know you're all right. So I know the baby has arrived safely. So I can transfer you some money, to buy things. I'll do it now,' he says. 'I'll go straight back upstairs and I'll put so much money in your account, Abbie, you and the baby won't want for anything.'

'Thank you, Sean,' I say, because anything else is pointless at this stage, when the driver is waiting politely and I reluctantly have a flight to catch.

Beg me to stay. Beg me to stay. We can work this out if you tell me you love me and you ask me to stay. Although if he begged me to stay, I'm not sure I could trust Sean to want us suddenly. Every fibre of my body knows this. I just need to relay that message to my brain.

His phone rings in his pocket and he reaches for it. 'I have to take this,' he says. 'Abbie, I'm so sorry.' I don't know if he's apologising for the way we've ended or because he has a work call that he needs to accept. I'm not going to stand here to find out.

I want to tell him I love him, before I say goodbye, but I look at him as he itches to accept his phone call and I can't say it. I'm not sure I'd mean it.

'Bye,' I say and I climb into the taxi.

He holds the door for me and then says goodbye, giving me a look of deep regret. And then he closes the door, holds his hand up to me and answers his phone. The taxi hasn't even left.

I want to be strong. I want to hold my head up high, but I can't. The taxi starts off. I'm having a baby in a few short months and I've walked away from my marriage. My heart hurts so much and the tears won't stop streaming down my cheeks.

Chapter 61

Abbie

June 2010

Today is my mum's birthday. I've missed celebrating her birthdays since we left London. I've missed celebrating so much. We spend the day at the RHS garden at Wisley and it's nice, walking around together and admiring the flowers and plants, the architecture of the buildings, the enormous glass hothouse. I'm going at a slower pace than usual, as the bump is enormous now. I look like I'm about to drop at any minute, but I've still got weeks to go.

Last month I walked out on my husband and I wish I could say that I regret it. But I don't. We've spoken, each telephone call laced with regret, all of our words never feeling final enough to have truly nailed the coffin lid down on our marriage. But I get off the phone each time to Sean and I know I've done the right thing. Each phone call makes it clear that he's not found the mental headspace to be part of our family. And I can't be with a man who is only 'there in spirit'.

I don't miss Sean because he wasn't there for a long time before I left. He's been asking me how I am over text messages, but these have dropped down to almost none per week now. He never asks how the baby is doing. He still doesn't see it as an actual being. To Sean, the baby robbed him of his wife.

I need to focus on myself and the baby. I need to be two parents now, and I'm OK with that. Or at least I will be, even if I'm devastated for the baby that it won't have a father who is present – who wanted to be present. But that is Sean's choice. I can't coerce someone into being a family man.

I can't talk about it to my parents any more because they are so angry at Sean's attitude to being a father. My dad wanted to book a flight and have it out with him. Behind my back, my mum even phoned him. But she got nowhere, a fact that surprised her. But not me. I'm resigned to it now.

We find the café and sit outside while my dad queues inside and loads up the tray with various cream-tea items. I need to work out my next plan. At least I can still freelance from here, but being the Asia editor means I'm going to be working in a strange time zone, trying to catch interviewees at the end of their working day the moment I've sprung out of bed in the UK. Once I've had the baby I'll hopefully get back into the swing of things.

I've been staying with my parents for about a month. I can't move back in and then force a baby upon them. That's not fair.

I tell my mum this and she sits up sharply. 'Don't you dare suggest moving out!' She speaks so loudly that pensioners enjoying a cream tea at the table next to us look over. 'Our house is far too big for the two of us, rumbling around in it. And we've only just got you back home,' she says. 'We missed you, Abbie.'

'I missed you too.' The fact that I get to see my mum on her actual birthday was something I thought would probably never happen again, if Sean had his way. 'But a baby . . . It's going to be noisy and stressful at night for a while, and you and Dad have to get up so early for work.'

'Yes, but we'll also be there to lend a hand. And you're going to need some help. You aren't being forced to do this alone. There are many women who, through no fault of their own, *are* forced into being a new parent alone,' my mum says. 'You are fortunate that you *aren't* in that position. So don't volunteer.'

I nod. 'OK. Thanks.' I'm sure we'll talk about this again, but I'm not going to argue now, on her birthday.

I *have* voluntarily put myself in that 'new parent alone' position by leaving Sean, haven't I? But in recompense for the way we ended, he has at least transferred about £30,000 into my bank account. For now, I'm going to take his money and keep it safe because when the guilt wears off, that money will stop. I know it. And then it will, unavoidably, lead to divorce. I can't imagine the ugliness that will bring. Sean isn't the kind of man to go down without a fight, but at least if he's on the other side of the world I won't actually have to see him. I don't understand how we got here. Or, rather, I do understand it. I can't *believe* we ended up here.

'Have you thought about catching up with some friends while you're here?' my dad prompts when he returns with the tray of sugary goodies.

'Not really,' I say, reaching for a scone and the mini pots of jam and clotted cream.

'Why not?' my dad asks, shooting my mum a look.

'I've seen Natasha,' I tell him.

'But no one else – in four weeks?'

I shake my head, slather on the clotted cream. 'You guys put jam on first, but I've always appreciated the structural stability of cream first, jam second. It means I can get more jam on this way. This baby is making me ravenous. I'm sure I'm putting on more weight than is normal. What do you think?'

'Why haven't you seen any other friends?' my dad persists, refusing to be drawn into my clumsy attempt to change the conversational direction.

'Just haven't,' I say.

I open the mini pot of Tiptree jam. 'Every time I went out for breakfast in Singapore these little pots of jam found their way onto the plate,' I remark in an effort to change the subject again. 'It was like a little piece of England followed me around from café to café.'

My parents watch me.

I sigh, knowing I can't avoid it. 'I'm embarrassed, OK? I'm humiliated. My marriage has collapsed. I'm heavily pregnant and I now live with my parents. I'm living the dream,' I say, trying to make light of it.

'You aren't living the dream now,' my mum says sagely. 'But you will be soon enough. You have a job, a family who loves you, a baby on the way and you're home, where you want to be and where you belong. This is where your friends and family are. Very soon, Abbie, this will feel like the dream.'

I'm unconvinced, but my dad spares me from answering as he says, 'Also, you left him. You made a brave decision to walk out on a situation that you knew wasn't going to get better.'

'It was only going to get worse,' I say adamantly, thinking of how lonely I already was, and how much worse it would have been with a newborn and an unsupportive husband. But I have to keep reminding myself it wasn't working, that there was a reason why I left. 'That's not the way marriage is supposed to be, *is* it?'

My mum and dad have been together for nearly forty years. They argue, sure. So it wasn't as if I had a rose-tinted view of how marriage should be. But it wasn't supposed to be *like that*, when it came to a baby obviously tearing Sean and me to pieces.

'No,' my dad says. 'It's not the way marriage is supposed to be. It's give and take, push and pull; it's love and . . . sometimes frustration; it's support and care. But without a shadow of a doubt, it's being there when the other person needs you.'

I nod. 'Every now and again I'm going to need you to remind me of that,' I say.

'Why don't you arrange to meet a couple of friends one day soon,' my dad suggests.

I nod. 'I might do.'

'How about Tom?' my mum offers. Dad keeps his eyes trained on me.

Tom. It's taken so long, but now I can finally think about him without every part of me clenching in some low-level form of distress. 'I'm not sure,' I say. 'It's been quite a while. It might be a bolt out of the blue.'

'You've not spoken to him at all since you went to Singapore?' Mum asks.

I shake my head guiltily. I think of the way I ignored all his messages, his calls after that night in his kitchen. I think of the way I saw him on TV, losing his job so publicly, and I still didn't message him.

'Did you speak to him?' I ask my dad, 'after that classic-car thing you went to?'

'No,' he says, equally guiltily, although it was inadvertently my fault that they stopped speaking. 'You seemed very upset that I was communicating with him, even though I only ran into him by accident, so I thought it best to leave it there.'

My mum cuts in. 'Your dad fobbed Tom off, and they haven't met since.'

I tut, but it's myself I'm annoyed with. 'You shouldn't have had to do that. I put you in an awkward position.'

'Tom didn't question it,' my dad soothes. 'He replied with a fairly upbeat "No problem, some other time" or words to that effect.'

This pushes a barb straight into my heart. The man just oozes goodness. 'Of course he did.'

My mum touches my arm. 'There's no pressure to see him if you don't want to. There's no pressure to see anyone.'

'But then again,' my dad says, reaching to pour us all a cup of tea from the warm pot, 'if, in a week's time, I find you lying about in front of the TV with no intention of ever leaving the house, we will obviously be staging an intervention.'

I look at my parents' resolute expressions. 'Noted.'

Chapter 62

Abbie

July 2010

'Is now a good time to tell you I always thought Sean was a bit of a cock?' Gary says.

'Hmm, maybe,' I reply, uncertain as to how much longer I might wish to continue this conversation. I've got the facts out of the way, but now it's clearly time for Gary's post-match analysis.

'Quite up his own arse.'

'Probably true,' I say. It's still painful talking about it. But given that I do actually want to see my friends this side of the apocalypse, I need to listen while they dispense their wisdom, even if it is a bit too late. And then once it's done, with each friend in turn telling me exactly what they thought of Sean – getting it off their chests – we can move on. Today is Gary's turn.

'Although he was very liberal with his money. Got the first round in a few times, as I recall,' Gary goes on, plumbing the depths of his memory.

'Yes, he was very generous with his money.' He still is. Another £10,000 has just landed in my account. Sean's buying his way out of being part of a family that he once said he wanted.

'Liberal with his cash, but not with his love?' Gary suggests.

'That's very astute,' I say. 'It's complicated. He loved me. But I'm not sure he loved . . .' I point to my stomach, where my baby is squirming around, trying to shift position.

He or she shoves what must be a hand, or it could be a foot, right into the space where my bladder wants to be, but is now squashed to the size of a marble. I have to clench tightly not to pee.

'I'll be right back,' I say and disappear to the loos.

When I return, a waitress has delivered our burgers and drinks.

'So your marriage has broken down, you've left a hot climate to return to living in freezing-cold England, with your mum and dad, and you're about to become a single parent?'

'Thanks, Gary.'

He grins. 'You know you just got really attractive.'

I raise an eyebrow.

He laughs. 'I'm joking. I'm joking,' he continues.

'And you thought Sean was a cock,' I say.

'Takes one to know one,' Gary replies. 'I mean it, Abbie,' he says in between chewing. 'Sean wasn't the be-all and end-all. You know that, right?'

'Yes, I think so. I'm sure in a few years I might notice that I'm a bit . . . single. But I'm going to have my hands full in the interim, so,' I shrug, 'I'll enjoy being a mum. I won't be joining all those internet dating sites you're signed up to.'

'Don't. It's a wasteland,' he says. 'Know any fit women you can send my way?'

'None that are single, I'm afraid.'

'How's your mate, Natalie?'

'Natasha,' I say.

'That's the one.'

'She's getting married in August.'

He swears and then takes a huge bite of his burger.

When we've finished our meals and finished bitching about all our old bosses, reminiscing about life as we knew it only a few short years ago, we settle up the bill and say goodbye. I can only ever seem to settle on lunch dates with friends at the moment, because I'm too tired to stay out late for dinner dates, and Gary has to get back to work. I should also be working from home, but I've filed all my copy and if I take an afternoon off, it's at my own discretion.

He hugs me goodbye as I walk him back to his new office at his new job on the east side of the City. We wave as he goes through the rotating doors and disappears inside the sleek steel-and-glass structure. There are so many new office buildings here since I left. I breathe in the smoggy London air, the heat of which is thick in my lungs. The pavement radiates warmth into the soles of my ballet pumps. It feels like such a long time since I've really appreciated my city. The last time I took in the atmosphere, truly, was when I was preparing to leave for Singapore. Even the final time when I was back here with Sean that Christmas I didn't stop to appreciate the city I'd always called home. I just careered my way around it by taxi, focused on seeing friends. I never took the time to appreciate it. Today feels like a good day.

The baby is getting heavier by the minute. But I wonder if I can get down to the river to take a walk down memory lane and then back home without too much hassle. It won't take long. I love the idea of these new pay-as-you-go Boris Bikes that are pinging up everywhere. Only the bump and I might not survive a fall off one of those.

I need to flag a cab to get me up to Liverpool Street to catch the overground back to Enfield. But maybe I could get a taxi down to the river first?

I walk along the street, waiting for a cab with an orange light, but one doesn't come for ages. I'm hot and bothered. I wish I could hold this baby bump up, just for a few minutes, to relieve the pressure on my hips, my waist.

'You are such a heavy little lump,' I say down to my stomach as I walk slowly. I'm sure I'm waddling. I dread to think what I look like from behind as I move along the pavement. I adjust my hands over my maternity dress. 'Only a few weeks to go, little one, and then we get to meet.'

I look behind me, waiting for a taxi to drive along, but the stream of traffic has died down. A taxi pulls around the corner and I raise my hand for it, then lower it when I notice the light is off and there's a passenger seated in the back already.

'Bugger,' I say and then pat my stomach. 'Don't repeat any of the sweary things Mummy says when you're older, will you?'

Mummy. It's the first time I've actually called myself that. A bit premature because he or she doesn't arrive for a while, but I cradle the bump again and smile. I *am* going to be a mummy; in a few short weeks my world is going to be whizzed upside down as this little person arrives and I become its mummy.

I walk on a bit longer, ambling slowly – because it's the only pace I can manage – with the freedom of having nowhere to be, turning back every now and again to check for a black cab sporting an orange vacant light. And then I smile because I realise where I am. Ahead of me is the McDonald's that Tom and I ended up in that night we went out together. I haven't had a Happy Meal since that day. I wonder if he's still got his Beanie Baby.

I haven't been back to this part of town in . . . for ever. If I keep walking, up ahead is St Paul's Cathedral, where Tom held onto me after pulling me from the wreckage of the derailed train. I'm cold, chilled to the bone – an arctic wave has risen towards me. I didn't feel this on the actual night, but being here, again, on this normal summer's day, I feel it now. Why? And then as fast as it came, the cold has gone.

I take a deep breath as I enter the garden around the churchyard. Because Tom and I had sat in there together the night we went clubbing, almost five years ago, dipping salty chips in sweet milkshakes and discussing our future selves, it holds good memories for me, not bad ones. Even though our friendship ended so emotionally, thinking of Tom now, I can only summon good memories.

I've sat in St Paul's Churchyard so many times, but never once stepped inside the building. I've got time to kill, so I join the throngs of tourists piling inside. I waddle around, admiring the sheer scale of the place, the gold columns and chandeliers, the offshoot chapels and war memorials to the fallen. It's sobering and I'm reminded – simply by seeing the memorials – that there are worse things in this world than my predicament, worse things than what happened to Tom and me the night of the derailment. It could all have been so much worse.

Despite the number of people in here, everyone is quiet, respectful, and so I take a seat in the moveable chairs and think about so many things. I'm reminded that on the night of the derailment I lived, and that Tom lived; we were the lucky ones. Others lost limbs, lost lives. When I think back to that night, which I try not to do too often these days, I wonder if I could have lingered over my drink a bit longer in the pub, not ended up on that train, not have been anywhere near it. And then I wouldn't have met Tom. Perhaps some things are meant to happen for a reason.

The cathedral is cool, even in this intense summer heat, and the ceiling high. I spend another moment taking in the beauty of the building's interior, admiring the way sunlight filters gently through the windows and onto the white floor. Everything is bright, dove-white, peaceful. It doesn't feel as if I'm in London.

I'm not remotely religious, but I say a little prayer for those who didn't survive. And then, even though Tom's not dead, I say a prayer for him: a sort of *thank you* prayer for sending him towards me that night, for making him the kind of man – a good man – who rushes forward in a crisis and helps people.

And then I rise slowly, my hand on my back to straighten myself, and I exit the sanctuary of the cathedral. The brightness of the sun shocks me, but I walk towards the patch of grass, find the place where Tom and I sat that night. Where Tom had knelt, pushing my hair from my face, examining my forehead, checking I was all right. Cocooning me in safety when I needed it most. I've still got the scar from that night on my forehead. Time is a great healer in some ways, and not in others.

I focus on the architecture, marvelling that while other old buildings get knocked down, replaced by skyscrapers in the name of progress, churches and cathedrals are afforded a special status. They stay put, remain resplendent, an everlasting beacon of hope for people who need it.

I don't know how long I've been here. But I'm aware that I should probably move on, back through the railings segmenting this ecclesiastical space from that of the financial world it inhabits. I'm pleased I've done it. I'm pleased I've stumbled across this space. I'm pleased I've sat here. It's almost as if it needed to be done, an unexpected reckoning; that I needed to encounter this memory and move on. I *am* moving on. In so many ways.

A little way down the road is Mansion House Underground entrance. I have mixed feelings, looking at the Tube station from this distance. My stomach wants to knot itself, only the baby is in the way of all my organs functioning as I want them to. I've been past countless Tube stations since that night without issue, but today, without realising it, I'm clutching hold of my bag tightly, my body stubbornly refusing to move as a cold wave settles itself over me.

Perhaps I need to put this hatred, this fear, this loathing of the Underground to bed, after all these years. I don't think it's a case of win or lose, but I do think I need to at least draw level with it. It's been so long, and I've been so scared of going anywhere near the Underground. I made Sean's life and mine so hard in Singapore because I navigated my way around it by taxi and bus. I refused to even consider boarding their version of the Tube, the MRT.

But it's only been five years. Perhaps I need longer. Perhaps I need never do it at all. I've been inside the cathedral,

I've sat in the churchyard, reliving Tom's and my own personal aftermath. That's enough, surely?

I watch people as they mosey to and from the station. It's not rush hour for a while yet, and so the pedestrian pace of movement isn't as frenetic as it soon will be. But still there's a steady trickle of people entering the station, pulling Oyster cards from their wallets, ready to tap and let the barriers usher them into the cavernous Underground system. Whatever I do next, I can't stay here all day as the world goes about its business.

I need to be brave. I'm going to have a baby soon, and I'm scared about that, but I know I will do it. This is a fear I need to conquer. I hardly ever come to this part of town. I'll probably never find myself in this spot again, or if I do, it might be another five years from now. I need to do this for me. I need to prove to myself that what happened that night hasn't damaged me for ever, that I can get on the Tube and it will be fine. I can go a few stops towards Liverpool Street. Then I'm in the right place to catch my overground back to Enfield. Five stops. That's all I need to do. Five short stops.

Deep breaths.

Across the road a black cab drops someone off and its orange light goes on. I'm saved. I can just walk over there and get in that taxi. I don't *have* to do this.

But I don't move towards the taxi. I force myself, with every shred of mental power I have, to stay rooted to the spot. Eventually the taxi leaves, and panic and relief hit me in one go.

I've made the decision now. There's no going back.

I cross the road, walk the short distance towards the Tube station and propel myself inside, to the glass screen that divides me from the uniformed vendor – the gateway between me and a ticket. I don't know what to ask for, so I mumble to the station worker that I want a Travelcard and, before I know it, I've paid and I'm clutching the little credit-card-sized ticket, walking towards the barriers, forcing myself to stop shaking. Inducing this level of worry today probably isn't the most sensible thing to do, given that I'm weeks away from giving birth, but it feels like a rite of passage. I have to do this.

I push the ticket into the barrier and watch as it's spat out for me to collect. I grab it and move through the open barriers before it's too late and they close on me.

And then I'm holding the handrail, forcing myself onwards down to the platform, where I look at the yellow-lit sign telling me that I'm one minute away from the next Circle Line train. One minute – I can do that without turning around and making a bolt for it. I count down: sixty, fifty-nine, fifty-eight, and on and on until I've gone past zero and attempt to amuse and distract myself, *minus four, minus five, minus six*.

The rush of air hits me first, indicating that a train is rocketing its way towards my platform. I stand firm. I'm not turning round now.

The train enters the platform, a set of doors open before me and people get out, fumbling for their tickets, ready for the barriers above us. It's now or never, and I get on, my feet crossing the threshold of the carriage. At this time of day there are seats available and I move to one, sitting down next to the glass partition, and although I don't need to hold the long vertical yellow handrail, I clutch it tightly anyway.

I look around, wondering if anyone else is giving off the same 'get me out of here' vibes that I must be. But around me the average commuters, students and tourists have their noses deep in books or newspapers or are fiddling with their phones or headsets. The doors close, the train begins moving and we leave Mansion House station behind. I've done it. I'm on the Underground. The automatic announcer tells us: 'This is a Circle Line train via Embankment and Victoria. The next station is Blackfriars.'

No, that can't be right. I've gone the wrong way. How have I gone the wrong way? I was too busy counting down the endless minutes instead of paying attention to which platform I should have been on, and now I'm on the wrong train.

Breathe in. Breathe out. It's OK, I can fix this. I have to allow the train to carry me onwards through the blackness and into the next station, knowing that I've got to get off and come back the way I've just been. I'm too tired and pregnant for this. But at least this is distracting me from what I was originally panicking about.

I'm accidentally doing a portion of my old commute. I wonder if I get off here and do my old walk to work, how that will make me feel. I'm here now. I might as well have a look around the courtyard that I used to work in, see if Gianni's is still there, remember all those blasts from the past. I'll get off, wander around and then get back on the Tube again to go home. Then I've *really* proved I can do it.

And after this, I never have to do it again. But . . . if for some reason I do have to get on the Underground in the distant future, then it'll be OK. I'll be calm. I *am* calm. Sort of. Let's see how I feel when I get off. At least I've stopped shaking.

The doors open.

It wasn't as bad as I thought it would be. It was the fear that I had to beat, not the train itself. I might need a few minutes of walking around my old haunts, though, before I get back on again.

I take a deep breath of smoggy London air as I emerge from the station. I process what I've just done, congratulating myself while I look round at my surroundings. I need a moment to digest the enormity of the last few minutes. *Deep breaths, Abbie. Deep breaths. You've done it. The worst is over. Next time it'll be easier.*

I'm so close to the Thames. I want to go down to the river, past all the places where I used to hang out. I want to take a look at my life from five years ago and, because it's so starkly different from how I'm going to live in a matter of weeks, bid it a fond farewell. Again.

I cross the road, walk towards the enclave of cobbled alleys and small streets, the pavements of which are too small for pedestrians, the road width very nearly too small for cars, although they venture through regardless.

The courtyard in front of the offices where Tom and I used to meet for illicit cigarettes in the early days of our friendship could be a cut-out-and-keep version from back then. Nothing's changed, except there are different faces outside each office now. The Victorian building where I used to work, before I went freelance, sits opposite the sleek financial building where Tom used to spend his days.

I look up at the window that I used to take great pains to avoid. There's someone else at his old desk now. There's someone at my old window desk too. I wonder if the two of them ever look across at each other. I wonder if they'll ever meet by accident, or if they'll pass each other in the street for years without ever realising who the other person is.

Around the corner I walk towards Gianni's. By now he might have closed up for the day, but as I approach I notice it's no longer even called Gianni's. 'Oh no,' I say to myself. 'Where's Gianni gone?' This isn't an old-fashioned, comfortable-but-badly-decorated Italian café any more. Instead it's a super-shiny artisan coffee bar.

Ahead of me, hanging baskets full of geraniums herald the ever-welcoming sight of the pub. At least some things have stayed the same. I wrestle with the idea of going in. I might grab a juice, have a well-earned sit-down, give the bump and me time to decompress before we head down to the river. But the day is still so hot, the sun working its magic on everyone as they filter out of their buildings for drinks before they head home. I miss that about summer in the City.

And then there's one place I want to see. Because I'm here now, and I probably won't be again for ages. I walk on slowly. It's only two roads away and I notice the hair salon that I went to is still there, still open, all bright lights and tub-thumping music. Office windows hold workers inside as they type, rifle through files. And then I'm there: I'm outside Tom's old flat, which he hasn't lived in for years. I just wanted to see it, really.

He hasn't lived there in so long. I think of him again the night he pulled me from the train, standing out here, wishing me well as my dad picked me up in his car. And I think back to the last time I was here, running out of this door as if my life depended on it, after having been rejected. But even after all that, I feel the connection to him sometimes pulls at me, a thread that's now been stretched so thin it's practically worn away. Tom is gone from my life. I let that happen.

Rain falls; clouds have blown slowly over the City without me noticing, sweeping over the Square Mile. The change in temperature is a welcome reset, following the day's sticky heat. I don't even have an umbrella.

Around me people are caught out, holding newspapers over their heads as they dash between coffee shops and dry cleaners, back to their offices or home early. My ballet pumps are quickly soaked, the silken material slopping underfoot. My summer maternity dress now looks wrong in this weather. I dive into the doorway opposite and decide to wait it out. After five minutes it's clear the torrent is unrelenting. I'm already soaked, so I might as well go for it.

Opposite me, Tom's old apartment-building door opens and a man walks out and pauses as he takes in the state of the weather.

In that moment, everything stops. I open my mouth to say his name. It's Tom. But it can't be.

Have I dreamed him? He doesn't see me and I think, *He's a mirage, surely*. I'm not going to speak. I'm going to let him keep walking. I'm going to let him go.

Behind him a little boy emerges, fumbling with an umbrella, and Tom turns, lifts it from his hands and clicks it open, the umbrella brandishing pictures of various animals from *Peppa Pig* on each side as he holds it in front of them, and then up, to shield them from the rain. How has Teddy grown so much? He is a proper little boy now. He looks like an incredibly young version of Tom, all blue eyes and dark hair.

And then everything stops as Tom stares straight ahead at me. He opens his mouth to speak, but is rendered as unable to communicate as I am. He looks at me, his gaze landing on my heavy-set stomach. His expression deepens and his eyes lift back towards mine.

A throng of people walk down the cobbled street, umbrellas up, taking their time, chatting and laughing and moaning about the weather. They pass in between Tom and me, momentarily breaking our view, separated as we are by a cobbled lane and five years of complicated history.

'Hi,' I say, when the lane in between us is empty once again, the rain crashing down against the cobbles.

Finally he speaks. 'What on earth are you doing here?' He finds his voice. It's so odd to hear it, after all this time.

'I think I could probably ask you the same thing,' I call from my position under the alcove.

'My flat,' he gestures behind him into the communal hallway. 'I've just re-let it. The agent couldn't find the keys to the windows. I had to get some cut and—' He stops speaking. Beside him, Teddy looks between us with a level of obvious curiosity. 'What are you . . .' Tom tries again. 'How are you *here*?'

I take a deep breath. 'It's a long story. How are you? You look—' I just smile. He looks wonderful. He always did.

'I'm great. We're great,' he says, nodding towards Teddy. 'How are you?'

'Fine. Pregnant.'

'I can see that,' he says. 'I'm glad, Abbie. I'm glad it all worked out.'

I'm not going to correct him – not here, not like this, while rain falls down around us. So I maintain my smile and acknowledge his comment. 'Thanks.'

He looks away from me. He doesn't know what to say now. And that's OK. Neither do I. So I say the only thing I can think of.

'I've just been on the Tube.'

Tom's eyes widen as he calls across to me. 'Really?'

'For the first time since . . .' I add.

'Wow,' he says, a small smile finding his lips. 'That's huge.'

'I know,' I reply.

Teddy looks understandably unimpressed by my story.

'How was it?' Tom asks.

'It was OK. I'm not sure I want to do it again in a hurry, but I know I *can* do it. So . . . that's the main thing.'

'Yeah, it is,' he says, wide-eyed amazement still on his face that I'm here.

Tom doesn't look a day older than when I last saw him – in his kitchen on the night of my leaving party.

Our conversation falters. I could say how much I've missed him, how I wish it hadn't been so long, and how I know it was all my fault that it was; that I wish things hadn't ended the way they did.

Instead I say gently, 'Bye, Tom. It was so lovely to see you again. And you, Teddy. Although you won't remember me.' I raise my hand to wave and, with the rain trying its best to destroy my ballet pumps, decide to brave it in search of a taxi. And as I say the words – as I utter my brief goodbye – it feels wrong. Because I know it will be years until I see Tom again. If ever at all.

Chapter 63

Tom

'Goodbye?' I call after Abbie as she starts down the lane. Is she serious? 'Is that it? You're just going to go?'

I step out from the doorway, holding Teddy's hand. Rain lashes down, but not on Teddy, who's cleverly clutching his umbrella.

She turns round. 'I'm not really sure what else there is to say.'

'There's plenty to say. You could tell me all about the baby, you could tell me what you've been up to, other than getting pregnant. We could . . . I don't know, we could talk about anything. Teddy's off pre-school today, which is good timing because today is—'

'It's my birthday today,' Teddy pipes up finally. *Nice one, son. Between us I'm sure we can keep her talking.*

'Oh, happy birthday,' she says. 'How old are you?'

'Four,' Teddy says. The rain's easing off a bit now, but we're so soaked it wouldn't matter if it continued for ever.

'Gosh. Time flies.'

'It does. He starts school in September,' I say.

'My God, Tom,' Abbie says. 'That's mad.' She directs her attention to Teddy. 'What presents did you get?'

She listens politely as Teddy reels off a list of items he received from me and from his friends who came to his birthday party at the weekend. Then he starts on the list of items Samantha and Ronald bought him. Abbie's face is so expressive, making 'wow' faces as she listens, totally ignoring the fact that she's drenched. Then she asks him something about one of the Transformer toys he's talking about, and Teddy lights up, grows animated as he explains how it moves. 'It's in my bag,' he says and points to his backpack. 'Do you want to see?'

'Sure.' And then, 'That's a lot of presents,' she says when he finishes showing her his toy and has worked his way verbally through his list. Above us, the rain has finished and the sun's making its way out, giving the cobbles an iridescent glow.

'Mummy and Ronald gave me loads of presents at the party at the weekend,' Teddy continues. 'But she saved all the Transformers for this morning, so I'd have something big to open when I woke up at their flat. And Daddy's giving me his presents tonight.'

I see Abbie frown as she computes Teddy's parental set-up, and then she understands and looks at me questioningly.

'Samantha and I aren't together any more,' I say.

She nods, her lips parting as if she wants to reply, but Teddy cuts her off.

'It doesn't mean Mummy and Daddy don't love me any more. They love me more than anything. They just don't love each other any more, which is OK because they're both *very happy now*.' Teddy's remembered my and Samantha's rationale word-for-word. We worked on how to phrase that for about an hour. It was an hour well spent. A shame we didn't spend all the other time we had together over the years being quite so cohesive.

Abbie looks at me, questioning this reasoning. Am I happy now?

I nod, smile.

'Well, that's good,' she says.

'It means I get two homes, because I see Mummy most weekends when she's not travelling, and I get two sets of birthday presents,' Teddy reasons.

'You can't say fairer than that,' Abbie replies.

I'm losing her now, I can feel it, and I look at my watch. Andy and Oliver are coming round to my house to celebrate Teddy's birthday and I don't want to have to leave to meet them just yet.

Abbie interprets the flick of my wrist incorrectly. 'I should go,' she offers. 'Let you guys enjoy the birthday fun.'

'We're having dinner with Andy and Oliver,' Teddy says, in his childish innocence not realising Abbie has no idea who these people are.

'My best mate and Teddy's best mate,' I clarify. 'They're coming round for takeaway and birthday cake.'

'Sounds lovely. Happy birthday again, Teddy,' she says and I know that's it. That's the end. 'Bye, Tom,' she says softly. She moves towards me and plants a gentle kiss on my cheek, and every brain cell fires up and shouts at me to keep her here a bit longer.

'Bye,' I say as she takes a step back, preparing to leave. 'Come for dinner,' I say suddenly.

'Sorry?'

'Come for dinner. Come for takeaway.'

'And birthday cake,' Teddy offers.

I silently thank Teddy, seconding my invite.

'Um . . .' She looks at me questioningly.

'Why not?' I ask. 'I haven't seen you in years. The next time we meet I may not be in a position to offer you cake.'

She laughs at this, and I wonder if I might not have lost her yet.

'Um . . .' She doesn't want to say yes. I know she doesn't. She settles on, 'Where? When?'

'My house. Putney. Now.'

She shifts from one foot to the other. Rays of sun shine on her blonde hair. God, I've really missed her.

'I don't know, Tom. It feels . . . odd.'

My brain screams to tell her that I know this. I know it's odd. How else was it ever going to be? But I don't say this. Instead I say, 'Why? It's just Andy and his son, and us. Small, intimate, low pressure. I've not seen you in so long, Abbie.'

'It's my birthday,' Teddy reminds her.

'It's his birthday,' I say with a grin, and she laughs again. 'Do those big eyes you do when I say no to a second ice cream,' I instruct Teddy and he does.

Abbie looks at Teddy's big, sad eyes, laughs. 'That's low, using a child like that.'

'Yeah, I know.'

She shifts from foot to foot again. 'OK,' she says. 'Maybe just for a bit. If you honestly don't mind?'

'I don't mind,' I say.

'I wasn't talking to you,' she says. 'I was asking the birth-day boy.'

'You can come if you don't eat all the cake,' Teddy reasons, looking at Abbie's stomach.

'I promise not to eat all the cake, and I didn't get this size because of cake,' she says. 'There's a baby in here.'

Teddy's eyes widen in happy surprise. 'In there?' he asks. Abbie nods.

'What kind of baby?' Teddy asks in awe.

'A really big one, I think,' Abbie replies, and that makes me laugh. She looks at me and I remember those eyes, which used to smile so much before they used to look at me like I was a piece of a shit, which I suppose I was.

'We can get a taxi,' I say, pre-empting any question that we might be getting the Tube.

She nods, visibly relieved. 'OK.' And then, 'How will I get home? Oh God, I've just realised I'll be miles away from home.'

'Where's home these days?' I ask.

'Enfield at the moment. I'm back with my parents to have the baby.'

'I'll drive you home later,' I say.

'You'll drive me all the way from Putney to Enfield?'

'It's not that far, in the grand scheme of things,' I tell her. 'Andy can look after the kids and I'll take you home. You won't have to get a train at night, or a Tube or wait for a taxi, or any of that.'

She crinkles her nose as she thinks. 'Really? You'll drive me home? I can't ask you to do that.'

'I'm offering. You're coming, right?'

She looks shy all of a sudden, uncertain. And then she smiles, a fraction. 'OK.'

Chapter 64

Abbie

'Oliver is my best friend,' Teddy tells me as the taxi pulls up outside Tom's house in Putney. I'd forgotten how huge his house is. The only other time I was here it was 1 a.m. and dark. I cringe at the memory of what happened and try to put it from my mind.

'And Andy is his dad, and he's nice but he swears a lot.'

'Ha,' I laugh as Tom splutters, 'What?' in response to Teddy's comment.

A man and a boy are waiting on the front step. 'About time,' the man calls. 'Where you lot been?'

When the taxi pulls away, Tom says, 'Andy this is Abbie. Abbie, this is Andy. Abbie and I are old friends. She's joining us for dinner.'

'Brilliant.' This stranger, Andy, accepts it without question. 'Are you hungry, Abbie, because I've already put the order in for a lot of pizza.'

'Sounds great. Thanks.'

Tom grins at me as he unlocks the door and Andy introduces me to his son.

The two boys immediately hurtle up the stairs at a pace that surprises me. 'I haven't moved that fast in what feels like for ever,' I say, resting my hand on my stomach.

'When's it due?' Andy asks as we enter the kitchen.

'When's what due?' I say, eyes wide and innocent.

'The baby?' Andy asks uncertainly.

'What baby?'

Andy turns white and mouths, 'Oh, shit' in Tom's direction.

'Baby's due in a couple of weeks,' I admit, saving him.

Andy stares at me and then at Tom. 'I quite like her,' he says. The doorbell rings and he goes to answer it, calling to the boys.

We sit down to eat, and it's lovely, casual, messy. Pizza grease coats our fingers as we discuss the new coalition government and how bonkers it is. And then Andy tells me about the children's cartoon that he and Tom have been working on.

'A cartoon?' I ask. 'That's incredible.'

'Tom's my money man,' Andy says, clearly proud of his friend. 'The brains behind the operation. He set us up with investor meetings that paid off, and now we're getting ready to record a pilot episode to take to market.'

I cast my gaze quickly in Tom's direction, and he glances back at me, smiles. He looks genuinely happy. I'm not sure I've ever seen him look like that. Tom and Andy continue telling me about how they're casting actors to narrate the voices.

'We don't know if we should try to hire really famous people, throw some serious money at it up front,' Andy says, 'or keep the budget slim and hope the concept sells itself.'

'Still to be decided,' Tom responds, throwing me a quick look that says, *The concept is going to have to sell itself*, before

Andy changes the subject and starts quizzing me about Singapore.

'So you've only just met each other again today, after three years?' Andy asks.

Tom nods, dropping a slice of pepperoni as he bites into his pizza. That's not the whole story, though. He gives no detail as to why we haven't spoken or seen each other and Andy doesn't probe, and I think it's best left that way. We sing 'Happy Birthday' to Teddy and cut his cake, each being given a slice and some forks by Teddy and Oliver – our proud waiters.

Then Teddy opens presents, and Tom's been thoughtful enough to buy Oliver one too, so he has something to open. The boys stay at the dining table and play.

'I'm sorry I didn't have anything to give him,' I say as Tom and I clear the plates.

'He's had quite enough, believe me. Father Christmas will have nothing left to give him at this rate,' he says.

Andy joins us in the kitchen and Tom says, 'Can you look after the boys when I run Abbie home tonight?'

'Sure. Teddy can come to ours for a sleepover, if you like, then you don't have to rush back and I'll take them both to pre-school in the morning.'

Tom looks grateful. 'I can come in and say hi to your parents,' he tells me.

'They'd like that. Oh, crap, I need to tell my parents where I am. They live in permanent fear that I'm on my own somewhere giving birth.'

I grab my phone, answer my mum's message, sent ages ago, about where I currently am with a very vague answer that assures her I'm safe. I can't say, 'I'm with Tom' without having to then engage in a text-rally with her as she quizzes me about it.

'So you moved to Singapore with a mate of Tom's from work and then got married?' Andy grabs a beer from the fridge.

I can't help feeling him being so at home here is a good thing. Tom never seemed to have any real friends before.

'Where's your fella tonight then?' Andy asks. 'Couldn't make it to Teddy's birthday tea?'

'He's not here.'

'Not in London?' Andy asks.

'Not in England,' I say.

The boys are playing Transformers at the end of the table, moving the pieces around to form cars, and then moving them back again to form robots.

'Not in England?' Andy asks.

I glance at Tom. He's looking directly at me, but he's not speaking. At a guess, he's waiting silently for Andy to keep asking questions.

'No,' I reply.

I was wrong about Tom, as he interjects sharply, 'Why not?'

I'm not hiding anything. It's no secret, but I feel very odd about saying it out loud. I feel even weirder saying it out loud to Tom while his friend is here. 'Sean and I aren't together any more.'

There's no register of shock or anger or . . . anything on Tom's face. Instead he lifts his water glass off the kitchen counter and drains most of it in one go and then puts it back down again. I can't tell what he's thinking. I force my gaze back to Andy, who I can see wants to probe deeper, even though he doesn't even know me. And when no one speaks, the awkwardness really sets in like a stain.

'We broke up,' I clarify, 'a couple of months ago. He wasn't into having a baby. He was into it, before it happened,' I ramble. 'And then he wasn't.'

Tom's face is still placid. 'And so, wait . . . what?'

'So I'm here on my own and I'm staying with my mum and dad, and I'm not sure what I'm doing, but whatever it is, I'm doing it on my own. Sort of.'

'On your own?' Andy says. 'He's not here?'

'He's not here,' I repeat. 'And he's not coming over for the birth, and instead every month or so a whole bunch of money drops into my bank account.'

There's a long pause and none of us speaks until Andy says, 'Fuck me sideways.'

'Yeah,' I say quickly. 'So there it is. I'm pregnant, I've left my husband – although I think you could say it was mutual – and in a matter of weeks I'm going to be a single mother.'

I can't see Tom's face. He's turned slowly, has started loading the dishwasher, although his movements are slow.

'Andy, tell me about you,' I say, to break the silence.

He launches in, only too happy to steer the conversation away from my predicament. He's saying something about the cartoon, but all I can focus on is Tom's clenched jaw as he moves to and from the dishwasher.

After an hour or so, Tom glances at the kitchen clock and then starts to round up the kids, with excited chatter about weeknight sleepovers. I say goodbye and happy birthday to Teddy as his football-shaped rucksack is heaved onto his shoulders, full of his overnight stuff; and his bag for pre-school is clutched in his little hands, ready for the morning. He really is a cute kid.

'Thank you for coming to my party,' he says to me, unprompted.

'Oh, thank you for having me,' I tell him and then I whisper in his ear, and he looks up at me and gives a huge smile.

Tom hugs his son and lifts him and his multiple bags into his arms, kisses Teddy on the head and then puts him down. 'Happy birthday, little man,' he says. 'Have a good sleepover.'

When Andy and the boys have gone, Tom closes the door and gestures for me to go back with him into the open-plan kitchen. I stand by the breakfast bar as he makes us both some tea.

'What did you whisper to Teddy?' he asks as he pours boiled water into mugs. 'Or is it a secret?'

'I told him I owed him a present and if he could think of something he'd like, then I'd like to get it for him.'

'He's going to be so spoiled,' Tom says. 'But thanks.'

'He's a lovely little boy,' I say. 'Genuinely. You've done really well, Tom.'

He shrugs. 'Ah, you know.'

'It must be tough, being a single parent.'

'You're about to find out,' he says.

'Yeah . . . I know. I'm not sure it's really sunk in yet.'

'You must have had a good reason to leave Sean,' Tom says. 'If you're sure you've done the right thing, then . . .' He doesn't finish the sentence.

'I am,' I reply. 'It worked when it was just the two of us. But I could see it wasn't going to work when we became a three. We weren't enough for him.' And because I can't stop myself, I tell him everything. I tell him how we could never match up to Sean's ambition; how he didn't want to move back home – ever, by the sounds of it; how much the power and the glory of his job had changed him; how lonely I was; how lonely I still am (although I wish I'd not said that bit), but how it was preferable to being with Sean, because in the end we were only going through the *motions* of being a happy couple while we were pregnant, because Sean wasn't happy. But it was too late to push the stop button. Until I went and pushed it anyway.

Tom sips his tea. There's silence.

'You're being really restrained,' I say eventually, when I can't bear it any more.

He runs his top teeth over his lower lip. 'Yes,' he says. 'I am.'

'OK, go on. I'm ready.'

'Ready for what?'

'I'm ready to hear what an idiot I am, or what an idiot Sean is – it's got to be on the tip of your tongue, right?'

'Has it?' he says.

I want to shake the restraint out of him. 'Yes, just say it,' I command. 'Get it over and done with. Say what you're thinking.'

'I can't fucking stand it!' Tom explodes. 'How can you bear this? How could he do that to you? How could he behave like that? I never understood how you two ended up together. The whole thing totally threw me.'

I'm not sure if I'm supposed to actually answer this or not. 'I liked him. I fell in love with him.'

'Fine. Whatever.'

I frown. 'I did.'

'If you say so.'

'What's that supposed to mean?'

'You honed in on each other because of me.'

I laugh and then realise Tom's serious. 'That's a bit vain,' I say. 'And that's not fair.'

'I reckon Sean knew I really liked you, and he went for you, regardless. He violated whatever code there was, whatever level of friendship we had; he downgraded us massively when he started dating you.'

'You two weren't even talking by then,' I retort. '*You and I* weren't even talking by then. As I recall, you and I almost slept together and then we stopped talking. And then you had a baby, and you became the star-billing in your own shitshow.' I can't stop the meanness.

'You think I don't know that?' he says. 'And so . . . what? Then you decide to go off with my friend? After what happened between us, that's a huge betrayal, all round. Was there really no one else in London you could have chosen? Did you choose each other specifically to fuck me off?'

'How dare you!' I shout. I liked Tom better when he was being restrained.

But he's still going. 'And then you come to my house the night of your leaving party and tell me you're in love with me, and then you run away and you don't answer your phone. I rang and I rang, and I messaged you and when I got a foreign dial tone I knew you'd gone with Sean, and then you disappeared entirely. You changed your number and you never even told me.'

'You were with Samantha. You had a baby together. What else was I going to do?'

'Wait. You could have waited. Even five fucking minutes. You could have waited for me to work out what the hell was going on. Instead you ran away.'

'I had to run away. I told you I loved you, and you said it back! It was going to ruin everything.'

'Of course I said it back. I meant it!'

I shake my head. I'm crying. I want to go home. Tom runs his hand through his hair, exhales and then rips kitchen roll from the dispenser and hands it to me.

I'm silent, and so is he.

I wipe my eyes with the scratchy kitchen paper. 'You should get some proper tissues in here for when people break down in tears in your kitchen.'

'You're the only person who cries in my kitchen.'

I feel a huge pull inside me. The baby. What's happening to the baby? I lift my eyes to Tom in horror and he springs towards me, swearing. He knows something's happened.

I look down in shock at the pool of liquid forming on the floor by my feet. All I can do is cry, 'What's happening?'

Chapter 65

Tom

I walk back into the room, where Abbie's dressed in a hospital gown and is holding onto the edge of the bed with gritted teeth. The midwives have been drifting in and out for the last few hours as her contractions have sped up. She's a terrible patient. They want to check how dilated she is, and it took every negotiation tactic they had to get her to lie down, so they could look.

She winced when they checked. I winced when they checked, but I held onto her hand tightly and she held onto mine.

And now she's practically refusing to lie down to let them assess her again.

'Where's my mum?' Abbie yells through contractions.

'I still can't get hold of her.'

'I'm not supposed to be here,' she cries and genuine tears roll down her face.

If she's about to spout bollocks about how she's meant to be in Singapore with that twat Sean, I'm . . . going to have to listen. I realise this is my job for now, to listen as she screams and shouts, swears and rants. Samantha was exactly the same, although her shouts were, 'It's all your fucking fault. It's all your fucking fault', much to the shock of the midwifery staff.

'I know you're not supposed to be here,' I say, rubbing her back. 'I know.'

'I'm not supposed to be at this hospital. I had it all planned. Did you tell my parents which hospital I'm in?'

'I left a voicemail.'

'Where are they? Don't leave me,' she screams as she bears down on another contraction.

'I'm not leaving you,' I tell her as her nails dig into my hand.

'Promise me,' she says when the pain passes. 'Promise me you won't leave me.'

There's sweat dripping down her face and she's red and panting. She's beautiful. I use my shirtsleeve to wipe her face. She looks tired already. She has no idea what's in store. Neither did I, until I stood here four years ago and went through this with Samantha.

'You men . . .' Abbie starts. 'You have the easy job. You just get to put the baby up there. We have to do *this*,' she screams as another pain shoots through her.

'I know,' I placate. 'We're shits.' This raises a laugh from the midwife, who then tries to look serious. 'If I could take the pain and do this for you, I would,' I say.

Abbie looks at me. 'You would *die*,' she cries. 'It hurts. You would die. Having a baby would rip you in half. I'm going to be ripped in half.'

Christ! 'No, you're not,' I tell her. 'You're going to be fine. Women do this every day. You're going to be fine.'

'You don't know that,' she cries and tears roll down her face.

'Are there any more drugs she can have?' I ask the midwife desperately.

'No!' Abbie cries. 'Gas and air. I only want gas and air.'

'We need to check again how dilated you are,' the midwife tells her.

'No,' Abbie cries. 'Not again. Please not again.'

If she can't cope with the midwives doing that, then she's going to be in for a shock, pain-wise, when the baby comes out.

'Maybe we should think about an epidural,' I suggest. 'I'm not sure gas and air is doing—'

'No!' Abbie shouts.

'OK,' I placate, helping her into position, 'OK.'

She grips my hand tightly, her eyes wide, boring into mine, as the midwife checks how dilated she is.

'You're not quite far enough yet, Abbie. No pushing until we say, remember,' she reminds her.

Abbie's sweating again. 'It's been hours,' she cries and grabs the mask to inhale on the drugs again. 'Why has it been so long? What is it *doing* in there? Why won't it come out?'

She lies back and stares at me, then a wave of calm descends over her and she wafts the gas-and-air mask around. 'It's really good,' she says. 'Do you want a hit?'

The midwife gives me a look as I say, 'Sure.' And then, 'No, no. I'm good.'

'Tom, it's so nice. Try it. Go on.'

I laugh. This is mental. 'Samantha couldn't wait to get an epidural. Practically put it in herself.'

'Samantha's his wife,' a drowsy Abbie tells the midwife.

'Oh,' she says and gives me a curious look.

'Ex-wife,' I say. 'Sort of. We're not divorced yet. Separated, though.' Stop talking, Tom. Too much detail.

The midwife looks between us, trying to work out what's going on here.

'We're just friends,' I say quickly. 'Abbie and me, I mean. Not Samantha and me. Although—'

'Shut up, Tom,' Abbie shouts and clenches my hand. 'I need to push.'

'Not yet, Abbie,' the midwife says. 'Soon, but not yet. I'm just going to go and get a colleague.'

'Why is she leaving?' Abbie looks at me desperately. 'Why is she leaving?'

'It's OK,' I tell her, but I don't know if this is a lie or not. This feels wrong. When Samantha's contractions were this close together, the midwives told her to push. Why isn't she dilated enough?

'I need to push,' she says conspiratorially. 'Can I push?' She wants me to say yes.

'Don't,' I tell her. 'Not yet. It'll be OK.'

Another midwife enters the room, bright and breezy. 'Hello,' she says, drawing out the word. She snaps on a glove, dives right in. 'I need to see what's going on up here.'

Bloody hell. I wince again. Abbie winces, her eyes boring into mine to make it all stop. I'm totally out of my depth here. I have no control over any of this. 'She's in a lot of pain,' I say unnecessarily, because Abbie screams again as a contraction hits.

'They're too close together, aren't they?' Abbie screams through her contraction.

The midwife doesn't comment.

'It's been hours,' I say. 'I know it's supposed to take a long time. But . . . is this right? It feels all wrong.'

'What?' Abbie asks. 'Why? Why?' I wish I hadn't said that out loud.

'You're not dilated enough yet, Abbie,' one of the mid-wives says.

They talk in hushed tones. Her contractions are coming too fast for how many centimetres she's dilated.

'Don't let them take me for a C-section,' Abbie begs. Her green eyes bore into mine. 'Tom, please. Help me. Don't let them put me to sleep. Promise me.'

'I can't promise you that,' I say. 'You need what's best for the baby and for you. But it will be OK.'

'Stop saying that,' she cries and then tears mix with sweat down her face and I wipe her red cheeks again. Her fingers wrap around my hand. 'Please, Tom,' she says weakly.

'Oh God, Abbie.' I hold her hand in return. 'We need to do what we're told and we'll be OK.'

'We?' she questions and then closes her eyes, briefly. 'Tom?' she says and her eyes ping open.

I nod.

'Why don't we talk any more?'

She's delirious on gas and air. 'We're talking now,' I say.

'Why didn't we see each other for all that time?'

'I'm here now. We're here now.' I brush hair from her face. Abbie looks calm. I think it's going to be OK.

'Abbie?' I say and she doesn't reply, just looks at me. 'Abbie?' I prompt.

'Mmm?'

What's going on?

'I can't do this,' she says.

'You have to. You've got no choice. You have to.'

'It's too hard,' she replies, and tears stream down her face as another contraction hits her and she clenches her face in pain.

349

'I know. But you have to. You are brave and strong and I love you, and you can do this because you have to.'

She doesn't answer and her face slackens.

'Abbie? Abbie? I love you. Don't go to sleep. You have to stay awake. Stay awake.'

The midwives rush me out of the way and listen to Abbie's heart, listen to the baby in her stomach. One tells the other to prep the surgical team.

'What's happening?' I ask.

'Emergency C-section,' the midwife says as she hauls up the sides on the bed and then rushes an unconscious Abbie out of the delivery suite and into the corridor.

I help push the bed and then an orderly rushes towards us and takes over, leaving me standing in the corridor. Abbie is sped away, through a set of double doors and then she's gone.

Chapter 66

Abbie

I open my eyes as I'm being wheeled on the bed through the corridor and see the glare of strip lighting as it blinds me and then it's gone, blinds me and then it's gone. Ceiling tiles and lights merge and swim above me, glare and fade. 'Where's Tom?' I ask.

The lighting overhead blinds. Bright, dark, bright, dark, bright.

He said he wouldn't leave me. Maybe he hasn't left me. Maybe I've left him.

And then everything goes dark.

Chapter 67

Tom

We argued and she's gone into labour early. I did this. Abbie's having the baby early – *weeks* earlier than she should be – because of me. I'm the worst kind of man. I look at my watch and see the hours have drifted into the next day. It's seven minutes past midnight. My phone rings. 'Hello?'

'Tom?' Abbie's dad says in a panic. 'We've been in the theatre and then at a bar with friends,' he rushes out. 'Abbie messaged to say she was fine and then . . . We've just found all your messages on my phone. We're on our way.'

I'm exhausted. I nod. 'Great.'

'What's happening?'

'She's still in surgery. They're giving her a C-section. She's been in for a really long time.' I'm crying. I'm actually bloody crying.

'She'll be fine,' Ken tells me. He can't know that. He's not here.

'Yeah,' I reply. I don't have the energy to say anything else.

'We'll be with you soon,' he says.

'OK.' I wipe my face, say goodbye and hang up. My eyes are tired, raw from all the rubbing. Abbie is in surgery, having a baby. What is taking so long? I've been so patient, but I can't do this any more. I stand up, walk towards the door of the little room they've put me in, full of plastic chairs and placid artwork.

A midwife enters the room as I'm on the verge of leaving. 'Abbie O'Hara's birth partner?'

'Yes?' I say quickly, because I suppose I am.

'The baby's been delivered,' the nurse says. 'A little girl.'

I make a strange noise from the back of my throat and fresh tears fall again, but I don't know why.

But her face is sombre.

'What about Abbie?' I ask quickly.

Her face says everything.

'Is she dead?' I think I'm going to be sick.

'She's not dead,' the midwife replies quickly. 'She is, however, taking a bit longer to come round from the anaesthetic than we'd like.'

Relief, sweet relief. 'OK,' I say. 'What does that mean? Taking longer to come round?'

'She's still asleep,' the midwife says.

'Like in a coma?' I ask, the horror of the situation dawning on me.

'No, not in a coma, but having a very long, very deep sleep. Anaesthetic can sometimes do this to people. Everyone wakes up in their own time.'

'She will wake up, though?'

The midwife is non-committal on this. She smiles. 'It's just taking a bit longer than usual. I'll keep you posted. She's being very well looked after. When she wakes up, we'll let you know.'

'Can I see her?' I ask. I feel this urge to check she's not dead.

'You can't see Abbie yet, I'm afraid, but would you like to see the baby?'

I stand up straighter. 'Can I?'

'Of course. Wait here and I'll get someone to take you through.'

I pace back and forth in the waiting room until the midwife who spent the majority of her time with us, checking how dilated Abbie was, arrives.

'Hello again,' she says brightly. 'Want to come and see baby O'Hara?'

'Yes,' I say, squirming a little that the poor baby has automatically been given Sean's last name, even though he's not around.

'You can give her a little bottle-feed if you like.'

'Really? Shouldn't Abbie do that?'

'Abbie's indisposed at the moment.'

'Right. Of course.' I'm shaking. Why am I shaking?

'Baby's a bit jaundiced, so she's under a lamp.' I'm led to a small side-room, where little plastic cribs are positioned at waist height, and three or four newborns are sleeping or stirring and making noises under lamps.

'Here she is,' the midwife says, double-checking the tag on the baby's ankle.

She picks up Abbie's baby and wraps a blanket over her, now that she's not under the lamp. Her little umbilical cord is clamped and bandaged, and she's wearing a small white hat and nappy. It occurs to me that Abbie doesn't have anything here for the baby, and so her little girl is wearing things donated by the hospital.

'Would you like to sit down and feed her?'

'Am I allowed?' I ask stupidly.

'Yes, we'll be here to help.'

'OK.' I sit down in a large pleather chair, and a tiny bundle of warmth is placed in my arms. 'Hi there,' I say softly and stare at this little thing that Abbie worked so hard at. 'Your mum's a bit busy at the moment, but she'll be here soon and then you can start giving her merry hell. Until then, it's me, I'm afraid.'

The baby is still; her eyes flicker open and she looks at me, begins crying.

'Girls always react like that to me,' I joke.

The midwife smiles, hands me a little bottle of warm milk. 'She only needs a bit for now, and then it's back under the lamp for her.'

I nod, tip it up, making sure there's no air in the teat, remembering all of this from when Teddy was a baby. It doesn't feel that long ago really. The baby settles in with the bottle, sucking milk down eagerly.

'Have you thought of any names?' the midwife asks conversationally.

I blink. 'It's not my place to think of names. Abbie's not . . . she's not my . . . we're not together.'

'Ah, I see,' the midwife replies as if she understands, and then she clearly doesn't, because she prompts, 'I heard you say you loved her, and so I presumed . . .'

'Yeah,' I say slowly after a few seconds. 'I forgot I'd said that. In hindsight, I probably shouldn't have done that. It wasn't the time or the place.'

'It was probably both the time *and* the place,' the midwife replies. 'But if it's any consolation, I don't think she heard you.'

'I don't think she heard me, either. She was a bit busy passing out.'

The baby finishes her bottle and the midwife instructs me to wind her. I place her up near my shoulder and rub her back, the way I used to do with Teddy. It's all coming back to me now. A little burp emanates from this tiny little thing, and the midwife takes her and puts her in the crib and the lamp goes back on. I stand there, watching her little face as she puckers her mouth, and then the expression on her face rests.

'She's so beautiful,' I say. I'm completely mesmerised by Abbie's baby.

The second midwife pops her head round the door as I stare at the baby.

'Abbie's awake.'

Chapter 68

Abbie

Tom stands at the door of the side-room where I've been placed.

The midwives have been so wonderful, making me comfortable, bringing me my baby. My baby. It feels so strange to think I have a baby. She's tiny, so adorable. I can't believe I grew her.

I'm holding her in my arms.

'She's beautiful,' Tom says, standing at the door with his hands in his pockets.

'Are you coming in?' I ask and he moves towards me, pulls the chair out next to the bed and sits down, gazing at us both.

'Jackie says you've already had a cuddle and a feed,' I say.

'Who's Jackie?'

The midwife who spent most of last night and the early hours of the morning with us gives him a look.

'Sorry,' he says, shamefaced. 'I was a bit busy worrying Abbie might be dead to be asking people for their names.'

'It's literally on her name badge,' I say, smiling. 'And I did say I didn't want a C-section. I react really badly to anaesthetic.'

'You neglected to mention that very important detail, and I kind of think there was no choice.'

'I was busy trying not to push,' I say.

'You did really well,' Tom says and tears suddenly fall down his face.

'Are you OK?' I ask. 'Why are you crying?'

'I thought you were dying.'

'Oh, Tom,' I say. I've got tubes and all sorts coming out of my hand and I'm clutching my baby. I can't reach out and stroke his hand, his hair, even though I really want to, so I just repeat softly, 'Oh, Tom. Thank you. Thank you for being here.'

'It's my fault you're here,' he says.

'What are you talking about?'

But he doesn't get the chance to answer because his phone rings and he answers it. 'It's your mum and dad – they're outside.'

'Visiting hours aren't for another five hours yet,' Jackie cuts in.

'Oh, yeah,' Tom says, unimpressed. 'I remember all this from when Teddy was born in the middle of the night too, at what the nurses deemed a thoroughly inconvenient time. Can she at least see her mum?' he asks.

'Don't worry,' I cut in, placating him. 'It's fine. They can come when it's time.'

Jackie gives Tom a withering expression. If he carries on like this, he'll get kicked out any second.

'Talk to your mum,' he says and holds the phone up to my ear.

I can't help but cry into it as I tell my mum and dad I'm fine, that the baby is fine and is going back under the lamp, now that we've had a cuddle, but will come back and we'll try breastfeeding soon. They say if I'm OK, they'll go back home and get changed and come back later in the morning, although they really don't want to leave.

'It's OK. Go home. I'm safe. I'm with Tom.'

'And Jackie,' Tom offers, trying to get the midwife back onside.

Jackie gives him another withering look and leaves the room for a moment when I say goodbye to my parents.

'Jackie and I were best mates up until three minutes ago,' Tom says knowingly.

'You didn't even know her name,' I point out as I gaze down at my little newborn.

Tom sighs, looks fondly at my little girl. 'Abbie, I was absolutely petrified you were going to die.'

'I'm sorry,' I say, still groggy. 'I passed out and had no idea about any of it.'

'Lucky for you. I've been through hell in that waiting room. I thought I'd killed you. It was my fault.'

'Why do you keep saying that?' I ask.

Jackie arrives again. 'Time to take little one back to the lamp, and time for you to get some rest, Abbie. If you want to try breastfeeding—'

'I do,' I say.

'Then we'll come back when she wants her next feed.'

I watch as my tiny little bundle is taken gently from my arms and carried away to be put under a lamp. Bereft, I start crying the moment she's gone, and Tom leans forward and holds me. He smells of cologne and sweat, and an evening spent in a hospital and . . . of Tom. I nestle in, my face against his chest.

'Having a baby is emotional,' I say, crying into Tom's shirt.

'You ain't seen nothing yet,' he laughs.

'Oh God, really? Isn't this the hard bit?'

''Fraid not. You'll spend the rest of your life stressing about that little girl – whether she's developing properly, whether she's sick or upset. My God, it's all a total rollercoaster. But it's wonderful as well.'

'It sounds absolutely awful,' I say and I cry heaving sobs into Tom's chest again.

He laughs. 'You'll be fine.' I feel him kiss the top of my head.

I lie back on the bed, drained. Anaesthetic has always messed me up. When I was fifteen I had to have my appendix out and it took two hours for me to come round from the procedure. General anaesthetics and I are clearly still not a match made in heaven.

'OK,' Jackie says, returning, 'baby is settled under the lamp and it's time for you to let Abbie rest,' she tells Tom.

'Don't leave,' I say, clasping his shirt. The thought of him leaving fills me with dread, sadness – as bereft as I felt when my tiny newborn was taken away, although I knew she was going to a place of safety.

Tom gives Jackie an uncertain look, pleading to stay.

'Sorry. We can't have men on the ward overnight. But you can come back at visiting time.'

'OK,' I say, resigned. I let go of Tom's bunched shirt. I don't have the energy to fight, and I could definitely sleep again.

Tom bends down and kisses me on the top of my head again. 'You did really well,' he says into my hair and then rises.

'Tom—' There's so much I want to say, and so much I don't want to say.

'Yeah?' he asks, turning back to me. 'I'll be back in the morning, if you want me?'

'I do,' I say quickly. 'I do.'

'OK. Get some sleep.'

'I'll try. Tom, thanks for being here.'

'Abbie, you're so very welcome.'

And then he's gone and I think I've lost the chance to say what I wanted to. But I'm so tired I've forgotten what it was.

Chapter 69

Abbie

'I can't think of a name,' I tell my mum and dad as they hold my newborn. 'I've been thinking of boys' and girls' names since I found out I was pregnant and there's nothing.'

'It'll come to you,' my dad says.

Despite being tired, I had drifted in and out of sleep and kept opening my eyes, expecting to see my baby being brought back in to me, expecting to see Tom in the chair next to me. But instead I was alone.

On her final visit to see me and help with breastfeeding, Jackie said goodbye as she finished her shift and a new, fresh and bouncy team of midwives arrived, who I hadn't spent the whole night trying to push out a baby with. I felt lost after Jackie went. Everyone had left me: Tom, the baby, no-nonsense Jackie – all gone.

But now the baby's back and I need to stop being silly, emotional. Tom's not back yet, despite saying he would be. I woke up and, alongside my little baby, he was all I could think about. He was wonderful yesterday and I tell my parents how amazing he was, how he drove me to the hospital, took me straight up to the maternity ward and helped me fill in paperwork while I was huffing and puffing. I must have looked a state. I felt a state.

'He held my hand the whole way through the labour until I was taken away,' I say and my mum smiles, but I think it's at the baby and not at my enthusiastic portrayal of Tom.

'He messaged this morning,' my dad says. 'Only two visitors allowed at a time, so he'll be here in the early evening instead, if you'd like.'

'Oh,' I say, disappointed he's not coming until later. 'Yes, I would like that.'

'I'll reply and tell him then,' my dad says.

Tom could have messaged me, and I look at my phone to check that I've not missed a text from him. I haven't.

I also realise that Sean hasn't replied. I sent him a message to tell him I'd had the baby early and that it was a girl. I didn't ask for help in choosing a name. I didn't ask if he wanted to come and see her. I didn't ask anything. I didn't expect him to offer anything, but I did expect a reply, an acknowledgement that our child had entered the world safely. I realise now that when I left him I gave him an 'out' and he's grasped it with both hands.

'Darling, we're so proud of you,' my mum says and my dad echoes it, and then they tell me about how they're going to handle the next few weeks until they break up for the summer holidays, trying to work out how to support me while not being able to take time off. They were relying on me giving birth nearer my due date, which would have taken them comfortably into the six weeks' holidays when they'd have been around.

My mum goes through the bag of stuff she's brought from home for me and baby – the nappies and a couple of white babygrows I'd purchased. I hadn't managed to buy anywhere near the right amount of items yet. I thought I still had a few weeks to go, and I had yet to undertake a huge blitz in Mothercare of neutral yellow and cream outfits, just to get us going.

And then visiting hours are over and I'm left alone, in time for a lunch tray to be brought to me. Baby comes back from the lamp and we breastfeed together again.

'We're alone, little one,' I say quietly as she sucks away. 'And I'm sorry to say it, but I think that's kind of how this is going to play out.' I stroke her little cheek, so soft, so thin and delicate. She's so small, being so early. 'It might be just you and me for quite some time,' I tell her. 'But that's OK, isn't it? We can do this. We'll learn together.'

Chapter 70

Tom

Abbie's sleeping when I arrive. I stand by the door and watch her. A ridiculous number of feelings rush through me, all at the same time. It's only Teddy, standing next to me quietly and tugging my hand gently, that shakes me out of my daze and into a slow action. I nod at him, usher him gently into the room.

The baby's been moved into a little plastic crib next to Abbie, and I guess it's because she doesn't need the lamp any more. She looks a much better colour. Abbie looks a much better colour too. She was ashen yesterday.

Teddy and I stare at the baby, marked 'Baby Girl O'Hara' on the end of her crib. She still doesn't have a name then. I wonder if Sean will turn up at some point and bestow one on the kid. He might be the hero of the hour, sweep in, declare undying love for Abbie and his child, whisk them back to Singapore and then I'll never see them again.

I'm not sure I could deal with that now, even though only twenty-four hours ago Singapore is exactly where I thought she still was.

'She's so small,' Teddy whispers, his hand still in mine.

'She is,' I whisper back. 'She's gorgeous too.'

He points to the bag I'm carrying. 'Can we give the baby the presents now?'

'Sure,' I say. 'Put them at the end of her crib, not up by her face.'

Teddy does as he's told, placing a little plush toy giraffe and an elephant at the end of the blankets. He's a bit put out that the baby can't see them and I have to go through the reasons why the toys can't be next to her face, and we agree that when the little one wakes up, he can hold them up to show her. We went into Mothercare after pre-school together and I bought things that I wasn't sure Abbie had: a few little newborn outfits, a pack of nappies, some of those pre-mixed milk cartons that might save Abbie's sanity in the middle of the night, if baby can't be bothered to latch on and breast-feed correctly. Those pre-mixed cartons saved my own and Samantha's mental stability in the early days. I should have bought shares in them.

'You're here,' Abbie says groggily.

'Of course,' I reply gently.

'You didn't come this morning.'

'I wanted to let your mum and dad come, and not have to be kicked out after a while to let me in. I didn't think you'd mind me not coming.'

She doesn't reply, and her face looks thoughtful. She looks towards Teddy, still peering into the crib. Abbie smiles at him. 'Hi.'

'Hi,' he says back. 'Can I hold her?'

I cut in, 'Oh, I don't know about—'

'Of course,' Abbie says. 'Maybe your dad can help you while you sit down and hold her on your lap?'

Teddy nods, jumps into the plastic chair by the side of Abbie's bed.

I pause by the crib. God, I'm a bit scared of picking the baby up. I stare at her little mouth puckering in her sleep and feel like someone's kicked me in the guts. What is this feeling? I can't tell if it is a good feeling or not.

'You OK?' Abbie asks.

'Yep,' I say, in a strangled version of what I normally sound like.

'You remember how to hold a baby, right?' Abbie asks, now genuinely concerned.

I held her yesterday, I want to remind Abbie, but I can't actually articulate that sentence. 'Yep.' *Why is my voice doing this?*

I pick the baby up, support her head, hold her in my arms, stare down into her little face. My guts rip in half again. 'Hi there,' I say to the sleeping baby, my eyes locked on her face.

'Dad?' Teddy prompts. He's already got his arms out, as if he's holding her.

'Yep,' I say and move towards Teddy, place the baby into his little arms and then keep my hands firmly around the newborn.

'Hello, baby,' Teddy says.

I cast a glance at Abbie as Teddy witters away to the baby about his day. He's almost whispering to her, so I can barely hear what he's saying.

Abbie smiles as she watches my son create a bond with her daughter. The baby slowly opens her eyes, locks on to Teddy and stares at him silently as he chats away at her. I regret not being able to give Teddy a sibling. There's not much I can do about that now. He'll have to suffer being an only child, as I was.

'Sorry,' I mouth at Abbie.

'It's fine,' she mouths back at me.

'Andy's on a book deadline, so he couldn't take Teddy. He's put Oliver on a late pick-up and it's full, so I couldn't put Teddy there. I left it a bit late to think about it.'

'It's fine,' Abbie reiterates warmly. 'It's nice to see you both. I've missed you.'

'Have you?'

She nods. I'm not sure what to make of that.

'Teddy and I went shopping. We bought some things for the baby.'

'Can I show her, Dad?' Teddy tries to wriggle off the chair and I lift the baby up to my chest, standing up, as he goes to the crib and extracts the giraffe and elephant.

'Look, baby,' he says and waves them around at her.

'Hold them still,' I say, 'then she can see them.'

'They're lovely,' Abbie says. 'They're her very first toys. Thank you, Teddy. And thank you for buying all those other bits. You really didn't have to, but I'm so glad you did. I've got barely anything.'

'Why isn't she taking them?' Teddy asks.

'She can't reach out for things yet,' Abbie says apologetically. 'She can only cry and suck down milk at the moment.'

'That's a bit boring,' Teddy decides.

Abbie laughs. 'Yes, it is a bit, actually.'

'She'll give you a run for your money soon enough,' I say. 'I remember when Teddy first started walking. We were on holiday when he began, and I thought, *Oh no, this is it. Freedom has ended.* And, sure enough, I spent the rest of the holiday running around with Teddy as he decided he needed to run and fall over absolutely everywhere. Now you hate walking. Always want to be carried.'

Teddy nods wisely. 'Daddy gives the best piggybacks, so I don't need to walk.'

'You're a victim of your own success,' Abbie tells me.

I smile at her and she smiles at me, and Teddy holds the giraffe up in the baby's eyeline and this moment – here, like this – is so perfect I never want it to end.

'I'm going home tomorrow,' Abbie says, heralding the end of perfection. In less than twenty-four hours' time we'll each go back to our lives, and that will be it.

'That's great,' I lie.

'*We're* going home tomorrow,' Abbie corrects herself. 'Not just me. I forget we're a duo now. A team.'

'You and baby-no-name?' I tease.

'Me and baby-no-name,' Abbie laughs back at me. 'I'm working on the no-name bit, though, I promise.'

'You're going to be a great team,' I say. 'Whatever you call her.'

'We're going to have to be,' Abbie says. 'Mum and Dad need to work every day, so it's only going to be me and baby-no-name at home for the next three weeks until their summer holidays start. And I really don't want to bother my parents in the middle of the night, given that they have to get up at six a.m. every day.'

'So what are you going to do?'

'Do what every other single mother does. Get up and do the nappies and feeds on my own every night. And then I'll go for walks to the park or the coffee shop, when I'm able to move properly. It might take a few days, though, before I can do all this by myself, with these stitches. You should see the line they cut through my stomach. Did you know they have to cut through muscle to get to the uterus? I mean, of course they did, but it didn't occur to me that's what would happen. I can barely move. I'm sucking down paracetamol like they're Smarties.'

'How are you going to get up in the middle of the night and run around doing nappies and feeds then, if you're in pain and can't move?'

'*Really, really* slowly,' Abbie says thoughtfully. 'I remind myself that single mothers do this, day in, day out. And I am a single mother now.'

'But you don't have to do it on your own.'

'What else am I going to do? I can't bother my parents all through the night every time she wakes up and cries for a feed or a change, or because she's got wind or whatever else is going on in that little body of hers. They'll be useless at work the next day. They're not spring chickens any more. I'm just going to have to dig deep and get on with it. It's only for a few weeks, until my stitches hurt less.'

I look at the baby in my arms, sleeping soundly again. Her lips are puckered, as if waiting for a kiss. Teddy's slipped his hand into the baby's and his mouth makes an excited O-shape as the baby's hand clasps his. Everything hurts inside again.

I drag my eyes away from the baby and look at Abbie, smiling at the scene in front of her.

'Stay with me,' I say quietly. 'Stay with us.'

'What?'

I clearly haven't thought this through, but I persevere regardless. 'Stay with us. We have a spare room that you can both sleep in. I'll hear her cry. I'm a father, I'm trained to hear babies cry,' I joke. 'I'll get up and down in the night and help lift her to you for feeds. I work from home, so it's not like I'm going to be late for work if I'm tired. We can do it for a couple of weeks, until your stitches start healing and your parents begin the school summer holidays.'

Abbie looks unsure. But she's not saying no. So I go in for the kill.

'We still have Teddy's bottle steriliser and his crib and bedding in the loft; and all his little white babygrows and vests, and hats and scratch mitts. I can wash it all tonight. And I can run out tomorrow morning after I've dropped Teddy at pre-school and before the hospital lets you go, and I can grab things you still need, so we're ready: new mattress for the crib, bottles, extra nappies or . . . whatever you don't have.'

Abbie's thinking, while Teddy moans that he wants to miss pre-school and go shopping for the baby again.

'And you won't be able to drive for a few weeks,' I continue. 'Because of the surgery, so during the day when your parents are at work I'll be there to ferry you around, if you need to go somewhere and can't walk it.'

I'm pretty certain I've got her now. I look at Teddy. His face is beyond excited. 'Is the baby coming home with us?' he asks.

'I don't know,' I say truthfully. 'Abbie, there's no stress. Really. It takes the pressure off your parents and means you don't have to risk ripping your stitches open, hauling yourself in and out of bed, trying to get to the baby before she wakes your parents each night.'

She nods, unconvinced. She's looking from Teddy to me. 'But it's weird,' she says. 'Isn't it?'

'It's weird if you make it weird.'

She rolls her eyes and then smiles. 'I don't know.'

'I can change nappies, I can hand her to you to feed and, if you're too tired, I'll grab a bottle and feed her while you sleep.'

'I can change nappies too,' Teddy volunteers. I give him a wink. *Well done, son.* 'And I can help feed her a bottle, if someone shows me how.' *Yes, Teddy. Nice one.*

Abbie's smiling. 'Tom . . .'

'What?' I say.

She's shaking her head, but she's still smiling at the same time.

'I'll be there to help when you most need it,' I continue. 'Let me help. Let us help.'

'You're ridiculous,' Abbie says, but laughter fills her face and at this point I'd be surprised if she says no.

Teddy reads her expression and laughs too, pleased to have been joint instigator in this not-very-well-thought-out plan that I've managed to conjure out of thin air like a magician.

'I don't know what to say,' Abbie confesses. 'Are you sure?'

I nod, look down at the tiny person in my arms. *What's happening to my heart? Only good things.* 'Yes. Yes, I'm completely sure.'

'Then . . . thank you. How about we try for one or two nights and, if you're put off by the constant baby screams, then I go back to my mum and dad's and we don't darken your door ever again.'

'OK,' I acquiesce. 'But that's not what's going to happen.'

She laughs again, mutters under her breath how mad I must be and watches as Teddy does a crazy little dance up and down, fuelled by sheer excitement.

I think Abbie's right. I must not be in my right mind. Because I am really looking forward to this.

Chapter 71

Abbie

After a couple of hours Tom and Teddy are ushered out by another knowledgeable but stern midwife whom Tom labels 'Jackie 2.0', and I spend the next few hours after they're gone rubbing my fingers back and forth over my rough lips, made dry by crying out through the labour that never was.

I look out of the hospital window as the summer beats down. I can't wait to get out of here. Baby and I have been feeding, cuddling and sleeping and now dusk threatens to settle, bringing another day to a close. We're a family of two, baby and me. I knew it was going to be that way, but I'm still feeling a strange mix of shock and disbelief that it's turned out like this.

Eventually Sean deigns to reply to my message, acknowledging the baby's arrival, asking how we all are, asking if he can phone me. I don't want to speak to him and, when I ignore his request, messaging to answer all his other questions, our texting comes to an end.

My mum and dad are relieved and enthusiastic when I call and tell them that Tom's stepped in to take the pressure off them. I can't help but agree when my dad tells me what a good egg Tom is. I say goodbye, and they say they'll come and see me at Tom's tomorrow afternoon when they've finished work.

Am I wrong for agreeing to stay with Tom? It's so generous of him. I think back over the time I've known him, the way we collided into each other's lives that night; the way we almost started something together five years ago; the way we almost started something again three years ago. And now look at us. Two failed marriages and two children between us. Yes, there have been imperfections there – too many to count. Tom has been practically riddled with imperfections.

But then so have I.

Tom opens the front door and carries the car seat holding my sleeping baby into his house, placing her in the sitting room, and then jogs back towards me as I move slowly down the path. He grabs my bags from the ground and helps me cross the threshold.

He was true to his word – driving us home to his house, even remembering to bring Teddy's old baby car seat, which it hadn't even occurred to me I would need. I'm obviously a slow learner, still groggy from strange sleep patterns and the always-there dull ache in my lower abdomen from the C-section.

'You've thought of everything,' I say, looking around his large open-plan kitchen. There's a changing table in front of the built-in bookshelves, laid out with baby wipes and a mat, nappies and mini muslins. I've no clue what to do with them.

'There's a changing table down here,' he says. 'And one in your room. The crib's in your room, and there's a bassinette basket-thing over there.' He points. 'I can't remember what they're called. But it means that if baby wants a sleep and you're down here, you don't have to climb the stairs to put her down.'

I go to speak, but Tom continues.

'There's freshly washed bedding, in that non-bio stuff Samantha always made me use when Teddy was small. And new mattresses, which are a must . . . apparently. Mothercare did very well out of me this morning.' I open my mouth to speak, but he steams right along, held on the crest of his one-sided conversational wave. 'Your mum and dad came over earlier for a cup of tea,' he says, which elicits a startled glance from me.

'Really?'

He nods. 'They brought all the stuff you'd bought for baby, and a load of your maternity clothes.'

'They've chucked me out then?'

Tom laughs. 'They don't like you having to be here,' he says.

'That's bullshit,' I offer. 'They love you. Adore you. My dad thinks the sun shines out of you.'

'He's not wrong,' Tom says with a grin.

His smile is infectious and I can't help but smile back.

'It's only for a few weeks,' he placates me.

I glance around. There is baby stuff everywhere. Some new toys with tags attached sit on the side, and others that must have been Teddy's look suspiciously cleaned and are already on a play mat, with items that dangle down for baby to look at. 'Really? A few weeks? It looks like I'll be here for ever. Tom, how much stuff did you buy?'

He shrugs. 'A bit.'

'How much did you spend?'

He laughs. 'A bit.'

I tut. 'Do I owe you huge sums of money?'

Tom shakes his head. 'It's my treat.'

'Tom . . .' I warn.

'Please let me do this,' he says softly.

'Buying all the stuff or housing us?'

'Both. All of it.' He leaves it there, and so do I.

I can't speak because I'm crying again. What is wrong with me? Why am I crying all the time? Tom walks towards me, soothing me by saying my name. As if in solidarity, baby wakes up and begins crying.

Tom changes direction and goes towards her while I stand wiping my eyes.

'There's a box of tissues on the island,' he says as he unclips baby and soothes her, holding her close and bobbing up and down.

'Are they for me?' I tease.

'A hundred per cent they're for you. They were top of the list when I went shopping today. I thought: what will Abbie need most of all? Tissues for when she inevitably cries in my kitchen.'

My tears turn to laughter as I wipe my eyes. 'You're a smug bastard,' I say, but I don't mean it. I hope he knows that.

Tom winks at me. 'Language! You're as bad as Andy. Fires his swear gun the very moment the kids enter the room.'

'You're lucky to have him as a friend,' I say as I move towards the man holding my baby. 'Even with all the swearing.'

'Yeah, he's all right. I have been lucky actually. Andy's a good person to have when the going gets tough. A like-minded soul. I hope I'm that for him.'

'It sounds like you are.'

Who is my like-minded soul when the going gets tough? Natasha, who wants so desperately to come over and see the baby tomorrow. I hope Tom doesn't mind. I look at him, bobbing up and down with my baby. My heart accelerates, not for the first time since he stepped out of his flat two days ago and found me standing in front of him. The baby starts crying again. I haven't been able to get up to change her nappy yet. The healthcare assistants did it for me when I was alone in hospital, and then Tom or my mum did it.

Tom moves over to the change unit and begins deftly removing her nappy with one hand and holding her legs up with the other.

'Can I?' I ask. 'I've not done it yet.'

'Sure. Sorry, am I taking over? Stop me if I'm becoming a little too much.'

'You're not,' I say genuinely. 'But you might have to show me what to do.'

I change my baby's nappy for the first time since she was born, standing up and trying to bend at the waist in order to stop my stitches tugging. Tom hands me damp muslin squares from a fresh pot of water to wipe and then dry her with, and then some nappy balm. He's thought of everything.

'You're a bit of a natural dad, aren't you?' I ask.

'No way. I had to learn. It was hard. Rock-hard.'

'I'm not sure I believe you,' I say as I pick up my little girl, freshly changed and back in her babygrow. Aware of my surgery, I slowly place her into the bouncer chair Tom has rediscovered from Teddy's baby days.

'Truly,' he enthuses. 'I'd never even held a baby until we had Teddy. And I didn't know anything about winding them.

I kept putting him straight down after a feed and wondering why he screamed blue murder. Samantha was equally clueless and we had to look it up on the internet.'

'That makes me feel a bit better,' I say.

'About what?'

'About not having a clue what I'm doing.'

'You will. And I'm here to do all the heavy lifting. And if you need a shoulder to cry on, when it all gets a bit too much . . .'

I finish his sentence for him. 'Then I can lean on your shoulder?'

'No way,' he says with a sideways smile. 'You can just mainline that box of Kleenex I've provided over there. I don't want to know anything about it.'

'Sod!' I say as something catches my eye over on the bookshelves. 'Tom, you kept it . . . all this time?' I say as I see the grey Beanie Baby propped up on his hindquarters.

Tom smiles and then says quietly, 'Of course.'

There's no *of course* about it. I don't know what to make of him keeping it. I don't want to read too much into it. I remember that day, that night with him, dancing in the club, the impromptu trip to McDonald's. I wonder if he attaches any significance to that or if it's me being ridiculous. After all, it's only a toy.

'I take it you didn't keep yours?' he asks casually, but his eyes are locked onto me.

'Of course I kept mine,' I say. 'I left it here when I went to Asia. But I kept it.' In truth, it was important that I left it in the UK – important that I did *not* take it with me, when I was supposed to be starting a new life with Sean. It stayed at Mum and Dad's. Out of sight. Out of mind. As Tom was supposed to be, but never quite was.

We're quiet for a moment.

'Shall I make us some coffee or tea or . . . ?' Tom asks, delicately slicing through what might have become an awkward silence.

'No,' I say. 'I'll make it and you sit down. You've earned it. After his protestations I begin hobbling around in the kitchen, familiarising myself with the layout and where the cups and coffee pods are kept. I'm desperate for something caffeinated. I can feel him watching me. For reasons that won't present themselves, I can't work out if I like it or not as Tom's eyes trail me around the kitchen. I glance at him and he smiles, then looks away, almost embarrassed. And then, when I glance back, he's crouched on the floor, trying to fit the overhead toys to the bar on the bouncer chair for my little girl to look at. My heart lifts itself into a place I didn't know existed. I look back at the coffee machine. Have I put in a pod already? I've driven myself into a state of confusion.

From the chair my little girl screams with ferocity, suddenly making even Tom jump.

'Boobs,' he says loudly over her crying, which makes me sputter with laughter.

'Is that shorthand for *the baby would like to be fed*?' I enquire.

'It is. It's faster to say.'

I can't help but chuckle again, and sit down while Tom lifts her out and lowers her down to me. It's so fluid, easy. Why is it so easy to be with Tom, like this, when our lives are now more complex than ever? It should have been easy back then, only it wasn't.

I'm thinking about this so much that I stop thinking about the process of breastfeeding – my movements now natural. It's become so normal to simply open my shirt, unclip my maternity bra and flop out a boob that I do exactly that now, without a second thought. Tom gasps audibly and spins round, crashing into the changing unit.

'Fuck! Forgot that was there. Sorry. I didn't mean to look.'

I can't reply because I'm laughing, and now baby's struggling to latch on because my shoulders are shaking so much at Tom's reaction. My newborn cries loudly with anger and rage that the boob she's so desperate for is just out of grasp, shaking as I laugh. I lower it into her mouth and she suckles me eagerly. Tom's still facing the corner of the room, like that scene in *The Blair Witch Project* that always wigs me out.

'You don't have to do that,' I say. 'I think about a hundred student nurses and doctors got an eyeful of my breasts and my nether regions over the course of my stay there. What's one more showing?'

'Yeah, but . . .' I think I can actually hear him swallow. 'It's your . . . I don't—' He stops.

None of those words made a sentence, and I close my mouth and make an unattractive snort from the back of my throat. I cover over the top of my boob, but there's very little I can do about the bit where her mouth is.

Tom turns round, his hands over his eyes, and tries to navigate his way over to the coffee machine. I'd forgotten I'd been halfway through doing that.

Maybe it *isn't* actually that easy being here with Tom, like this. Maybe this is going to be odd, awkward. It kind of *is* already odd, awkward, and to spare his blushes I say, 'Do you know they put a catheter up me?'

'What?' he says, spinning round and catching sight of my half-uncovered breast and then spinning immediately back towards the coffee again.

'I didn't even know,' I say, attempting to keep some level of normality between us. 'One of the nurses came in to change it, and I had to confess I didn't even know one was up there.'

He makes a whimpering noise and his stance at the coffee machine changes. He closes his legs tightly and I laugh again. Is Tom a bit squeamish?

'Explains why I didn't need to use the loo for twelve blissful hours,' I continue. 'Then they took it out and made me get up and walk.'

'The bastards,' Tom chuckles as he pushes Go on the coffee machine.

'I know. It's almost like they wanted me up and moving, recovering and getting home.'

I look around me. I'm not at home. But it feels like home. It's homely. Perhaps that's what I mean. I'm comfortable here. I don't feel as awkward being here as I thought I would. Other than the boob situation.

'Tom, you've made such an effort. Thank you.'

He places my coffee away from the baby and perches in front of me on the footstool.

He shrugs. 'It's nothing.'

'It's not nothing. You're wonderful.'

He shrugs again. 'Anyone would have done it.'

I watch him as he sips his coffee. These are the exact words he said to me after he pulled me from the train.

'I disagree,' I say. 'Most people would not have done it. They'd have rung an ambulance and waited it out. You drove me there. You held my hand the whole way through. You waited for me. You went shopping. You volunteered to house me and the screaming, hungry one for a few weeks. Anyone would not have done that.'

'Anyone who knows you would.'

'Hmm,' I say. 'I'm not sure I can see Natasha housing me for a fortnight, coating her and Will's blissful shag-pad in a layer of baby sick and breast milk.'

Tom smiles.

'You're a good man, Tom Archer.'

'I'm not,' he replies and the tone has changed somewhat.

'You are,' I say quietly. 'You're one of the best men I've ever met. Obviously my dad's in pole position, but you . . .' It's my turn at shrugging now. I can't finish my sentence, but I think Tom needs it, so I try. 'You're the second-best man I've ever met.'

'I feel sorry for you that you've not met anyone better.'

'Be quiet,' I chastise.

And I don't know what else I can say to convince him, but he surprises me by saying, 'You went into labour early because of me. Because I argued with you.'

'I argued with you too,' I say softly.

'We're not very good at this, are we?' he suggests.

'Good at what?'

He looks right into my eyes. 'Being friends.'

'I don't know. This is . . . friendly.'

'This is recompense,' he says.

I'm a bit taken aback by that and have to think before speaking. 'No, it's not. This is us.'

'Me banging into changing units because I've caught sight of your boobs?'

'Just one boob actually. I'll save the other for later, see what else I can get you to crash into.'

He laughs.

'I married a man who was nowhere near as good a person as you,' I say softly. I don't feel disloyal saying this now. I would have done, a while ago. But now I know it's the truth.

'I can't argue with that,' Tom says coolly.

'You're a good man,' I repeat. I want him to know this. It's important that he acknowledges this. 'Have you ever spoken to anyone – properly, I mean – about that night on the train?' This has been bothering me for five long years.

He shakes his head. 'Have you?'

'No. I'm still not sure if I need to. Not now. I probably did before, but . . . I needed to overcome the fear of getting on the Tube again, mostly. I think I'm over halfway there. Or I very soon will be. I guess my experience of that day and yours were very different.'

'You do like to sleep your way through hellish events,' he deadpans.

I issue a small smile. 'Tom,' I nudge.

He won't look at me. Instead he looks at the floor.

'I feel a bit funny about talking to people I don't know. It may have escaped your attention, but I don't have a great deal of friends, and my parents and I . . . we aren't exactly close. We don't talk about things like that.'

'What do you talk about?' I ask.

'It's a good question. We don't really talk much. "Stiff upper lip" is pretty much the family motto.'

'It's a terrible motto,' I say.

He laughs at this. 'Maybe. I don't know. They're not very emotional, you know. They don't show emotion.'

'So if talking to your parents won't help, would talking to mine, maybe? Not specifically about this, but . . . in general. My parents are good for life advice.'

He doesn't answer. He's thinking about it, though.

'My dad really likes you,' I offer.

'Yeah, he's nice. One of the good ones.'

'He is. Why don't you give him a ring? Meet up. He's a good listener.'

Tom thinks for a few seconds. 'Maybe. I mean . . . I'd actually quite like that. Would you mind?'

'Of course not.'

'The problem is . . .' he starts.

'Yes?'

'If you and I don't remain friends . . .'

'We will,' I say emphatically. 'We will and if we don't, you can have joint custody of my dad and I need never know about it. When and if you want to talk to him, or go for pints or whatever, please do it, Tom.'

He looks at me. 'I'd like that, if you really don't mind and if he doesn't.'

'Are you kidding?' I ask with an eye-roll. 'I think over the past few years he's missed you more than I have.'

And then I wonder how true that is. Because I missed Tom. I missed him more than I could ever say. I just think I need to work up the courage to actually tell him this.

Chapter 72

Abbie

It's 1 a.m. If I had any energy, and if I could actually move without it hurting my lower abdomen, I would be pacing back and forth in my room right now. Instead I'm lying in bed, wide awake, as feelings of confusion and tiredness wash over me.

Being near Tom feels good. Being in his company feels good. It was something I thought, when I ran out of his kitchen years ago, that I would never, ever get the chance to do again. I really wish I knew what to do about this. Perhaps it's best to do nothing. Perhaps it's best just to be friends. 'Oh God.' I throw the palms of my hands up to my tired eyes and push gently, rubbing for good measure.

How am I here, in Tom's house, with my baby and about a billion little stitches in my stomach? If the universe has a plan, it has a weird way of letting me know about it.

Next to me my little girl cries again, so I start to move. I really need to think of a name for her. Why is it so hard? I want Tom to know how much I value his presence in my life. Even when he wasn't present, he was always there, under the surface, under my skin. I loved him. I loved Sean too, but I never stopped loving Tom. These feelings don't simply die because we want them to, because we think it's for the best. And now I'm here and I still can't make them stop. If anything, it's getting worse.

Thomasina. Is that a good name for a baby? Will Tom know how much I value him, how much I care for him, if I name the baby after him? Thomasina. I try it out on my tongue. That'll piss Sean off nicely. Maybe the name will grow on me. But what if Tom and I get close and he rejects me again, then my baby has his name? That'll piss *me* off.

Baby's crying is really ramping up now. It's taking for ever, but I finally swing my legs out of bed very slowly and lean over the cot. I can do this. My stomach muscles tell me, in no uncertain terms, that they are not happy. I cry out, but I'm determined and then Tom runs in.

'What are you doing?' he cries.

'I didn't want to wake you,' I protest.

'Christ, this is exactly what I'm here for.' He picks her up. He's in his boxer shorts and I'm totally awestruck by this. I can't look away. I can't stop staring at his chest, his legs, his strong arms as he holds my baby. I need to look away.

'Sorry,' he says, noticing my harlot eyes scanning him. 'I couldn't find my pyjama bottoms in the dark and you cried out, so I just ran.'

'OK,' I say. I'm anything but OK.

Tom tells me he's going to change her nappy first, even though she's screaming for milk. He says he nailed this practice in about a minute when Teddy was small. 'It means she'll fall asleep after her milk, and I won't have to pull her around and make her angry by changing her nappy after she's all ready to go back to bed. Makes putting her down so much easier.'

'OK,' I say over the noise. I really need to think of something else to say. 'Thank you.'

I make myself comfy in bed and shortly after my freshly changed baby is in my arms and bashing her face on my breast, ready for milk. She suckles eagerly.

Tom stands by the end of the bed and looks towards the door of the spare room I'm in. Teddy's standing, looking curious and nervous.

'Sorry, mate,' Tom says. 'Did we wake you?'

Teddy nods. 'It's OK.' He's clutching a book in his hands, which makes Tom smile, until he realises the time and wonders why Teddy's holding a book at 1 a.m. when he should be sleeping. 'Can you read me a bit to get me to sleep?' he asks Tom.

'Maybe a couple of pages. It's late, buddy.'

But Teddy's moved on, as he gazes at the baby. 'Can I watch her feed? How does it work?'

I explain it to Teddy and he automatically curls up in bed next to me and the baby while he listens. It's nice, the feeling of Teddy nestled against me in this big double bed, surrounded by muted tones. He strokes the baby's hair while she feeds.

'OK if I go put some trousers on?' Tom asks me, gesturing towards Teddy as if I might not be able to cope with a four-year-old snuggled quietly with us.

I smile. Of course I'll be fine. 'Sure.'

Tom leaves and returns with pyjama bottoms on, still shirtless. In amongst being superdad, I assume he still finds the time to work out. Teddy and I are reading a page of his book: *Matilda* by Roald Dahl. I feel this book is a bit old for him, but he seems keen.

'Samantha bought it for him,' Tom says. 'She's got no idea how reading ages work.'

'Ronald loves Roald Dahl,' Teddy says and I look at Tom for any hint of a grimace, but he seems content as he smiles at Teddy's enthusiasm.

Teddy continues, 'I've already read *George's Marvellous Medicine* and *Fantastic Mr Fox* with Mummy and Ronald. I didn't like *The BFG*. Too many words I didn't understand.'

'*Matilda* was my favourite when I was a child,' I say.

'Was it?' Teddy asks. 'I really like it. She's got special powers.'

I nod sagely. 'She has. Shall we keep going?'

Teddy nods. He holds the book and turns the page when I tell him to, as I've got my hands full holding the baby. Tom sits on the end of the bed and watches us, thoughtfully or sleepily. I can't tell. He looks like he wants to nod off, but I sort of need him to put my little girl back in her cot. And then he has to get Teddy back off to bed. Poor man. He's going to be exhausted in the morning. I feel so guilty. I really hope I start feeling better soon.

We stop reading at the end of the next page and I glance at Tom, who looks like he's itching to get Teddy back to bed.

'What do you think of Thomasina?' I ask, desperate for his approval.

'Who's Thomasina?' he asks, rubbing his tired eyes.

'This little one, maybe.'

'That's not a real name,' Teddy says.

I laugh. 'It is a real name.'

'It's not a name for a baby,' Tom says. 'Why would you do that?'

'I want to name her after you, so you know how much you mean to me, to her – what you've done for us. Not just five years ago. But now as well.'

'No. Sorry. I'm not having that. Thank you. But no. I've got a man's name. She's a girl.'

This makes me laugh. 'Thomasina is a girl's name.'

'You know what I mean,' he says. 'It's a punishing name for a baby. Such a mouthful. Do you love it? The name? If not, don't do it for me. Call her something you actually love.'

'I don't love anything,' I whine. Now I think about it, I'm glad Tom didn't like the idea of naming the baby after him, but I hope he appreciates the gesture.

And then Teddy cuts through with his own thoughts on the matter. 'What about Matilda?' he says, gesturing to the book.

I look at Teddy and then I look at Tom. Tom mouths the name, and so do I.

'It was your favourite book,' Teddy suggests. 'Do you like other names?'

'No. I don't think I do.'

'You could shorten it,' Tom suggests. 'Matty or Tilly?'

'Tilly,' I say. 'I like that. Matilda, and for short . . . Tilly.' I look down at my baby. I can't tell if she suits it or not. 'Tilly,' I say thoughtfully. She opens her eyes and then closes them, continues sucking. 'Tilly.' I nod. 'I like that.' I might need to think about it a bit more, but in the interim I say, 'Well done, Teddy. You clever thing.'

He yawns.

'OK, you,' Tom says, picking up his protesting son. 'Bed. No arguments.'

Teddy waves at us from his position in Tom's arms as he's carried off to bed and I wave back, then I look down at my baby. 'Tilly,' I say, deciding I do actually really like it. And then I whisper, 'Oh, thank God, you've got a name.'

Tom knocks on the open door a few minutes later. 'I think Teddy's asleep.'

I smile. 'You can come in properly, if you want.' I realise I want him to come in. I want him to stay. Just a bit longer. He sits on the end of the bed for a few minutes, looking tired. 'Tilly's finished feeding,' I say, using her new name.

He smiles. 'OK then, Tilly. Let's get you back to bed too. And then I'll be right back here in about two hours, when the fun begins again.'

He winds her, places her back in her cot and starts to leave.

'Don't go,' I say. 'Why don't you stay here for a bit?'

He looks at me, says nothing. And then, 'I don't know if that's a good idea.'

'Why not?' And I genuinely mean this. I'm in maternity pyjamas and I am definitely *not* the svelte fifty-laps-every-morning size I was when I got pregnant. I'm huge now, desperate for my I've-just-had-a-baby stomach to retreat back from where it came.

'You must know why not?'

'Tom,' I say, 'while the connotations are very flattering, I know you don't mean what I think you mean. I'm the least attractive I've *ever* been. You're in no danger here.' I simply want to spend some time with him. I want to be near him. I'm reminded of a conversation with Natasha about knowing that she loved Will because she wanted to be *with* him.

'You're kidding, right?' he says. 'You're the most beautiful I've ever seen you. I'm in all kinds of danger here.'

'You're lying,' I whisper.

'I'm not, Abbie.' He sits on the edge of the bed, puts his head in his hands. 'And please remember something: we did this before. Or we almost did.' He corrects himself and then looks back at me. 'Twice. At varying stages of our friendship, and both times it's what ended us. I thought it had ended for good last time. I'm not falling into that trap a third time. I don't want to lose you as a friend.'

'We messed with each other's hearts,' I say. 'We messed with our own hearts and our heads. We chose all the wrong timings. Or the wrong timings chose us. Which sent us on different paths.' Because I know – I've always known – that I love Tom. I never stopped.

'But you're here, now. And, amazingly, I've not lost you,' Tom says. 'We're friends again. Let's not fuck that up.' He sounds as if he means it, as if his decision is final.

'OK,' I say uncertainly. I don't know what's just happened. Have I been rejected again?

And then I try again. I have to. *This is Tom.*

'Us being together isn't going to ruin things. It's when we try and *stop* being together that everything is ruined. Has that not occurred to you?'

He sighs. 'Abbie . . . Over the years I can't help going back to that night you stood in my kitchen and told me you loved me, hours before you got on a plane and disappeared. I analyse it all the bloody time: what I could have done to stop you leaving, what I should have done to buy us some time to work things out—'

'I love you,' I tell him and his chest stops moving as he pauses breathing for a moment. 'I still love you. And I'm putting my heart on the line again, and all of my dignity again, might I add, by telling you this . . . yet again, Tom: that I love you. And I want you. And I don't think I ever stopped loving you. If you hadn't been with Samantha, if I hadn't been with Sean – I think things might have been different.'

'I don't,' he says. 'We'd still have messed it up.'

'I don't agree,' I say, but I feel I'm losing him.

He's not saying anything. Just watching me. And exactly like last time I told him I loved him, I keep talking, because I'm all in now. If Tom rejects me again, I really will need a stern talking-to from someone.

'Do you still love me?' I forge on. 'Do you want me? Because if not – if you don't want me, and if it's because you genuinely don't have feelings for me any more – then that's OK. I mean, it's not OK, but I'll get on with it. And if it's because I've just had someone else's baby and you don't want anything to do with this messy situation, even though I *assure* you Sean is out of the picture and firmly staying that way, because I don't love him, I love you . . . then that's fine too. I understand.'

'You're an idiot,' Tom says. 'You really think I don't love you? You really think I haven't fallen for that little person over there, as well as having already fallen for her mother?'

I breathe in hard, lift my shoulders and drop them down. 'Really?' I whisper.

'Really,' he says. 'And I want you in my life.'

'I'm right here,' I say. 'Don't reject me again.'

He's thinking.

'What's stopping you?' I whisper tentatively.

'I don't want to lose you when I fuck it up,' he says. 'Because I couldn't bear the thought of losing you again. And now . . . there's Tilly. And Teddy. If we're going to do this, there's little people to consider. We can't mess it up, because we'll mess them up. We have children.'

'We do,' I say.

'I'm still not even divorced,' he tells me.

'Neither am I.'

'What if we fuck it up?' he says, his voice shaking.

'Why are we going to do that?' I ask softly. 'I've seen you at your worst. You've seen me at mine. And I'm so in love with you.'

'I'm so in love with you too,' he says.

I smile. Everything has brightened. 'Being away from you has been horrible,' I go on. 'Trying to put a stop to whatever was happening between us – that was what messed us up.'

'I know,' he says desperately. 'And trying to sleep with each other too soon. As I recall, that was what started all this mess off.'

'I have good news on that front,' I say softly. 'Or bad news, depending on how you really feel. I can't sleep with you.'

His eyes narrow and a horrified expression falls over his face. 'What . . . ever? You're joking?'

I can't help but laugh. 'Not never. Just for the next few weeks. It's in the leaflet I was given about dos and don'ts after having a C-section. And the leaflet is probably spot-on, because I can't even stand up straight without everything hurting, so sex is probably off the cards for a while.'

'OK,' Tom says slowly. He shuffles forward on the bed, sits opposite me. 'It's probably for the best. It gives us time to get to know each other properly again,' he continues, brushing my probably wild-looking bed-hair back from my face. 'Are we actually going to do this?' he asks. He looks shocked, amazed, joyful.

'Yes, please,' I say, because I never say the right thing at the right time. And then, more appropriately, '*How* do we do this?' I ask, scanning his face.

He looks awed, baffled, confused, happy. He looks all the things I feel.

'Like this.' He leans forward, strokes my face, my jaw, and I close my eyes as he touches my lower lip with his finger, before kissing me the way I remembered him kissing me, five years ago – and now today. I hold his face in my hands as I kiss him back. I don't want to be without this man ever again.

He looks at me far too longingly for a man who can't sleep with me for another few weeks.

I look back into the eyes of the man I love. I feel as if we're magnetised. Only, for so long the magnets were dysfunctional, pushing apart, repelling us, instead of drawing together, the way we were supposed to be.

'I think we should start again,' he says. 'From the very beginning.'

'So do I.'

And then I smile as he repeats words he said to me years ago, in a pub that we used to drink in, back in another life we used to live.

'Hi,' he says, holding his hand out for me to shake. 'I'm Tom.'

I laugh, hold my hand out to shake his.

He's looking into my eyes so intensely that I think he must be looking into my soul, my very being, the way I'm looking into his. And I love him all the more for it. Because it's Tom.

'Hi, Tom,' I say and I can't help laughing again as I shake his hand. 'I'm Abbie.'

And maybe it wasn't our time before. But it is now.

Epilogue

Tom

Two years later, August 2012

It's late afternoon and Abbie's been reading one of our books at Teddy's school summer-holiday club – or, rather, she's reading one of her books, as Teddy's teacher invited her to. It turns out Abbie's calling wasn't in journalism at all, and when our idea for the new children's TV series took off, she started writing books to accompany the show. I told her it might be easy: fifty words on a page rather than 500 for the articles she used to write. Apparently it's not. It's hard. But she loves it, especially on a day like today, when Teddy and Oliver are obviously proud to show off their connection to the cartoon. None of us expected it to take off quite the way it did.

Last week we secured a deal with a TV channel in Japan. I've lost count of how many countries are broadcasting it now. Being sort of back in the world of finance, co-owning an animation studio, isn't quite where I predicted my life would head, especially after I lost my last financial job the way I did. But I love this. It's better. In every way possible.

After Abbie's finished reading, she takes Oliver and Teddy to collect Tilly from nursery and they come to see us in the studio, before she goes out for dinner with Natasha.

Teddy takes Tilly's little hand and they go and play in the kids' area, where all our new merchandise sits. Working in an office where every now and again a small child comes to hang out for the day has its benefits – Andy always makes a beeline for the kids to find out what they're into, so that he can storyboard ideas.

He's dating Tilly's nursery teacher, Lizzy, now, which is a bit awkward, but Abbie and I didn't want him to be alone for ever. He met her while picking Tilly up for me one evening. When I reminded Andy of his thoughts about dating at the nursery, he happily replied, 'Oliver doesn't go to nursery any more, so if it all goes wrong I'm not making it hard for me any longer, I'm making it hard for you.' Which is fair enough, I suppose.

They make a great couple actually. Lizzy has secretly told Abbie she loves Andy, and I think Andy might be in love with her too, even if he hasn't worked that bit out yet. He will, though. He's just slow to catch up.

Later on Sean is coming to collect Tilly to take her for a picnic in the park and a push on the swings. He's been back and forth from Singapore a few times since she was born. Whenever I see him we're civil, but it's still awkward. At least he shows a genuine interest in the child he helped to create. I wanted that for Tilly. I wanted that for Abbie too.

I've stalked Sean briefly on Facebook. Each time he posts a photo update, he's with a different woman. They're all Abbie lookalikes. He's chasing something he knows he can't have. He let her go – and I thank my lucky stars every day that he did.

Samantha and Ronald take Teddy every other weekend and some nights after school. Ronald's quite decent. It annoys Samantha something chronic that he and I get on so well.

The last time they came round to collect Teddy she stood looking mildly disconcerted as Ronald, Teddy and I stood over the engine of his latest supercar, muttering about horsepower and drooling over the engine. We shook hands and that was the start of a beautiful friendship. They've got him this weekend, which has worked out well for us, because Abbie and I have got our second baby scan tomorrow.

Abbie finishes reading through the latest episode scripts and walks over to me. 'This is so funny,' she says. 'I just snorted. Andy said it's the most awful thing he's ever seen me do.'

'He's wrong,' I say, nuzzling into her and placing my hand on her stomach, where our tiny little baby grows inside day by day, getting ready to join our slightly chaotic family. 'The most awful thing you do is leaving one spoonful of ice cream in the tub and then putting it back in the freezer.'

'I'll try to eat all of it next time.'

'You trooper,' I say, kissing her again because I can't help myself.

Tilly toddles over and hands me one of the toys. I say thank you and she heads off to bring me another. On the TV in the background Andy and the scriptwriting team are watching the London Olympics. They shout loudly all of a sudden and jump up and down – Andy swearing as usual, as Great Britain takes gold in yet another event.

Abbie and Teddy cheer and Tilly claps, although I'm not certain she understands what's going on.

I look at Abbie as she walks over to the toys and glances at our latest, a soft toy train, which is something one of our little dog cartoon characters is heavily into. A fleeting memory of how we were first thrown together enters my mind; and then of the forces that pulled us apart. Now, seven years after we were first brought together, we have each other.

And a family.

And they're our everything.

Acknowledgements

Firstly, thanks to Becky Ritchie, the best agent a girl could have. Dedicating a book to you was long overdue as I always say, I have the easy job but you have the hard job. And I stand by that. I just write the books, you have to go and find homes for them! Thanks for all the complicated things you do that I don't see and the hours you put in to reading and re-reading my manuscripts, my dreaded synopses and all those half-baked outlines, along with everything else. You really are a shining star.

Thanks also to Oli Munson, for taking over temporarily from Becky and inheriting me for a while like an errant step-child. Not long now Oli. Not long now. You've been truly amazing, lightning fast at emails and say all the things I dare not say. Your authors are *very* lucky to have you. Also at A. M. Heath, thanks to Jack Sargeant, as always, who holds my hand through the joy of foreign tax forms and thanks to Harmony, Gosia, Tabatha, Prema and Alexandra.

Thanks to my wonderful editor Emily Griffin who took *The Last Train Home* in its original guise without question and became an ace collaborator of plot and character. You know how to make a book better while also delivering any and all news in such a calm and relaxing way that I'm instantly put at ease. And to all involved with design, sales, PR, marketing, foreign rights and all the behind-the-scenes things I don't see, thank you. Thanks also to Laurie Ip Fung Chun who nurses me through the technical stages and to Mandy Greenfield for copyediting genius.

To Steve, thank you for everything, as always. And to my wonderful family Emily, Alice, Mum, Dad, Luke, Cassie, Natalie, Sarah and Nicky for all your love and support.

Thanks to Savvies and writing buddies Jenny Ashcroft, Iona Grey, Rachel Burton and Mandy Robotham for words of advice and encouragement. For the Rayleigh Writers and Write Clubbers: monthly meets for cake and critique is sanity-inducing and just the best thing.

And to all the lovely readers who've bought *The Last Train Home* or any of my other novels, downloaded them on audio or borrowed them from a library, thank you most of all. If you're one of the ones who tags me on social media posts showing pictures of you reading my books on a sun lounger, on the commute or curled up on the sofa with a pet, double thank you. Messages and emails, social media posts and tags make my day! Do get in touch and say hi. I love it and will always reply. Likewise, if you have a moment to leave a review on Amazon or Goodreads (or both!) it's just the best thing for authors and helps readers find new books to read.

Join me on social media and sign up to my newsletter via my website to win books and stay informed about what's coming next from me. I write two books a year under two names, Elle Cook and Lorna Cook so there's always something going on!

Until next time . . .

Lorna/Elle

www.lornacookauthor.com
Facebook: LornaCookWriter
Instagram: LornaCookAuthor
Twitter: LornaCookAuthor